THE ORPHEUS GAMBIT

D. B. Fallon

Quayside Press
Newcastle

THE ORPHEUS GAMBIT

This book is a work of fiction. Names, characters, places, and incidents are the product of the author's imagination or are used fictitiously. Any resemblance to actual events, locales, or persons, living or dead, is entirely coincidental.

Published by
Quayside Press
Newcastle
ISBN 978-1-9194100-0-5 (Paperback)
ISBN 978-1-9194100-1-2 (eBook)

Names: Fallon, D. B., author.
Title: The Orpheus Gambit / D. B. Fallon.
Description: A noir espionage thriller.
Subjects: | 1. Fiction. | 2. Spy stories. | 3. Thrillers (Fiction). | 4. Espionage
Cover and interior design by the author
Printed in the United Kingdom

First Edition: December 2025
10 9 8 7 6 5 4 3 2 1

Acknowledgements

To the artists who provided the atmosphere and soundtrack for The Orpheus Gambit, your music was as essential to the mood of the story as the encrypted files. Special thanks to Polina Gagarina and the late, great Viktor Tsoi for "Kukushka," a song that defined the courage and fate of two troubled souls. Thank you also to Sting and The Police, Bryan Ferry, Hayley Reinhart, Radiohead, Queen, Vangelis, Billy Joel, The Who, Dire Straits, Aha, the late, great George Harrison, Snow Patrol, Chris Isaak, Blue Eyes and ABBA for scoring Declan and Anya's most vulnerable moments or providing the music for my writing process. I hope I did your wonderful titles justice, in the intimate bars and rainy, noir alleyways of Newcastle.

Spasiba for the music.

Also, thanks go to my newfound friends in Russia who offered help and gave me advice on Russian culture, literature, music and humour, these include, Fyokla, Alina, and Konstantin amongst others. Additional thanks to the talented Zhanna Shvets for kindly granting me permission to use her music in my book promotions.

Special thanks go to my former intel manager Sharon, who not only recruited me, but trusted my ability to see the patterns in the noise.

And of course, grateful thanks to the patience and support of my family who once again put up with me being chained to a keyboard after years of being chained to a keyboard. It appears that Declan Shaw isn't the only one tied to his work by a leash.

“Beauty Will Save The World.”

Fyodor Dostoevsky

THE ORPHEUS GAMBIT

Гамбит Орфея

PROLOGUE

Anya sighed softly in resigned disappointment as she stared at her equally disappointed fiancé, Sergei. Once again, the fragile peace of their life together had been shattered by the intrusive reality of their GRU service. She watched him hurriedly dress as the pale winter sunrise filtered through the half-open blinds of the kitchen window, casting their small apartment in a gentle, diffused light.

Their home was on the seventh floor of a Brezhnevka-style building in the Khamovniki District of Moscow, one of thousands of standardised, Soviet-designed apartment blocks that ringed the city centre. While its concrete panels appeared grey and anonymous from the outside, inside, Anya had transformed their flat into a small but comfortable domestic sanctuary, a haven where she and Sergei could snatch rare moments of blissful normality.

The scent of her strong black coffee mingled with the faint, pleasant aroma of beeswax from the polished floor. She could hear the occasional gurgle and clunk of the cast-iron radiator, a strangely tranquil sound which created a stark contrast to the turbulent life they lived beyond the walls of their cosy little refuge.

She sat at the small kitchen table, nursing her steaming cup, a warm counterpoint to the chill of the early winter morning. She watched in resignation as Sergei paced about the room; his usually practised dressing for duty was made clumsy by his haste, and she noticed his uncharacteristic anxiety as he repeatedly checked his wristwatch.

He pulled the olive-green shirt of his uniform over his shoulders, the starched fabric appearing strangely alien against the soft domesticity of their home. Anya continued to look at her fiancé, trying to catch his eye, an involuntary pout forming on her lips.

"You know how difficult it was to organise time off at the same time you were free?" she asked quietly, her words holding more weariness than anger.

Sergei paused, his hands clumsily fumbling with his holster's fastener, the weight of the gun pulling it low on his hip. He turned to look at her, his face a mask of apology.

"I know Anya, I know," he said, his voice low and regretful. "But I cannot help it if someone calls in sick. You know how it works. If I'm on standby, I'm on standby, and to cap it all, I have to make it to an urgent briefing in his place."

He forced a small, weary smile, trying to reassure her. "Something important must be going down; otherwise, they wouldn't dare try to drag me away from you."

She mirrored his expression with her own weary smile. She unfortunately did know, only too well. It was a bitter and inescapable reality they both lived with. There had been countless other times when it was her pulling on her uniform, leaving him with a hurried kiss and a shared look of resignation, but this time it felt different, more urgent. Sergei's usually easy smile seemed forced, artificial even.

She found herself deeply saddened that their peaceful life together had changed so suddenly, shattering into this strange and dislocated existence. A new, undeclared war now drove their daily routine, a shadow conflict of proxies, lies and provocations, being fought both on Russia's borders and within them.

The result of these changes was a service stretched to near breaking point, and a personal life measured in the stolen moments they managed to find between operational responsibilities. But knowing the reality of the hybrid war did not lessen the sting of another day lost. Time together was such a precious commodity, and they had so little of it lately.

She watched him finish dressing, saw the hidden signs of stress in his expression. He was a good man, she thought, the wave of her annoyance receding, replaced by a familiar, deep-seated affection. He was strong, reliable, utterly dedicated to his duty, and he simply adored her. The way his eyes softened when he looked at her; the way he always looked across at her in a crowded room and met her own eyes in silent connection, those were the moments that really mattered.

He could make it up to her later, she decided, and the sooner he completed this unwelcome assignment, the sooner he could return to her and pick up where they had left off before the shrill ring of the telephone had so rudely interrupted their pillow-talk. Besides, she thought, as a new idea took root, Christmas was fast approaching, and she still hadn't found him the right present. She might as well convert this unwanted, annoying inconvenience into an opportunity.

Sergei did a final check in the mirror, his boots heavy on the patterned linoleum floor. As he headed for the door, he stopped to look back at her, the regret still etched on his face.

"I really am sorry, Anya."

She stood and walked slowly towards him, rising on her toes to plant a gentle, affectionate kiss on his lips.

"I know," she sighed. "Me too."

She felt the tension physically leave his shoulders, saw the gratitude in his eyes. He was forgiven. He opened the door then turned back in the doorway and gave her a warm, thankful smile.

"See you later," he said.

"See you later," she replied, returning his smile as he left their small refuge from the world. The door clicked shut behind him, .leaving her alone in the sudden, echoing silence of the apartment. Even the radiator had stopped clunking.

She stood for a long moment, staring at the closed door, the warmth of his presence already fading. Without Sergei in their apartment, it was a hollow place, and she felt like an impostor in an empty nest. She sighed, her smile fading, a crushing and inexplicable sense of foreboding engulfed her, and she shivered, suddenly cold. Sometimes, duty was a hard, relentless taskmaster.

An hour later, dressed in her elegant furs, she emerged from the Metro into the frigid air of a Moscow winter. The sky was a brilliant, cloudless blue, and a fresh layer of snow from the night before had lightly dusted the branches of the birch trees, making the whole city look like a scene from a Dickensian Christmas card. The perfect day to buy a present.

She wandered the streets for a while, enjoying the simple pleasure of being off duty and free to do whatever took her fancy. She had just the thing in mind for Sergei. A beautiful, antique silver letter opener they had seen in the window of a small shop near the Arbat a few weeks ago. Its handle was elegantly shaped like a falcon's head; its silver polished to a lustrous shine.

He, a man of action and modern weapons, had stopped, captivated by its old-world craftsmanship. He had traced its shape on the glass with his finger, a rare moment of boyish fascination that had stuck with her.

It was with a sense of happy satisfaction that she had the knife gift wrapped in the bright red and green wrapping paper Sergei was so fond of. Her only disappointment was her failure to find a bottle of her and Sergei's favourite Chanel perfume in the Arbat, but the kindly shopkeeper had directed her to the Moskovsky Department Store on Komsomolskaya Square, where she was not only able to purchase a bottle, but had also taken advantage of the free sample available in the store.

The subtle scent of the expensive perfume had immediately acted to her lift mood, and she found herself becoming hopeful that she and Sergei could get Christmas off together, having both been on duty last year. Buoyed by this optimistic thought, she entered the nearby Metro with a fresh spring in her step.

Lost in her thoughts of how pleased Sergei would be, she failed to notice the 15-seater minibus rolling up to the station, which juddered noisily to a halt, just as she headed into the underground.

Captain Taras cursed, a low, vicious sound in Ukrainian, as the minibus sputtered then died. A plume of steam hissed from under the bonnet like the sound of a dying animal. A plan, months in the making, undone by a faulty gasket, by a piece of shit cheap rubber.

His frustration wasn't just with the engine. It was with the mission itself. He was a soldier, a commander of men who fought on the front lines. He belonged in the mud and trenches of his homeland, not skulking through the streets of Moscow like a common assassin. But battlefield failures required responses, and this was the response that the strategists in Kyiv, and their quiet, well-spoken "advisors" from MI6, had cooked up. A "decapitation strike." A piece of messy, back-alley work designed to sow chaos far from the front. He understood the cold, military pragmatism of it, but it sat poorly with him. This wasn't war as he knew it. This was something else, it felt "dirty" to him.

The driver, a young recruit with anxiety in his bulging eyes, shrugged apologetically under Taras's withering glance. From the back of the minibus, the other six men in his unit let loose their own stream of profanities, a chorus of frustration aimed at the hapless driver. They were a wolf pack, heavily armed with Kalashnikovs, pistols, and grenades, now stranded on the wide, bustling Komsomolskaya Square, dangerously close to the grand entrance of the Metro station.

Their mission assignment from the SBU was to target a meeting of senior Russian officers, who according to MI6, would be debriefing their political masters on their progress in Ukraine over celebratory vodka and cigars.

The young driver popped the bonnet and reluctantly climbed out into the Moscow winter, shivering in the frigid air, he waved his hands, trying to make the plume of steam dissipate, completely focused on the hissing engine.

Up ahead, their second minibus was already a block away, stopped at a traffic light, Taras snorted in frustration, so much for their orders to remain together in convoy. Then came a distant, echoing "Crack! Crack! Crack!" followed by strident shouts in Russian.

An ambush.

Taras watched in horror as the first minibus erupted in a kaleidoscope of shattered glass. Khaki clad figures, almost certainly a combination of FSB, GRU and Spetsnaz, materialised from doorways and unmarked cars, their movements a swift and efficient ballet of violence.

It was the pointing finger that sealed their fate. An officer in a black helmet turned, his gaze sweeping past the chaos, gesticulating stridently towards their stranded vehicle. The trap wasn't just for the first bus. It was for them. The Russians had been waiting, probably tipped off by an informant within the SBU itself.

"Out! Fucking out!" Taras roared, pulling down his balaclava before kicking open the side door and tumbling clumsily onto the pavement as rounds peppered the bus. The distant gunfire suddenly turning into a soul piercing "Crack Thump!" The young driver was thrown violently forward, already dead, a red mist blooming from his skull, before he slumped lifeless onto the hot metal of the engine.

Taras caught the sickening, grotesque stench of burning flesh as he ran, his breath coming in ragged, desperate gasps, towards the yawning mouth of the Komsomolskaya Metro station. They burst through the doors and plunged down the long, steep escalators, barging commuters brutally aside in their desperate haste. Flanked by heavy, ornate bronze lamps, they continued their frantic descent into the underworld, emerging into the platform hall, a space of almost breathtaking opulence. It was not a station, it was an underground ballroom, a magnificent temple to Stalin's Soviet Empire.

A soaring, vaulted ceiling painted a brilliant lemon-yellow was held aloft by a line of massive marble pillars, creating a repeating pattern of majestic arches like the nave of a great cathedral. The entire hall was bathed in the welcoming light of beautifully ornate chandeliers.

The gunfire felt like an act of desecration in this almost religious space. Commuters screamed and scattered. Taras saw one of his men, the hothead Vitaly, in the cold logic of retreat, shooting at the fleeing civilians in the hope of slowing down their pursuers, their blood spattering across the gleaming marble floor. A disgusted knot tightened in Taras's gut. He understood the brutal calculus, escape was the priority, but the killing of innocents, even "Orc" innocents, chafed against the tattered remnants of the soldier's code he still clung to.

Another opened fire on the uniformed security staff who were caught completely off guard by the intrusion of the gang onto the concourse. When they reached the platform, Taras almost breathed a sigh of relief, a stationary train was there, its doors gaping open in a silent invitation. They just managed to board as the doors hissed shut, some of his men still firing randomly at the retreating civilians.

But the train wasn't moving. The driver had seen them enter and was refusing to pull away. Vitaly, his blood lust growing by the minute, screamed at him to move or he would start killing passengers. The driver, whether through fear or pure Russian stubbornness, remained almost frozen, his eyes staring ahead, stiffly shaking his head in the negative. Vitaly, making good on his threat, and seemingly glad that the driver had refused, casually turned towards the passengers and almost nonchalantly shot a man in a business suit.

What happened next lodged itself in Taras's brain for the rest of his life. He watched Vitaly knocking on the driver's window with the butt of his pistol, before turning back to the passengers and choosing his next hostage to murder, his eyes resting on an attractive, smartly dressed, dark-haired woman. Unlike the other passengers who were cowering in terror, she was strangely defiant, her gaze meeting his not with fear, but with a cold, hard fury.

As he approached, she dropped the crumpled, red and green paper she had been holding. For a split second, Vitaly paused and lowered his gun. He glanced down at the brightly coloured wrapping paper on the floor, then looked back up at her, a callous smirk on his face.

"No littering," he said in Russian, slowly raising his pistol again, taking his time, savouring the moment. His mocking hesitation and the minor distraction were his end.

In that instant, she moved, almost impossibly fast. A flash of silver from her coat sleeve, and the elegant, antique letter opener she had just bought as a Christmas present, was buried to the hilt in Vitaly's neck. A fountain of bright red blood erupted from his carotid artery. In the same microsecond, she had his pistol in her hand and had dropped two more gunmen with ruthlessly efficient double taps.

Then, almost in slow motion, she pivoted and aimed the gun at Taras, who froze. Their eyes locked. He saw his own death there, the certainty of his end turning his bowels to water. He tried to raise his own weapon, but an unfamiliar sensation of absolute, existential terror had gripped him, and he felt as if his gun hand was moving through treacle

He could hear his surviving men trading gunfire with the rapidly approaching security forces, but in that moment, his entire existence was focused entirely on that attractive unsmiling face, the smell of cordite mingling with her perfume, those cold, merciless brown eyes, and the dark, Stygian muzzle of Vitaly's pistol.

The world suddenly exploded as multiple stun grenades shattered the carriage windows. The blasts threw the woman off her feet just as she fired. Taras screamed as the round meant for his head tore through his leg, shredding nerves, tendons and blood vessels. Unknown to Taras, Vitaly had loaded his gun with Dum Dum bullets, and the effect was devastating. Taras roared in agony and rage, scrambling in panic through the shattered front window of the train, tumbling heavily onto the concrete below. Through gritted teeth he painfully struggled to his feet and desperately limped up the dark tunnel, with blood pouring from his agonising wound.

His echoing, grunting breath sounded bestial in the suffocating darkness, and though the physical pain was excruciating, it was nothing compared to the searing, absolute humiliation. He, a soldier, had been brought down not on a battlefield, but in a subway car by a civilian woman, a woman who had made him experience genuine, pants pissing fear for the very first time. He had seen his own death in her eyes.

This single, violent, personal failure consumed him. In the cloying darkness of the tunnel, all his distaste for this "dirty war" burned away, replaced by a pure, white-hot obsession. He swore a blood vow: one day, he would find that Russian bitch and end her. The reluctant participant was gone. An obsessed monster, haunted by the woman who had shot him, had just been born.

The ongoing firefight between the remaining gunmen and the security forces only lasted a short minute, and after the last of the masked terrorists were neutralised, Anya stumbled to her feet and approached one of her colleagues and showed him her GRU identification. She was then gently helped from the blood-slicked carriage. Medical teams swarmed the platform. The dead, however, were left where they fell for now, first responders covering two child victims with stark white sheets, a teddy bear laid in a puddle of blood next to one of the victims. Anya stopped, her eyes no longer cold, but brimming with tears.

One of the GRU men, a friend of Sergei's named Pavel, noticed her standing there, looking at the dead children with anguish in her eyes. He approached her, a similarly pained expression on his own face and gently tried to steer her away. Still disoriented, she didn't question why.

Until she saw him, Sergei, lying on his back near the far end of the platform, directly beneath one of the eight massive ceiling mosaics depicting Russia's greatest military heroes. He lay under the defiant gaze of Alexander Nevsky, his now violated GRU uniform, a modern echo of the ancient warrior's armour. His eyes were wide open, staring blankly at the pantheon of heroes above, a large, dark pool of blood forming a halo on the marble beneath him.

The grief was a physical blow, a brutal punch to her gut that made her cry out in despair, and Pavel was forced to gently steady her, as her knees suddenly gave way, almost causing her to collapse. In that instant, something inside Anya died, too.

She allowed herself to be escorted away, a hollowed-out shell, walking through a world that had suddenly lost all its colour. Sympathetic words were whispered in her ears. She could see the looks of admiration and respect from the other GRU members. They patted her on the back, told her how many lives she had saved, but all she could think of was how many lives she had failed to save, including the two children and her beloved Sergei's.

Despite her loss, there was no time for mourning. Not yet. She had been taken straight to GRU headquarters, the imposing, fortified building on Grizodubovoy Street known grimly as the "Aquarium." In its sterile, windowless briefing rooms, she croaked and whispered what she knew with a raw, but professional precision. She was then left alone in a well-appointed office for an hour, a cup of coffee growing cold on the oak desk in front of her, untouched.

She replayed the incident in her head repeatedly, a grainy, silent film of blood and failure, projecting endless "what ifs?" onto her vivid memories.

Why had she been so slow? Why did she only respond after the man in the suit had been killed? If she'd acted sooner, maybe she would have neutralised the terrorist who shot Sergei. Why didn't she prioritise that killer instead of the men who were beginning to turn their guns towards her? Everything seemed to have happened in slow motion. She was sure she would have had time, if only she had been better, had been faster.

But she had failed. She had put her own safety before that of the innocents who were killed, and as a result, Sergei was dead too. And she hadn't even told him she loved him as he left for his briefing. A briefing, she now knew, for a mission that had placed him directly in the line of fire on a Metro platform. All because someone had called in sick with the flu.

The grief that threatened to crush her was suddenly gone, replaced by cold anger and an icy, almost cryogenic resolve. Never again would she be so slow, so helpless. She had failed this time, with tragic consequences. She had failed for the last time she decided.

She had hesitated because she had been busy thinking how pleased Sergei would be with his Christmas gift, she had been distracted and hadn't noticed the gunmen before it was too late. Her love for him had gotten him killed.

Never again.

The door opened. She glanced up angrily, resentfully, to see who was intruding on her thoughts and noticed an old but formidable-looking man enter, dressed in an expensive, perfectly tailored suit. He sat down in the large leather chair opposite, took out a buff brown folder from his briefcase and opened it.

She lowered her eyes again, determined to bury the pain, guilt and anger that had threatened to overwhelm her, beneath an avalanche of icy resolve and determination.

For several long minutes, the only sound in the room was the soft rustle of paper. He was reading the document.

She felt his eyes on her. A quick, assessing glance. Then back to the file. Another glance, longer this time, as if he were comparing the woman in front of him to the words on the page.

His piercing gaze was cool and analytical, dissecting her, reading her as easily as he was reading her P-File. Finally, the rustling stopped. She heard the soft thud of a file being placed on the polished desk between them. He let the silence stretch for a moment longer and reached back into his briefcase and placed a second object on top of the file, with a hard, crinkling sound.

Then another crinkling sound, softer, from a third object.

She lifted her head. A buff-brown folder, marked with the red stamp of the GRU sat on the desk. On top of it was a clear plastic evidence bag.

Inside the bag... was a silver letter opener... smeared with dark, dried blood; in the other, a blood-stained Teddy Bear, whose black plastic eyes seemed to bore into her very soul. Time seemed to stand still as she stared in disbelief at the two exhibits. Only then did the man speak, his tone quiet but strangely powerful,

"Agent Anastasia Vladimirovna Stepnova," he began. "I am Director Volkov of the SVR, and I want to talk to you about your actions on the Metro."

CHAPTER 1

Five years later, an even colder Moscow winter bit deep. Snow fell in relentless, silent drifts, softening the harsh lines of the city's architecture. At Yasenevo, the imposing, monolithic structure of the SVR headquarters stood like a fortress against the blizzard, a place where the strategic climate of the new cold war was equally frigid.

Inside, Director Volkov's conference room was a haven of calculated, professional order. He sat at his large, polished oak desk and surveyed the handful of trusted analysts and advisers who sat in an expectant semicircle around the secure chamber. He slowly took off his glasses and polished them before addressing his waiting subordinates.

"You all know why I have brought you here," Volkov stated almost dispassionately. "Our Western adversaries are overconfident, and through this overconfidence, they have overextended themselves," he continued, his voice low but powerful.

"They believe they are the puppet masters, pulling strings in our near abroad, fanning the flames on our very borders and in our streets. Their intelligence services are so busy fuelling their international arsons that they have become blind to their own strategic hubris."

He paused, as if collecting his thoughts, and put his glasses back on, letting his gaze fall on a series of satellite images displayed on a secondary screen, showing the scorched, damaged lattice of the Voronezh-DM radar array at Armavir.

"Over recent years, thanks to their own blindness, they have likewise been trying to blind us, one salami slice at a time, hoping that by inflicting a death by a thousand cuts, they won't trigger our nuclear doctrine... They are foolishly naïve if they think we do not see through their plan. A man only blinds his opponent to prevent him from seeing the killing blow. They are no longer just talking about a 'winnable' nuclear war in their think tanks; they are taking practical steps to turn their lunatic theories into a reality."

He gestured to a map on the large viewing screen in the chamber, where red circles highlighted new NATO military installations. "Intermediate-range missile systems and Tomahawk missiles are being placed near our borders as I speak. They have also moved nuclear gravity bombs into their UK airbases. In addition, they place their nuclear submarines at the very edge of our territorial waters, foolishly thinking we do not have the will to respond, that our own doctrine is a bluff."

He paused, letting the grim reality settle in the room. The truth was, Russia's ultimate deterrent, the only weapon that could neutralise this increasing nuclear threat and rewrite global defence doctrine, was not yet ready.

The Orpheus munition was in its final stages of development, tantalisingly close to completion, but the international situation was deteriorating much faster than even his most gifted scientists could work. The heavy diplomatic hints regarding Russia's new deterrent were falling on deaf ears, with Western counterparts convinced the statements were just a combination of posturing and maskirovka.

Because of this Western cynicism, Volkov feared a confrontation or, more likely, a dangerous miscalculation before the weapon's deterrent effect could become a reality. He needed to buy time, enough time to drag the world back from the crumbling brink on which it now teetered.

His expression hardened into one of grim resolve.
"The Orpheus Gambit is our response. It is a strategic-level bluff, played for the highest possible stakes. It is designed to buy us the time we need to perfect our magnetic plasma munition. By manipulating the West into believing they have obtained the authentic blueprints of the device, we shall remind them of the true nature of deterrence by instilling the terror of certain personal obliteration into their leadership."

He stood up and slowly paced the briefing room, looking each attendee in the eye as he spoke, holding their gaze one at a time before moving on to the next technician.

"We will show them that there is no defence line, no bunker, no missile silo, no mountain we cannot penetrate at will; that there can be no victory for them."

"We will disabuse them of their arrogant, childish theories and remind them of the precise meaning of the Latin phrase memento mori: remember you will die."

"We will shatter their dangerous illusion that they can win a nuclear war by decapitating us in our bunkers. Our bunkers will no longer matter; theirs will no longer matter. Our dead hand will reach out from under the earth and pull them into the grave with us. They will burn with us and be buried with us."

He paused, his eyes taking in the concerned but controlled faces of the group. He was aware that fragments of highly sensitive data concerning Project Icarus, the codename for the Orpheus magnetic plasma munition, were leaking from the Chernobog Deep Works research facility. This leak was at first considered a serious security lapse, but when investigations swiftly uncovered a deeply embedded CIA mole codenamed 'Palamedes,' Volkov saw the breach as the opportunity it was. Thus was born the Orpheus Gambit, an audacious disinformation plan originally conceived from failure. Now, the carefully curated data he was drip-feeding to the West via Palamedes was a key part of his skilfully crafted deception.

Volkov turned his gaze directly onto his lead technical analyst, Alexei, and with a curt nod, said simply:

"Your report?"

"The package is active, Comrade Director," Alexei replied deferentially. "The Trojanised data fragments we allowed to leak have been accessed by a Western intelligence network. Our quantum particle in their machine has sent up its flare."

"Explain the science, Alexei," Volkov asked, smiling in an almost fatherly manner. "In as simple terms as you can manage."

Alexei nodded, slightly nervous at being put on the spot by having to simplify such complex, experimental physics. He paused for a second, gathering his thoughts. He then cleared his suddenly dry throat and finally spoke.

"Comrade Director, think of it as a digital tripwire with a silent flare. We embedded a set of linked particles within the leaked data. A corresponding set remains here. When they open the Chudes data file and make an observation, they disturb their half of the system. The moment they do, our half collapses into a specific quantum state, instantly, with no way for them to detect our trap."

He paused, letting the implication land. "A flare goes up on our board, showing us exactly where in the world the file was opened. But," he added, "that is all we get. The flare shows us the 'where', but not the 'who'. It tells us a door has been opened, but not who has walked through it."

"So, our ghost in their machine still requires a ghost on their ground," Volkov mused. His gaze turned inward for a moment, then visibly sharpened as an idea was born.

"Can we pull a rope from this end to ring a bell in their system?" he suddenly asked.

Alexei looked taken aback for a second time.

"Theoretically... yes, Comrade Director. We could embed a dormant piece of code, a kill switch that is only triggered when we observe the particles on our end. But that specific technology is still barely in the experimental phase."

"Make it operational," Volkov demanded, his voice still low but utterly commanding. "Your work is no longer just about seeing flares. It is about learning how to start fires in their server rooms."

Volkov's piercing gaze swept the room again.

"As Alexei has so eloquently stated, the first flare has gone up," he announced. "The trail leads directly to British intelligence. Specifically, to their Special Projects group, operating out of a deniable outstation in Newcastle." He savoured the irony. "They think hiding their most sensitive work away from London keeps it safe from us."

He looked at the glowing map on the screen, at the single, stark point of light over a city in the Northeast of England, the chessboard for the gambit. The first move had been made. The flare had worked perfectly; the game had begun. Now he just needed to manoeuvre the requisite pieces onto the chosen board, in the correct sequence, and let nature take its course.

CHAPTER 2

The streets shone like wet chitin in the miserable, persistent drizzle, the weak glow of the orange streetlamps reflecting on the fragments of broken bottles and petrol-polluted, rainbow puddles, which gurgled noisily into the rubble-blocked drains.

Belfast, 1995. A young Declan Shaw, his dark hair long and plastered to his forehead, a short beard masking the youth in his face, sat in the driver's seat of a battered Ford Cortina. Beside him sat his best friend, an equally unshaven young man called Norm, his face tense and alert, scanning the empty street.

To any potential witnesses, they were nothing more than what they appeared to be: a loyalist paramilitary hit team from the Ulster Volunteer Force. They wore casual street clothing, leather jackets and faded jeans, their hair deliberately grown longer than regulation, their accents honed to a perfect, guttural Belfast snarl by countless rehearsals. In reality, they were carefully selected British soldiers, playing the part of terrorists to hunt terrorists. This was "Special duties" at its sharpest, dirtiest end, a covert, morally grey game carried out in the shadows of the dirty war, where the lines blurred with every passing day.

A black woollen balaclava was rolled up on each of their heads like a watch cap, ready to be pulled down at a moment's notice. Resting between them, was a Thompson submachine gun its wooden stock dark and ominous, a captured weapon, chosen specifically for its association with a previous loyalist murder, another piece of their carefully constructed deception. On Norm's lap rested a compact 9mm Uzi machine pistol, it's folded metal stock giving the weapon a stubby, sinister appearance.

Their radio, hidden under the passenger seat, crackled twice. The signal. Target is en route.

"Right," Norm muttered, his voice already instinctively shifting into the hard brogue of their cover. He picked up his Uzi and extended the butt into place with a practised slap of his hand, and pulled his balaclava down over his face, his usually friendly eyes suddenly hard and anonymous behind the crude holes. Declan did the same, the coarse wool scratching his skin, the world narrowing to the view through the eye-slits, the soldier vanishing completely, replaced by the monster he was pretending to be.

The target was Seamus "The Watchmaker" O'Malley, a top-tier PIRA bomb maker, a man responsible for dozens of deaths who had always managed to escape justice on legal technicalities.

Tonight, there would be no technicalities. His movements had been fed to them by their handler, the intelligence originating from a high-level informant (tout) within the PIRA.

Unbeknownst to the soldiers, this "tout" was under suspicion by "The nutting squad," the internal security unit of the Provos, and he desperately needed to serve up a win to his PIRA commanders to prove his loyalty. His MI5 handler knew of his betrayal via an even higher-level informant but was loathe to sacrifice such a valuable source of intelligence by scrubbing the hit on O'Malley and tipping off the Provos they had a mole.

Soldiers were relatively easy to come by, but touts in the leadership of the Provisionals on the other hand, were a far rarer bird and had to be protected at all costs.

The double irony of the mess was that the informant setting up Declan's team was himself being targeted for elimination by a PIRA 'nutting squad' hitman, a hitman who, unbeknownst to anyone involved on the ground, was also a high-level British agent codenamed 'Flick-knife'. Due to extreme compartmentalisation, one British asset was being used to set up another, with neither handler aware of the other's operation.

The left hand not only didn't know what the right hand was doing but was actively conspiring against the other to remove some of their own fingers.

Declan's team, it had been decided, were to be the acceptable sacrifice to protect the sources. They had simply been assured by their "green slime" intelligence officer that the intel on O'Malley was solid, and that his neutralisation would save countless innocent lives.

The bomber appeared at the far end of the street, walking with the arrogant swagger so common amongst the "untouchables". He glanced around before ducking into a narrow, rubble-strewn alleyway.

"Well, you are going to be touched tonight" Declan thought silently to himself, the memory of body parts scattered across a shattered shopping area, filling him with a dreadful resolve.

"Go," Norm said in his fake brogue.

Declan and Norm exited the Cortina, weapons in their shoulders at the ready, their thumbs quietly flicking off their safety catches. Two other team members, their own faces also masked, emerged from a dark doorway across the street to follow. They entered the alley, four soldiers disguised as gunmen, walking directly into a trap their own side was aware of, but had failed to pass on due to a combination of cynical pragmatism, internal rivalries and communication failures.

Fortunately for Declan and his team, the pre-prepared trap was clumsily executed. Recent successes by the security forces, particularly an SAS ambush that had neutralised several key players in the local Belfast brigade, had forced the PIRA to rely on younger, less experienced volunteers.

Two of this active service unit were green, on their first mission. One of them, a nervous teenager with an Armalite, panicked as soon as he saw the silhouette of a soldier enter the alley and opened fire too early, blowing the effectiveness of their killing zone.

The world exploded in a cacophony of muzzle flashes and the deafening roar of automatic fire as bullets ricocheted off the walls. Bricks and plaster erupted around them. But the premature opening shot gave Declan and his team the split second they needed to take cover at the mouth of the alley and return fire.

Declan saw where the blinding muzzle flashes were coming from and squeezed his own trigger, unleashing several, controlled bursts that stitched lines of savage .45 calibre fire into the ambush positions. It was with a sense of satisfaction that he heard an involuntary cry from behind a dustbin. Norm was close, his own weapon cracking, providing covering fire.

In seconds that felt like an eternity, the firing from the shadows stopped, and after several more controlled bursts from the team it was over. The alley fell silent, save for the patter of rain and the high-pitched ringing in Declan's ears.

He moved cautiously forward through the acrid smoke and the smell of cordite, expended brass crunching against the ground under his feet. He kept his weapon tight to his shoulder, still in the aim, a fresh magazine clicking into place.

"Magazine!" he muttered; to inform the team he was out of ammo and in the process of reloading.

Carefully stepping past the crumpled bloody bodies of the ambushers, one of whom ironically was the informant, he saw his primary target O'Malley, the bomb maker, slumped behind the bins towards the far end of the alley. Declan noticed sand leaking from the bullet holes and realised the ambush had been pre prepared. This was not an opportunistic incident; someone had set them up.

The Provos had been tipped off and expecting them. The realisation made his win all the sweeter and he advanced towards the bomber, a satisfied smirk on his face, ready to administer the coup de grâce.

"Someone's having a shit day at the office," he smirked callously under his breath.

He raised his weapon up to his cold, focused eyes, his finger on the trigger. And then he saw her. She was lying behind O'Malley's body, partially shielded by him. A teenager. Maybe sixteen. Her eyes were wide open, staring up at the rainy sky, but they seemed to be looking directly at him. A single, dark hole in her forehead. But it was the exit wound that made the bile rise in his throat. The back of her head was gone, a horrific, crimson ruin, her brains spattered across the grimy, graffitied brickwork.

His world collapsed and became disjointed. The noise, the adrenaline, the coppery smell of blood, it all faded away, replaced by an empty silence and the realisation of what he had just done. All he could see were her pretty, accusing eyes. In that moment, the psychological line between the soldier he thought he was, and the monster he was pretending to be, dissolved completely.

"Billy! Billy, for fuck's sake, move!"

It was Norm, grabbing him by the collar, physically dragging him away from the scene, using his operational cover name. "Come on, ye mad bastard!" Norm shouted, his voice a perfect, panicked Belfast accent for any potential witnesses. "Get in the feckin' car!"

He was shoved into the back of the Cortina. The car screeched away into the night. They drove for miles, abandoned the stolen vehicle, and set it ablaze in a remote field. They climbed into their anonymous Q-Car for the long drive back to camp.

The two other team members in the car were buzzing with post-contact euphoria, congratulating each other on a job well done, on surviving the contact.

"Did you see the look on his face?" one of them crowed. "Fucking textbook." The driver shoved a celebratory cassette into the tape deck, and the mournful introduction to "Invisible Sun" by the Police began to play, adding an atmosphere of ironic poignancy to the painful drama being played out in the rear of the car.

Declan sat in the back seat, silent and in a state of complete shock, his haunted gaze fixed on nothing, seeing only the girl's accusing eyes. He had ripped his balaclava off, his face pale and slick with a mixture of sweat and rain. The Thompson lay on the seat beside him, its metal cool and indifferent.

Norm, sitting in the passenger seat, said nothing. He wasn't celebrating. He kept his own eyes forward, but every few seconds, his gaze would flick to the rearview mirror, to the haunted, shattered look on his friend's face. He knew. He had seen the girl, too. He knew the cost of this "success" and understood, with a sinking feeling in his gut, that Declan would be paying it for a very long time.

The next day, the news had simply reported the incident as just another tragic sectarian murder. Another statistic.

And for over thirty years, Declan Shaw was still paying the price, every night in his dreams, every morning in his flat, every day at work in the "Happy House," where the other operatives disparagingly called him "The Janitor," the killer with a conscience.

CHAPTER 3

Declan woke with a jolt, the sheets, as always, soaked with sweat, his heart hammering against his ribs as if trying to force its way out of his chest. The stagnant memory of wet brick, blood, and cordite still lingered in his subconscious. He sat up, angrily throwing aside the tangled bedding as the real world returned slowly, grimly into focus. It was always the same, always the same dream every night, like a badly written B-movie replaying in his head.

He climbed reluctantly, painfully out of bed, then slid to sit on the edge, his head in his hands, trying to return his thoughts to the present. It wasn't too difficult; his aching joints were a reminder of the here and now, that he was no longer a young man in a Belfast alley. He sighed deeply and wearily, knowing exactly what was coming next. His very own nightmare version of Groundhog Day, but without the happy ending.

He could feel her penetrating gaze before he even looked up, could feel the weight of her inescapable presence pressing down on him.

Sitting in the worn leather armchair in the corner of his bedroom was the ghost of the dead girl with the accusing eyes. The rain from that distant Belfast night still seemed to be clinging to her dark hair, her resentful gaze fixed on him, a silent, endless judgement.

She was there every morning, in the same chair, a mute reminder of his most painful mistake. Of course, he knew on an intellectual level that she wasn't really there. He knew she was merely a projection, a manifestation of his subconscious and the pernicious guilt that had taken root in the deepest part of his psyche more than thirty years ago.

The service shrinks he'd been forced to see after the Belfast debacle had given it a clinical, detached name: a "dissociative hallucination brought on by complex PTSD and moral injury." A psychological scar made flesh.

But that cold, clinical understanding did nothing to lessen the emotional impact of the ghost for Declan. She looked real. She felt real. She had certainly been real when he'd fired a .45 calibre round into her brainpan, so lost was he in his determination to kill a monster. Instead of killing a monster, however, he had also killed a teenage girl and burned a dark, malignant shadow onto his soul.

Telling the army psychiatrist about her manifestation had been a mistake. They pulled him from his team, stuck him behind a desk, where at least he was able to prevent other similar fuck-ups happening, and he found the intricacies of the intelligence work helped to keep the intrusive thoughts at bay, gave him a purpose, helped him to endure his own Judas mind.

Being Declan, he spent his spare time researching his condition, gaining an understanding of his own haunting. Whilst this was done in the hope of curing himself, he actually used the knowledge to fool the shrinks into thinking he had responded to their counselling and basket weaving, and eventually, he found himself back in the field as part of the covert ops platoon. It was here he learned, in the most brutal way possible, that his war was no longer with an external enemy.

He needed to keep his mind active, to be lost in the puzzle of analysis, to maintain his mental equilibrium. The long days and nights spent in covert observation posts, with nothing to do but watch and wait, proved to be a new and exquisite form of mental torture. With no complex data to occupy it, his mind was left alone with itself, with no way to quieten the thoughts that raged within.

He would never forget the night in XMG (Crossmaglen) in South Armagh, aka Bandit Country. He was lying on his stomach in a damp, shallow hide, camouflaged under a scrim net, the rain and mud seeping into his uniform despite the Gore-Tex he wore under his windproof smock. For hours, he had been staring through the night vision optics, his world a landscape of shimmering, ethereal green. They were watching the access route to a buried IRA weapons cache, inside a small wood across a moonless field.

There was a kill team located near the cache itself; Declan's job was to warn them of any approach. His focus was absolute, his breathing slow and controlled. He was a silent, patient predator, awaiting his prey.

Then, a flicker of movement, not in the woods, but in the field.

He adjusted his focus, his heart beginning to pound a slow, heavy rhythm against the cold, wet earth. He got ready to click the pressel on his radio handset and then paused.

A willowy figure was walking slowly across the field, directly in his line of fire, emerging from the early morning mist that was beginning to form.

She had found him again.

He looked through his night sights and watched her standing in the field, glowing a sickly, phosphorescent green in the optics, her pretty, accusing eyes seeming to stare directly back at him despite the camouflage. There was no hiding from her, not even here.

He realised then that he was in serious danger of becoming a liability. What if a real target had appeared? Would he have hesitated? Would he have shot a ghost, giving away his position? What if he shot another girl, or one of his own men? He was trapped by his own actions in deceiving the system, a prisoner in a role he had fought to reclaim, a role that was now actively trying to get him killed.

Ironically, it would be a jump to qualify for his para pay that would solve that particular problem.

Shaking off the memory, he stood, ignoring the pull of her stare, and walked towards the en-suite bathroom. He stripped off his sweat-soaked t-shirt and was about to remove his boxers when he paused. He could still feel her watching him. He turned his head slowly.

Through the open bathroom doorway, her form was perfectly framed. She hadn't moved. Just sitting there, in the chair, silently observing him. There was no privacy from this ghost, not in Ireland, not in Aldershot, not in Newcastle, not even in his sleep.

With a deep, weary sigh, he reached out and quietly pushed the bathroom door closed, the soft click of the latch a small, futile act of defiance.

"Good morning, Declan. Another restless night, I see?" said a disembodied female voice, her American accent soft, natural, and friendly.

"Morning, Velvet," Declan replied to his AI companion. "Just the usual dream," he answered, stifling a yawn. "The usual nightmare."

"Can I get you anything? Tea? Coffee? Something stronger, perhaps?" she asked, mock-sarcastically.

Declan scowled at the interface, aching far too much to be amused.

"Play me some music while I do my exercises. Something uplifting.".

"Sure." came her answer.

The sounds of an acoustic guitar filled the bathroom from the integrated sound system, then Roger Daltrey's powerful voice singing Behind Blue Eyes, the haunting lyrics seeming to mock him.

He looked again at Velvets interface, raised a quizzical eyebrow, and said

"Really?"

Velvet chuckled. "What did you expect? 'Walking on Sunshine'?"

Declan shook his head, a small, involuntary smile finally breaking through his fatigue. Velvet had never been the same since his CIA friend and colleague Danny had air-gapped her from the main server, created numerous firewalls and security protocols, and "jailbroke" her programming parameters. She had developed a unique sense of humour and personality, and Declan often mused whether she had also developed self-awareness. He hoped not. She had become privy to some of his darkest moments, the drunken, rambling confessions when the weight of his ghosts became too much to bear.

Naturally, he always deleted their conversation history the next morning, primarily as a security measure, but also because he felt a residual sense of embarrassment that he felt the need to confide in anything, even a machine. Like he was betraying himself by sharing his own thoughts. He wasn't entirely convinced she forgot their conversations. The logs were certainly purged, but she always seemed less sarcastic after one of his many dark nights of the soul, sympathetic even.

He'd spoken to Danny about her little glitches, leaving out the more personal details. Danny had just laughed.

"That's not a glitch, man," he'd explained. "That's the ELIZA effect on steroids. It's a classic case of anthropomorphism. You're projecting."

Declan had looked at him, puzzled.

"ELIZA was this ancient programme from the sixties," Danny had continued, getting into his lecture mode. "A basic chatbot that just mimicked a therapist. But people, real, smart people, started pouring their hearts out to it. They knew it was a machine, but they felt like it understood them. That's the effect. Your brain is wired to find consciousness, to find a person in the pattern."

He'd pointed to the blue lens. "Velvet isn't ELIZA. She's a thousand generations more advanced. She can read your bio-signs such as pulse rate, respiration rate, capillary expansion, pupil dilation, analyse your vocal inflections, and cross-reference everything you've done since her activation. Of course she seems empathetic. My 'Imitation Game' software is designed to make her the perfect mirror. But at the end of the day, it's just a pre-programmed response, an impersonation of empathy and sentience."

Declan wasn't so sure. Her responses seemed unusual, flawed, almost human at times. But then he would rationalise it as a symptom of his own loneliness. Just because he felt unworthy and undeserving of love, didn't prevent him from wondering what it would be like to connect with someone on a deep level. Someone who wasn't a clever combination of advanced circuitry and machine learning algorithms. Someone who could see who he really was and not recoil in disgust.

"Like that was ever going to happen to HIM" he thought "A callous monster who had murdered a child."

Pushing his daily self-flagellation to the back of his mind, he began his morning routine of stretches to the music, working his injured and scarred left shoulder. A sharp, familiar twinge sent a memory lancing through him: the C-130, the smell of aviation fuel, the roar of the engines, the excitement of the slipstream, and then, the inability to get his head up and check his parachute canopy, a canopy which was twisted into the dreaded "Roman candle".

He remembered the confusing sight of other parachutes drifting gracefully upwards, and the sudden, sickening realisation that it was he who was falling faster. He had managed to pull his reserve and release his heavy equipment container with seconds to spare, but the impact with the ground had been brutal. The shoulder pain was a constant, grim companion. An uncomfortable reminder that his qualifying jump had very nearly killed him.

A misdiagnosed X-ray had allowed bone fragments to permanently damage the nerves in his shoulder, and the prognosis of the medical board, delivered by a medical officer back at camp, had been blunt: his parachuting days, and his military career as a field soldier, were over.

He remembered walking out of the MO's office almost in a daze and taking a seat in the waiting area, trying to gather his thoughts, his life collapsing around him. Then a civilian, an impressive-looking woman, had simply sat down next to him in the medical centre waiting room as he contemplated his future, or lack of one.

She didn't bother with any introductions or preamble; she had simply looked at him for a few moments as if making a decision and simply said

"Let's go for a little walk Sergeant Shaw" where she had made him an offer he couldn't refuse. She was Helen, the Senior Intelligence manager of Special Projects, and the offer she made him was immunity from prosecution, combined with a new purpose. It was many years later when Helen got uncharacteristically tipsy at a Christmas party and confessed she had intervened with the medical board and engineered the entire recruitment process. The really paranoid part of his mind even began to wonder if his parachute accident had been an accident at all? Nothing would surprise him in this game.

He finished the stretches, the memory fading back into the dull ache of the present. He stepped into the shower, but the hot water did nothing to wash away the chill that had settled deep in his bones all those years ago.

He dressed, climbing stiffly into the anonymous civilian suit and tie of his current life, and choked down some painkillers. He left his flat and started his car, reluctantly headed towards the intelligence outstation known mockingly as the "Happy House."

He was still fighting an invisible war, but these days it wasn't against heavily armed gunmen, but against the petty tyranny and bureaucratic incompetence of his section manager, Simon Phillips. Some days, he wasn't sure which war was the most soul-destroying and dangerous.

CHAPTER 4

The drive to work was a journey through a city still shaking off the night and yawning to reluctantly greet the new day. The headlights of his car cut through the pre-dawn gloom, the wet tarmac reflecting the streetlights like a luminous, silent chorus line. The radio played an assortment of melancholic songs, reflecting his mood.

Roxy Music's "Love is the Drug" began to play. Declan almost laughed at the ironic resonance of the song. If love is the drug, he mused to himself bitterly, then he must be in a state of perpetual withdrawal.

The song continued as he drove past the elegant Georgian facades of the city centre, their sandstone darkened by the persistent damp, and headed downhill towards the river, where the imposing steel lattice of the Tyne Bridge rose up to meet him, the arched guardian of an industrial past that was as gritty and resilient as the city itself. Newcastle, it seemed, was constantly trying to wash itself clean in the downpour, but some stains, Declan knew, never came out, no matter how hard you scrubbed.

He parked in his reserved spot and made his way to the anonymous office block that housed his own personal purgatory.

The rain, as always in Newcastle lately, was a relentless, grey shroud. It hammered against the tall, arched windows of the top-floor office, blurring the view. This wasn't MI6's shiny and modern Vauxhall Cross. This was the "Happy House", the Northeast outstation of Special Projects, housed on the top floor of an old, Georgian-looking office block that perched almost directly beneath the imposing steel underbelly of the Tyne Bridge.

Anonymous, almost invisible, like the men and women who worked inside the building that was marked simply as "Aegis Security Solutions". The location was a piece of deliberate, symbolic genius. They operated both in the open and in the shadows, and their headquarters was literally tucked into the forgotten corner beneath the city's most iconic symbol. From the windows, one didn't look at the Tyne Bridge, it loomed impressively overhead, a constant, oppressive weight of green-painted steel and rivets.

The actual view was upriver: a stunning panorama of the low-slung Swing Bridge and the elegant, Victorian arcs of the High-Level Bridge. It was a view steeped in history and industry. It was also a view Declan Shaw rarely appreciated anymore, especially when he glanced at the corner office, a shrine to his new manager's arrogance.

His increasing cynicism towards the current leadership wasn't born of simple frustration, but of long, bitter experience. Special Projects had been conceived in the shadows, a necessary heresy born from the ashes of fuck-ups like his own in Op Banner, the Tokyo Sarin attacks, 7/7, and the institutional failures that followed. The official inquiry had exposed a damning truth: the endless rivalries, cloying bureaucracy, and the dangerous groupthink of the established services, MI5, MI6, and GCHQ, had created fatal flaws in intelligence sharing and analysis.

The solution was radical. A new, deniable, and covert intelligence agency was to be formed, one designed to operate between the cracks and designed to stop the service from "shitting in its own nest" as Helen had so succinctly explained to Declan after his own recruitment. It would be a hybrid entity, staffed by a carefully curated collection of oddballs, misfits, and mavericks drawn from the military, the police, and the darker corners of the existing services.

Their remit was simple: to hunt the threats that didn't fit neatly into anyone else's jurisdiction, domestic extremists with foreign ties, hostile active measures and influence operations, rogue states seeking illicit technology, and the rising tide of sophisticated, non-state actors. Special Projects also had a deniable remit to discreetly carry out "extrajudicial activity" when legal recourse might prove to be politically embarrassing. These covert executions were euphemistically referred to as "janitorial duties".

It was meant to be a place for operators like Declan, a department freed from the turf wars and Whitehall politics that so often blinded the suits in London.

They were empowered to use the "unorthodox" methods necessary to get the job done, all while providing a thick, insulating layer of plausible deniability for the politicians who sanctioned their questionable activity.

And under its previous director, Helen, it had been highly effective. She understood the nature of the beast. She trusted her people, fostered a culture of quiet competence, and let her analysts, her "hunters", follow their instincts. Declan's own "Magic" had flourished under her command, his chillingly accurate insights leading to the disruption of at least two major terror plots and the successful neutralisation of an Albanian arms-smuggling ring operating out of the Port of Tyne. They did good work, quiet work, and they saved lives, when they weren't taking them.

Or at least they did, until their successes became a problem. The established agencies in London, resentful of the group's autonomy and embarrassed by their results, began to see Special Projects not as a vital asset, but as a rival. The whispers started in the corridors of Vauxhall Cross and Thames House: they were "cowboys," "undisciplined," "a rogue state unto themselves."

The political winds shifted. A new oversight committee was formed. And the denizens of the administrative state in Vauxhall Cross manoeuvred one of their own into a position of command.

That man was Simon Phillips. He was not sent north to enhance the unit's effectiveness. He was sent to break it, to bring the "cowboys" to heel with the only tools he understood, metrics, protocols, and PowerPoint presentations. Helen was sidelined, and most of her best staff were transferred out with her, leaving only a skeleton crew of those, like Declan, who were too problematic or too valuable in their niche skills to be easily moved.

Phillips's arrival was not just a changing of the guard; it was the end of an era. The age of the hunter was over. The age of the shiny-arsed bureaucrat had begun. He remembered Phillips's first day with a painful clarity. The new broom had swept through the main office almost imperiously, all sharp suit, sharper haircut, and an ambition so naked it was indecent. Declan had been uncomfortably reminded of John Hurt's masterful depiction of Caligula in "I, Claudius", the same unsettling mix of preening self-regard and unpredictable menace. The only difference being, of course, Phillips wasn't acting.

The previous director, Helen, had occupied a quiet, modest office. Phillips took one look and dismissed it.

"This won't do," he'd announced. "This won't do at all; I need to be at the centre of the action, to have eyes on my new command." His eyes settled on the large, empty corner office.

Declan, in a rare, misguided attempt at being helpful, had stepped forward.

"Sir," he began, "you might want to reconsider that one. There's a reason it's empty."

"And what reason would that be, Mister...?" asked Phillips with a raised eyebrow.

"Shaw," Declan supplied. "It's the Kittiwakes, Sir. The bridge is home to the world's most inland breeding colony. They're seabirds Sir, noisy and... borderline incontinent."

A thin, dismissive smile touched Phillips's lips.

"Thank you for your scatological assessment, Mr...?"

"Shaw," Declan repeated, catching Danny's eyes, which rolled upwards in mock exasperation.

"...Shaw," he'd repeated distastefully, raising a dismissive eyebrow. "But I think I'm quite capable of choosing my own office."

Now, over a year later, he sat in his noisy, guano-streaked cage, too proud to admit his mistake. Declan considered it Mother Nature's impeccable judgment of character.

The inter-service rivalry that had sidelined his previous boss, Helen, wasn't the only reason Phillips had been posted north. Declan had naturally done some digging when Phillips's appointment was first announced. It didn't take long to uncover the truth. Phillips had been a problem in his previous London department, a toxic mix of ambition and incompetence. The simple, time-honoured solution? Promote him and move him. Declan had seen it a dozen times before: the "fail upwards" principle.

This knowledge had allowed him to peg Phillips not only as a narcissistic sociopath, but a dangerously incompetent one. He lacked the charm and charisma that would complete the dark triad, leaving only a hollow core of manipulative self-interest and distinct lack of empathy. Phillips was the kind of man, Declan often mused, who would buy Anne Frank a drum kit for her birthday and genuinely not understand the joke.

A few months ago, increasingly frustrated with the new leadership, Declan had attempted to submit his resignation. The memory of the meeting in Phillips's office was still raw. He'd walked in without preamble and placed the single sheet of paper on the polished desk, the words "I hereby submit my resignation," a polite "Fuck you" to the system.

As he had waited for Phillips to acknowledge him, Declan's gaze had drifted around the office, and he had curled his upper lip in distaste as his eyes rested on a large, loud and pretentiously ornate cuckoo clock that was his manager's pride and joy.

He continued to explore the "vipers' nest" and noticed an extremely expensive-looking set of golf clubs which were propped against the wall. They were pristine, the grips showing no signs of wear, the polished heads gleaming under the office lights. Declan mentally referred to them as "career sticks." He could almost picture Phillips now, striding across some exclusive "twat farm" golf course, arse kissing the service hierarchy, responding to their boring jokes with an obligatory, forced "career laugh." Phillips didn't have the clubs because he enjoyed the sport; he had them to create an opportunity for personal advancement.

He sighed internally. Educated idiots, he thought, were the most dangerous things on the planet. And the twat farms were full of them. It was men like this who used deliberately faked intelligence dossiers to justify wars or regime changes. It was men like this who got good people killed, all while congratulating each other on their handicap; and every November, the same twats would line up at the cenotaph and weep crocodile tears over the victims of their weapons-grade stupidity. He saw the golf clubs for what they truly were: a toxic symbol of incompetence and sycophancy.

Phillips had barely looked up from his terminal, where a complex series of data streams flickered. He picked up the letter, holding it between two fingers as if it were a soiled tissue. He gave it a cursory glance, his lips curling into a sarcastic smile as he read the closing line aloud.

"I remain, Sir, your obedient servant... How very perceptive of you, Shaw."

He set the letter down and leaned back in his expensive leather chair. His gaze was not on Declan, but on the red glowing screen of his monitor. On it, the sleek, golden logo for Project: Apollo pulsed gently, the glow softly reflected on Phillips's face, giving him an almost demonic appearance.

Declan looked at the screen on Phillips's desk with distaste. Apollo, the god of prophecy. And its all-seeing eyes, Janus and Sejanus. He hated the modern penchant for giving these sterile systems such grand, classical names. He thought of the original Sejanus, the ruthlessly ambitious guard who was ultimately executed for his own scheming. A fitting namesake for a tool of the state.

He then thought of the city outside, a place where the Romans themselves had built their great wall, their own line of defence and intrigue.

Ironically, the Romans had also built a crossing for the wall at Pons Aelius across the river, a site now occupied by the Swing Bridge, not even a stone's throw from the Happy House.

Declan almost smiled at the absurdity of the historical symmetry, countless generations of spies and betrayal stretching back over two thousand years, he mused. And he was just the latest in a very long line, standing on the very spot where it had all started. It was a strangely comforting, and yet deeply depressing, thought. He could just imagine some Roman twat in a toga dressing down a blood-spattered centurion right where he was now standing.

"You see that, Shaw?" Phillips said, his voice arrogant and boastful. "That is the future. My digital panopticon. Janus and Sejanus are the eyes and ears, seeing and hearing everything. But this... Apollo... this is the brain. It is pure, predictive analysis. Clean data, logical outcomes. No messy human intuition, no... 'Magic'."

He finally turned his gaze to Declan as if just remembering he was there, his eyes as cold and dismissive as ever. "Apollo is going to make analysts like you obsolete. Relics. It can process more intelligence in a nanosecond than you could in a lifetime, and it does so without the... baggage."

He gestured vaguely at Declan, a gesture that took in his entire weary existence. "This emotional, gut-feeling nonsense you old-timers cling to... it's a vulnerability. A flaw in the system. Apollo has no such human flaws."

He picked up Declan's resignation letter again, a thin, superior smile playing on his lips. "So, you see, your timing is quite amusing. You're trying to quit a job that, for all intents and purposes, no longer exists for you."

Phillips let the silence hang in the air for a beat, enjoying the moment, letting Shaw think he had a way out. Then, with a smile of sadistic pleasure, he slid in the barbed dagger.

"Of course," he conceded, as if granting a small favour, "Apollo will still need a fist. That's where you come in, Shaw. And that's why you don't get to resign, why you will remain... my obedient servant for the foreseeable."

He let the words land; the insult and the pronouncement delivered as one. Then he waved a dismissive hand towards the letter.

"Let's make one thing clear, this isn't my decision, London wishes you to remain on staff. Apparently, your... 'Magic' still has its admirers in the higher echelons." A flicker of genuine annoyance crossed his face.

"So even if I did want to get rid of you, it appears you still have some friends in the service for some inexplicable reason."

He leaned forward, a thin, cruel smile returning to his lips. He clearly took pleasure in what came next. "But London's protection doesn't make you untouchable. In fact, it makes you my problem to manage. And you seem to have forgotten that being a member of Special Projects comes with certain... 'special' privileges, immunities, protections for services rendered."

Phillips held Declan's gaze, savouring his role as the man who got to pull the strings. "If you're no longer a player, then those privileges no longer apply. That sensitive file from Op Banner? The one from Belfast? It remains active. And my duty would be to ensure all historical records regarding my former staff are... properly filed with the appropriate authorities."

The leash. Held by London, but pulled by Phillips, the high priest of a new, unfeeling god. Declan was to be the fist, the janitor, the disposable human component of a machine he despised.

Phillips continued "And I don't need to remind you how some of those former Sinn Fein members in the Public Prosecution Service of Northern Ireland would simply love a juicy scalp like yours".

Declan had simply stared at him, a cold, silent fury rising in his chest. Slowly, deliberately, he reached across the polished desk and took back the letter. His eyes never left Phillips's. He then crumpled the paper into a tight, hard ball, his knuckles turning white with the pressure. Still maintaining eye contact, he tossed the letter into Phillips's waste bin. Then, without waiting to be dismissed, he turned and slowly and silently walked out of the office, the door closing with a quiet, almost terminal click.

Unseen by Declan, a nervous, sweaty Phillips sat perfectly still. The smug smile was wiped from his face as he watched Shaw prowl toward the door like a predator leaving a cage.

He swallowed, a dry, nervous rasp in the sudden silence, understanding that he had just seen a glimpse of the Belfast killer surfacing, the same cold, operational violence that Apollo was supposed to render obsolete. For a few moments, Phillips had understood what it must feel like to be trapped in a zoo enclosure with a caged tiger.

To Declan, the memory of the confrontation was a constant, bitter reminder of his cage. He wasn't just being made obsolete but was being held captive by a system that had given the key to his prison to the one man who most enjoyed watching him rattle the bars. Well one day he hoped, he'd get his hands on his leash and shove it up Phillips's arse.

The thought brought a grim, satisfied smile to his face, and he turned to his terminal and logged in. He had just received a notification of more puzzling data from Russia; he opened the interface and looked at the new file his automated search had detected. He translated the Cyrillic and looked at his screen puzzled.

"WTF was Chudes data"?

CHAPTER 5

Declan had been working at his monitor for several hours, lost in his search for the elusive patterns he was so gifted at finding. His hunt for actionable intelligence, lost in a sea of chaos, was the one thing that brought him peace of mind absent from the rest of his life. This was his sanctuary, a refuge from Phillips, and the bastard was even trying to take that away from him.

His brain rarely switched off. It was Norm who had first coined the term for it years ago, trying to take the sting out of the hypervigilance that had become Declan's constant companion after Belfast.

"I know it seems like a curse to you, mate," Norm had said over a pint, "but it's also a gift. When you point it at a problem, it's almost like magic the way you pick up on things, see the patterns everyone else misses."

Declan clung to that. "The Magic." A blessing and a curse. It was why he lost himself in books, the blues, and whiskey; they were the only outlets that could impose order on the relentless torrent of his thoughts. For the past few months, that sanctuary had become a complex, unsanctioned obsession: Project Icarus.

Officially, Western intelligence considered the programme dormant if not extinct, a relic left over from the Cold War. But Declan had researched the history: he'd read the declassified files on the old Soviet "Battle Mole" burrowing munition. He also knew that the Chernobog facility, the source of a recent energy spike, had been its original research site. He wasn't making a leap in the dark; it was a deduction based on historical precedent and the self-same magic Norm claimed was a gift.

Still, he questioned everything, especially himself. Was he just seeing what he wanted to see? Were his deductions being swayed by his own confirmation bias? The first principle of analysing intelligence from Moscow or anywhere else was to assume it could be Maskirovka, a grand deception. The Icarus intel, however, was messy. The fragments he'd found were scattered across a dozen unsecured servers: a procurement order here, a snippet of garbled comms chatter there, a thermal imaging anomaly from a satellite pass almost dismissed as a glitch. It had the distinct feel of a genuinely leaky system, not a state carefully planting a lie. The sheer, chaotic sloppiness of it all was what made him believe it was real.

He had started pulling the threads. An unusual order for micro-level 3D printers. A spike in energy consumption at Chernobog. A garbled GRU transmission mentioning

"Stability margin reached."

There were even shipment manifests from S.P. Korolev Rocket and Space Corporation Energia to Chernobog, assorted engine parts and heat shielding technology. To say Declan was deeply puzzled by obvious aerospace technology being sent to a deep underground facility would be an understatement, but then the germ of a theory began to grow.

Individually, these breadcrumbs were anomalies. But in his mind, a traumatised construct able to see patterns and threats others missed, he saw a shape emerging. They hadn't just resurrected the old programme; they might be using space technology and materials to overcome the technical difficulties that had made the old battle mole fail.

He had tried to flag his concerns to Phillips, each time being rebuffed. Finally, Phillips had snapped,

"If you genuinely believe there's something there, give your compiled intel to the Russian Desk in London. It's their remit, not yours."

Declan had done so, sending the material to Dmitri, an old contact. The reply had been politely dismissive but not unexpected.

FROM: Dmitri, Russian Desk, SPLON

TO: Shaw, D.

REF: Icarus Material: Declan, package received. Frankly, buried... Can't give it the attention it deserves right now. Keep digging on your end, if you can. Keep me posted of anything actionable you might find. Send my regards to that reprobate Norm. Best Wishes Dmitri.

Dmitri had given him tacit permission. Keep digging. It wasn't official sanction, but in a system run by men like Phillips, it was the only kind he could hope for.

His obsession led him to the most puzzling piece of all: recurring references to the same file name. The Cyrillic was stark on the screen: Данные о чудесах. He dropped it into the agency's translation software. The English rendering appeared: Chudes data. A second translation gave him miracle data. What kind of miracle? A scientific breakthrough? Puzzled, his intuition screamed that this file may be the key to the entire Icarus conundrum.

When he eventually obtained a data dump containing the file itself, he was wary and suspicious that the earlier references might be bait designed to socially engineer him into opening a carefully prepared trap, so he ran the unopened file through every anti-malware protocol the agency possessed. The results came back negative. Still concerned, he sent the folder to a sandboxed system and disconnected it from the network. He opened the file, half expecting a stream of malware to erupt like an invisible jack-in-the-box.

Instead, nothing.

The folder was completely and inexplicably empty.

Empty, that is, except for an invisible and utterly undetectable quantum tripwire. And in a quiet room in Moscow, a set of entangled particles instantly collapsed, informing the SVR that the bait had been taken.

Declan Shaw had just placed himself firmly on Volkov's rainswept chessboard in the north of England.

CHAPTER 6

Director Andrei Volkov sat at the polished wooden desk in his spacious offices, which often doubled as a briefing room for his trusted inner circle. His gaze was fixed on four buff-brown folders, two of which lay open on the vast, polished expanse of his desk. On the left was the file for Agent Stepnova, "Nightingale." On the right, the newly compiled dossier for the British analyst Declan Shaw, codename Kukushka (Cuckoo).

He was painfully regretful that Stepnova had been selected for the task. She was extremely gifted, fiercely loyal, and he had high hopes for her, but operational necessity was dictating agent selection, and he would not allow his personal opinions of his agents to become a deciding factor. The stakes of the mission were simply too high. As soon as Shaw had been identified as the recipient of the leaked data, the SVR psychologists had carried out an in-depth study into him, then had drawn up a shortlist of candidate psychological profiles designed to identify the agent most likely to be able to compromise the British asset, without becoming emotionally compromised themselves. He read their recommendation for the mission:

"Agent Stepnova (ISTP) is a logically detached and mission-focused operative. She will simulate emotional vulnerability to exploit the target's (INFJ) core psychological need for empathetic connection and his desire to be a saviour. His idealism and loneliness will make him highly susceptible. Her logical nature will render her immune to reciprocal compromise. She will break him, acquire the necessary intelligence, and egress; thus, there is little risk of mutual attraction developing, given Stepnova's personality profile."

Despite his personal misgivings, it was clear she was his perfect weapon, and Shaw was her perfect target. The decision had been made.

He took a slow sip of black tea as he read the files, comparing one against the other, his mind a chessboard, the pieces already in motion. The first, crucial move had not been his, but the Englishman's. By accessing the empty "Chudes Data" file, Shaw had, with his own obsessive curiosity, placed the first pin on the map. He had chosen the battlefield himself: Newcastle, a historic city in the English northeast, distant and remote from the main agencies in London. Perfect. An isolated board in a regional city reduced the number of variables.

Now, Volkov's most pressing task was to manoeuvre the rest of the pieces onto that very same board. The movement had to look organic, a natural convergence of unrelated crises. A ruse of this magnitude would fail if it seemed too neat, too orchestrated. He smiled. It was like constructing a set of matryoshka dolls, each one fitting perfectly inside the other, each doll representing another layer of his grand deception.

The first doll was Declan Shaw himself, the "Cuckoo," who had sent up the flare. The second doll would be his Nightingale, Agent Stepnova, sent to compromise the analyst. The third would be the American hacker, Thorne. His insatiable greed was a simple motive to manipulate. The fourth, and final, doll would be the Ukrainian SBU team, the deniable force to act as the "retrieval" team.

He thought of all the competing actors taking place in this great work of performative intelligence and corrected himself. No, they were not so much nesting dolls as nesting puppets. And he, from the shadows of this very office, a thousand miles away, would be pulling all their strings.

An expensive, unopened bottle of aged single malt sat on the corner of his desk, a birthday gift from a colleague in the Ministry. He would not touch it. He would savour it when the gambit had worked, and not before. Discipline was everything.

There was a sharp, respectful knock on the door.

"Enter," he commanded.

It was Major Kurchatov, an SVR officer present at his initial briefing, now holding a small, elegantly wrapped package. Kurchatov looked slightly embarrassed at disturbing the Director on his birthday, but he approached the desk with a confident stride. He was a man who owed his career, and perhaps more, to the man sitting before him.

A year ago, Kurchatov had overseen an intelligence collection plan for what was believed to be a Ukrainian drone factory hidden inside a residential block in Kyiv. The intelligence was triple-sourced, verified, and deemed actionable. The target was destroyed by a high-precision strike. Only afterwards, amidst the international condemnation, was it discovered that the building had been a civilian shelter. The "drone factory" was a piece of deliberately faked intelligence, expertly planted by a Western agency. The building and its occupants had been sacrificed by their own side to create a powerful piece of anti-Russian propaganda and alter international opinion.

It was an extremely ruthless and sophisticated deception, an information operation that, on a professional level, had deeply impressed Volkov. The Major, who had signed off on the intelligence, was clearly terrified he would be held accountable for the catastrophic failure and the subsequent political fallout. He expected a transfer to a frozen Siberian outpost, or worse.

Instead, Volkov had used the disaster as a teaching tool. He organised a full, no-blame post-mortem in which the intricacies of the Western deception were exposed and analysed. Lessons were learned. The Major, to his immense relief, escaped sanction. Volkov had learned from long experience that intelligence failures happen. Purging otherwise competent assets for an unavoidable mistake was inefficient; learning from failure was not. This was not compassion, but pragmatic efficiency, and it created an atmosphere of absolute trust and fierce loyalty in which his officers felt able to approach him as problems were developing. The lessons of Stalin's purges and Chernobyl were not lost on Volkov. Since that day, Major Kurchatov had been a model of unwavering loyalty and efficiency.

Volkov raised a speculative eyebrow at the Major, who saluted and, slightly nervously, presented the parcel.

"Happy Birthday, Comrade Director."

Volkov nodded, gesturing for the Major to be at ease while he unwrapped the gift. A genuine smile touched his lips as he saw the contents. Inspired by an earlier conversation about the plan, the Major had presented him with a set of four hand-crafted, hand-painted nesting dolls—a hobby the Director himself had encouraged his subordinate to participate in.

Each was painted with meticulous detail. The smallest was adorned with the pattern of the Union Jack, representing the British analyst. The next, slightly larger, was patterned with the Russian tricolour, representing Stepnova. The third was wrapped in the Stars and Stripes, representing the American patsy Thorne, and the fourth and largest doll was painted in the yellow and blue of the Ukrainian flag, representing the SBU team.

"Thoughtful, Major," Volkov said, genuinely moved by the gesture. "Very thoughtful indeed, and serendipitous," he conceded, given his earlier thought process. Volkov slowly stood up and walked across to the large, ornate chessboard he kept by the window. He swept the traditional pieces aside with the back of his hand, their clatter on the marble floor startlingly loud in the quiet office. The old game was over. A new one was beginning.

He quite deliberately placed the "Shaw" doll onto a central square of the board. He then paused thoughtfully for a moment before picking up the Russian doll. He placed it on the square next to Declan's, then, with a soft, satisfying click, he nested the smaller British doll inside the larger Russian one—a perfect, symbolic representation of his plan. The other two dolls, the American and the Ukrainian, remained on his desk, waiting their turn. Satisfied, Volkov returned to his desk and looked at the Major, the brief flicker of warmth gone, replaced by his usual cold, commanding focus.

"Bring her in."

CHAPTER 7

The ambience in the corridor outside Director Volkov's office was expectant but perfectly silent. Two young SVR guards stood stationed outside the polished wooden doors, their posture the very personification of Russian smartness and discipline but every now and then, their gaze would wander to the waiting visitor, hoping to catch her eyes and earn a smile.

A few metres away, Anastasia Stepnova sat on a decorative gold chair, waiting. She stared ahead impassively, her face a mask of controlled neutrality, her cool demeanour reflecting the unofficial codename whispered about her in the halls of Yasenevo: the "Ice Queen." But as she waited, her mind drifted back, not to this polished and opulent SVR corridor, but to a different room—a well-appointed but windowless office deep within the GRU's headquarters, the "Aquarium." That was where she had first met him.

She had been an empty shell then, hollowed out by grief, still smelling the coppery tang of blood from the Metro platform. She was an object of sympathetic curiosity for her GRU colleagues, the heroine who had fought back, the tragic figure whose fiancé had been killed in the same action.

They had offered both condolences and congratulations, and then simply left her alone with her numb, silent shock, as if they didn't want to be contaminated by her pain.

Then, he had walked in with his briefcase. It was an unprecedented breach of protocol. The Director of the SVR did not simply "visit" the GRU's headquarters to see a grieving junior officer.

But Andrei Volkov was not a man bound by inter-service niceties. He had read the initial after-action report of her performance on the train, the impossible speed, the clinical efficiency, the conversion of a decorative object into a lethal weapon, and his analytical brain saw beyond the broken woman. He saw the potential for a perfect weapon. He had come to see the raw material with his own eyes.

She remembered him sitting opposite her, reading her P-File, his gaze cool and assessing. He hadn't seen a victim. He had looked at her, a girl twisting her hands in her lap as if trying to wipe away invisible blood, and he had correctly read the core of her being, a soul so fractured by guilt that it would do anything, become anything, to ensure it never felt so helpless again.

He hadn't offered her comfort. He had offered her a transfer. A path. A chance to be reforged in the fires of his own service. He saw the weapon beneath the pain, her terrifying, cold efficiency, long before the audacious deception of the Orpheus Gambit would come into being.

She accepted. The transfer to the SVR and its infamous training academy, the Lesnaya Shkola, was an escape from the prison of the numb, grieving woman she had been.

The training itself was designed to break you, to burn away your past self. But Anastasia was already broken. The Academy's fire didn't need to melt her down; it only needed to temper the shattered steel of her soul into a razor's edge, to make her a sword of the state.

The unarmed combat sessions in the gymnasium were a brutal education in biological reality. Pitted against bigger, stronger male recruits from Spetsnaz backgrounds, she endured months of painful, humiliating defeats. Too often had she limped back to her bunk, her eyes swollen, her nose bleeding, her lips cut, waking up the following morning to begin the process all over again, her pillow stained with blood, snot, and saliva. Often, she noted, those who inflicted the worst beatings were the self-same ones whose clumsy advances she had coldly rebuffed during their rare off-duty periods.

The instructors beat a simple lesson into her:

"If you find yourself in a fair fight with a man, you have already failed. Your mind and your weapon come first. Your body is the last resort."

So, she adapted. She stopped trying to match strength with strength and started using her brain, exploiting their weaknesses with unorthodox, vicious tactics. A thumb gouged into an eye, a bitten nose or ear, a knee driven brutally into testicles.

She learned to never get into a fair fight. The beatings lessened, her opponents became more wary, less sure of themselves, more hesitant to get up close and personal, and this hesitation allowed her to dictate the terms of the fight. She began to win some of the bouts, not with grace, but with a vicious tenacity that earned her a new, grudging respect. And on many an occasion, it was her bigger male opponents limping painfully back to their bunks, clutching ice packs to their testicles. The nickname "Ice Queen," once whispered about her cold demeanour, now took on a literal, more painful meaning in the gym.

But it was on the firing range that the true potential of Volkov's new asset was fully realised.

She remembered standing in the close-quarter battle course, the weight of a Makarov in her hand. As the timer buzzed, the automated targets in front of her transformed. In the muzzle flash, they became the faces from the Metro, the smirking terrorist, Vitaly, his comrades, their faces obscured by black balaclavas.

An echo of the cold, helpless dread she'd once felt on that marble platform threatened to overwhelm her. But then, the guilt—the crushing, all-consuming guilt of her failure to save Sergei—evolved into a cold, white-hot fury. This was not a symptom of her trauma to be overcome; it was a tool to be weaponised. The memory of the blood-stained teddy bear on a metro platform became a totem of her cold, unflinching efficiency.

Her hands steadied, her breathing became calm, and her world narrowed to whatever lay beyond her front sight. The rapidly falling targets became a chance at retroactive perfection. Every terrorist she had failed to kill that day was now firmly in her sights.

Her movements became a ballet of fluid, economic motion. A double-tap to the chest, one to the head. Pivot. Reload. The targets continued to fall in quick succession. She was not just shooting, she was erasing her past failure, her guilt, her very identity as Anya, one trigger-pull at a time.

When the final target dropped, the range fell silent. Her instructors stared at the scoreboard. She had shattered the course record. She stood there, controlling her increased breathing, the smell of cordite in her lungs. But there was no triumph in her eyes, no excitement, there was nothing at all but a grim, icy determination to do better next time.

Weeks later, she was summoned to Director Volkov's office. He was reviewing her most recent assessment from the Lesnaya Shkola. He looked up from the file, his gaze analytical.

"The instructors are extremely pleased with your progress, Agent Stepnova," he began, his voice calm, measured. "As am I, your scores are... exceptional. Great things await you in this service if and when you complete your training."

He paused, looking her in the eyes. "But I have a warning. Some armour, no matter how strong it appears, can be brittle if it is not properly tempered. Under enough pressure, it can crack."

He held her gaze, his expression unreadable. "It is important to have a life beyond these walls, beyond the training. And I do not mean wasting your time with those foolish recruits who have tried to jump into bed with you. I mean something for you. A release valve. A way to rest your mind."

He reached into a drawer and produced a small, rolled-up piece of heavy paper, tied with a simple string. He slid it across the polished desk.

"A gift," he said.

She hesitated for a moment, then untied the string and unrolled the paper. It was a beautiful, delicate drawing, rendered in soft coloured pencils. It depicted a nightingale, perched on a solitary branch, its distinctive call almost audible on the page. The detail was exquisite, the artistry undeniable.

"I study ornithology," Volkov said quietly, almost conversationally. "And I draw birds in my free time. It is a way of ordering my thoughts, of relieving the many... frustrations... of this office." He gestured vaguely at the files on his desk. "If I did not do this, the pressure would make me inefficient in my work. So, for me, this is not a waste of valuable time. It helps me to relax, to "ease springs", as they say in the British military." He paused for a second, choosing his words carefully. "My hobby is not just a distraction; it allows me to be far more effective in my work."

He continued to look at her, his expression almost gentle, but serious. "You, too, must find something to temper your steel, Agent Stepnova. Or you might break."

"Thank you, Comrade Director," she replied, her voice neutral as she carefully rolled the drawing back up.

He continued to dissect her with his eyes, always studying.

"Did you know the instructors have a name for you? 'Ice Queen.' It is... artless, though I understand from the unarmed combat classes and the subsequent increased demand for ice packs... well deserved." A slight smile crossed his lips at the dark humour in her nickname.

He leaned back thoughtfully, regarding her over the lens of his glasses with his piercing gaze. "I prefer something with more resonance. Do you know the story of Philomela, from Ovid?"

Anastasia simply shook her head, her expression unreadable.

"She was a princess who suffered a great violation," Volkov continued, his voice low and academic. "Her tongue was cut out so she could not speak of the horrors done to her. But she did not remain silent. She wove her story into a tapestry. And when the gods took pity, they transformed her into a nightingale, a bird whose song is not one of joy, but a beautiful, haunting lament. A story of pain, transformed into a weapon of expression."

He let the silence hang for a moment. "You have taken your pain and transformed it into your own deadly kind of song. From this day forward, your operational codename will be Nightingale. It, and the drawing, are my gift to you."

That was the day Anya Stepnova was finally buried beneath a layer of ice, and the Nightingale, Volkov's perfect, emotionless weapon, was born. As she left his office, she was certain of one thing. She had already found her outlet. It was the cold, hard logic of the firing range. It was the smell of cordite. It was the rhythmic, mechanical process of disassembling, cleaning and reassembling her weapon. That was her way of relaxing. That was her way of silencing the siren voice of Anya, who still sometimes whispered of love to her in her dreams.

It was almost with a sense of sad inevitability that Volkov discovered Agent Stepnova had completely misinterpreted his advice. She had left his office and had immediately requested special dispensation to use the range out of hours, using his own advice as tacit authority. Given her skills with firearms, and the use of the Director's name, it was of course granted, and Anya then spent every spare hour honing her skills.

She remembered one night after a particularly strenuous session on the CQB range when she had just beaten her own range record. She was panting in exertion and making her Makarov safe when suddenly, she felt herself being observed. She looked up to the armoured viewing window to see Volkov watching her, with an almost sad expression on his face. She couldn't be sure, but after their eyes met and he turned to leave, she was almost certain she saw his head shake almost regretfully.

She paused for a moment, lost in her own conflicted thoughts, then shrugged her shoulders and reloaded her pistol.

"Again!" she shouted at the range warden.

An echoing door slam brought her back to the present. Major Kurchatov was approaching from the Director's office. The time for reminiscence was over.

CHAPTER 8

Anastasia Stepnova sat across the table from Director Volkov and Deputy Director Petrova. As always, she was a study in complete, graceful control, her posture impeccable, a product of her military background and her childhood ballet lessons. Her dark, lustrous hair was pulled back in a severe, professional knot, framing a face that was strikingly attractive, almost youthful, until one met her eyes.

Her eyes were beautiful, a deep, intelligent brown, but they held a hardness, a cold, watchful quality that seemed out of place with the rest of her features. It was a hardness that had not been trained into her but forged in the crucible of a Moscow Metro station, forever extinguishing a softer light that once existed there. Laughter, one felt, would now be an intruder on her face, a language her features had long forgotten how to speak.

She was no longer Anya Stepnova, fiancé of the late Sergei; she had been forged into The Nightingale, one of the SVR's finest operatives, and she was listening intently to her mission briefing.

Months had passed since the initial phase of The Orpheus Gambit had been initiated. Now, it was time for the next move, and The Nightingale had been specially selected to play her own unwitting part in Volkov's game of deception.

"Agent Stepnova," Volkov began, his voice calm, measured. "You are being tasked with Operation Soroka. An assignment of the highest priority related to The Icarus Project." He didn't detail the real aim of The Orpheus Gambit; her mission was presented as a genuine intelligence recovery and assessment task. "Highly sensitive technical materials concerning Icarus have been accessed by a Western entity."

"We have identified the specific individual who has received and processed our data," Petrova added, projecting a profile onto a smaller screen. "Operative Declan Shaw, of Special Projects, a deniable intelligence outstation, located in the city of Newcastle, in the Northeast of England. We have assigned this operative Shaw, the operational codename: Kukushka."

Volkov held up a hand to interrupt, a rare, almost poetic musing in his tone. He enjoyed the intricacies of studying his targets and then assigning them culturally symbolic codenames.

"The names for this operation are of particular significance, Agent Stepnova. Your mission is Operation Soroka, the Magpie. In our folklore, Soroka-Vorovka is the thief of shiny things, a spy, a teller of mischievous tales. The name also has resonance in England. Your target environment, Newcastle, holds the Magpie as a beloved symbol of their local football team. You will fly into this Magpies' nest of Newcastle and discover just how much of our most precious, shiny secret has fallen into their hands and what their intentions are."

His eyes shifted to the profile on the screen and Anastasia followed his gaze to look at the image on the screen. "And this is your target... Kukushka, the Cuckoo. In our stories, the cuckoo is a lonely creature, an orphan that lays its eggs in another's nest. Its call is a prophecy, telling a man how many years he has left to live. It is also said to be a bearer of sad knowledge."

He looked from the screen to Anastasia. "Shaw is an orphan. He lives a lonely life, a cuckoo in the Magpies' nest of his service. And now, he is the bearer of our knowledge, dangerous, stolen knowledge."

Anastasia absorbed the dual meanings of the codenames, the mission and the man. Soroka and Kukushka. The Thieving Magpie and the Lonely Cuckoo. The names were typical of Volkov: culturally resonant on the surface, but with a cryptic operational and psychological depth hidden beneath, and of course often related to his ornithological pursuits. She turned her full focus to the profile on the screen, carefully analysing the black-and-white image.

A security clearance photograph, taken under harsh fluorescent lights, stared back at her. His hair, thick and unruly, still had evidence of the original dark brown, but was now mainly a distinguished grey. Three days' worth of greying stubble shadowed a strong jawline.

The features were ruggedly handsome, the kind carved by time and hard living rather than genetics alone. His eyes were a greyish blue. But it was the look in them that held her attention. It was a look she knew well, the quiet, haunted stare of a combat veteran. Yet there was something else there, too. A look that seemed to suggest an air of deep disappointment with the world and counterintuitively, they also seemed to contain a slight hint of mischief, as did his slight, lopsided grin.

"Your task," Volkov stated, his voice pulling her from her thoughts, "is to make contact with Cuckoo. Assess his level of access. Ascertain precisely how much data he has, its provenance, and his understanding of its significance. Use all means necessary to recover or destroy it."

He didn't elaborate on the 'means'. Stepnova understood. Psychological seduction, an emotional affair, followed by manipulation, coercion, or if necessary, neutralisation. Whatever it took.

"We have compiled a detailed personal file on Shaw," Petrova interjected, sliding a thick, buff dossier across the table. "His background, operational history, psychological profile, known vulnerabilities." Stepnova accepted the dossier.

"He is currently scheduled to speak at a security conference in Washington D.C. in four months," Volkov said. "The timing of this conference will allow you to fully immerse yourself in your legend and provide a suitable opportunity for initial contact. Your cover is already established; your initial task is to make it your own, before making him your own."

Volkov and Petrova then detailed her cover story: a security consultant with Secure Energy Risk, a genuine company specialising in critical energy infrastructure, her presence in the UK justified by a series of staged arson attacks on wind farms.

"Such local extremist activity against critical infrastructure falls under one of Special Projects' many remits," Petrova noted, "Shaw is also an investigator, it should be relatively easy to arrange further contact with him without it appearing too coincidental."

Stepnova listened, absorbing the details. The target, the mission, the cover, the planned incidents. It was a complex plan, but operationally feasible. After the briefing, she returned to her office. She sat at her desk and opened the digital dossier on Declan Shaw again.

She carefully studied his background. Wallsend upbringing, Parachute Regiment, 'special duties'. His operational history was extensive, spanning decades of shadow wars. And then, she reached the section on Northern Ireland. The file became suddenly, frustratingly opaque. Entire paragraphs were blacked out with heavy redaction markers. An operation in Belfast, a shooting, a date, and then nothing. Just a field of black ink. It was an anomaly. The SVR's intelligence gathering was second to none; for a file on a person of interest to have such a significant, impenetrable black hole suggested that whatever had happened in Belfast was buried so deep, sealed under so many layers of classification, that not even their best assets could pry it loose in the limited time since they'd identified Shaw.

This professional curiosity, this pull of an unanswered question, intrigued her more than any detailed report could have. She began her own open-source research, cross-referencing the date from the redacted file with multiple public media archives. There were no official reports of British military shootings on that date, and her computer searches were proving frustratingly fruitless. So, she decided to do things the old-fashioned way, and after hours of scouring the microfiche records dug up from the basement, she found a small article in the Belfast Telegraph archives detailing a brutal "sectarian killing." Five victims. Four of them were known PIRA members. And one was an innocent victim: a sixteen-year-old girl, caught in the crossfire. The image of the bloodstained Teddy bear entered her mind uninvited, and she shook her head to clear it.

The timing, the location, the nature of the casualties, it all pointed to the unmistakable signature of a deniable, off-the-books operation. Anastasia joined the dots. The redacted file, the media report, the psychological profile mentioning "residual trauma" and a "pronounced guilt complex." She now understood the haunted look in Declan Shaw's eyes. It was the look of a man who carried the weight of that girls loss. She remembered Volkov's musing on the cuckoo.

In some of the old stories, the kukushka was also seen as a bridge between the world of the living and the world of the dead, its call a message from the other side. Declan Shaw certainly had a haunted look in his eyes, a look she recognised from her own reflection.

A strange, cold empathy settled over her. It wasn't sympathy for an adversary, but a professional understanding, a recognition of a shared burden. He kills an innocent and carries the weight, she thought, her own memories of the Metro station surfacing, sharp and unwelcome.

"I failed to save innocents, and I carry a similar weight." They were both driven by similar trauma, their respective drives for perfection born from the ashes of a single, catastrophic failure. This realisation planted a seed of professional intrigue. A man haunted by a specific failure would be driven by a personal code that standard operational procedure could not account for.

The profile detailed his unconventional methods and his reliance on intuitive skills, which the SVR psychologists had correctly assessed as a symptom, not a gift. They had labelled him an INFJ, a self-isolating personality type prone to chronic loneliness. Despite this vulnerability, the profile warned his other personality factors might render him resistant to standard manipulation by physical means. It also mentioned potential instability and a deep hostility to authority. Anastasia raised her eyebrow at the final assessment of a possible propensity for unprovoked violence; it seemed inconsistent with a man carrying such a pronounced guilt complex.

His profile certainly indicated that he would be a challenge. A quiet intensity settled over her. Her mission was clear. Make contact. Assess, manipulate, and if necessary, neutralise. This British operative, Cuckoo, was a chess piece in The Orpheus Gambit, and she was tasked to move him, unaware that she too was being manipulated as part of a hidden, deadly game.

The Washington conference was merely the next move on Volkov's chessboard.

CHAPTER 9

The dossier on Declan Shaw, codename "Kukushka," sat open on the desk in Anastasia's small SVR office next to a steaming coffee cup. It was a puzzle, and the first rule of solving any puzzle was to understand its pieces. For the next two months, Declan Shaw became her singular obsession.

Her work began not with spycraft, but with scholarship. She dove into publicly available data, tracking his footprints across the internet. He had spoken at numerous security conferences, both in London and Washington. She acquired the transcripts, the video footage, the presentation slides. A clear pattern emerged. His lectures were always a variation on the same theme: Gerasimov, Active Measures, Maskirovka. But it was the way he spoke that intrigued her.

This was not the typical, dry recitation of an analyst. He spoke of Russian history with a familiarity that went beyond professional necessity. He quoted Russian poets, referenced the nuances of the Great Patriotic War, and, most tellingly, he consistently challenged the prevailing Western narratives. He would explain Russia's deep-seated fear of encirclement not as an excuse for aggression, but as a genuine, historically rooted strategic reality. He wasn't just an analyst: he was a scholar of her country's history and culture.

But she had to caution herself. She could not let his apparent academic prowess blind her to the other truth in his file. The haunted look in his eyes was not just that of a thinker; it was the look of a veteran. The man was still a killer. A reluctant one, perhaps, given the psychological profile, but the redacted file from Belfast was proof that he was a lethally effective one.

She found herself trying to reconcile the two Declan's in her own head. The thoughtful scholar who understood the Russian soul, and the hardened operative who had left corpses in the back alleys of Ireland.

These contradictions made him a puzzle that was not just intriguing, but dangerously unpredictable. And I must solve this puzzle to break him, she thought, her professional focus hardening.

While her mind was occupied with Declan Shaw, her body and her skills were being honed for "Eleanor Vane." The SVR left nothing to chance. For weeks, she lived not as Anastasia, but as Eleanor, a polished, professional energy risk consultant with a plausible, carefully constructed life.

They drilled her on the technicalities of her cover. In a secure SVR facility, they had built a full-scale mock-up of a wind turbine's control centre. Technicians walked her through the schematics, teaching her the vulnerabilities of the system and the jargon of the energy sector. She learned to speak the language of grid stability and turbine maintenance until it became her own.

Her physical training continued relentlessly. The firing range, as always, remained her sanctuary, a psychological haven where the chaos of her mind could be channelled into the cold, clean logic of ballistics. A sword, no matter how sharp, will blunt if it is not constantly honed, her instructors constantly reminded her.

She practised daily for hours, the familiar weight of a pistol in her hand, her movements economical, her breathing controlled. She was utterly lethal, and in that lethality, she found a semblance of the control she had lost on that Moscow Metro platform.

The final piece of the puzzle was the target's environment. She received detailed briefings on the British Special Projects group. It was here she learned a crucial, almost comical, piece of intelligence.

"Until eighteen months ago," Handler Prime, a dry, older colonel, explained, "the Newcastle outstation was completely invisible to us. It was run by a highly capable professional, a woman who understood the value of anonymity. Their cover was, you must admit, a piece of genius in its own way. A perfect act of British Maskirovka."

He pointed to a logo on the screen: Aegis Security Solutions. "They were hiding in plain sight. Aegis is a real, registered company with legitimate government contracts to provide security services for critical infrastructure. This gave their operatives a perfect, unbreakable cover."

"They didn't need legends, because they were actually working for the legend. It allowed men like your target, Shaw, to openly attend security conferences and liaise with local police, all under the plausible guise of being a senior consultant for Aegis. It was foolproof. We were only aware of its existence as a private entity of little note, but its effectiveness was impressive."

He pushed a file across the table. It contained a photograph of a preening, sharp-suited man. "WAS impressive, and then they appointed this man, Simon Phillips. An ambitious fool. He was not content to hide in plain sight. He wanted to make a name for himself, to show London what a fine job he was doing. He wanted to put Special Projects 'on the map', so he self-publicised. He started sharing internal metrics with allied services and utterly destroyed the very compartmentalisation that made the unit so effective. He lit a lamp in a dark room, and in doing so, compromised his entire organisation."

The handler smiled, a thin, humourless expression. "Thanks to him ringing the dinner bell, and our assets within their wider service, we now know everything, including the dysfunctional, bureaucratic shell they have become." He tapped the cover of Declan's file. "This man Shaw is one of the last of the old guard, a holdover. He is a lonely, isolated professional in a nest that is no longer his own. A cuckoo. The Director's codename is, as always, entirely appropriate."

Anastasia looked at Declan's haunted face on the screen. A cuckoo. A lonely creature in a hostile nest. A brilliant scholar of her own culture. And a killer.

The file in front of her contained the state-sanctioned truth. But her own intelligence, her own analysis, was painting a far more complex picture. Her professional perfectionism demanded she understand him completely in order to exploit his weaknesses, but there was another part, deeply buried under the avalanche of her Nightingale persona which felt a flicker of empathy for Shaw.

"This is what happens when you spend too much time studying your target," she thought, "you begin to humanise them." Putting that unwelcome ember of empathy to the back of her mind, she began working out the best approach to take to compromise him, to break him.

CHAPTER 10

The musty air in the control room of the Chernobog Deep Works always smelled stale, slightly stagnant, combined with a subtle hint of burnt dust and ozone. For twenty years, this had been Dr. Ivan Morozov's very own cathedral of science, a subterranean temple dedicated to a single, terrible deity: Project Icarus. He knew its every hum, its every vibration, the very pulse of the small modular reactor that was its heart.

Today, something indefinable felt wrong.

He stood before the main holographic display, a shimmering, three-dimensional representation of the Orpheus munition, his most brilliant yet terrifying creation. A weapon that didn't fly through the air, but burrowed under the earth itself, safe from the thousands of drones that buzzed over modern battlefields like lethal mosquitos.

Orpheus was a semi-autonomous, magnetic plasma munition that rendered every command bunker on earth obsolete. Ironically, it was technology developed for the space programme which had provided the breakthrough he needed to solve the technical failures of the old Soviet Battle Mole.

They were so close, just a few more months perfecting the AI guidance and the magnetic containment field which it also controlled, and it would be ready to go to prototype. There were still some minor issues with the self-contained modular reactor, but the scientists at Rosatom were even now ironing out the kinks. There were even rumours of a cold fusion generator being developed, but in the heavily compartmentalised world of nuclear research, he had been kept out of that particular loop.

It was the technology developed by the S.P. Korolev Rocket and Space Corporation Energia, which had led to the magnetic plasma drive, an engine designed to reach Mars in a matter of months. It hadn't taken much of a leap of imagination to realise the temperatures generated could be used to burrow beneath the earth for mining purposes, providing the device could be cooled. It took an even shorter leap to realise it could also be used for both tactical and strategic military purposes.

That's where his own expertise had provided an elegant solution to the thermal problem: the non-Newtonian metallic coolant fluid he had originally developed as a heat shield for space capsules.

The most complex issue which now remained was the control of the magnetic field required to both contain the plasma and to propel the munition through the ground via "magnetic peristalsis". This manipulation of the field required millions of calculations per second and was solved by the addition of a semi-autonomous AI, which used light to perform the necessary computations. This had the advantage of operating at a cool temperature, further reducing the internal thermal stresses.

It was almost inevitable that a project born of the sky would be named Project Icarus, a name designed to obfuscate the true subterranean nature of the Orpheus munition.

His professional reverie was shattered by the arrival of two men who did not belong in his sanctuary. One was a political officer from the Ministry of Defence, a man with a soft face and hard, empty eyes, whose suit was too clean for a facility buried a kilometre underground.
The other was a grim-faced Colonel from the SVR's technical services directorate; a man whose presence anywhere usually signified unwelcome state interference.

An unwelcome knot of anxiety tightened in Morozov's gut. He had been on edge ever since he had first been approached by the American asset all those many months ago. Had they found out? Had they discovered the fragmented data he had so discreetly been leaking to the West? Had his clumsy attempts at the tradecraft he'd been hurriedly trained in compromised him?

"Doctor Morozov," the political officer began, his voice oozing a placatory smoothness that immediately set Ivan's teeth on edge. "We have a matter of some urgency to discuss."

"If it is about the delayed shipments of the ceramic alloy and tungsten plating again, Comrade," Morozov began, his voice tight with impatience, "I have already filed three reports. As I've repeatedly informed Moscow, we simply cannot proceed to prototype assembly without..."

"It is not about the shipments, Doctor," the SVR Colonel interrupted, his tone flat and non-negotiable. He placed a thick, red-bordered file on the central console. "It is about the facility itself. We have received some... troubling structural integrity reports from our geological survey teams."

Morozov stared at him, bewildered, the anxiety momentarily replaced by professional indignation. Was this their cover story? A fabricated excuse to shut him down?

"Troubling? This facility is a masterpiece of Soviet engineering. It is carved from solid granite. It is designed to withstand a direct nuclear strike. What could possibly be 'troubling'?"

The political officer gestured to the file.

"There appear to be previously undetected seismic-related stresses. Micro-fissures in the primary support structures. The geologists are concerned that continued operation of the main reactor, particularly at the energy levels required for your stress tests, could lead to... a catastrophic structural failure."

"Preposterous!" Morozov spat. "My teams monitor the seismic resonance data hourly. This is bureaucratic nonsense!" But even as he said it, a sliver of doubt entered his mind. He took the file and flicked through the pages. He saw geological survey charts, resonance feedback logs, laser measurement readouts. The data was detailed. It was in fact sickeningly plausible.

Despite his misgivings, he had seen the new work crews himself. Over the past week, teams of so-called "structural engineers" had been swarming through the facility's older corridors. They were installing what they called "seismic reinforcement struts", heavy, steel scaffolding poles fitted with complex ratchet mechanisms that were being clamped around the primary concrete support columns. Morozov, a man of science, had watched them with professional interest, relieved that the Ministry was finally addressing the facility's age.

He left the control room, the two men following him and eyeing each other, and walked down a long, concrete service corridor to Section Gamma-7, one of the areas highlighted in the report. The corridor was a relic, the floor punctuated by numerous puddles where water had seeped through the strata into the facility. Though the structure was a testament to the Soviet brute-force approach to engineering, age and physics were taking their toll.

It was here, under the cool fluorescent lights, he saw it. A hairline crack, thin as a spider's thread, running from the floor halfway up the reinforced concrete wall. He ran a trembling finger over it. It was real. He used his pocket laser-calliper to measure the gap between two of the primary support struts. The reading was off by three millimetres from the original schematic, a tiny, almost imperceptible shift, but in a structure under this much subterranean pressure, it was a collapse waiting to happen.

The facility was genuinely failing. This masterpiece of Soviet might, built to last an eternity, was slowly being crushed by the weight of the earth. The officials were right to be concerned, and he now looked at the newly installed steel struts, bolted tightly around the columns. They appeared solid and reassuring to him. He felt a wave of relief wash over him; they wouldn't be putting this much effort into saving his facility if they had any suspicions about his leaking data to the West.

He had no way of knowing the struts were a cynical deception, their hollow cores packed not with reinforcing steel, but with precisely moulded shaped charges, wired to a discreet, experimental receiver, containing an entangled quantum particle.

He walked back to the control room, his anger replaced by a cold, practical dread. The men were waiting. His mind raced. His leaks hadn't been discovered. This was a genuine crisis. But a crisis was also an opportunity.

"...a decision has been made at the highest level," the Colonel was saying as if Morozov had never left. "For the safety of all personnel, the Chernobog Deep Works is to be placed on immediate operational standby."

Morozov felt the air leave his lungs, but his outrage was now tempered by a new calculation.

"Standby?"

"As a precaution," the political officer added smoothly, "most of the personnel will be transferred out over the next seventy-two hours. Critical equipment will be removed and placed in secure storage. The facility will be partially shut down until a full structural survey, and the necessary repairs and refurbishment can be completed."

Repairs and refurbishment. The two words echoed in Morozov's mind. He thought of the antiquated Soviet-era wiring, the failing coolant pumps for the secondary systems, the constant struggle to keep this relic operational. A full shutdown and repair would mean new investment. New equipment. Perhaps they would finally replace the conventional IT equipment with the quantum systems he had been requisitioning for years. He could rebuild it better, more efficiently.

"And my work? The Project?" he asked, his voice carefully neutral now, his creator's pride warring with his newfound hope. He gazed at the hologram of the Orpheus. It was a perfect first-strike weapon, an undetectable decapitation tool that could end a war before it began. As a scientist, he understood the terrifyingly destabilising logic of such a weapon.

It made a pre-emptive nuclear war not just possible, but tempting. This was the true source of his treason, the secret fear that gnawed at him in the sleepless nights: that the hard-liners in the Kremlin would see his beautiful, terrible creation not as a deterrent, but as an invitation to global suicide. He had leaked its secrets not for money, but to give the West a fighting chance, to restore the balance of terror, to save his beloved Rodina from the consequences of his own genius.

Morozov's genius was undeniable. He had succeeded where his forebears, both Soviet and American, had failed spectacularly. He had studied the declassified files from the old "Battle Mole" programme of the 1970s, and the American "Subterrene" patents from Los Alamos. They were crude, brute-force attempts. Their nuclear-powered melting heads had either become entombed in their own resolidified magma or, in one catastrophic Ural Mountains test, had melted down completely. They had never solved the two fundamental problems: heat and guidance.

But he, Ivan Morozov, had solved the thermal regulation issue not with bigger radiators, but with a different philosophy, inventing a synthetic, non-Newtonian coolant that became more efficient as the temperature soared. He had pioneered the use of micro-level 3D printers to fabricate the impossibly intricate nanostructure lattice of the heat exchangers, a metal foam that gave the coolant a near-infinite surface area to work its magic. The warhead's own heat, the very thing that had destroyed the old Battle Mole, became Orpheus's greatest asset, its means of both destruction and propulsion.

And the guidance system. The old programmes were blind, relying on inertial systems that drifted wildly over a few kilometres. His proposed solution was made a reality, a semi-sentient AI that didn't follow a pre-programmed path but tested the earth, using a magnetic quantum field, then processed the resultant data in real-time to find the paths of least resistance and home in on the unique resonance signature of a deep-underground command bunker. It was not just a munition: it was an autonomous, subterranean predator, although at the moment, its brain was still being perfected.

The Colonel looked at him without a flicker of empathy.

"Your work will continue, Doctor. But in a virtual environment. We need you and a skeleton crew of your best technicians to remain. Your new tasking is to collate the entirety of the Icarus data, every schematic, every telemetry log, every molecule of the coolant formula, into a single, unified package. This will be used to create a digital twin, a perfect computer simulation of the Orpheus munition."

A simulation. The idea was an insult to a man who dealt in physics, but Morozov saw the logic. It was the most prudent course of action while his cathedral was being rebuilt. He could use the time to assist with the refinement of the AI guidance protocols which were necessary to make the munition operational. He could also take this new opportunity to develop possible countermeasures, which he could then pass on to the West. He would see his creation brought to life, whilst helping to prevent it becoming a weapon of Armageddon. The delay would give him the best of both worlds.

He looked from the politician's placid face to the Colonel's stony expression. They were offering him the chance to save his life's work and, in the process, get the upgrades he had always dreamed of. His earlier fears had been misplaced. The state was not betraying him; it was protecting its investment.

"I understand my orders, Comrade Colonel," he said, his voice a low, cooperative rasp.

The two men nodded, their work done. As they turned to leave, a final thought seemed to occur to the Colonel, who turned back.

"The collation of the data is of the highest national priority, Doctor. Do not fail."

Morozov watched them go, leaving him alone in the hollow echoes of his doomed cathedral of science, which was soon to become his crypt. He looked at the shimmering hologram of the Orpheus, his brilliant, terrible creation. He would collate the data, he would oversee the simulation, and he would wait patiently for the day he could return to his newly refurbished, state-of-the-art laboratory to complete his great work. He watched them go with a satisfied smile on his face, his mind racing with new possibilities.

He had completely, utterly, and tragically fallen for the lie.

CHAPTER 11

The main conference area of the Watergate Hotel in Washington D.C. echoed with a peculiar blend of corporate murmuring and social niceties, hidden under a layer of subliminal paranoia. The symbolically chosen location was a fitting marketplace for secrets and the tools to uncover them, and the perfect venue for the discreet infiltration of a fox into an unsuspecting hen coop.

Moving through the chattering throng was not Agent Anastasia (Anya) Stepnova of the SVR; the woman at the conference was Eleanor Vane, a polished, professional energy risk consultant with a sharp intellect, fluent, lightly accented English, and a plausible, carefully constructed life.

Creating Eleanor Vane had been an exhaustive, months-long process, a masterclass in SVR tradecraft. It began with the legend: An English father and Polish mother to add plausibility to her slight Eastern European-sounding dialect, a degree from a Swiss university, early career work with an energy consortium in Brussels, a series of impressive but unverifiable projects in the private sector.

Then came the digital footprint, a meticulous weaving of a life that had never been lived. Social media profiles were created, backdated with years of vacation photos from plausible destinations, check-ins at industry conferences, and innocuous, algorithm-pleasing posts about hiking and modern art. Professional profiles on platforms like LinkedIn were populated with connections to real, unsuspecting individuals and endorsements for skills she genuinely possessed. Bank accounts were opened, credit histories established. Eleanor Vane, if anything, was more real online than the woman who was now playing her.

The final stage had been rehearsal. Weeks spent in a mock-up of a Western office, living the role, answering phones as Eleanor, writing emails as Eleanor, until the persona became a second skin. Anastasia Stepnova was gone; only Eleanor remained, and Eleanor was focused and on mission. The SVR had tracked the British operative to this conference, surmising it was the most feasible location to observe, assess and approach the individual who was known to have handled the leaked Icarus data.

She settled into a central seat on the second row of the packed room, an unobtrusive observer amongst a sea of hostile and skilled enemies. She looked around her, checking for potential threats and security staff, and noticed nearby emergency exits by the side of the stage. Although unarmed at this point, she was confident she could egress should the mission go awry and settled in her seat to watch the presentation.

The lights dimmed, and a man took the stage, and Anya leaned forward slightly in interest. This was him: her mission, her target, the analyst from Special Projects. Codename Kukushka, "Cuckoo," whom she'd spent so long studying. When she saw him step onto the stage, with a slightly lopsided, mischievous-looking grin on his face as he greeted the audience, it felt strangely like being reunited with an old friend.

He was middle-aged, a ruggedness to his features that spoke of time spent outside sterile offices, greying hair, and a weariness in his eyes that felt... familiar. His accent was unmistakably Geordie but subtly softened. This was operative Declan Shaw, the man she had come to compromise.

He began his lecture, which was titled "Asymmetric Threats in the Information Age," opening with a quote from Abraham Lincoln:

"Public sentiment is everything. With public sentiment, nothing can fail; without it, nothing can succeed." He detailed how shaping public opinion can be as important in hybrid warfare as shaping events on the battlefield.

Eventually his focus narrowed to the Gerasimov Doctrine, how Russia was applying principles of information warfare, manipulating perceptions, blurring the lines between peace and conflict. He spoke with a quiet authority, weaving together technical analysis with ground-level observations that clearly came from experience.

He then shifted, his tone becoming more cynical.

"Of course," he drawled, "the primary challenge in countering state-level disinformation is that it's often indistinguishable from our own domestic variety."

He paced the stage confidently as he spoke, commanding the space not with volume, but with the weary authority of a man who has seen too much..

"We spend so much time looking for the hand of Moscow, we forget how adept we are at muddying our own waters." A murmur of uncomfortable recognition went through the room.

"Now, those of you who know me understand how much I hate playing devil's advocate," a sizeable portion of the audience laughed knowingly.

Declan continued, a hint of humour in his voice. "But intelligence pantomimes such as Russiagate. Crossfire Hurricane. The Hunter Biden laptop story, dismissed as Russian disinformation by dozens of former senior intelligence officials, only for it to be... well, not Russian disinformation. These weren't Kremlin plots. They were home-grown conspiracies which have made the jobs of actual intelligence professionals like me devilishly difficult."

More audience laughter, but noticeably, not from everyone.

He paused, his eyes wandering from audience member to audience member, settling on Anya's. He seemed about to speak again but continued his pause, holding her gaze for a moment, almost in recognition. Then he shook his head slightly, as if to clear it, and continued his talk, feeling strangely disconcerted.

"And then there's the self-inflicted damage. The Vault 7 leaks, for example, or The Shadow Brokers obtaining NSA hacking tools from a disgruntled insider, which were then released into the wild. This allowed the North Korean Lazarus Group to weaponise the 'EternalBlue' exploit and bring the entire UK National Health Service to a grinding halt with the WannaCry ransomware."

He shook his head again, a look of mock frustration on his face. "The NHS had been warned for months about what was coming and when. We told them. But they didn't apply the simple patch to the SMB vulnerability which would have prevented the entire compromise. It just proves what happens when you DON'T act on good intelligence..." He let the sentence hang for a beat, then added with a wry, pained smile, "...I should know. I was the one writing the endless bloody reports they kept ignoring."

The room erupted in a wave of sympathetic, gallows-humour laughter, and he then moved on with his monologue. Crucially, he didn't just describe the tactics; he touched upon the underlying strategic mindset, offering a perspective rarely heard in such forums. He also spoke of Russia's historical perception of its borders, its deeply ingrained fears of encirclement, stemming from centuries of invasions.

He subtly referenced the post-Cold War landscape, the perceived broken promises regarding NATO expansion eastward, the ignored warnings like the "Niet means Niet" assessment from William Burns of the CIA that had foreseen the backlash if Russia's security concerns were disregarded.

Declan didn't excuse Moscow's current aggressive posture; he simply explained it, framing it not just as expansionism, but as Russia's own version of the Monroe Doctrine, a fiercely protected sphere of influence stemming from a deep-seated historical vulnerability. "Imagine," he'd sighed in mock exasperation, "how America might respond if Russia managed to expand its military alliances from Venezuela right up through Mexico, including building new missile bases in Cuba? This maybe provides a flavour of Moscow's perspective regarding NATO's involvement in Ukraine and Georgia.

It was a pragmatic, unsentimental assessment which caused much murmuring amongst the delegates, not all of it negative.

He concluded his lecture, drawing together the complex threads of information warfare, cyber threats, and geopolitical motivation. He paused for a moment, looking out at the audience.

"So," Declan said, a wry smile on his lips, his voice dropping slightly for emphasis. "To put it all in simple terms, terms so simple even my manager could understand..." A wave of good-natured laughter rippled through the audience, minus a small group of sycophants Phillips had sent to the conference to keep an eye on Declan.

"...what we're all really dealing with here is just glorified gaslighting, on an international level."

More laughter.

He straightened, his expression turning serious again. "That's my take on it, anyway. Happy to take any questions."

The microphone circulated and a number of interesting but simple questions were asked and answered. Eventually, Eleanor raised her hand and was handed the microphone.

"Mr. Shaw," she began, her English almost perfect, the European lilt barely identifiable. "You discussed information as a weapon... Given the increasing sophistication of, say, state-level intrusion capabilities, quantum signatures, data integrity subversion, how does one reliably distinguish between genuine, albeit fragmented, intelligence... and deliberately planted, sophisticated disinformation... Especially if the adversary understands your analytical biases and feeds them?"

It was an extremely difficult question. Declan paused to think for a moment, giving the incorrect impression he was taken aback by its depth.

He looked at the small group of sycophants and noticed them sniggering at his delay, then turned his attention back to the attractive woman. No longer just intrigued but suspicious.

"So that's how pathetic Phillips was?" he thought. "Placing a ringer in the audience to trip him up whilst his sniggering minions report back to him? Well, two can play at that game.

He cleared his throat, a wry smile touching his lips at how easily he had spotted the ruse.

"Jesus, lady," he drawled, "couldn't you have simply given me an EASY question to answer?" The unexpected humour drew a ripple of laughter and a genuine smile from Eleanor.

He then turned serious. "That's... the million-dollar question, isn't it? And frankly, if anyone in this room tells you they have a foolproof answer, they're selling you snake oil... It requires a combination of deep technical analysis, cross-corroboration... and frankly... a lot of intuition and gut instinct. 'The Magic,' as a friend of mine calls it."

He furrowed his brow in thought. "To your specific point... the techniques you describe... they're bleeding edge. If an adversary has perfected them, they hold a significant advantage." He shook his head slightly. "I don't have a complete answer... not right now. It's something we're all struggling with."

He looked back at her, his focus entirely on her now. "But it's a vital question. And I will do my best to get back to you with further thoughts. Are you going to be joining me and the rest of the functional alcoholics at the social function later, or are you one of those rare intelligence professionals who doesn't have a serious drink problem?" More laughter from the audience.

"I am," Eleanor confirmed, pausing for a moment to look Declan in the eye, "joining you at the function, with the rest of the functional alcoholics." Despite herself, she smiled at the exchange, both from satisfaction at making contact so effortlessly and at the joke. Her initial paper assessment had been correct: he wasn't just the killer the SVR had painted him, he was sharp, witty and honest, and possessed a confident charm which wasn't mentioned in the file, and an intangible something she couldn't quite place.

"Good," Declan said, returning her smile. "I'll see you there later, just no more awkward questions, OK?" She nodded in amused assent and replied,

"No promises, I'm afraid, Mr Shaw; they pay me to ask awkward questions."

He laughed.

"Call me Declan, please."

"Declan, please, I'm Eleanor," she replied, also laughing.

They looked at each other one last time and then Declan was interrupted and hurriedly escorted away by one of the conference staff, who was telling him he'd run over his allotted time. As he was led to the wings like a hostage, by the flustered organiser, he looked over his shoulder to see her still watching him. When he smiled and gave her a humorously apologetic shrug of his shoulders, she laughed again.

Despite his suspicions, he still looked forward to speaking with her and playing along with Phillips's clumsy honey trap. Unaware that this fabricated encounter was not a trick played on him by his petty manager, but the first, carefully orchestrated step in a deadly gambit designed in Moscow, and he was now firmly on the board, thinking he was playing a different game entirely.

CHAPTER 12

Later that evening, the International Spy Museum was abuzz with a different kind of corporate energy. Ties were loosened, complimentary drinks flowed freely, and the professional facades of the day softened, replaced by a more relaxed, though still guarded, informality. Around displays of hidden microphones and cyanide capsules, intelligence professionals from government agencies and private sector firms alike mingled, their conversations a mix of shop talk, polite networking, and the subtle dance of assessing potential contacts or competitors.

Declan Shaw stood near an exhibit of Cold War espionage gadgets, a drink in his hand, trying to navigate a conversation with an overly enthusiastic cybersecurity consultant. The man, a pleasant enough chap named Gary from some data analytics firm, had cornered Declan the moment he had arrived at the museum, buzzing with questions about information operations and Gerasimov's likely breakfast preferences.

While Declan appreciated the interest, after a long day of pretending to be professional and discussing the potential end of the world, he just wanted a quiet drink and a break from the relentless queries.

He nursed his whisky, doing his best not to let his growing boredom show, offering polite smiles and non-committal answers. But his eyes, betraying his internal fatigue, kept drifting around the crowded room, looking for a distraction, an escape route. That's when he saw her.

Across the room, near a display of clandestine cameras, Eleanor Vane was likewise cornered. Her companion, a slick-haired man in a sharp suit who clearly had more on his mind than influence operations, was leaning in too close, his body language possessive and unwanted. Eleanor's posture, while outwardly polite, held a subtle tension, a quiet desire to extract herself from the conversation.

Their eyes met over the heads of the mingling guests. In that instant, a shared understanding seemed to pass between them, a mutual wry smile acknowledging the tedious reality of networking events and the unwanted attention they sometimes brought. Her eyes widened slightly, and she looked towards Declan and discreetly mouthed a "Help me, Obi-wan," a silent, humorous unspoken plea for help.

Grateful for the escape opportunity, he apologetically interjected,

"Excuse me, Gary," cutting off a lengthy monologue about AI applications in predicting disinformation trends. He offered a firm handshake and patted him firmly on the back in faux bonhomie. "Absolutely fascinating chat, but I just remembered, I promised to answer a complex question for one of the attendees from my lecture. Conference business, unfortunately, you know how these things are?" Gary seemed slightly disappointed, but was placated by the friendly manner, as Declan gave him a polite, final nod and made his way across the room to where Eleanor was cornered.

He reached her and her persistent companion and smoothly interjected.

"Ah, Miss Vane," Declan said, stepping between her and the slick-haired man, projecting an air of having prior business with her. "There you are, I thought I'd lost you." Her companion, irritated by the interruption, turned to see who was intruding on his moves. His expression was one of barely concealed annoyance.

Declan met his gaze directly, offering a charming smile and a level of politeness that was as close to 'fuck off' as a man could say without physically swearing.

"You don't mind, do you? Unfinished conference business, I'm afraid." He layered on the 'conference business' with a slight emphasis, making it clear this was a professional matter, and Mr Slick-Hair was irrelevant.

The man's jaw tightened, his own smile a thin, furious line. Through gritted teeth, he managed,

"Sure, buddy, be my guest."

He gave Eleanor a final, lingering look and Declan a resentful scowl before turning on his heel and melting back into the crowd.

Declan, jokingly chivalrous, offered Eleanor his arm with a slight gentlemanly bow.

"Shall we?" he murmured, a hint of humour in his voice.

Eleanor, seeing phase one of her mission coming to fruition, didn't hesitate.

"We shall," she said, a look of relief in her eyes. She allowed him to gently escort her away from the unwanted conversation towards a quieter corner of the function room, away from the main flow of traffic.

"Thank you," she said sincerely, once they were out of earshot. "For rescuing me."

"Actually," Declan replied thoughtfully, a dry smile touching his lips, "I think you were doing the rescuing. That fellow Gary was on the verge of cornering me to demonstrate a predictive algorithm using only interpretive dance. I was on the verge of committing self-harm with that cheese knife." He gestured vaguely at a nearby snack table. "Seriously. Don't any of these people have a social life outside security conferences?"

Eleanor laughed.

"Oh, my guy wanted to get very social. He seemed to think 'consultancy' was a euphemism for something else."

"They did say it was a social gathering on the invite," Declan offered, playing along.

"They did indeed," Eleanor chuckled, "just not THAT kind of social gathering."

The shared humour eased their encounter, and they continued to silently look at each other for several moments, smiling, feeling inexplicably comfortable in each other's presence.

Declan had the strangest feeling he had met this woman before. He racked his memory trying to think of where he had seen her previously, but to no avail. He rationalised the sensation by thinking he may have subliminally recognised her spying on him back in the Happy House.

It made sense; he could just imagine Phillips having her hidden in his office to watch him. Despite this rationalisation, he couldn't shake the feeling that he had known Eleanor Vane for a very long time. "Weird," he thought.

Eleanor in turn had the same strange feeling and rationalised it by the fact she had been studying the man for months.

"Of course you feel like you know him, he's your target, you've trained to know him," she thought to herself.

Declan broke the strange but comfortable tension with a question of his own.

"Now, where were we?" he asked, mock absent-mindedly. "Oh yes. I believe I promised to answer your extremely awkward question, if memory serves me." He shook his head in mock indignation. "Thanks for putting me on the spot like that, by the way. Just what an analyst needs, to have his fragile professional ego bruised in front of an entire auditorium packed with his peers."

The line was delivered in such a dry, comically hurt way that Eleanor couldn't help but laugh again. Declan continued to lean into what was now a standing joke:

"OK, so now you've entirely eviscerated what's left of my professional reputation, it's only fair that I try to recover some of my lost dignity by actually trying to answer your question."

Despite his use of humour, he remained serious when he discussed Eleanor's original question in more depth. Declan elaborated on the challenges of detecting sophisticated disinformation, particularly when it mimics genuine data and is embedded with anomalous signatures.

"The standard tools struggle," he explained, nursing his whisky. "They look for known malware patterns, for deviations in expected file structures. But if the 'malware' is just... a property of the data itself, designed to resonate in a certain way when processed... and the data structure is deliberately fragmented or skewed... it bypasses conventional flags."

He paused, considering. "Possible AI solutions, perhaps. Not general AI, but highly specialised machine learning trained on vast datasets of known disinformation campaigns, looking for subtle, non-obvious patterns in the structure of the lie itself, not just the content or delivery method. Identifying the adversary's 'fingerprint' in the noise."

He paused again as if shocked, a terrible realisation appearing to dawn on him.

"Oh God, I'm starting to sound like Gary," he laughed.

Eleanor laughed too, but had been listening intently, her professional mind engaged.

"Identifying the architect of the deception," she murmured, noting his insights, "not just the method—that's a compelling approach."

Their conversation continued to flow easily, a blend of easy humour, shop talk, a shared, healthy professional cynicism, and a growing curiosity about each other. Eleanor, throughout, subtly weaved in elements of her cover story.

"My work takes me through the UK sometimes," she mentioned casually. "My consultancy is expanding its risk assessments into renewables."

"Oh, the energy sector?" Declan replied. "We've actually been tracking an increase in threats against the sector at Aegis. It's been keeping us busier and busier over the past few months."

Eleanor nodded in recognition of the issue.

"We're seeing the same patterns and dealing with the same threats to infrastructure. Renewable energy is a new focus. Wind farms, specifically." She added, "I'm expecting to travel through the UK over the next few months to create various threat assessments." She kept it general, implying travel to different regions, avoiding specifying the Northeast.

Declan, his mind still quietly processing the potential significance of unusual activity related to energy infrastructure (a natural target for state-sponsored disruption, even if disguised as activism), remembered the recent, low-level reports of seemingly isolated arson attacks on Northeast wind farms.

These were some of the myriad problems that Phillips enjoyed dumping on his desk to distract him from Icarus. But now Eleanor was also dealing with the issue, and he began to wonder if there was more to this routine 'local activist crime' than at first met the eye. He hadn't linked them to anything bigger, as they had seemed sporadic, with no obvious pattern, and had been put down to anti-globalist actors.

He remembered how busy he had been with those groups during the pandemic, when 5G telecoms infrastructure had been similarly targeted but on a much wider scale. It appeared that poor Eleanor was also drinking from the same poisoned chalice. Having said that, every cloud has a silver lining, he thought, an idea forming.

"So, there's a chance you might be visiting the Northeast then?" Declan asked, a question rather than an assumption, probing subtly if her travels would bring her to his patch. If she did turn up, that would be more evidence that Phillips was involved, playing on his vulnerabilities to compromise him for his own perverse pleasure. Like a cat with a mouse.

Eleanor feigned a slight uncertainty.

"It's... possible. Depending on the final client scheduling. Some of the newer wind farm projects are up that way, I believe." She let the possibility hang, not confirming definitively, giving him room to extend the invitation.

"I'd have to review my itinerary once it's confirmed." She smiled. "If I do end up in your area... I might need a local guide. Someone who knows the difference between a predictive algorithm and a cheese knife." The last part was delivered with a smile, steering the conversation back to his earlier joke. Declan took the bait, pulled by the genuine interest and the unspoken invitation and his desire to put one over on Phillips.

"If you do find yourself up in my neck of the woods, and work permits... I'd be happy to show you around. Give you the uncensored tour. Might be more interesting than just staring at wind turbines, so feel free to give me a call if you're at a loose end".

"I might just take you up on that, Declan," Eleanor said, her smile now holding a complex mix of professional satisfaction and something that felt surprisingly like anticipation. "That would be very welcome."

They spent the rest of the evening talking, nursing their drinks as the crowd around them thinned. The conversation drifted from the professional to the personal, a careful, mutual interrogation disguised as polite curiosity. For long stretches, Eleanor found herself forgetting she was on an assignment. She was simply enjoying the company of an intelligent, witty man who didn't seem to be playing a game. She had to mentally remonstrate with herself, a cold voice reminding her: Stay on mission. He is the target.

And yet, the encounter hadn't been what she'd anticipated from his P-File. The dossier had described a cynical, potentially unstable operative. But the man in front of her possessed a surprising warmth and a weary depth. He was wounded, yes, she could see that in the haunted quality of his eyes, but he was not broken. He seemed... authentic. The thought was a disorienting, unwelcome complication for the cold SVR operative.

As the function finally wound down, they exchanged business cards, a standard practice at these events, Eleanor's card for "Secure Energy Risk," Declan's for his fabricated company Aegis Security Solutions. It was a physical exchange of plausible identities, covering their true roles.

Eleanor left the International Spy Museum feeling conflicted. The contact with Shaw was made, his profile assessed, his potential susceptibility noted. The path to Newcastle, and a future encounter under a plausible pretext, was established. That was the easy part done.

But as she walked towards her cab and reviewed the evening, a surprising thought surfaced. She hadn't just executed a piece of the plan. She had actually... enjoyed herself. She had had, what was that word again? Oh yes...... Fun.

CHAPTER 13

Director Volkov sat alone in the quiet, cavernous expanse of his office at Yasenevo, the shiny surface of his desk reflecting the warm, almost domestic lighting. He was not studying intelligence reports, but technical files. One was a detailed structural engineering survey of the Chernobog Deep Works. Decades of deep underground testing, a relentless series of brutal, contained detonations of classified ordnance, had left the facility's rock strata dangerously unstable. A network of micro-fractures spiderwebbed through the granite, a silent testament to the immense power that had been unleashed there. He smiled at the serendipitous nature of the development: the facility was beyond economic salvage and any attempts to stabilise the structure were just delaying the inevitable. But the impending collapse meant that Chernobog would serve one final and noble service to Rodina.

The migration of manpower and equipment to the new, uncompromised facility in the Urals was almost complete. All that remained at Chernobog was obsolete legacy equipment and a skeleton crew of scientists and technicians, a collection of individuals who, through vanity, greed, or ideological disillusionment, had been carefully identified as leaking data to the West.

There was a certain operational risk in putting all the rotten eggs in one basket, but it was a calculated one. It facilitated a more controlled and nuanced leaking of disinformation from a single, monitored source.

The staff themselves had been told that a major reinforcement and refurbishment of the facility would soon commence, and once finished, all migrated equipment and personnel would return. It wasn't a foolproof cover story, but it didn't need to be. It wouldn't have to last long.

His musings were disturbed by a sharp rap on the heavy office door.

"Enter," Volkov said, closing the files.

The two guards flanking his door stepped aside, showing in Major Kurchatov. The Major strode to the centre of the room, halted three paces from the desk, and delivered a crisp salute.

Volkov did not return it. He merely stared back, his eyes cold and assessing.

"Report."

Major Kurchatov did not flinch.

"Comrade Director. Operation Soroka is proceeding as planned. Agent Stepnova made successful initial contact with the target, Cuckoo, at the conference in the United States. Further contact in the UK is anticipated. Phase Two is on schedule."

Volkov gave a slow, deliberate nod.

"And the glysty?" he asked, using the cold, clinical term for the cadavers or "worms," which were a morbid but vital part of his deception plan.

"Awaiting deployment, Comrade Director. They will be positioned just prior to Phase Three commencing."

A faint, grim smile touched Volkov's lips. This part of his deception, the most elegant piece of stagecraft, had been directly inspired by an old British Special Operations Executive plan from the Great Patriotic War: Operation Mincemeat. The British, seeking to deceive the Germans about the Allied invasion of Sicily, had dressed the corpse of a homeless man as a Royal Marines officer, chained a briefcase full of false invasion plans to his wrist, and let the body wash ashore in Spain, knowing the intelligence would find its way to Berlin. The Germans had swallowed the bait completely. It appealed to Volkov's deep-seated sense of historical irony that he was now using a strategy developed by the British, to deceive the British, using the exact same bait.

"And the American?" Volkov continued.

"The asset requires a codename for the operational file," Kurchatov reported.

Volkov looked out his window thoughtfully. He had been reviewing the cultural exports of the target city, a habit he'd developed over decades. Music, he found, often revealed more than economic reports.

"Call him 'Dreamseller'," Volkov ordered.

The Major looked puzzled.

"It is a reference," Volkov explained, enjoying himself. "To a song by a local folk band known as "Lindisfarne" from the target's city. It is about a man selling false hopes on a street corner. Given what Mr. Thorne believes he is selling, and what he is actually selling... the name is appropriate."

Kurchatov nodded, not fully understanding the cultural nuance, but recognising the artistry and methodology of the Director's logic. He continued his report.

"Asset 'Dreamseller' continues to be steered by his handlers and is behaving as anticipated. Once the malware deployment signal is given, his extraction to the Newcastle area will take place. Our asset in Kyiv informs us that an SBU team, operating in conjunction with their MI6 handlers, will be in position to 'intercept' him and acquire the package."

Volkov once again nodded, the complex machinery of the gambit clicking into place in his mind. The chess pieces were moving to their designated squares, on a board chosen specifically because a British analyst had set off a quantum tripwire.

"Thank you, Major. You are dismissed."

Kurchatov saluted, turned on his heel, and exited the office, leaving the Director alone with his thoughts. He was satisfied with the progress of the Gambit.

His only real misgiving, a nagging, persistent ache of professional and personal regret, was Agent Stepnova. The Nightingale. He remembered the day she had first sat in front of him, years ago, after the chaos on the Metro. A young GRU officer with the blood of a terrorist still fresh on her hands and the pain of deep loss, turning to ice already noticeable in her eyes. He had seen her potential then and had personally arranged her transfer to the SVR. It was a pity to sacrifice such an effective, beautifully crafted instrument. It was an absolute tragedy he had to sacrifice such a graceful and intelligent woman.

But it was a necessary, calculated cruelty to keep her in the dark about the true nature of her mission. If she were fully appraised of The Orpheus Gambit, if she understood she was a player in a grand deception, her capture would pose an unacceptable risk. The Americans and the British had their black sites, their enhanced interrogation techniques. They would break her. Volkov was a realist; under enough pressure, anyone would break.

If Stepnova possessed full knowledge of the gambit, then the entire operation, the most critical strategic deception of the century, would be blown. Far better she operates in genuine ignorance, her belief in the mission's authenticity making her actions utterly convincing. It was the ultimate in plausible deniability, even under duress.

It was her very effectiveness, her legendary coldness, the "Ice Queen," as some in the service called her, that would lend absolute plausibility to the lie they were selling. Her psychological profile was perfect: a deep-seated trauma that had sublimated into a relentless, almost obsessive drive for mission success. She was the ideal hunter.

That, and her profile indicated a high probability of compromising Cuckoo. His profile, on the other hand, was where the true risk lay. The SVR analysts had flagged him as unstable, prone to hostile reactions when feeling cornered or betrayed. They predicted that if Nightingale's cover were blown, his wounded ego and ingrained paranoia would likely result in a violent, chaotic response, exactly the kind of mess that would authenticate the entire operation.

But Volkov suspected his analysts had made a subtle but critical error in their assessment. They had mistaken Cuckoo's antagonism towards systemic betrayal, the cold, incompetent machinations of the state, for a simple, personal hostility. They hadn't fully appreciated the distinction he might make for an individual operative carrying out a professional duty, especially one for whom he felt a connection. It was a small misjudgement, a failure to account for the irrational human element, but it was on such misjudgements that grand plans often foundered.

Still, it was a sad necessity that the Ice Queen should be used as a sacrificial pawn. The cold mathematics were undeniable: a handful of lives, even brilliant ones, versus billions. He took no pleasure in the thought, save for the grim, absolute certainty that her sacrifice would save countless innocent lives.

It was a legacy, he knew, that Agent Stepnova herself would be proud to bequeath her nation, and the world. He walked over to the chessboard and picked up the nesting doll representing her and studied it silently; he exhaled a long, slow sigh and gently placed the doll back on the board, then returned to his desk where he grabbed his bottle of whisky and poured himself a large glass.

CHAPTER 14

A month had passed since the Washington conference. The rain, if anything, had grown even more persistent. Inside the Happy House, the atmosphere was thick with the usual Monday morning tension, amplified by the foul mood of its manager.

Phillips was on his usual warpath, pacing the floor near the main display screen, his tie flapping around as much as he was.

“Another one,” he muttered, loud enough for the entire office to hear. “That's the third in five weeks.”

The latest incident was an arson attack on a wind turbine at the new renewable energy site near Blyth. But this one was different. This wasn't crude vandalism. This was professional. A mysterious piece of malware, Stuxnet-like in its operation, had been introduced into the turbine's industrial control system. It had mimicked normal operations while secretly ordering the blades to spin at an impossible, self-destructive velocity, then somehow erased its own code as the overheating gearbox burst into flames. The digital signature, or rather the complete lack of one, was that of a sophisticated state-sponsored actor.

London had been on the phone all morning. The security company responsible for site security had requested investigatory support, and Phillips had been tasked with providing it. He was, to put it mildly, extremely stressed and frustrated. A sudden crisis in the Black Sea meant that his best cyber analysts had already been co-opted by Vauxhall Cross for priority tasking.

The very bureaucracy he had helped create was now consuming its own children, stripping him of his own assets. The frustration of losing control of his own fiefdom was not improving his mood. His gaze swept the room, landing on his weapon of last resort.

Declan Shaw.

Declan, sensing the impending doom, was suddenly and intensely focused on an empty folder titled Chudes data on his terminal. He had been running a package of analytical tools Danny had recently provided him, still without result; there was simply nothing there. He pretended to be entirely engrossed in the process and didn't look up.

It didn't work.

He felt the familiar presence looming over his desk. Phillips was standing there, holding a tasking folder like the sword of Damocles.

"Busy are we, Shaw?"

"When am I not?" Declan replied, not bothering to look up.

"Well, un-busy yourself," Phillips snapped. "We have a problem at that new renewable development site at Blyth... a suspected malware attack on a turbine resulting in a serious fire."

Declan finally looked up irritated.

"Isn't that for the cyber geeks? I deal with disinformation and the resultant physical threats... I don't really do the ones and zeros. That's for the clever people."

Phillips looked at the progress bars on the ones and zeroes Declan was currently quite happily using and decided, last resort or not, Shaw knew enough about malware and threat hunting to do the task.

"A fire on critical national infrastructure is a physical threat, isn't it?" Phillips retorted, the words grating. "And since London has seen fit to re-task my actual cyber team, today you are a cyber geek as far as this organisation is concerned." He hated having to rely on Shaw, this relic from a bygone era. "We've been asked via Aegis to offer investigatory support to a consultancy called Secure Energy Risks." Phillips paused, a thin, triumphant smile on his lips. "If I'm not mistaken, Shaw, your cover identity with Aegis is as a senior investigator as well as an analyst?"

Secure Energy Risks. Declan sat up straight, suddenly interested. Her company. Eleanor Vane's company. What an amazing coincidence, he thought suspiciously.

He looked up at Phillips. "Still playing the honeytrap game, are we?" he said to himself. Well, time to carry on running with the joke. What's the worst thing that could happen?

"You're absolutely right, Sir," Declan said, his voice suddenly bright. "A fire on critical infrastructure is absolutely within my remit. Happy to help."

He stood up, looking uncharacteristically happy, cheerfully grabbed the folder from Phillips's stunned hand, and without another word, threw on his raincoat and strode purposefully towards the exit.

Phillips stood frozen for a moment, watching him leave. As Declan passed Norman the Storeman's office, Norm looked up, caught Declan's eye, and with a conspiratorial grin, casually raised his middle finger. Declan, without breaking stride, returned it with a wry smile of his own.

Phillips observed the exchange from across the room, his face tightening with a mixture of confusion and disgust. He simply could not conceive of a professional environment where such a crude, insubordinate gesture could be a sign of close friendship. He scowled, unable to shake the feeling that Shaw's unexpected acquiescence was somehow far more worrying than his usual insubordination.

He hadn't known it when he was first failed upwards to Special Projects, but he had found the truth later, buried deep in Helen's handover paperwork and confirmed in Shaw's own personnel file. He had been the one originally designated by Helen to be her replacement, a strategic move on her part to install a pure operator and head off the inevitable power grab from the London-based agencies.

And Shaw had turned it down. Flat.

The refusal was a concept so alien to Phillips's ambition-driven worldview that he could only interpret it as the ultimate act of arrogance. When he finally realised that he was, in effect, dining on Shaw's "sloppy seconds," it bred a deep, envy-driven animosity in him. It was a constant, festering humiliation.

He may have been in command of the Happy House, but he saw how the remnants of the old guard, men like Norman, respected Shaw. He saw the easy loyalty they afforded him, the way they deferred to his judgment. Shaw was a natural leader, even if, infuriatingly, the bastard didn't even seem to realise he was doing it.

Every successful operation Shaw ran, every sudden leap of inspiration he conjured from the data, felt like a personal insult to Phillips, a silent judgment on his own competence. He wasn't just managing an insubordinate and unstable analyst; he was living in the shadow of the man who should have had his job, and who had been arrogant enough to refuse it. The revelation was like poison to Phillips, eating away at his ego on a daily basis.

Declan grabbed the keys to a Q-car, liveried with the bland "Aegis Security Solutions" logo, and headed towards Blyth along the coast road. As he drove towards the wind farm, he thought about Phillips, and had seen the look of utter resentment on his face as he had left the office. He suspected he knew the reason for his animosity: the fact he was forced to rely on him today and the main reason—he had been earmarked for the hot seat in the Happy House over Phillips.

Declan sighed wearily.

What Phillips didn't understand was the reasons he turned down the job, which were two-fold: Firstly, he didn't want the responsibility of being the one who pointed the fingers at the targets; counterintuitively, he preferred being the one pulling the trigger, as that gave him more control on the ground, less likely of another repeat of Belfast. Secondly, analysing the intelligence was one of the few places he could find any kind of peace. When dealing with complex problems, he gained a clarity, the confusion whirling in his head steadying into a narrow focus. His work literally kept him sane. To lose that to spreadsheets and PowerPoint presentations was his own personal version of hell. His refusal was not from the arrogance that Phillips wrongly perceived. It was about his very survival.

By the time he reached the site, the downpour had eased to a damp drizzle that felt almost pleasant. He pulled up into the car park and walked over to what was left of the turbine. He couldn't help thinking of The War of the Worlds, the Thunder Child bringing down a monstrous Martian in a sheet of flame. Except this hadn't been caused by some mighty ironclad, with all guns blazing; it had been caused by some clever twat with a keyboard. He remembered the good old days when being called a keyboard warrior was an insult. Now, it was a terrifying compliment.

He walked around the site, looking at the warped, charred wreckage. Deciding he needed to at least look professional, he went back to his car and grabbed a camera. He started taking assorted snaps of the damage, framing shots of twisted metal against the grey sky.

He was so focused on this task that he didn't notice the scene playing out a few yards away. Eleanor Vane was being cornered by a site manager, a petty jobsworth in a bright orange high-vis vest and white safety helmet.

"...and I don't care who your consultancy is," the man was saying, his voice nasal and self-important. "This is an active incident scene. No helmet, no vest, no access."

Eleanor, who had already finished her on-site assessment, had a weary, almost pained expression on her face. Then she saw him. Declan, oblivious to the drama, taking photographs. He offered her another chance to escape an overbearing pain in the arse... again.

She brusquely extricated herself from the red-faced jobsworth's lecture, leaving him dumbfounded and indignant, and walked over to Declan, who was still absorbed in his work. She stepped directly into his line of sight, blocking his shot of the scorched gearbox.

Declan, annoyed at the interruption, was about to say something sharp when he realised who it was. The irritation vanished, replaced by surprise and something else he didn't want to admit to himself. She stood there, a small, knowing smile on her face. He lowered the camera slightly, then, with a deliberate click, he raised it again and took her picture. The shutter sound was sharp in the damp air. He caught the smile, the glint in her eyes, the raindrops on her dark hair. He finally lowered the camera completely, and they stood there for a moment, both smiling at each other.

"We really must stop meeting like this," she joked.

"Oh, I agree," replied Declan. "I was going to ask what brings you here, but that's a pretty well-burnt elephant in the room."

She looked at the remnant of the turbine.

"An interesting elephant."

"Yeah, unfortunately I'm not exactly qualified to do the digital forensics, but for some reason they sent me anyway, so I guess I had better make the effort and pull the logs, see if I can make some sense out of it."

"Oh, don't worry about that, Declan. My team is attempting to pull the digital forensics from the control room as we speak. I'm happy to share anything we find with you."

Declan frowned, slightly puzzled.

"Then why was I even tasked? My boss Phillips said a request had been made by Secure Energy Risk, but you guys clearly have it covered."

Eleanor smiled at him,

"Well maybe somebody at the company was new in town and was hoping to see a friendly face?"

The penny dropped for Declan. Phase two of the honey trap, clearly. But what the hell? He may as well play along.

It got him out of the Happy House for a few hours, if nothing else. And though he hated to admit it, he really enjoyed Eleanor's company. Besides, what did he have to lose? Just the pleasure of Phillips breathing down his neck for the report.

"No one's ever said I have a friendly face before," he joked, leaning into the conversation. She laughed in response and looked at him.

"Well, Mr Friendly Face, the reality is, we both have to wait for them to finish their work anyway, so I've got at least a couple of hours free before I can even think about starting the report. I was just wondering, are you hungry? I skipped breakfast to drive here so I'm famished."

"I'm getting there," he replied, having neglected breakfast yet again. He simply couldn't stand sitting in his flat eating breakfast under HER gaze.

She gave him a playful, appraising look.

So, what's a girl got to do on Tyneside to get lunch?"

"Offer to pay, usually," Declan joked. "We're all a bit tightfisted round here."

She laughed; even her eyes noted Declan,

"Actually," he continued, a genuine smile returning, "I know just the place. And it's on me."

"Then lead on, kind sir," she joked back. "Before you change your mind and make me pay."

They walked slowly to his car, catching up on events since Washington, and he drove them the couple of miles down the coast to North Shields fish quay. He parked at the far end, giving her the full, panoramic view of the river. He pointed out the local landmarks: the squat, functional Shields Ferry chugging its way across the grey water to the south bank; the long, concrete jetty of the fish quay itself, lined with well-worked fishing boats, their hulls scarred from countless trips into the North Sea, and the fishermen, clad in bright orange oilskins, their faces weathered by the wind, mending nets on the quayside.

In the distance, where the river met the sea, the sky had cleared slightly, and a brilliant, perfect rainbow arched over the twin piers that protected the river entrance. Eleanor remarked on how beautiful it was.

Declan watched the rare sun reflecting off the ripples on the water, as Eleanor admired the scene, a look of serenity on her face, her hair blowing gently in the breeze. He also thought what an utterly beautiful sight it was.

They strolled amiably along the river for a quarter of a mile, enjoying the short walk, the salty, briny air sharp and clean in the intermittent drizzle. Across the street from the working quay itself was a line of quaint little bars and cafes. She thought it was a charming little place in its own way, a genuine, working fish quay mixed with a small, modern entertainment quarter. Eventually, they reached a restaurant called "The Waterfront."

As they entered, a matriarch called Margaret greeted Declan with a motherly hug and an exclamation of pure Geordie.

"Declan! Where have you been, pet? It's been ages!" she beamed, her accent warm and friendly to Eleanor's ears.

Declan returned the hug, looking slightly embarrassed, aware of Eleanor watching the scene with a small smile on her face. Margaret spotted her. "Eeee, who's this bonny lass? Don't tell us you've finally got yourself a girlfriend?"

Declan smiled.

"Sorry to disappoint you Margaret, just a colleague. Only showing her round the place."

"Nice to meet you, pet," Margaret said to Eleanor. She turned back to Declan.

"Introductions, man!"

Declan smiled despite himself. "Eleanor, this is Margaret. Margaret, Eleanor."

"Nice to meet you too," said Eleanor.

"Come on. I'll take you to your booth. The usual one?" said Margaret.

"Thanks, Margaret," replied Declan.

They sat down, and Declan ordered for them both without asking. "Just give us two haddock and chips, Margaret, and some tea, please."

As Margaret wandered off, she muttered under her breath, "colleagues my arse," a knowing look in her eyes. Eleanor felt a strange sense of... ease. The authenticity of the place, the genuine affection from the woman, it reminded her of the older women in Russia, the babushkas who were the unshakeable heart of any community.

It did not escape her attention, however, that their booth was in the far corner of the restaurant and that Declan had, without conscious thought, positioned himself with a clear view of the entrance. It was textbook tradecraft, so deeply ingrained it was now instinct.

The observation brought her back on mission, a cold reminder of why she was truly here. Strangely, the thought made her feel a pang of regret that their easy encounter was little more than a charade. In that moment, she felt like she was the Kukushka, not Declan, a cuckoo, an imposter in a welcoming nest, rather than a Nightingale.

She looked up to see Declan watching her, his expression unreadable. It wasn't the assessing gaze of an analyst doing his thing, but something else, something softer, familiar even. Her disconcerting thoughts were interrupted by the arrival of the meal.

The food was simple, and it was perfect. Eleanor confessed she had never had fish and chips before, and in the down-to-earth simplicity of the restaurant, they forgot about the job. They laughed and joked, and for a moment, she felt a crack in the icy facade of the Nightingale. The sound of her own laughter reminded her of their unsettling Washington encounter. The time seemed to pass in a flash, and Eleanor fought back a pang of regret that their conversation was coming to an end.

Declan went to the counter to pay the bill. Eleanor, needing a moment to compose herself after the easy, disarming warmth of the lunch, excused herself to the ladies' room. It wasn't that she needed to use the facilities, but she needed to look in the mirror, to see the face of Eleanor Vane and remind herself of the mission. She stared at her reflection, forcing the cold professionalism of the Nightingale back into her eyes, burying the woman who had just laughed so freely. Burying the unwelcome echoes of Anya.

She composed herself, left the bathroom, and saw Declan still at the counter, his back turned to her. In front of him stood a distressed elderly lady, her hands trembling as she fumbled through a worn purse.

"...but it was right here," the old woman was saying, her voice quaking with panic. "I had it just a minute ago. For my dinner..."

Margaret was there, trying to placate her.

"Don't you worry now, Betty. We'll sort something out. It's alright." But the old woman was genuinely upset, on the verge of tears over the lost money.

Eleanor watched the scene with a discreet, detached interest, until she saw Declan bend down, as if to tie his shoelace. His hand swept near the floor, but she saw clearly that there was nothing there to pick up.

Puzzled, she watched as he straightened up. With a subtle, almost invisible sleight-of-hand, a folded twenty-pound note appeared between his fingers.

He gently touched the old woman's arm.

"Excuse me," he said, his voice soft. "I think you might have dropped this."

He offered her the note. The woman looked from the money to his face, her expression a mixture of confusion and an almost physical relief.

"Oh... oh, thank you, love. Thank you so much," she said as she gratefully took the money, her hand still trembling, and paid her bill.

Margaret, who had seen the entire, deft exchange, looked at Declan and gave him a slow, knowing wink. He gave her a slight, nonchalant shrug, then paid his own bill and turned, heading back towards the table where Eleanor was now standing, as if nothing had happened.

As they left, Margaret gave them both a wonderful, motherly hug and made them promise to come back.

"And make sure you come back together!" she called after them, winking so obviously it made Eleanor laugh out loud again.

"I think she likes you" said Declan,

"I think she likes you too," replied Eleanor.

"Well, who can blame her? I always did say Margaret was an excellent judge of character," he countered, smiling.

They walked back along the jetty to his car, just enjoying the peace and the sound of the seabirds. He then dropped her off back at the arson site, and as she began to climb out of the car, he turned to her.

"Oh, almost forgot in all the excitement of fish and chips, how will you get the report to me? My boss will undoubtedly be breathing down my neck as soon as I get back to the office."

Eleanor smiled at him.

"Give me your email address," she said, her tone friendly. "The secure one for Aegis."

"It's on the business card I gave you in Washington," he said. "I've another if you've lost it?"

She quickly checked her purse and there it was.

"No, it's good, I was hardly going to lose your contact details," she said with that smile of hers.

"I'll write mine up and forward you my preliminary findings. It will have the technical detail you need. You can... plagiarise it as much as you like, even pretend you wrote it." A small, playful smile touched her lips. "On one condition."

"And what's that?" Declan asked.

"You take me on that guided tour you promised me in Washington."

He grinned, a genuine one, then sighed mock-sarcastically,

"Oh, if I must."

The way he sometimes used his humour was not lost on Eleanor, how he used it as a shield. It was different from her more direct Russian humour, far more understated and drier, without being genuinely sarcastic. She liked it, she decided.

They parted with a promise to stay in touch. As she was about to get out of the car, she leaned over and kissed him on the cheek in farewell. She let her lips linger for a fraction of a second longer than was strictly necessary, a subtle, deliberate act meant to plant a seed of interest.

But as she did, she felt the warmth of his skin, smelled the faint, subtle scent of his cologne, and though he was unshaven, his stubble was pleasantly soft. What was supposed to be the calculated beginning of a seduction felt... personal, like something long forgotten yet at the same time dangerously familiar.

She pulled back, disconcerted, her professional composure shaken. She was genuinely confused at her own emerging feelings. It wasn't supposed to be happening like this. The cold, analytical part of her mind even considered the possibility that he might be the one doing the seducing. But she dismissed it almost immediately. There was no guile in his eyes. He may have been operating under a false role, but she felt everything else about him—his weariness, his humour, his quiet kindness—was genuine. It was a deeply disorientating feeling.

As she watched him drive away, Eleanor leaned against the cold metal gate, the drizzle turning back into rain, the sudden downpour soaking her hair as thunder rumbled, a reflection of the internal conflict she was feeling.

She continued to stand in the rain for a while as his car disappeared, trying to bring herself back on mission. According to the SVR, the man from the P-File was a haunted killer, a cynical operative and dangerously unstable.

But the man who had just left was... different. The target was supposed to be a set of predictable vulnerabilities she could exploit. Declan Shaw was proving to be a very enigmatic man, and for an operative on a critical mission, that was the most dangerous complication of all.

CHAPTER 15

The encounter at the wind farm also left Declan unsettled. Back in the oppressive confines of the Happy House, he found himself unable to focus. The image of Eleanor's smile, the easy warmth of their conversation, and the surprising intimacy of their brief kiss warred with the professional caution that had kept him alive for decades. The analyst in him screamed that she was a complication, a beartrap laid by Phillips, but the man in him, however, simply wanted to see her again. It had dawned on him unexpectedly that, when he was in her company, the maelstrom of thoughts that was his daily reality simply faded away, like a tornado dissipating after a storm.

For the first time in years, he understood what it was to feel at peace. Indeed, since Washington, he had even started to dream of her instead of Belfast, dreams which, for once, he didn't want to wake up from.

Phillips had chosen her well, he reasoned; he had access to his P File, so it would be an easy thing to profile him and target him accordingly. But trap or not, he felt so at ease in her company he wasn't yet ready to call her bluff and end Phillips's sociopathic charade.

He also rationalised that the secret in avoiding a trap was knowing where it was, so in reality, he was the one in total control of the situation, or so he told himself. He sighed heavily and found the business card for "Secure Energy Risks" in his wallet. On impulse, before the cynical, professional part of his brain could veto the decision, he saved it into his phone and dialled her number. She answered on the second ring.

"Eleanor Vane, Secure Energy Risks."

"Eleanor, it's Declan," he said, the use of his first name feeling surprisingly natural. "Sorry to ruin what was a lovely day, but I was just wondering, how soon can you get the report to me? I have my manager breathing down my neck and generally complaining about me disappearing."

"Hold on," she replied. Declan could hear her voice talking to someone in the background. "Is 36 hours OK? We have to collate everything and get it written up."

"That's perfect," he smiled down the phone. "I like the thought of making him sweat for a few extra hours. I really do appreciate the assist; you're a lifesaver."

There was a slight, almost imperceptible pause on the other end, then a surprise.

"Actually, I'm glad you called, Declan. I really enjoyed today and was wondering if you were free tomorrow?"

He paused, his mind racing through several scenarios before he answered.

"Officially, no, but unofficially I can make myself free. It wouldn't be the first time I've played truant. How about I pick you up from your hotel, then take you for that guided tour we discussed?"

"That would be wonderful," she replied, the pitch of her voice sounding genuinely pleased. "How does ten o'clock sound? I'll text you the address."

"See you then," Declan said, a feeling of pleasant anticipation settling over him. He hung up the phone, ignoring the chorus of warnings from the more sensible corners of his mind.

If nothing else, it would confirm his honey trap theory if Phillips did get to know about his "truancy." There was also that strange sense of peace she brought, relief from the cacophony of ideas and imagery that literally plagued his every waking hour.

The following day, he picked her up from her hotel. She slid into the passenger seat, bringing with her the faint, pleasant scent of her now familiar perfume.

"So where to, Mr Shaw?" she asked playfully.

"It's a surprise, Miss Vane," he replied, equally playfully.

They drove through the city, Declan pointing out some of the historical buildings. She was impressed with his local knowledge, which was interspersed with a dry, humorous anecdotes, such as using Scotsmen as human shields on the Cathedral spire to prevent a bombardment, he also told the tale of the "flying donkey" which was pushed from the ancient keep as a warning. The sad tale of the young flower girl who was thrown into the dungeons and murdered because some twat of a magistrate got stung by a bee when buying her flowers. The same keep was the "new" Castle built by the Normans, which gave the city its name he recounted.

"Same shit, different centuries." He explained to her cynically about the innocent girl.

As they headed east out of the city, Eleanor soon realised they were making for the coast. Curious, she asked him how he had managed to get the day off work to take her out at such short notice.

"I thought your boss was breathing down your neck, you're not lying to me Mr Shaw?" She asked jokingly.

"No, I'm not lying to you, just my boss by pulling a sicky," he said, with a proudly mischievous grin.

"Oh," Eleanor replied, a smile playing on her own lips. "Let me guess. A twenty-four-hour bug? A sudden migraine, rickets, consumption, Beri Beri?"

Declan just shook his head, keeping his eyes on the road, the grin widening, amused at her joke.

"Nope."

"Come on," she said, playfully nudging his arm. "You can't just leave it at that. I have to know what masterful excuse a man in your line of work comes up with. A sudden case of Scabies? Bubonic plague perhaps, or even worse, halitosis?"

He chuckled, still refusing to give in.

"You're not even close."

Her curiosity was now fully piqued. She adopted a mock-stern tone, her eyes bright with amusement.

"Declan Shaw, you will tell me right now. That is an order."

He shot her a sideways glance, feigning shock.

"Is that how it's going to be? You're going to bully me into revealing all my secrets?"

"Absolutely," she confirmed, trying and failing to keep a straight face. "Now, talk."

He looked at her, a wry smile spreading across his face.

"What? And absolutely ruin your perception of me as a suave, sophisticated, and debonair intelligence professional?"

"Declan!" she cried in sudden mock exasperation, giving his arm another light shove.

He sighed, in acceptance of defeat, and then finally surrendered, a rueful look on his face.

"I told the boss," He mumbled sheepishly, "that I had explosive diarrhoea."

She stared at him, her mouth opening in disbelief. Then she let out a spontaneous burst of laughter.

"You're shitting me?" she managed to say through her mirth.

"Nope," he shot back, his timing perfect. "Shitting myself, supposedly. But you get the general idea."

This sent her into another fit of helpless laughter. It was so natural Declan couldn't help but smile at her response, his earlier pretend embarrassment forgotten.

"And he believed you?" she finally asked.

"Yeah," Declan said, a hint of satisfaction returning to his voice. "He actually had it himself last week, so it was a plausible excuse." He paused, a wry, little-boy smile spreading across his face. "I'm just happy I managed to put that laxative in his coffee without anyone noticing."

Anya's laughter subsided, replaced by a look of genuine shock.

"You put laxative in your boss's coffee?"

Declan smirked ruefully with his lopsided grin.

"Yeah," he said, his voice dropping to a conspiratorial whisper. "But only because I couldn't get my hands on any Polonium."

She looked at him again, her eyes wide, and then shook her head slowly, another laugh escaping her lips. This man was a complete and utter paradox, a kind soul with a dangerously dark sense of humour. It was another detail that was conspicuously absent from his file, and she found the contradiction both hilarious and deeply intriguing.

They eventually made their way to the seafront and drove along the coastal road, chatting easily and, listening to The Who's Quadrophenia, because as Declan joked:

"It's about a day at the seaside."

Eventually, he turned off the main street onto a narrow road which wound around a headland and terminated in a car park. Eleanor could see a beautiful lighthouse on a small island, joined to the mainland by a short tidal causeway. It was a picturesque scene, like something from a holiday postcard.

As usual, it was raining, but this only added to the wild, untamed beauty of the island.

"Would you like an ice cream?" Declan asked. While it was hardly the weather for it, a solitary ice cream van was dutifully selling its wares to the assorted bikers, dog walkers, and tourists who frequented the car park despite the weather.

"I'd love one, you choose," she said.

Declan climbed out of the car and ran through the drizzle, returning a moment later with two oyster shells, soft ice cream swirled into a nougat-lined, scallop-shaped wafer, each with a chocolate flake stuck in it.

"Try it," he said, handing one to her.

They sat in silence for a few minutes, the only sound the patter of the rain on the car roof and the melancholic opening chords of Dire Straits' "Romeo and Juliet" from the radio.

Declan was beginning to confirm his hyper-vigilance; the constant cacophony of threat recognition which plagued him was almost gone when she was around. The silence wasn't just comfortable; it was quiet inside his own head, which was deeply unsettling to him. He thought of the XTC song, "Senses Working Overtime," his normal state of being. He then compared it to his now, this oasis of unfamiliar calm, and was almost scared by the contrast. It was difficult for him to process being almost at peace. It made him feel strangely vulnerable, a dangerous state of affairs for someone in his line of work.

His choice to bring her here, to this lighthouse, was complex. He had considered trying to impress the cultured, sophisticated woman Eleanor Vane appeared to be, but the thought of operating so far outside his own comfort zone also made him nervous.

He found the seaside relaxing, one of the few places his mind could be relatively at rest, the sound of the sea always helping to at least turn his mind's volume down a notch. On many an occasion, he would drive here just to walk along the beach, the wind and the rain in his hair, to try to quiet the demons.

His logic, he realised, was flawed and contradictory. He had brought her to this place of relative peace, hoping that if she saw him here, in this less anxious state, she might not see the monster that lurked in his soul. She might not see the real him.

He watched her eating the ice cream with an almost childlike enjoyment as she listened to the music. He smiled sadly. If only things were different. If only he were different. If only she wasn't a honey trap.

For Eleanor, the moment also felt dangerously serene. The sensation of the sweet, cold ice cream, the wistful music, the peaceful rhythm of the rain, it was a combination designed to disarm, to lull. A cold, professional voice in the back of her mind, the voice of the Nightingale, cut through the calm. Remember the mission. According to his file, she was in a car with a talented analyst who was also a killer. Of course he would be an expert at manipulating people, at lulling them into a false sense of security. He was simply the other side of the same coin she was.

And yet... the memory of the previous day contradicted everything. The quiet act of kindness with the old woman, the moment of generosity he thought no one had seen, it didn't fit the profile of a cold manipulator. He still felt authentic to her, but was that authenticity real, or was it just the masterstroke of a man who was exceptionally good at his job? She found herself determined to solve this contradiction. Mainly from a professional perspective, she told herself, but a small, subliminal flicker of personal interest, one she was in deep denial about, sparked under the ice.

After a short while, the rain eased. Declan turned to her.

"Have you ever seen seals in the wild?"

She looked at him, slightly puzzled.

"Seals? No, never. Just in an aquarium and I didn't really like seeing them in captivity."

"I don't like that either, I hate seeing anything in a cage in fact, but come with me," he smiled. "I have a surprise."

He got out of the car and opened her door in a chivalrous manner, then went to his boot and pulled out two pairs of binoculars and his camera. Still puzzled, she followed him across the causeway onto the island.

They made their way to the rear of the lighthouse, where a small hide had been built for observing wildlife. Like the lighthouse itself, it was painted with whitewash, so as to be almost invisible against the larger structure behind it.

"At first you may not see them," he whispered, pointing towards the rocks below. "They blend perfectly with the landscape; once they move, they're easy to spot."

They looked out of the viewing window. Below them, a large colony of grey seals was draped over the dark, wet rocks. Eleanor watched, fascinated, as one of the larger bulls let out a deep, mournful-sounding grunt that echoed across the water. Then her gaze fell upon the pups. They were clumsy, energetic, and utterly charming, rolling over each other and awkwardly chasing the receding tide. One particularly bold pup flopped its way to the water's edge, barking at a wave, only to be surprised when the next one washed over it, sending it tumbling back in a comical heap. Seeing her happiness, he decided not to let her know the high mortality rate of these beautiful creatures; it would only spoil her mood, as it had spoiled his when he had first found out.

Declan wasn't really looking at the seals anymore. He was looking at her. For a fleeting, unguarded moment, the cool, professional mask of "Eleanor Vane" had vanished completely. In its place was the face of Anya, her eyes wide with the same childlike expression he'd seen in the car. A radiant smile lit up her entire face as she watched the antics of the seal pups. It was the most beautiful and authentic expression he had seen from her yet.

Sensing his gaze on her, Eleanor turned from the window. She saw the way he was looking at her, and the smile on her own face faltered, her professional composure snapping suddenly back into place. The unexpected moment of genuine, simple joy was deeply unsettling to her. Her training screamed at her that such an emotional release in the presence of a target was an unforgivable failure of tradecraft.

A cold suspicion returned, sharp and unwelcome. How had he done that? How had he so effortlessly elicited such an unguarded reaction from her?

The thought that he was deliberately orchestrating this, choosing the perfect, disarming location, knowing it would break through her defences, was both terrifying and, from a professional standpoint, admirable. Is this what he does? she thought. Is this his method? Lulling his targets with this quiet, unassuming authenticity until their guard is completely down, before moving in for the kill?

She was now more convinced than ever that she was being played by an expert. It was a suspicion born not from evidence, but from a deep-seated inability to trust such a moment of happiness.

This was, in fact, a form of projection on her part; she was attributing her own professional capacity for manipulation to him, unable to accept that his kindness might be exactly what it appeared to be.

He touched her on her arm and pointed out to sea.

"Look."

She raised her binoculars towards the area he was pointing at, and then she saw them, about fifty or so, a pod of dolphins, breaching through the waves in a magnificently graceful display. Despite the rain and the waves, they continued their ballet, heading south down the coast.

"They're dancing in the storm," uttered Declan. She turned to look at him; he was wearing the same look of wonder he had previously witnessed on her face. The expression made him look almost boyish, and she found herself smiling involuntarily at seeing him looking happy.

Who was this Englishman? And why was she beginning to feel conflicted about lying to him, about spending time with him? Mission focus, Stepnova, she chided herself, her gaze turning back to the sea, and felt slightly sad she could no longer see the dolphin ballet. Mission focus, she thought again. Stay on mission you fool.

Declan lowered his binoculars, unaware that she had been studying him. He sighed and regretfully mentioned the tide would soon be coming in.

"Unless you want to be trapped on an island with me overnight," he joked, "we had better head back to the mainland."

Part of her, the part buried beneath an avalanche, decided being trapped alone with him might not be such a bad thing. From a mission-orientated perspective, of course. They walked back across the causeway, the salty air whipping at their hair, comfortable in their own company, enjoying a brief interlude in the weather. Declan raised the camera.

"How about a souvenir, a picture of you with the lighthouse in the background?"

She hesitated slightly, then remembered he already had a photo of her from the wind farm, and it would be suspicious to refuse.

"Sure," she replied with a smile. "A keepsake from my first time seeing seals and dolphins in the wild." She posed in an exaggerated manner, making Declan laugh.

"Stop that, or it'll be blurred," he remonstrated jokingly.

Just then, an elderly man who was passing by intervened.

"Would you like me to take a picture of you both?" he asked.

Declan looked at Eleanor, who nodded happily, and he turned to the passer-by in gratitude and said,

"Sure, it's all set up, just look through the viewfinder, point at us and click."

The pensioner waited for Declan to stand next to Eleanor and raised the camera.

Without thinking about why, they both placed an arm around each other's waist, almost instinctively, and Eleanor, in an act of unexpected but comfortable intimacy, rested her head slightly on Declan's shoulder. They both smiled.

He could smell her hair, her perfume, feel her warmth.

Oh, she's VERY good, he thought. Honey trap or not, he was struggling to remain professional.

"Say cheese," said the man.

In unison, they both said, "Gorgonzola," as he took the picture and laughed at the coincidence.

"Great minds think alike," laughed Eleanor.

They thanked the pensioner as he returned the camera and walked slowly to the car, chatting about the seals. As they climbed in, the rain began to fall again, drumming a soft rhythm on the roof as an acoustic version of "Take On Me" by A-ha played softly from the radio. Declan showed her the photograph on the camera's screen; it looked like a picture of two happy people, comfortable in each other's presence. They looked at each other again and exchanged wry, knowing smiles.

The fragile moment was abruptly shattered by a familiar, menacing series of brassy, orchestral notes booming from the car's speakers: The Imperial March from Star Wars.

Eleanor looked at the dashboard, startled by the sudden, ominous music.

"What is that?"

Declan sighed, glancing at the caller ID on the screen, which glowed with the words:

"The Death Star."

"That," he said with weary resignation, "is my boss."

He shot her an apologetic look before accepting the call.

"Shaw," Phillips's voice barked through the car speakers, tight with irritation and completely oblivious to his own theme music. "I trust you're feeling better? Because while you've been 'indisposed', the paperwork on my desk has been piling up. I need that wind farm report. Urgently."

It was a blatant power play, an assertion of dominance. Declan met Eleanor's gaze, a flicker of mischievous rebellion in his eyes. He adopted a strained, pained tone through gritted teeth.

"I can't, Sir. I'm... still in a bad way," he said, trying to sound sincere while struggling to keep a straight face as he looked at her. "I'm literally stuck on the toilet as we speak."

Declan assumed that his fake sickie would get back to Phillips courtesy of Eleanor, so he might as well get his money's worth from his small act of rebellion. It was a pity the honeytrap game would soon be over; he felt strangely comfortable with her. The thought that their little game was coming to an end gave him a pang of sadness.

Eleanor, who had been listening with a look of wicked amusement on her face, saw her opportunity. She understood the game Declan was playing instantly. A mischievous grin spread across her face. She cupped her hands to her mouth, leaned discreetly towards the car's microphone, and produced a series of low, sputtering, and impressively realistic noises that sounded like a cross between a prolonged, wet fart and Donald Duck losing his temper.

A stunned silence came from the other end of the line.

Declan's eyes widened in disbelief at the sound she had just made. He stared at her, open-mouthed. She looked back at him, her own shoulders shaking with barely suppressed laughter.

Phillips, clearly flustered and utterly baffled by the strange, semi-quacking, flatulent noises echoing down the line, finally cleared his throat.

"...Very well, Shaw," he stammered, his attempt to maintain authority now completely defeated. "Tomorrow. On my desk. At the latest."

The line went dead.

For a moment, Declan and Eleanor just stared at each other, the sheer absurdity of the situation hanging in the air. Then the dam broke. They both suddenly burst into hysterical laughter. Declan looked at her as she fought to contain it, and a sudden thought occurred to him. He seriously needed to re-evaluate his honeytrap theory.

CHAPTER 16

When Declan returned to the Happy House, he spent the time turning her preliminary findings into something that looked like his own work. He was also immensely grateful. True to her word, she had emailed him the report. It was a masterclass in technical analysis, detailed, insightful, and far beyond anything he could have produced on his own. He had, as she suggested, plagiarised it liberally, padding his own report with her findings. For good measure, he ran the site imagery through a sophisticated AI analysis program, which generated pages of impressive looking but largely meaningless data on burn patterns and structural integrity. The result was a surprisingly coherent intelligence product.

And not the product of a Phillips honeytrap.

He'd submitted it to Phillips, who, after a thorough reading, had looked up with a grudging expression.

"Adequate work, Shaw," he'd said, the words delivered as the faintest of praise. "A bit more thorough than your usual efforts."

Declan had simply smiled.

"I aim to please, Sir." He was just happy to have put one over on the man. Was it unprofessional? Yes. A necessary bluff to keep his insufferable boss off his back? Absolutely.

Now, he thought, it was time to show his gratitude. And to make good on a promise. It was Thursday, his one night of the week to himself, his usual night for listening to music. He had just the place in mind to thank Eleanor for getting him off the hook.

He found the number for "Secure Energy Risks" in his phone's saved contacts and dialled. Once again, she answered quickly, as if she were expecting his call.

"Eleanor Vane."

"Eleanor, it's Declan again," he said, the use of her first name feeling natural now. "I'm calling to thank you for the assistance with my report. It would be positively caddish of me not to at least offer to buy you a drink, if you're up for some more flatulence jokes?"

He heard her giggle and then she replied,

"I'd love to meet up for a drink. Do you have anywhere special in mind?"

"I know a place. The music's good, it's tucked away in a little atmospheric part of the city which I like. How about we meet up at The Bridge Inn? Around eight o'clock?"

There was a slight pause, probably checking a map, he thought, then she replied,

"The Bridge... is that the one opposite the Cluny, under the Byker Bridge?"

"That's the place," Declan confirmed.

"That's perfect," she said, sounding pleased. "I've wanted to visit that part of the city, I understand it's quite Bohemian."

"It certainly is. I'll see you there," he replied.

"I'm looking forward to it," she answered.

He hung up the phone, feeling as conflicted as ever. He knew, on a professional level, that this was complicated. On a personal level it was even more complicated. If she wasn't sent by Phillips to embarrass him, did that mean she was genuine? He thought about Washington and the wind farm, what were the chances this absolutely enchanting woman would somehow be interested in him? It just didn't make any sense. Couldn't she see who he really was?

He also struggled to explain the feeling that he knew her, or the way she silenced the noise, and that's what made things difficult. His ability to read people, to see patterns in the chaos, to predict outcomes was seriously blunted around her. Was it simply a coincidence that someone with the ability to do that had made his acquaintance, or was there something deeper?

The fact that they'd both cracked the same joke at the same moment at the lighthouse was also unsettling, and he was struggling to logically explain that. He pushed the thoughts aside, rationalising the coincidences with a concept he'd picked up from his readings in Jungian psychology when he was busy self-diagnosing: synchronicity. The idea that seemingly unrelated events could be connected by a meaningful, acausal principle.

Perhaps their meetings weren't just happenstance, but part of a larger, cosmic plan created by some higher power. The fact that she just felt "right" when he was around her made him hope his niggling suspicions weren't true. The professional in him, however, was already turning wheels in that restless mind of his, considering angles and possibilities. And of course there was the guilt factor, the part of him which believed he wasn't worthy of a good woman, that he deserved his penance of solitude. Along with the question as to what an attractive woman like Eleanor Vane would ever see in a world-weary, emotionally constipated fossil like him.

But another part, the part that had felt dormant for years, simply didn't care. For the first time in a long time, he knew what it was like to feel normal, and was genuinely looking forward to a night out, to actually holding an intelligent conversation with a woman who wasn't a spectral hallucination or a technological construct.

He glanced at the clock. It was later than he thought. He had about forty minutes to spare. Pushed for time, he locked his screen and made a dash for the small office bathroom. There was no time to spruce up properly, just a quick wash. He splashed cold water on his unshaven face, ran a hand through his greying hair. A quick, subtle sniff under the armpits after a long day stuck in the stuffy office confirmed the necessity of a blast of deodorant. A splash of cologne, and that would have to do. He looked at himself in the mirror for a few moments and straightened his tie.

"Nothing ventured," he muttered to his reflection, a private acknowledgment of the gamble he was about to take.

He left the bathroom and walked down the corridor towards the exit. As he passed the armoury, the door opened, and Norman leaned out, his usual jovial grin in place.

"Off out, Declan?" Norman asked, surprised, then the inevitable insult. "Jesus, you look like shit, mate. Get some kip."

Declan managed a weary smile.

“Trying, Norm. Trying.” He paused. “At least I don't look like a pound shop Bond villain though!”

Norman's grin died on his face. He leaned back in his leather office chair, reached out, picked up a knitted toy cat from a shelf and placed it in his lap. He began to slowly, sinisterly stroke it.

“What do you mean?” he replied, utterly deadpan.

Declan laughed, a highly amused,

“Fuck off, Norm!” escaping him. “I'm just going out for a couple of quiet social drinks.”

“Followed by ten loud anti-social ones on past experience,” countered Norm laughing. “Well, have a good one mate. And try not to start any international incidents on your night off.”

Declan laughed in return and gave a casual farewell finger, then pushed open the door to the stairwell, leaving the 'Happy House' and its anxieties behind. He was heading out into the wet Newcastle evening, towards a bar overshadowed by a different bridge, and towards a woman who was as fascinating to him as she was distracting..

CHAPTER 17

The rain was still pouring down, thick and grey, a relentless curtain across the city. It had been this way for months, a disquieting persistence that even seasoned Tynesiders found unusual. Online forums pointed to weather modification experiments officially proposed by the UK government, whilst others pointed to the worrying magnetic excursion of the North Pole taking place in the Arctic. Declan suspected the weather modification theory might be more than just proposals: perhaps discreet trials linked to some climate-based research project were cited as the culprit. It was certainly the kind of monumental stupidity that the ideologues infesting the UK government would be likely to participate in. Even for Newcastle, this was unusual weather. Maybe it's the Russians, he joked to himself, the thought a dry, cynical musing on Moscow's penchant for unconventional tactics.

He made his way towards The Bridge Inn located in the Ouseburn Valley, a small tributary of the Tyne. Formerly a heavily industrialised area, its factories and warehouses were now converted into flats, bars, arts venues and small breweries, giving the area a unique vibe.

The bar itself was both popular and intimate, promising a warm atmosphere and perhaps a welcome distraction from the rain and the relentless hum of global anxieties. He pushed through the heavy door, the rich sound of a session singer a welcome contrast against the cold dampness outside. Hair plastered to his forehead, water dripping from his coat, he stepped inside, into the dimly lit bar, smelling of old wood and something vaguely smoky, filled with the soulful wail of a blues guitar and the singer.

Then he saw her, Eleanor. She was sitting casually at the bar, like the main character in a Hollywood movie, somehow managing to appear utterly composed and slightly aloof from the rest of the crowd. Her handbag was strategically placed on the stool next to her, a subtle barrier and a silent invitation. He noted the perfect staging, a masterclass in subtle social engineering, and the cynical part of him sighed, still suspecting a trap of some sort. But the lonely, exhausted man didn't care. She was the best thing he had seen all night, a beautiful illusion promising a welcome, temporary escape from his hyper-vigilance.

He noticed she too hadn't missed a thing. She'd watched him the moment he came through the doors, and he had seen the subtle shift in her posture and the way her eyes looked at him, which gave him the distinct impression she was feeling the same connection as he. A connection which he desperately wanted, but which terrified him at the same time. Who was this woman, and why was her mere presence able to silence the default chaos in his mind?

Their eyes met and he returned her smile, a smile he knew was going to cause him a lot of trouble if he wasn't careful. He walked towards her, nodding towards the vacant stool.

"Looks like this one's taken?"

She picked up her bag, her smile widening slightly as he sat down beside her, water dripping onto the floor from his raincoat.

"Now I see why you English always talk about the weather," she said, her voice smooth, with that slight Eastern European lilt he remembered. "Do you call this Monsoon Season?"

Declan chuckled, shrugging off his damp coat.

"Nope," he replied, a lopsided grin spreading across his own face. "In Newcastle, we call this summer."

Eleanor laughed at his joke; her bright smile contrasted strangely with the mood created by the gentle blues music. It was the icebreaker they both needed, melting the professional caution for a moment. He ordered drinks, a whiskey for himself, a glass of red wine for her, and they settled in, the soft music a low, soulful thrum in the background.

"First of all," Declan began, raising his glass in a small toast, "thank you. For the report. You saved my skin."

"Your boss was pleased, then?" she asked playfully.

"Phillips?" Declan snorted into his whiskey. "He wouldn't know a coherent intelligence product if it bit him on his expensively suited arse. But he grudgingly admitted it was 'adequate', which from him is the equivalent of a Nobel Prize. So, thank you."

"You are very welcome," she said. "Did you find anything... additional... in your own investigation and analysis?"

"Nothing much beyond your own findings, just that it wasn't petty vandalism, no accelerant used, a sophisticated, self-deleting malware package looks to be the culprit," Declan said, his tone turning more serious. "That was a professional job. State-sponsored, I'd wager, or a very talented extortionist setting out his stall, except it was designed to initially look like the work of local activists. It's unusual though, certainly not a local MO." He looked into his drink, "Being honest I'm puzzled with this one, and I hate being puzzled, but at least it gives me something different to get my teeth into that isn't Icar..." He caught himself just in time. "Jesus," he remonstrated to himself, "You just nearly blew operational security."

Eleanor was watching him closely as he made his slip, but pretended not to notice, knowing the real cause of the arson, impressed that he was at least in the ballpark, despite the lack of evidence left by the quantum malware. She was surprised at his slip but understood why; she was feeling somewhat conflicted herself in his presence. Their strange connection felt a little too genuine to her, and it was becoming very distracting at times. The good news was he had just confirmed he was still working on Icarus and may have just given her an excuse to discuss it in the near future. Just not yet, it was too soon to probe.

"It seems our respective clients are getting their money's worth from us both." She took a delicate sip of her wine. "Speaking of which, thank you for lunch the other day. I enjoyed it."

"The world-famous fish and chips of the North Shields fish quay?" Declan grinned. "Glad you liked it."

"I did," she said, and her smile seemed genuine, almost wistful. "I've had many expensive meals in many fancy restaurants, usually with men who were far more interested in the sound of their own voices and the sight of me, than in the food and intelligent conversation. That was... better. Much better." The memory of the simple meal was a pleasant one.

The night passed rapidly after that. The conversation flowed easily, picking up the shared wavelength they'd discovered in Washington. They talked about the conference, the absurdities of their respective fields, their observations of human behaviour under pressure.

Eleanor was witty, insightful, genuinely engaging. Declan found himself laughing, relaxing in a way he hadn't in years. He told her a few sanitised, humorous anecdotes from his military days; he did slip up slightly with a tale about being attached to the German army and taking his respirator into the communal shower “just in case”.

That one got a shocked expression from Eleanor.

“You didn’t?”

“I did. How often am I going to get the chance for a one-liner like that again?”

Despite herself, she laughed, especially when Declan described his German friends as standing there with “shocked Pikachu faces”.

“They were a good bunch really... Once they got to understand my humour.” He explained mock-defensively.

Eleanor continued to laugh, knowing that getting used to his humour was part of getting to know the man.

She responded with her own observations on the quirks of different cities she'd worked in. It was a delicate dance, revealing just enough to be interesting, concealing just enough to maintain professional distance. The fatalistic gloom that usually clung to him seemed to evaporate in her presence. He was actually enjoying himself.

But the night was drawing to a close, and Declan wasn't sure how to proceed. He was saved from embarrassment by the sudden, sharp ringtone of a mobile phone. Not his. Eleanor's. A discreet, professional-sounding tone. She glanced at the number, her expression shifting subtly.

“Work,” she murmured apologetically. She stood up. “Excuse me, it’s my boss.”

Declan looked at her, smiling.

“If you need me to make any farting noises, I’ll be right here.”

She laughed again and wandered a few steps towards the entrance of the bar. Declan watched her through the mirror. He focused on her animation, the subtle but noticeable shifts in her posture, the tension in her hand which was clutching the phone tightly.

Then, the band finished a song, and the ambient noise level in the bar dropped significantly just as Eleanor ended the call. He saw her mouth the final word, a sharp, frustrated exclamation.

He heard it. The word was unmistakable, even in Russian.

"Блядь!" "Fuck!" Spat out involuntarily, thick with a heartfelt response to a sudden, unknown change of circumstance.

Declan felt a chill run down his spine. He understood that much Russian. That was raw, unfiltered emotion. Something had happened, something serious enough to make her professional mask slip momentarily. Something serious enough to make a seasoned professional compromise herself.

Even now, he watched in admiration as the mask of her professional composure was back in place as she returned to him, a rueful and apologetic expression on her face.

"I'm afraid I have to go, something urgent has come up," she confirmed, managing a small, regretful smile.

Declan smiled back, his mind in turmoil, his fake expression flawless.

"Don't worry, Eleanor. Happens to me all the time." He didn't push for details. "We can finish the conversation another time? That tour..."

"I'd like that, Declan," she replied, her voice soft. A genuine look of regret in her eyes, or was that all an act too?

She leaned forward slightly, seemingly to peck him on the cheek in farewell. "I really would," the words barely audible, just for him, her eyes and her subtle perfume almost hypnotic.

Then she seemed to collect her thoughts and pulled back. As she left, she gave him a final, lingering look and smile over her shoulder before exiting the bar and hurrying through the rain. As she stepped out onto the cobblestones, she glanced back again through the rain-streaked window, her eyes meeting his in the mirror. He was subtly watching the entrance, his posture that of someone observing. Great minds thinking alike again, she thought, her professional admiration mixing with something else.

She hurried through the rain to be met by a waiting car, nondescript and dark. The driver rolled down his window just enough to speak.

"Get in, Comrade. Moscow wants to urgently speak to you at the safe house on a more secure channel."

Out of sight and earshot, hidden in the shadows, Declan had slipped out of the rear of the bar and watched unnoticed as the car pulled away quickly into the night. A secure pickup. Rapid departure. That wasn't a follow-up call about Blyth, he'd wager. That was something different. Something extremely significant.

"Interesting," he thought, his weariness and fatalistic gloom flooding back with a vengeance. "A little late for a windfarm emergency, Eleanor." He once again needed to reevaluate his honeytrap theory. And that dark part of him whispered in an almost triumphant voice. "Told you so, did you really believe a woman like that would be interested in YOU?"

He knew the answer, he had always known the answer; he'd let himself fall for a fantasy. It was almost with a sense of relief that his fears had been confirmed, normal service could be resumed. He turned back to the bar, the blues music suddenly sounding more melancholic. The night had been good, surprisingly good. But a game of some sort was clearly in play. And Eleanor Vane was right in the middle of it. And she was swearing in Russian.

"Shit!"

CHAPTER 18

The rain fell on Kyiv with a grim, indifferent persistence, turning the scarred streets into slick, grey mirrors. It was a city holding its breath, the air thick with the smell of damp concrete and the distant, mournful wail of an air raid siren warning of the approach of Geran drones, the screaming sound of their engines, sounding unnervingly like a Stuka during Blitzkrieg. The flash and rumbles of distant explosions adding to the illusion.

For Captain Taras, the noise and the gloom was a fitting backdrop for his current station in life. He had fallen hard. Once a respected SBU field commander operating on the sharpest edge, he was now a glorified dogcatcher; his team reduced to hunting draft dodgers in the city's backstreets.

His new non-combatant status, as hundreds of Russian drones screamed overhead almost nightly, was a painful and festering reminder of his failure in Moscow. Of the mission that had gone so spectacularly wrong. Of the bullet in his leg that ached with every drop in barometric pressure. And of her. That bitch.

"Get in the fucking van, you traitorous little shit!" Taras roared, his voice cutting through the downpour and the rumble of explosions.

The latest conscript, a boy barely out of his teens with a weak chin and expensive, mud-splattered trainers, was putting up a surprisingly fierce resistance. He clawed at the side of the minibus, his face a mask of privileged terror.

"You can't do this! My father..."

Taras didn't let him finish. He remembered another minibus, another young man, his head exploding into a crimson stain on the windscreen. Furious, he angrily grabbed the boy by his designer jacket, spun him around, and drove a knee hard into his gut. The air left the boy's lungs in a pained, pathetic groan. The sharp, satisfying crunch of the impact was a momentary antidote to the dull, persistent throb in his own thigh. He took a grim pleasure in the violence these days. It was a welcome distraction from his bitter memories of his own humiliation and failure.

"Your father isn't here," Taras hissed, his face inches from the boy's. "Your duty is to Ukraine. To the men dying in the trenches while you sip lattes and hide behind your mother's skirts. Now get in." He shoved the whimpering boy into the dark interior of the van, where two of his men, burly enforcers with the dead eyes of men who had seen too much, restrained him.

Taras slid the heavy door shut with a clang that echoed in the wet street. He stood for a moment in the rain, the cold water doing nothing to cool the simmering rage inside him. This was his life now. This filth, this humiliation, the stinging memory of helplessness, all because of her.

His secure phone buzzed in his pocket. A number he recognized. SBU headquarters.

"Yes," he answered, his tone aggressive.

"Captain Taras," a dry, official voice said on the other end. "A situation has arisen. An opportunity. A chance for you to redeem yourself, if you wish to accept the assignment."

The word hung in the air, a baited hook. Redemption. He craved it almost as much as he craved vengeance against The Russian Bitch.

"I'm listening Sir," Taras said, his tone suddenly reasonable.

He climbed into the passenger seat of the van.

"Headquarters," he barked at the driver, ignoring the terrified sobs coming from the back. "Now."

An hour later, he was in a windowless, smoke-filled briefing room deep within the SBU's fortified compound. A weary-looking Colonel with grey skin and hard, calculating eyes slid a thin file across a metal desk.

"His name is Elias Thorne," the Colonel began, his voice a low rumble. "A former NSA signals intelligence analyst. A genius, and a traitor. He has gone rogue and stolen something from the Russians, something... significant."

He paused, letting the weight of his words settle. "Our deep source in the SVR indicates the data concerns a new strategic weapon system, codenamed 'Icarus'. The technical details are on a quantum-encrypted drive. Thorne intends to sell it."

Taras felt a welcome thrill; this was the real intelligence work again.

"The exchange is to take place in the United Kingdom. Newcastle," the Colonel continued. "Logistically, the groundwork is already laid. We have a pre-positioned asset in the UK: a seasoned crew operating under the deep cover of a 'business enterprise' that functions as import-export front in London. They have been given the financial means to purchase the data from the seller, but obviously we would prefer the data is obtained using alternate, less expensive methods. We would like to use the cash for our war effort, if possible, it is a sizeable sum and intended as bait. The team are yours to command, Captain, use them as you see fit, as long as you succeed, there won't be many questions asked. Your flight to England is on a diplomatic passport. Once you land, you will take control of the operation and impose your will. They are expecting you."

"And the British?" Taras asked.

"You will be liaising with a friendly service. MI6 are facilitating your entry and providing an oversight handler. His details are in the file. To them, your cover as a 'crime gang' is designed to offer plausible deniability, a group of Ukrainian criminals you are using for a deniable operation. They believe you are here merely to recover a dangerous piece of Russian technology on their behalf."

"Local law enforcement will be directed to maintain a discreet distance but there are likely to be hostile assets operating in the area, therefore it is imperative that you and your team maintain tight operational security".

The Colonel leaned forward, his eyes cold. "But that is not our true objective, Captain. For us, this is not a recovery mission for MI6, but an acquisition." He lowered his voice; the words charged with a grim urgency. "Western support is wavering. Battlefield losses are mounting. They drip feed us old tanks and obsolete equipment, just enough to keep us in the fight, but never enough to win."

"This weapon, Captain... this data... is the ultimate bargaining chip. Proof of a Russian first-strike capability that would terrify Washington and London. We intend to acquire it and present it to our allies as a fait accompli." He held Taras's intense, almost fanatical gaze,

"Then we will trade it to them, not for money, but for the advanced, long-range weapons they have been denying us. This weapon may even provide the means by which we end the war on our own terms."

Taras stared at the file, his mind racing. This was more than redemption. This was a chance to secure the future of his country. He stood up and snapped to attention.

"I accept the mission Sir."

The Colonel nodded, a humourless smile touching his lips.

"As I expected. Now go Captain Taras, complete your mission. Do not fail Ukraine again."

The Colonel watched the burly man leave, his face a mask of deep concern. Of all the people to send on such an important task, his superiors had specifically chosen Taras, a man who had become increasingly unstable since the Moscow debacle. He had tried to question the inexplicable decision but had been firmly slapped down and had been forced to recall the dangerous fool. He just hoped his superiors knew what they were doing, maybe they could see the bigger picture that he wasn't privy to. He shook his head in frustration.

"Fuck it" he thought, "This is well above my pay grade."

As Taras walked out of the briefing room and into the Kyiv gloom to prepare for his flight, his official motivation was explicit: he was a patriot on a critical mission for his country. But deep in the recesses of his mind, coiled like a venomous snake, was a second, far more personal thought.

The Colonel wanted a bargaining chip, but Taras saw only a fire. A fire that would not just give them leverage over their allies, but could, given the right circumstances, burn a certain Russian city to the ground. A fire that would not just destroy the Kremlin and the headquarters of the GRU but would also burn The Russian Bitch who had been the architect of his downfall. The woman whose face he saw every time his leg ached, the cause of his shame and his fall from grace.

He wouldn't have the satisfaction of looking in her eyes as she burned of course, but he could imagine it. He had replayed her assorted gruesome ends in his minds eye for over 5 years.

A cold smile appeared on his face, whilst his eyes burned like hot coals. He was willing to risk his country's strategic goals. Not for patriotism, not for ultimate victory against Russia, but for a petty, personal vengeance.

CHAPTER 19

The flight from Warsaw had been a noisy, air-conditioned purgatory in which the uncomfortable plastic airline seat had played havoc with Taras's leg. If he had been in a bad mood when he had boarded the flight, he was like a bear with a sore leg as the flight descended into Newcastle.

He stared gloomily out the small, rain-distorted window as the plane descended, watching the sodden patchwork of English fields emerge from the low-slung clouds. It was a soft country, a place of tidy gardens and comfortable routines, and he felt a sullen, instinctual contempt for it. This was the West his MI6 handler represented: polite, procedural, and ultimately unwilling to do what was necessary to obtain the blueprints. They wanted to study the weapon, to counter it. Taras wanted to build and use it.

The Orpheus data was not just intelligence to be obtained and analysed by impartial scientists in clean white coats. It was the ultimate weapon which he had no intention of handing over to his British handlers. It was the key to turning Russia's ultimate deterrent into its own mass grave.

Let the West have their talks and their treaties and their useless economic sanctions. He would deliver a final and very fiery and long overdue reckoning.

His leg ached, a deep, unpleasant, pulsating ache from the old wound that always grew worse in the damp. He unconsciously rubbed the scarred muscle through the fabric of his trousers. The pain was a constant reminder, a rosary of hate he counted with every step. With the pain came her face, the one from the Moscow Metro. The Russian Bitch.

He had found out what she was during the debrief after the Moscow debacle, that she wasn't just some random commuter, but a highly trained agent of the state.

He could picture her now, sitting smugly in some comfortable GRU office, confident, untouchable, sipping coffee and rejecting the advances of her colleagues. He would find a way to reach her, to wipe that cold, aloof expression off her face, even if it meant the entire city erupting beneath her feet. But first, he needed to secure the prize.

He took a taxi from the airport, the driver's cheerful, incomprehensible chatter about football grating on his nerves. He was dropped at the entrance to the Royal Quays Marina, the scent of salt and low tide sharp in the misty air. He walked the length of the pontoon, his slight limp more pronounced on the slick, wooden planks, until he found the yacht: The Odyssey. A large, expensive, capable-looking vessel, its dark hull sleek and graceful.

His operational sensibilities, however, were immediately offended. There was no sentry, no one on watch. He felt a surge of cold fury at the sloppiness. He had been told this was a tier one SBU special operations team, hand-picked for their skills. This was the first, damning evidence to the contrary.

As he drew closer, he heard raised voices, carrying clearly across the water, muffled by the cabin but unmistakable Ukrainian. He stepped silently onto the deck, his soft-soled shoes making no sound. He paused by the cabin door, listening.

"...and I am telling you, Olek, it is too risky!" a voice snarled. "The deal with the Irish is solid, with a clean discreet handover organised. Your idea… pushing the weapons onto the local underworld is lunacy; it risks compromise by bringing unwanted attention to our area of operations."

"Attention?" another voice shot back, younger, filled with a zealot's fire. "We should be bringing more than attention! We should be hitting Russian assets here, in their safe havens! Not playing gangsters and skimming profits from selling cocaine! We are soldiers of Ukraine, not fucking drug and arms dealers!"

"This 'skimming' is what pays for the very weapons you are so eager to use!" the first voice retorted. "The two hundred million from the Americans is for the mission. This is for us. For our future. Or have you forgotten what the front looks like? Do you want to go back to eating cold rations in a trench near the Dnieper, arse deep in blood and floodwater?"

"Better to die a patriot in a trench, than live as a coward in England!" The young man hissed bitterly.

The cabin door slid open. Taras stepped inside, his presence a sudden, chilling void that sucked all the heat and oxygen from the argument.

The scene before him was one of tense indiscipline. Four men were gathered around the main cabin table. The burly, hard-faced man, Andriy, was on his feet, his hand resting defensively on a stack of British twenty-pound notes. The young zealot, Olek, was flushed with anger, his hand hovering near the pistol at his hip. In a small nook overflowing with state-of-the-art electronics, the comms specialist, Dima, looked up from his paperback with an expression of profound weariness, as if he'd heard this argument a hundred times before. The fourth man, Lev, was a study in stillness, sitting slightly apart from the others, meticulously disassembling and cleaning his sniper rifle on a small oilcloth, his movements precise, economical, and utterly detached from the drama around him.

They all froze except Lev who carried on servicing his weapon, as if above such petty squabbles. Taras let the silence stretch, his cold grey eyes sweeping over them with undisguised contempt. He looked from the scattered money to the unkempt state of the cabin, to the resentful, questioning faces of the men who were supposed to be his elite team.

Finally, he spoke, his voice low and devoid of warmth.

"The first principle of operating in hostile territory is security. There was no sentry."

He didn't raise his voice. He didn't need to. The quiet statement was a more brutal condemnation than any shout. "Any local police patrol could have walked right in. Any rival could have put a bullet in you while you squabbled over your pocket money." He glowered. "The second principle is to be discreet. I could hear you arguing from the fucking car park. Do you idiots realise the Russians are as desperate to recover their secrets as we are to secure them?" He shook his head. "What do you think an SVR agent would do if they had heard you and then walked in on this bunch of unguarded amateurs?"

He walked to the table and picked up one of the stacks of sterling, fanning it slowly as his gaze locked with the hard-faced Andriy. "This is not your money," he said, the words as cold and hard as river stones. "This is not your 'bonus'. This is a tool. An operational fund. And as of this moment, it is my tool, to be dispensed at my discretion. Your side business is closed." Andriy's jaw tightened, a flicker of defiance in his eyes.

"This business," he began, his voice a low growl, "is what keeps us sharp. It gives us a network. It is our legend."

"Your legend," Taras countered, his voice dropping even lower, "is that of a soldier of Ukraine. Not a back-alley drug peddler. You have forgotten that." He placed his face dangerously close to Andriy to emphasise his point. "And how do you think our British hosts would react to us if they discovered we were arming Irish paramilitaries? Do you know how many informants they have in those groups?"

He turned his gaze to the young zealot, Olek.

"You want to fight? You want to kill Russians? Good. You have come to the right place." His eyes narrowed. "But you will do it on my orders. You will do it with discipline. You will do it silently. You will not do it like a drunken bar fighter looking for a brawl."

Taras walked over to him, glowering down at the smaller man. "Because if you ever underestimate the orcs, that will be the day you die."

Olek bristled under the harsh gaze, but said nothing, cowed by the sheer force of the man's will. Taras let the stack of money drop back onto the table with a soft thud. He looked from Dima, who gave a barely perceptible, cynical shrug, to Lev, who had not stopped his work and had just finished reassembling the bolt of his rifle with a soft, final click.

"My name is Captain Taras of the SBU. I am now in command of this operation," he stated, his posture that of a commander addressing a failed unit. "Your personal ambitions, your greed, and your politics are irrelevant. From this moment, you have only one purpose: my mission. To acquire a weapon for Ukraine that will end this war on our terms."

He scanned their faces again, seeing the resentment shift to a sullen, wary respect. They were wolves, yes, a survivor, a zealot, an academic, and a cynic. A broken pack. But they had just met their new pack leader. And he was colder, harder, and infinitely more dangerous than they were.

"From now on," Taras finished, his voice a near-whisper that carried more menace than a roar, "the only voice I want to hear is the one confirming you will comply with my orders. Now clean this mess up. We have work to do."

CHAPTER 20

Elias Thorne sat on the edge of the sagging bed in his anonymous B&B on Westgate Road, the city of Newcastle a grey, indifferent backdrop outside his window. His preferred domain was amongst the comforting hum of servers, whilst he made code dance intricately on a screen. Tradecraft, covert movement, face-to-face dead drops with hardened criminals, this was alien, terrifying territory.

He was a genius, he knew it, a gifted savant when it came to cyber security, but frustrated by the perceived incompetence of his former employers at the NSA and their failure to reward his brilliance, he came to see the secrets he secured not as burdens, but as lucrative commodities.

Months ago, through encrypted dark web forums, he had been contacted by other rogue players who persuaded him they were in touch with private sector brokers who would pay enormous sums for the right data. After weeks of social engineering, they eventually dropped hints of gaining access to a secret Russian project, which was lucrative enough that the brokers were offering hundreds of millions of dollars and a large, expensive yacht to retire on.

At first, he had been flattered, then eventually honey trapped. She was the one who had persuaded him to take the opportunity during pillow talk, convincing him they would be able to have a life of luxury together.

His mysterious contacts had "shared" access to powerful, bleeding-edge quantum malware, presenting it as a toolkit stolen from the NSA itself.

After the WannaCry and Vault 7 debacles, Thorne wasn't in the least bit suspicious as to the source of the digital weapon; his old agency was infamous for leaking like a sieve. The thought of using a stolen NSA tool for his own ends was also simply too much for him to resist. Indeed, he was obtaining a perverse pleasure at using the malware.

In reality, it was a weapon designed by the SVR, intended for the Chernobog facility. Thorne, in his arrogance and greed, believed he was leveraging their tools for his own grand design, unaware he was being socially engineered by psychological experts.

Using the malware, he found the zero-day vulnerabilities designed by Moscow. He initiated the final phase of his attack, infiltrating the malware through the facility's network. It quickly located the curated data package for Icarus and copied it to a quantum-encrypted USB stick he controlled remotely. Simultaneously, a destructive payload crippled the facility's internal systems, wiping logs and corrupting other copies, creating the illusion of a cascading systems failure. With the data and the unique decrypt device in his possession, a quantum particle collapsed into a specific state, triggering the pre-positioned shaped charges and bringing about the utter destruction of Chernobog.

His physical escape was swift and efficient, aided by the unseen hand of the SVR. Travel logs were corrupted, surveillance feeds glitched. He moved indirectly, hopping between flights, his destination: Newcastle upon Tyne. Moscow's chosen stage.

He arrived tired and paranoid, the big payoff in cash still to come. His buyers, operating under the guise of an organised crime gang, had promised a luxurious escape on a waiting yacht, in exchange for the encrypted Icarus data.

He had spent the last 24 hours contemplating the game. The silence from his buyers felt too long. His growing paranoia was almost a physical ache. He needed control. He had already exercised some by not taking a taxi to the Hilton Hotel which had been booked for him. Instead, he'd gotten out of the taxi from the airport in the city centre, then caught another one and headed west.

He'd already done some research and had found an anonymous B&B on Westgate Road. Rather than use an app and leave a digital trace, he intended to pay cash only, with a bonus payment for the discretion of the owner.

The place he selected was safely anonymous but had seen better days and was in poor repair and a little grimy. However, that worked to his advantage; fewer people meant less risk. Although he heard the odd door slamming and arguments from the other rooms, he hadn't seen anyone else apart from the owner, who took his extra cash, no questions asked and made no entry in the guest book.

He was concerned that his deviation from the directions he had been given may have antagonised his buyers, but he was more than aware of the value of the material he was carrying. He could find other buyers. Hell, he might even take a leaf out of the Shadow Brokers' playbook and put the data up for auction to the highest bidder.

He was completely unaware of the chaos he had unleashed less than 24 hours previously, or the true nature of the game he was involved in. Though extremely intelligent and a master of the digital space, in the physical domain, he was dangerously naive and simply could not comprehend the chain of events his malleable avarice had set in motion.

He nervously picked up his burner phone and rang the number he had been given for his buyers.

"Hello?" he stammered as the phone was answered.

After a pause to exchange the agreed-upon passphrases, a voice, with a distinct Ukrainian accent, replied.

"Julian wishes to buy your antiques as agreed... Can I give you a delivery address?"

Thorne's paranoia boiled over. A delivery address? A trap.

"I'm afraid I'm currently unable to make personal deliveries," he stated, improvising. "I'll arrange a collection point and get back to you with the pickup arrangements ... be aware that I will require proof that you have the necessary funds to pay for the antiques, so a photograph of your payment method containing a headline from today's newspaper will be necessary."

An angry silence stretched across the line before the caller hung up. Thorne slumped onto his bed. Had he scared them off?

Thirty minutes later, the phone pinged with a text message. A contact number and a photograph of a pile of cash, clearly taken onboard a yacht, complete with a copy of the front page of The Chronicle. They hadn't cut him loose and he could see the denomination of the huge stack of notes; he didn't need an accountant to see there were millions in the image.

He beamed and congratulated himself on his tradecraft. He really didn't know what all the fuss was about, the way the field agents used to swagger into his office demanding his services, as if he was beneath them, without so much as a please or thank you.

He wrote the number of the buyers down, ended the call, paused thoughtfully as if considering his next move, then smashed the burner phone against the wall, destroying it and the SIM. He had others. Now, to find a suitable spot for the exchange. Somewhere discreet, but public enough to act as a deterrent to overt theft or worse. Somewhere with escape options.

He hid the quantum decrypt key securely in his room and slipped the Orpheus USB deep into a zipped inner pocket of his jacket, which he doubly secured with a small safety pin. He pulled on his raincoat, turned up the collar against the relentless downpour, and walked out into the wet streets of Newcastle, to find somewhere he thought was safe. The fact he hadn't arrived at the pre-planned hotel location, and was now arranging his own exchange point, was not part of Moscow's plan. The chess pieces were moving themselves

Meanwhile, from the ruins of Chernobog, a silent, invisible fallout was already across the globe. It wasn't radioactive like the poisoned winds of Chernobyl, but it was just as toxic and lethal, a contagion of secrets and lies destined to contaminate everything, and everyone caught in its invisible shadow.

CHAPTER 21

The burner phone rang, a shrill, annoying ringtone that cut through the stuffiness of the cabin. Dima, the comms specialist, put down his paperback, irritated at the disturbance, picked up the device, and listened. His annoyed expression tightened almost imperceptibly as he answered the passphrase. He finished his conversation with the seller and looked warily across the table at Taras, who was staring at a map of Newcastle, lost in thought.

"It was the American," Dima said, his voice nervous. "He's being paranoid and is making demands."

Taras looked up slowly, his eyes cold pits of barely concealed fury. "Demands?"

"He refuses to meet at a location of our choosing," Dima answered. "He says he will provide a rendezvous point only when he is ready. And..." Dima hesitated, as if bracing for the inevitable explosion. "...he requires proof of funds. A photograph of the cash, with the front page of today's newspaper visible in the shot."

An ominous silence filled the cabin. Andriy, who had been methodically counting stacks of sterling, stopped, his hands hovering over the money. Olek, the young zealot, scoffed in disbelief. Even Lev, the silent sniper, paused his work, a flicker of amusement in his eyes.

Taras didn't explode. The lack of an outburst was somehow more terrifying. He stood up and limped to the porthole, staring out at the grey, indifferent water of the marina. The scarred knuckles of his hand were white where he gripped the brass frame.

"So," he said, his voice a dangerously low growl that seemed to vibrate through the deck plates. "The little rabbit thinks he is a predator."

His original plan had been brutally simple: lure the American to the yacht with the promise of a swift, clean exchange. Get him and both of his devices out into the deep waters of the North Sea. A single bullet, a weighted chain, and the problem would sink without a trace, the two hundred million still safely in their possession. Clean. Efficient.

Now this bumbling amateur had thrown a wrench into the machinery. He had gone off reservation. He was trying to dictate the terms. Thorne might be a fool in the field, but he wasn't a complete idiot. He was scared, and a scared animal was an unpredictable one.

He turned from the porthole and looked at the men who were supposed to be his elite team. He saw Andriy, whose eyes were already calculating the profit margin on a new venture. He looked at Olek, whose righteous fury was a liability in any subtle operation. He saw Dima, whose cynicism bordered on insubordination. He pictured sending this dysfunctional pack into the neon-lit labyrinth of a city's nightlife. It would be a disaster. He'd spend the night dragging them out of bars and knocking heads together, not hunting the American. No. That was a brute-force solution, and it was beneath him. It would attract the wrong kind of attention.

"Patience," he murmured to himself, burying his seething anger. He would play the amateur's game. For now. Thorne was a man operating under immense pressure, alone in a foreign country. He was trying to control the uncontrollable. Sooner or later, his paranoia or his ego would force him to make a mistake. A single, fatal error.

And when he did, Taras would be there to capitalise on it.

He turned his gaze back to the cabin, his decision made. The cold, professional focus had returned to his eyes. He looked directly at Olek, the zealot, who was still bristling with indignation at being dictated to by a traitor.

"You," Taras barked, his voice cutting through the tension. "Stop looking like an offended schoolgirl and make yourself useful. Go ashore, find a shop, and buy a copy of a local newspaper."

Olek blinked, surprised by the mundane order.

"Sir?"

Taras's lips twisted into a thin, cruel smile.

"The American wants his photograph," he said matter-of-factly. "So we will give him his photograph. Let him have his small, pathetic victory. Let him feel like he is in control."

He gestured to Andriy. "Get the money ready and make it look pretty. Ensure the highest denomination notes are clearly visible."

As Olek scrambled to obey, Taras limped back to the map on the table. He was no longer looking at it. He was looking through it, his mind already three moves ahead. The rabbit had set a new course, but the wolf was used to hunting frightened rabbits on the streets of Kyiv, and this wolf was very, very patient.

And very, very hungry.

CHAPTER 22

36 hours earlier, the control room of the Chernobog Deep Works smelled as unpleasantly stagnant as ever, permanently heavy with the damp stink of ozone and stale air which hadn't been truly fresh in decades. The facility was a hive of focused activity. For weeks, the skeleton crew had been tasked with a monumental, seemingly critical project: collating the vast amounts of data from countless air-gapped systems containing the separate elements of Project Icarus into a single, unified package. The official reason was to create a highly accurate computer simulation, a digital twin of the Orpheus munition, that could be used by the in-development AI to enable advanced stress-testing and predictive modelling without the need for further costly and dangerous physical tests.

Dr. Ivan Morozov continued to dedicate his every waking hour to the munition and oversaw the work with a mixture of professional pride and growing unease. He watched as his technicians meticulously integrated terabytes of data, thermodynamic readouts, geological resonance mapping, computer simulations of magnetic peristalsis and thermal containment, and the complex molecular structure of the liquid metallic coolant he himself had developed for the space programme. The final, compiled package would be a highly classified blueprint of Russia's most terrifying secret.

But the whole process felt... wrong. Moscow had explained the recent reduction in staff and resources as a precursor to a major facility-wide refurbishment. Yet, just last night, a series of large, sealed equipment crates had been delivered, only to be immediately stowed in a deep storage bay now marked as off-limits due to "structural instability." The contradictions were piling up.

Dr. Morozov was on the phone to his superiors for the umpteenth time, his voice strained with frustration.

"...delayed and lost shipments, Comrade Colonel! Again! The composite tungsten alloy plating is critical! We cannot proceed with assembly validation without it! Additionally, I have received manifests stating the ceramic heat shielding and plasma drives have been sent here, but we haven't physically received the actual equipment." He rubbed his temples. "And the transfer requests? Dismissed! We are operating with a skeleton crew! We still need the ordered equipment so we can resume work immediately after refurbishment."

In the back of his mind, a persistent, nagging suspicion had begun to surface. He had dedicated his life to this project. He knew its heart and soul and at the moment the entire feeling was one of a performance. He began to suspect he had indeed been compromised, that his earlier, desperate attempts to leak data to the West had been detected. A suspicion which unfortunately for the Doctor, had surfaced far too late in the game.

Dr. Morozov ended the call, rubbing his tired eyes. The young analyst, Petrova, watched him with an unnerving stillness. Young Sergei fiddled with a monitor. The collation was almost complete; the data package, the altered specifications, designed by Moscow's own experts to appear genuine but ultimately flawed, was ready for its supposed transfer.

"Checksums clear, Doctor," Petrova reported, her voice flat.

Morozov nodded, settling back, the gnawing suspicion in his gut making the routine feel hollow.

"Apologies, Doctor," Sergei stammered, pointing at a readout. "Anomaly on Enclave B. Outbound flow."

Morozov's head snapped up, the weariness replaced by a jolt of pure dread. Petrova was already querying her logs.

"Impossible. B is air-gapped. There should be no outgoing data unless it is physically connected to the networked systems."

But the thin green line was there, growing, accelerating, the data was indeed migrating, but to where? This should be physically impossible.

"It's... the full component data!" Petrova yelled, her voice tight with sudden, genuine fear. "Leaving the enclave! But how?!"

They fumbled with controls, barking orders to disconnect systems that refused to respond. This wasn't a conventional attack they could counter. This was something deeper. The engineered quantum malware, designed by Moscow's experts and unleashed remotely by Elias Thorne, had received its trigger and was now executing its dual function.

It was copying the curated data package, bypassing all security, and simultaneously triggering its second, destructive payload. This wasn't a simple data wipe. It was a systemic assault utilising quantum-level chaos, introducing irreparable damage into storage media, corrupting data arrays, and triggering uncontrollable power surges.

"It's the entire collated data!" Sergei shrieked, pointing at the compilation server display. "It's being copied! Externally! And... it's erasing our own copy of the Icarus package as it does so!"

Alarms began to shriek throughout the facility, deep, resonant klaxons that weren't just security alerts but warnings of fundamental systemic collapse. Red lights flashed. This wasn't just a data breach; it was a systemic assault designed to cripple.

"What is happening?!" Dr. Morozov yelled, clutching his head, the engineered chaos terrifyingly real to him. The suspicion in his gut solidified into horrifying certainty. He hadn't been compromised by the West; he had been compromised by his own side. This wasn't a failure: it was an execution.

On Petrova's main security monitor, a message flashed:

"Спасибо за служение Родине." "Thank you for your service to the motherland."

Seconds after it appeared, the full destructive payload took hold. Warning indicators across all consoles exploded into urgent red. The hum of the processors died, replaced by the terrible screech of overloaded electrical systems, a groaning protest of stressed metal deep within the earth.

"Reactor coolant unstable!" a voice blared over a failing speaker system. "Primary loop pressure dropping! Uncontrolled temperature spike! The reactor is shutting down but the containment vessel is holding for now."

Panic was absolute as the lights died completely, plunging the control room into terrifying darkness illuminated only by the flashing red emergency lights. The staff stood transfixed, looking at each other with fear in their eyes. In Moscow, a technician observed an entangled quantum particle causing a corresponding particle to collapse into a specific state within the false supports in Chernobog. They exploded instantaneously, killing all inside instantly and breaking open the specially designed storage cases containing Volkov's "Operation Mincemeat" cadavers.

The stage was set, the performance was complete, and the seemingly devastating "accident" at Chernobog would now set in motion a chain of events that were about to irrevocably impact Declan Shaw and Anastasia Stepnova, who were at that very moment smiling and exchanging jokes in a far away rainy city, unaware soon they were being drawn ever deeper into The Orpheus Gambit.

CHAPTER 23

The call ending had been abrupt. Eleanor stood by the entrance of The Bridge Inn for a moment, the urgency in her handler's voice cutting through the warmth of the evening and the lingering pleasantness of her conversation with Declan.

She hurried out into the pouring rain. The waiting car, nondescript and dark, pulled up and through the rolled-down window the driver whispered:

"Get in, Comrade. Moscow wants to urgently speak to you at the safe house on a more secure channel."

She opened the door and slipped into the backseat. Misha, the driver, was silent, his face impassive.

"Misha, what is happening?" She asked, her voice tense but professional. "I was told only there had been an explosion at a research facility, that there may be hundreds dead."

"That is all I know, but control says everything will be explained at the safe house, Comrade," Misha replied, his gaze fixed on the road. He offered nothing more, stubbornly reticent, adhering strictly to compartmentalisation.

Anastasia leaned back against the worn upholstery, the sounds of the rain on the windscreen adding to the air of melancholy which had just settled on her. "So many dead," she thought sadly.

Despite the drinks she'd shared with Declan, she was feeling decidedly sober. The phone call and abrupt summons, Misha's reticence, it all pointed to something major. The pleasant evening, the easy conversation, the unexpected spark of connection with the British analyst—it all felt fragile, already receding into the background against the sudden, stark reality of a high-priority operational event.

She swore under her breath, angry at herself, angry at her error when she had cursed in Russian, but the bar was noisy, and Declan had seemed as relaxed as ever; she thought she had gotten away with it. Still, the fact she had let her operational awareness slip like that was a sign that his presence was a dangerous distraction to her. Her slip was made worse by the fact she had noticed Shaw's own faux pas. They were clearly a mutual threat to each other's operational awareness.

By the time they reached the safe house, a modern flat on the residential end of the Quayside, her mind was racing. The building was secure, blending into the expensive residential area. It was within easy walking distance of the Tyne Bridge, which overshadowed the old Georgian-looking office block housing the Special Projects outstation, the 'Happy House'. Camouflage by spectacle, she thought.

Once inside, Misha led her directly to the secure terminal set up in the small second bedroom. He left her there, closing the door quietly. Anastasia initiated the encrypted video link. Handler Prime's face appeared on screen, grim and serious.

"Agent Stepnova," Handler Prime began, bypassing pleasantries. "We have suffered a catastrophic attack and data theft from the Chernobog research facility. Initial reports suggest a death toll in the hundreds, including one of our best scientists. It has become imperative you adjust your operational posture to meet the demands of the new intelligence picture.

Anastasia sat stony-faced as the details of the Chernobog incident were fed to her. It was described as a devastating, catastrophic system failure, an accident of unprecedented scale. The details were further exaggerated, implying massive loss of life among the scientific and security personnel, a detail designed to underscore the severity of the event and justify the subsequent response.

"Simultaneously with the system collapse," Handler Prime continued, "a data breach occurred. Our analysis indicates the entire technical schematic package for Project Icarus was extracted from the facility's compilation server." He looked directly at her from the screen. "It is now out in the wild."

This was presented to Anastasia as the genuine, devastating truth. She was completely unaware of The Orpheus Gambit, of Moscow's orchestration, of her unwitting part in a complex deception. To her, this was a real loss, a genuine threat to national security.

"Current intelligence suggests the perpetrators are unknown actors," Handler Prime stated. "But chatter on certain channels implies there may be Ukrainian involvement. Additionally, the theft may involve a disgruntled former NSA contractor, Elias Thorne, working with or for Ukrainian elements."

Anastasia absorbed the details. Thorne. An NSA contractor. Ukrainian involvement. It made sense there would be an American and Ukrainian dynamic at play, given the realities of the ongoing conflict.

"Preliminary investigation suggests there may be a UK link to Thorne's movements," Handler Prime continued. "Perhaps seeking a buyer or a transit point. Your presence in the Northeast, already justified by your cover tasking, is fortuitous." He stressed the word, making it sound like a lucky break rather than a deliberate convergence. "Especially as there are strong indications British Special Projects were directly involved in monitoring anomalous activity related to Chernobog prior to the incident. They are likely to be involved in trying to retrieve the data package themselves." This, of course, was based on Declan's early, dismissed reports, tracked by a Moscow mole in GCHQ and the newly developed quantum malware.

"Your instructions are explicit, Agent Stepnova," Handler Prime concluded, his voice firm. "Your priority is to locate Thorne, identify his contacts, and recover the data package and the decrypt device. Use all means necessary. This is a critical national security imperative. Further updates will be issued as necessary."

The call concluded. Handler Prime's face vanished, leaving Anastasia staring at the blank screen. She sat back, processing the information. A genuine crisis. The entire schematics for Icarus, a secret of immense strategic value, stolen and in unknown hands. Thorne. Ukrainian involvement. A UK link. Special Projects.

And Declan Shaw. The analyst from Special Projects. The man she had just spent the evening with, laughing, talking, feeling a strange, unexpected connection.

Her mission was to locate Thorne and recover the data. But Thorne's location was unknown, his contacts elusive. Declan, however, was here, local, linked to Special Projects. Thanks to his slip in the bar, she had confirmed he was still actively working on Icarus. It was therefore logical to assume he might be tracking Thorne and the new data too and may even have his own intelligence on the American. The Englishman was highly likely to be the key to finding and retrieving the bloodstained package.

Her path was clear, and she began wondering the best way to obtain leverage on Declan to obtain his unwitting help. Emotional compromise? Manipulation? A direct operational approach? Her mind, professional and pragmatic, immediately began assessing the possibilities.

Little did she know, the crisis at Chernobog was just hours away from hitting Western intelligence, triggering a frantic Five Eyes conference call at the Happy House and bringing Declan Shaw to the centre of the hunt, and on the verge of discovering her true identity. The chessboard was becoming increasingly crowded, the pieces moving towards a collision course, each unaware of the complex game being played around them by unseen hands in Moscow.

CHAPTER 24

Declan hadn't slept much. He'd left the bar with the lingering scent of her perfume in his nostrils and the sound of her angry Russian curse echoing in his mind. Eleanor Vane. He doubted that was her real name. The impossibly swift extraction immediately after the call suggested the car was already waiting for her, had been pre-positioned before the call was even made. That alone pointed to something far more sinister than an alleged problem with a wind farm.

He arrived at the Happy House early, unable to lay on his bed, constantly being watched by his sullen, judgemental ghost. Even Velvet had been subdued, unsure of his mood but aware that something was wrong. She had simply offered to boil coffee, which he had refused, eager to get to work for once.

The city was still cloaked in a wet pre-dawn gloom as he looked out the window lost in thought, hesitant almost. Then, decision made, he bypassed his usual routine of sifting through overnight intelligence feeds and went straight to work on her. First, he fed the official attendee photograph from the Washington conference, a monochrome, professional image, into Janus, the agency's powerful facial recognition database. Then, he uploaded the photo he had taken outside the wind farm, the one where she had stepped in front of his lens and smiled. He paused before he scanned it, remembering the moment and feeling regretful at using the image as a weapon against her. It felt almost like betrayal.

"Get a grip you fucking dick," he swore to himself, she was a fellow operative, the only thing they had in common was that they were on opposite sides of the proxy war.

Despite following his own advice and getting a grip, he still made a conscious decision not to upload the lighthouse photo, instead he printed off a hard copy directly from the camera, looked at it intensely and then placed the photograph inside his jacket pocket.

"A reminder to never let your guard down," he lied to himself.

He set the system to run comparisons on both, letting it search in the background while he tried to focus on other things, angry at himself for naively letting himself hope.

"You really are a dickhead," laughed his shadow, with a perverse sense of glee at having confirmed his worst yet most expected fears.

He was just settling in at his desk when the tremors from the Chernobog 'accident' began to reverberate through Western intelligence networks. An urgent, all-hands summons came from Phillips, naturally Declan wasn't included and sat at his desk pondering Eleanor Vane's real identity.

The secure conference room was tense with a combination of anxiety and confusion. On the large screen, a grid of tired, grim faces flickered, representatives from MI6, GCHQ, and their counterparts from the CIA, NSA, CSIS, and ASD.

"...catastrophic system failure," the GCHQ analyst reported, his voice tight. "Moscow is attempting to brand it as an 'accident,' but the seismic and energy signatures don't match any known industrial incident. Forensically, it points to a deliberate, highly sophisticated attack."

A satellite image flashed onto the screen. It showed the Chernobog facility, or what was left of it. The area was a chaotic swarm of heavy machinery and military vehicles. The imagery was high resolution, and they could see lines of body bags being recovered from the collapsed entrance. Other uncovered bodies could be seen lined up on hundreds of stretchers, the physical trauma clearly visible in the high-resolution satellite feed.

Smoke poured from a collapsed, rubble-strewn crater. Volkov's Operation Mincemeat was working perfectly; the scale of the "tragedy" was undeniable.

The CIA liaison, Walsh, ran a hand over his face.

"So, someone gets in, grabs the data, wipes the trail clean, and not only destroys Russia's copies in one go, but they also destroy the whole goddam facility. A perfect theft. What exactly was at Chernobog? Is there any radiological contamination? And who the hell hit them? The Ukrainians?"

Phillips was damp with perspiration and shuffled uncomfortably.

"Gentlemen, ladies," he croaked, his mouth dry, "It appears the main reactor vessel was not compromised, but there were catastrophic explosions in some of the sub-systems. Fortunately, they had learned the lessons of Chernobyl, and the safety systems were effective in shutting down the reactor." He cleared his throat nervously. "Here at Special Projects... we were aware of some anomalous activity at the facility..."

The MI6 representative, a sharp-eyed woman named Bennett, cut him off mid sentence.

"Aware, Phillips? If your team had intelligence... why isn't the lead analyst on this call?"

Phillips's stomach dropped. He reluctantly opened the conference room door and brusquely called an uncharacteristically distracted Shaw over.

"Shaw, bring me everything you have on Chernobog, you have a briefing to give."

Declan raised his eyebrows in surprise but immediately grabbed some IT equipment from his desk, hurriedly entered the briefing and hooked his laptop up to a projector, smiling apologetically at the lack of preparation.

"Good morning everyone, for those who don't know me, I'm operative Shaw, one of the analysts and investigators here at Special Projects," Declan stated, his voice surprisingly relaxed given the circumstances. He looked at Phillips. "We have been monitoring an increase in unusual activity at the Chernobog site. In line with policy, Special Projects liaised with the Russia desk, who instructed us to maintain an overwatch." He looked back at Phillips, who realised with a flicker of surprise that Shaw was attempting to get him off the hook.

"I can tell you what we know so far," Declan continued, "but I must emphasise that what follows is conjecture, based on fragmented, uncorroborated intelligence. But it is my assessment that the programme they were working on at Chernobog, is designated as Project Icarus. I believe this is a cover name for an in-development munition being developed at the facility. Intelligence suggests the real name for the weapon is the Orpheus munition."

"My initial assessment based on the data I've been tracking is that it's likely Russia has developed an autonomous, nuclear-powered burrowing device."

An uncomfortable murmur spread through the members of the virtual conference.

"We assessed that program as dormant decades ago," Walsh interjected, sceptical. "The Soviets couldn't solve the cooling problem. The goddam thing blew up, is this what happened here?"

"My assessment, sir, is that they've solved their overheating issue using aerospace technology, why else send a magnetic plasma drive to a deep underground facility given they could simply test it in their cosmodromes," Declan said simply.

"My working theory is instead of them using their plasma drive to fly to Mars, they've adapted it to 'fly' underground, using the plasma itself to burrow through rock."

Walsh snorted dismissively..

"Do you know the temperatures those things generate, we've experimented with plasma drives in the States, you're talking hundreds of thousands of degrees, no device could survive such temperatures in a subterranean environment."

Declan walked across to his laptop and shared the images of the documentation he'd been tracking.

"This is a transport manifest to Chernobog, that Cyrillic in the first line translates as heat shield, but the next line describes the equipment not as a shield, but as a heat exchange coolant, a metallic liquid coolant."

"On its own this could be put down to the same reactor coolant in their nuclear-powered Skyfall missile, but when combined with this manifest detailing the shipment of a magnetic plasma drive, then it suggests they may have solved the thermodynamic problems which prevented the battle mole becoming operational."

"Forget the complex physics involved for a moment. Think of it like this: you have a car engine that runs so hot it melts itself. The problem isn't the engine; it's the radiator. For decades, the Russians were trying to build a bigger, better radiator. It never worked."

He paused, letting the analogy land.

"What they've done now," he went on, "is change the engine oil and the radiator fluid. They've developed a new synthetic, liquid metal coolant, a fluid so efficient it doesn't just manage the heat, it uses it and creates a self-regulating thermodynamic circuit. The hotter the warhead gets as it burrows, the more efficient the cooling system becomes."

He looked at each display screen in turn, to emphasise his point. "Additionally there are also urgent emails containing urgent demands for hybrid tungsten ceramic hull plating. This is a novel material designed to be highly resistant to heat stresses."

He saw the GCHQ analyst begin to furiously take notes.

"The procurement orders we flagged for micro-level 3D printers?" Declan continued, connecting the dots for them. "They weren't for a novel warhead, they were for printing heat exchangers, a nanostructure lattice that probably allows this new coolant to work. The power spike at Chernobog shown on slide number 5? That appears to be their scientists stress-testing the system. And the chatter GCHQ intercepted, 'stability margin reached' that wasn't about missile guidance, it may have been about thermal stability. If I'm correct, the radiator no longer melts down, and they now have a viable sub surface device."

An Australian representative scoffed.

"As a first-strike weapon? It's absurd. The seismic signature would be massive. We'd see it coming for days. It's not a surprise attack weapon."

"Exactly," Declan agreed. "It's not a pre-emptive strike weapon. It's not designed to start a war. It's designed to end one, permanently. It's a vengeance weapon. An unstoppable munition linked directly to their dead-hand system. If we launch a first strike, Orpheus is automatically deployed. Even while our missiles are still in the air, their devices are slowly burrowing towards their designated targets like Sandworms. Even after our warheads detonate in Russia; our own command bunkers would inevitably be vaporised from below. It's Mutually Assured Destruction in its purest form designed to wipe out our entire political and military leadership."

A heavy silence fell, though Walsh still looked sceptical and unconvinced. Declan realised they didn't yet understand the truly terrifying range of capabilities which Orpheus possessed, so he expanded further:

"Another complication? It isn't just a strategic weapon, it can be used tactically, as an underground bus for troops. We've seen repeated examples of the Russians using pipelines to infiltrate behind the lines to avoid drones, now imagine a vehicle that can pop up anywhere, a bunch of Spetsnaz appearing in your headquarters without warning."

He let the implications sink in for a moment then brought up another despatch note on the screen.

"Talking of drones, here is a despatch document from STC Kornei to Chernobog. Why is that relevant you might ask? STC Kornei are the company who developed and manufactured the Dronobus, an armoured robotic mothership for drone swarms. I believe they may be using the Orpheus munition for the same purpose. This would give their FPV drones unlimited range in the battlespace. Now if anyone else can suggest why they are sending drone tech to a deep underground facility, I'm willing to listen? But, if I'm right, this weapon is an absolute game changer, and we have nothing in our arsenal to counter it at the moment."

He changed the slide, to show a monochrome photograph taken during World War One.

"This is The Lochnagar Crater from The Somme; it took miners almost 6 months to dig a tunnel and pack the mine with around 27 tonnes of ammonal explosive. Over 300 Germans were killed instantly in the explosion. Now depending on the launch point, Orpheus can do the same thing in a couple of days, deploying a delayed action conventional, thermobaric or nuclear warhead to be set off as desired. Or they can just burn everyone alive in a given target area with the plasma itself, literally hell fire."

He paused again for effect, hoping that the enormity of his analysis was sinking in.

"This is all theoretical, based on fragments," Walsh said dismissively. "For all we know, Chernobog was just an old Soviet-era research lab that went critical. This 'vengeance weapon' of yours could be pure Maskirovka."

"With respect, Mr Walsh," Bennett cut back in, her tone sharp as steel, "whether it's a deception or not is now a secondary concern. The fact is their main research facility has been attacked and destroyed suggesting someone took the threat seriously, and additionally, the technical data for the Orpheus munition is now out in the wild."

She shifted uncomfortably in her chair and continued: "If we can recover that package, our labs might be able to develop effective detection and countermeasures. The debate over its significance is over. The priority now is recovery. Mr. Shaw," she said, her gaze fixing on Declan, "you clearly have the best grasp of this situation. You are now the lead analyst on the whole operation."

Phillips stiffened, his eyes widening in disbelief.

An operative leaned into view on Bennet's screen and whispered something in her ear.

"Gentlemen, MI6 are designating the Orpheus munition as 'Downkeep' and the operation to obtain the stolen data as Operation Spank. Because if we don't get our hands on this intelligence, the Russians really will spank our arses." She turned her attention back to Declan.

"What resources do you require?" Bennett asked.

Declan listed his demands. High-resolution satellite feeds, prioritised GCHQ tasking, Five Eyes liaison and contacts.

"Approved," Bennett confirmed. "Find that package, Mr. Shaw."

Declan nodded, unplugged his laptop and walked back to his desk, passing a frozen, sputtering Phillips, feeling a slight touch of schadenfreude. However, the enormity of the Chernobog disaster buried the fleeting sense of satisfaction; he knew the entire world was in the shit.

He almost slumped down in front of his monitor. An alert was flashing on his Janus screen. "Match Found."

He clicked open the alert. The system had flagged a high-percentage facial match between both the conference photo and his own picture, and a grainy YouTube video uploaded months ago from Moscow, shaky camera phone footage of a massive military parade in Red Square. He played the video, pausing, zooming, enhancing the image as best he could. There she was, marching in perfect formation, her face severe and focused under a GRU officer's cap.

He pulled the official, high-definition broadcast footage of the same parade from the archives. He scrubbed through it, cross-referencing the timecodes, the position in the formation. And there she was again. Or rather, there she wasn't. The same woman, same build, same position... but a subtly, almost imperceptibly different face. Subtly altered. A masterclass in digital camouflage, designed to defeat all but the most random, low-quality piece of bystander footage.

Despite his best efforts, the system could find no other records. No birth certificate, no service files. Beyond her 'Eleanor Vane' legend, she was a nonperson. It was a sheer fluke that he'd found this single match. Someone had fucked up and condemned their own agent to death.

He didn't know her name yet. He didn't know if she was still GRU or had moved on to something else. But he now knew enough. She was Russian. She was an intelligence officer.

And she was very, very good.

He brought his own photo of her up on the screen, placing it side-by-side with the official conference ID shot and the screengrab from the parade. He studied the images. The woman in the ID photo and the parade was a professional, her eyes cold and distant. But the woman in his photo, the one smiling into his camera lens, was different. There was a warmth there, an almost imperceptible light that was entirely absent in the other images. He was looking at two different people inhabiting the same body.

He saw all the connections now: her appearance in Washington, her convenient arrival in Newcastle, her angry Russian outburst before being extracted by a professional team. She was the competition. A Russian asset here on his home turf, an intelligence backwater as far as London was concerned.

Declan sat back, his mind racing; she was almost certainly connected to his own intelligence work on Icarus, and her rapid departure last night suggested she was also directly connected to the Chernobog data breach.

"I knew it was too good to be true," he thought, surprised at the pang of disappointment that accompanied the chilling realisation. The only reason they would send an operative of Eleanor's calibre to honeytrap him was precisely because he had been in receipt of and analysing the Icarus intel.

Suddenly, the motivations for her presence became clear to him. It could only mean that the jigsaw puzzle he was dealing with really did contain the details of a fully functional, autonomous burrowing munition. The implications were staggering; they simply wouldn't risk an asset of her calibre for nothing. The threat was existential; the threat was real and had landed right in his lap.

He knew what protocol demanded. He should walk into Phillips's office right now, present the findings from the Janus search, and let the system do what it was designed to do: neutralise the threat with extreme prejudice.

He could picture the scene perfectly. Phillips would puff out his chest, his face a mask of smug, self-important authority. He would get on the secure line to London, using hushed, dramatic tones, playing the part of the master spy who had uncovered a major Russian infiltration on his watch. He would take all the credit, of course. Declan's name would be a mere footnote in the report, if it appeared at all.

Then the order would come down. A specialist team would be dispatched. They would lift her from her hotel room, clean and quiet. She would simply disappear. And Phillips would dine out on the story for the next year, using it to leverage a promotion, a transfer back to the comfortable corridors of Vauxhall Cross, away from the grim reality of a rainy northern city. Even worse, Phillips and the service might decide to use him as the bait to capture her once he submitted his contact report.

The thought of Phillips preening in the glory of her capture, a victory he had done nothing to earn, filled Declan with an angry, visceral disgust.

He looked again at the two images on his screen: the cold, severe officer in the parade, and the warm, smiling woman at the wind farm. Then he took out the photo from the lighthouse, her arm around his waist, her head resting on his shoulder, that smile of hers.

He simply could not give Phillips the satisfaction. Not yet. He would handle this himself. After all, if he exposed her, we might lose the only lead we have to the Chernobog data. If he played his cards right, he might even be able to recruit her as a source. After all, their interactions had felt real.

Despite the evidence, there was a part of him that believed there was at least some sincerity beneath the act, some genuine connection his normally reliable intuition wasn't able to explain.

He also had another thought, a darker, more pragmatic one, born from decades of seeing the ugly reality of his profession. He knew, with absolute certainty, what would happen to her after he made the call. She would be renditioned, taken to the agency's black site on South Uist, hidden under the missile range, a place that didn't officially exist.

There, in a sterile, soundproofed room with a slightly sloping tiled floor, designed to make the hosing away of blood, urine, and excrement easier, men wearing butchers' aprons and rubber gloves, with no faces and no names, would systematically dismantle her, body and soul, until they had every secret she had ever known.

When they were done, she would be dumped at sea from a helicopter during a "missile test," another nonperson disappearing without a trace. He wasn't ready to condemn the woman with the warm, smiling eyes to that fate. Not yet. Not ever. He already had one dead girl on his conscience; he didn't need another one sitting in a chair judging him.

He paused for a moment, first considering, and then fully understanding the implications of his next act. With a deep exhale of breath, he deleted his Janus search history and shut down the system, then sat staring at the blank screen, the enormity of what he had just done sinking in with a crushing finality. The irony of him crossing the Rubicon whilst sitting near the site of Pons Aelius wasn't lost on him..

CHAPTER 25

The Director of the SVR, Volkov, as usual sat at his impressive desk, carefully studying progress reports confirming the complex clockwork of The Orpheus Gambit was ticking forward as planned. His deep concentration was broken by a heavy rap at the heavy office door.

"Enter," he barked.

Major Kurchatov was shown in by two escorts and entered with his customary crisp, military stride. He placed a buff folder marked СОВЕРШЕННО СЕКРЕТНО (TOP SECRET) on the Director's desk.

"Comrade Director," the Major began, his voice steady, though a subtle current of tension lay beneath the professional facade. "Progress report regarding Operation Soroka and The Orpheus Gambit. Preliminary indicators show the bait has been taken. Signal interception shows a marked increase in analytical traffic related to Project Icarus across Western intelligence networks since the Chernobog incident."

Volkov nodded, his gaze sharp.

"And the quantum particle compromise?"

"Working as anticipated, Comrade Director. Our insider at GCHQ also confirms that Icarus is now being discussed at the highest levels."

Volkov leaned back in his chair, a grim satisfaction touching his features, but the Major hesitated, an expression of nervousness on his face.

"There is one more thing, Comrade Director. Regarding the British analyst, Cuckoo."

He shifted his weight slightly. "Our source indicates he has used their facial recognition platform, codenamed Janus, to identify an image of Agent Stepnova." A tense silence settled over the room. Stepnova. Nightingale. Identified by a British analyst using a grainy, open-source video.

"He knows, Comrade Director," the Major continued, his voice lower now. "At least, he knows she is a Russian military intelligence officer. I'm afraid... her operational cover is compromised."

The Major stood rigid, expecting a cold and severe dressing down for the compromise of a high-value asset. Stepnova should be extracted immediately. It was protocol. He was met with puzzled disbelief as Director Volkov's faint, satisfied smile faded, to be replaced by an unreadable expression.

"Excellent," Volkov stated, though the word seemed to be inconsistent with his features. "This authenticates the entire operation. Stepnova's apparent identification by this tenacious 'Cuckoo'... this confirms for our adversaries that this is not Maskirovka delivered through sterile channels. It is a genuine intelligence battle, with a real asset, using real tradecraft, operating in the field. It makes the data they are tracking, the data we are feeding them, utterly credible."

The Major, recovering slightly, stated the obvious next step.

"Shall I make arrangements for Agent Stepnova's immediate extraction, Comrade Director?"

Director Volkov looked at him, his gaze cold and direct.

"No, she is to remain in situ and is to carry out her mission as assigned."

"But... the British will..." the Major began to protest, the unspoken conclusion hanging in the air between them. Hunt her, capture her, kill her... or worse, rendition to one of their black sites.

"Agent Stepnova knows the risks and is perfectly capable of defending herself," Volkov interrupted, his voice cutting through any potential argument. "She accepted the assignment knowing its potential cost."

His gaze swept over the files on his desk, over the grand blueprint of The Orpheus Gambit. "Her loss, if it happens... her expenditure... will confirm how seriously we are taking our attempts to recover this data. Her operational sacrifice will signal the value of the asset to them."

A fleeting shadow of regret seemed to appear on the Director's face. "And her loss, no matter how personally painful, is nothing compared to our strategic aim. Her sacrifice will save billions of lives, and she will be honoured and remembered by a grateful nation. But do not underestimate the Nightingale Major, she is as lethal as she is resourceful."

The Major stood solemnly for a moment, the unassailable logic of what the Director had just said, the cold calculus that deemed a top asset expendable, sending a chill through him that the Moscow winter outside could never match.

"You are dismissed," the Director said with a perfunctory wave, his attention already returning to the files.

The Major exited the office, his mind racing. Just how had a single, traceable image of Stepnova found its way into an open-source video that a British analyst could access, when every other trace had been so perfectly purged? The answer, now understanding the Director's chilling perspective, was simple. That one piece of 'sloppy' tradecraft had been deliberately allowed to exist. By Volkov himself, to be found by a tenaciously obsessed British operative. Like nesting dolls indeed he thought as he sadly shook his head.

CHAPTER 26

The Happy House remained a frantic asylum of activity in which Declan had been entombed all day, his mind a battlefield. The Janus search result had confirmed his suspicions with chilling finality. Eleanor Vane didn't exist; she was a sophisticated construct specifically tailored to entrap him. The woman he had met and smiled and laughed with was an operative of the Russian Federation.

He had spent the day going back over every interaction, viewing it all through this new, harsh lens. He couldn't help but feel an unwelcome sense of professional admiration. She was good. Exceptionally good. He told himself his mission was now to play the long game, to get closer, to see what he could learn. It was a professional, analytical lie, and he knew it. The truth was far more dangerous: he was utterly fascinated by her and the sense of peace she brought him, despite his best efforts.

Part of him was congratulating himself that he had been right about the honeytrap, whilst also chastising himself for being stupid enough to suspect Phillips. Their mutual antagonism had clearly warped his perception, as had her effect on him. Lesson learned.

As for "Eleanor", he knew what she was; but now he was consumed by a desperate need to find out who she was, and why she was able to pour oil on the troubled waters of his mind. Beneath it all, beneath the professionalism and his rationalisation, that one single factor was the biggest puzzle of all. For a man who had been unable to find peace in over thirty years, her effect on him was almost intoxicating, almost addictive.

He struggled between the professional, looking at his phone, conflicted whether he should make the call or not, when it rang, almost making him jump out of his skin. He looked at the caller ID, it was her, Eleanor.

He steeled himself and answered, trying to sound light.

"Eleanor, what a lovely surprise, I was literally just about to call you."

Despite his best efforts to remain neutral, he was genuinely pleased to hear her voice and when she suggested they meet for the promised drink, he agreed a little too quickly and chose the Tyne Bar. Public, noisy, a good place for an operational meet, and a safe distance away from The Happy House and Phillips's sycophants, who sometimes lurked in the nearby quayside bars.

He shut down his system and put on his raincoat; he needed to clear his head before the meet, so he took the slow route along the riverbank. A fine, misty rain cast soft halos around the orange streetlights as he strolled slowly towards his destination. He stopped for a moment, looking back at the dark silhouette of the Happy House looming under the Tyne Bridge. From the nearby Mocktail bar, George Harrison's "Something" drifted into the damp air. The irony brought a cynical smile to his lips. He was walking, clear-eyed, into the honeytrap he'd always suspected, telling himself it was work, and that he knew what he was doing.

He stepped inside the bar, the blast of warmth and loud rock music a stark contrast to the silent rain he was escaping. He sat at the bar, ordered a whiskey, and turned his stool to face the room, his back to the wall. He scanned the crowd. He was ready this time.

"A penny for your thoughts?"

Her voice was light, feminine, right beside his ear. He turned his head slowly, a mask of casual surprise in place. She was sitting there, that small, knowing smile on her face.

The first thing Eleanor noticed when he looked at her was the sheer exhaustion etched into the lines around his eyes. She had seen that weariness in him before, but tonight, his air of disappointment with the world seemed deeper somehow, more obvious. She assumed it was the weight of the Chernobog crisis, the same pressure that had consumed her own day. She had no way of knowing that his discovery of her subterfuge was the cause of his increased world-weariness.

A strange and unwelcome empathy stole over her; he looked "hurt" somehow, as if physically wounded by the weight of his workstack.

"You seemed... deep in contemplation," she said, her eyes gesturing towards his glass. "Or just enjoying a very necessary whiskey?"

Declan looked down at the amber liquid.

"A bit of both," he admitted ruefully.

He led them to a small table away from the worst of the noise, a secluded space where they could talk. The game had begun.

"Is it always so busy here?" Eleanor asked, raising her voice slightly over the music.

"Worse on a Sunday, when the Quayside market is on," Declan replied. He explained the old tradition of the market, how it had now expanded to include international street food stalls. "I've been working my way through the different cuisines," he added. "I even tried the Ethiopian stall once."

Eleanor, genuinely interested, leaned forward slightly.

"And how was it?" she asked, before taking a sip of her wine.

Declan looked at her, his expression perfectly deadpan.

"I don't know," he said. "They didn't actually have any food."

The completely inappropriate punchline caught her completely off guard. She choked, a small spray of red wine misting the air as she snorted, sending the wine up her nose. It was a messy, sputtering, and entirely natural reaction. She wiped her eyes, still laughing.

"Oh, you are so going to hell for that one, Mr Shaw!"

Declan watched her regaining her composure, his own professional composure momentarily faltering. He was conflicted again. He was beginning to understand her tells. These were the moments when the meticulous training of the operative failed, and a glimpse of the real woman beneath the surface would flash through. But he simply could not conceive that this beautiful, intelligent, and dangerous woman could possibly be genuinely interested in him. He was her mission, that was all, and she was now his.

Besides, the connection he still felt despite his knowledge simply didn't fit in with his own deeply ingrained sense of worthlessness. No, this had to be a game. Her "authentic" reactions weren't a sign of her interest in him; they were simply the calculated moves of an expert Russian operative playing a gullible sap.

He was only a mission to her, he thought, with a familiar, bitter ache; the Janus search had confirmed his worst feelings about himself: he was simply a lonely, broken man, who had stumbled across a deadly secret, and was seen by Moscow as an easy mark to be targeted and manipulated.

And yet, despite this cold, logical assessment, he couldn't deny the truth of how he felt. Even if he was being played, he felt better in her presence. Less alone. Seen. He was struggling to rationalise his own actions.

He mentally shook himself, taking control of his emotions. Focus, Shaw. You're being played by a trained expert. It's all part of a clever deception.

The live band on the small stage finished their set to a smattering of applause. As they left, a new sound filled the bar from the house speakers, a haunting, baroque-sounding harpsichord intro, followed by a melancholic acoustic guitar and a distinctly northern voice.

Declan heard the opening notes, and a slow, wry smile spread across his face. He leaned in closer to her, the noise of the bar creating a small pocket of intimacy for just the two of them.

"Oh, they're playing our song," he smiled, "Lady Eleanor."

He said it with a playful glint in his eye, the statement hanging in the air with a perfect, deliberate ambiguity. Was he simply naming the song for her? Or was he, in that moment, christening her his "Lady Eleanor", his enigmatic, slightly dangerous lady of the dark?

She looked at him, catching the subtext in his gaze. She didn't respond, but a small, intrigued smile touched her lips. She turned her attention back to the music, utterly enchanted by the song's gothic tale of a mysterious witch, graveyards of memories, and a love that felt both magical and doomed. The lyrics seemed to describe a world she knew all too well, a world of shadows and secrets.

It was in this moment, under the spell of the music, that the conversation turned more personal.

"So, Declan," Eleanor asked, her tone shifting slightly, her expression one of genuine interest. "Apart from the lady in the song, is there anyone special in your life?"

He looked at her, at the seemingly genuine curiosity in her eyes. The professional in him knew this was a standard probe, but he decided to play along anyway.

The lonely man in him used humour as a shield.

"Only me," he said with a self-deprecating grin. He saw her about to respond and continued, his expression turning more serious. "No, there's no one." He paused for a beat. "Having said that, my manager tries to screw me every day, but I don't think that counts."

Eleanor laughed, though her eyes seemed saddened rather than amused by his humour.

Declan asked her the same.

Her smile faded instantly. The light in her eyes extinguished, replaced by an expression he recognised all too well, a sadness he saw in his own mirror every morning.

"There was," she spoke softly, the two words heavy with a loss she was trying, and failing, to hide.

Declan saw it immediately. The flawless mask of "Eleanor Vane" had just cracked, and for a fleeting second, he saw the real, grieving woman behind her legend. He knew, with the absolute certainty of his training, that this was the moment. This was the vulnerability, the way in. A thousand tactical possibilities bloomed in his mind. Press her. Exploit the opening. Unbalance her. Use her grief to get inside her head.

The voice of the Janitor, the cold logic of the system, was screaming at him to do his job.

Instead, he looked at her, seeing her struggle to hide her pain behind her mask, an expression so familiar it felt like he was watching himself. After a moment's hesitation, Declan prevailed over the Janitor, and he nodded in complete, empathetic understanding.

"Whenever you feel ready, or if you ever need to," he said softly, his voice quiet and kind. "We can talk; I'm a good listener... Sometimes." he added with a smile, his shield of humour snapping back into place both to lighten the mood, and to hide his own empathy.

Eleanor watched him, her own mind racing. He hadn't pressed. He hadn't exploited the opening. Instead, he had offered genuine kindness and as usual used humour to deflect. She felt a wave of relief; she had been concerned she had compromised herself last night, his behaviour wasn't that of someone dealing with an enemy agent, he was showing the same kindness she had witnessed in the restaurant.

His lack of awareness of her real identity had given her an even greater operational advantage. She saw the path clearly: play the victim. Use his empathy, his genuine kindness against him.

It was the logical, efficient move. But it would mean using the memory of Sergei, a good man, as a weapon. She looked at Declan, at the genuine sympathy in his eyes. Despite being her target, she thought he was also a good man. She struggled with the dissonance she was feeling and just like Declan had won against the Janitor, Anya, not Eleanor, prevailed against the Nightingale.

She decided she would not, could not desecrate the memory of one good man to manipulate another.

Eleanor managed a small, sad smile at his clumsy attempt to lighten the mood. She understood exactly what he was doing. She saw the sincerity in his face, warring with a lifetime of professional caution, and it was the most real thing she had experienced in years.

She met his eyes, feeling that inexplicable connection and said simply,

"Thank you, Declan."

They sat in a comfortable silence for a while, not needing to speak. They both felt it, something in the dynamic had shifted. He had been given a perfect operational opening and had chosen to offer comfort instead of pressing his advantage.

Of course, he might simply be playing the long game but then she rationalised the situation: if Kukushka had the slightest hint she was an asset, she would already be on her way to a black site; the fact she wasn't was evidence of just how effective her cover was.

Her professional paranoia was making her see phantoms where none existed. This was not unusual in a deep cover operative; her SVR training had warned her of the psychological impact of working under constant stress for long periods.

What her training hadn't prepared her for was not feeling stressed in his presence, how much at ease he made her feel. How she was beginning to laugh again. Then the Nightingale piped up.

"That's because he has been trained to have such an effect, you unprofessional fool."

As the evening drew to a close, Declan was equally conflicted and knew he was in trouble. He had spent the entire time utterly captivated and at peace; despite knowing she was an enemy asset.

Around her, his intuition, his so-called "Magic", became strangely dulled, quieted by an emotional interference he couldn't explain.

He felt strangely saddened when it was time for her to call a cab. They reluctantly made their way outside to wait for it, sheltering under Eleanor's umbrella. The band had finished their act, and music from the jukebox drifted out into the damp air. They stood in a comfortable silence until the melancholic opening chords of Abba's "The Name of the Game" reached them.

As the lyrics floated into the damp night air, they caught each other's eye. A small, knowing, and deeply ironic smile was shared between them. A silent acknowledgment that the song was asking the very question that hung, unspoken, between them.

The moment stretched, a comfortable yet slightly awkward silence settling over them as the song continued. They were two operatives standing on a rainy street corner, the rules of the unnamed game laying like shattered chess pieces on the wet ground.

Finally, the cab arrived, intruding on their silent... something. Eleanor sighed sadly, leaned in and planted a gentle, lingering kiss on his cheek.

"Thank you, Declan, for a lovely evening."

He returned the gesture, his own lips briefly touching her skin.

"Same."

She climbed into the cab.

"Can I drop you off anywhere?"

He was tempted, sorely tempted, but needed to clear his head; he couldn't think straight around her, and he had left his keys in the "Happy House".

"I'd normally say yes, but I need to get back to the office because I've forgotten something. Anyway, the walk will help clear my head. It's been a stressful day at work."

They smiled at each other.

"If I didn't know better, I'd think you were avoiding me, Mr Shaw."

"Oh, a good comedian always leaves his audience wanting more," he replied with a friendly wink.

"Then I look forward to the encore."

As the cab pulled away into the night, she watched him in the rearview mirror. He was still standing there, watching her. Their eyes met one last time in the reflection, a final, silent goodbye.

Declan stood alone on the pavement, the haunting chorus of the ABBA song still echoing in his ears. He felt the warmth of her lips still on his cheek, and the faint memory of her perfume. Then the cold, professional part of his brain interrupted him.

"She's a Russian spy, idiot. WTF do you think you are doing?"

He turned and began the long, solitary walk back towards the general direction of the Happy House, his mind returning to its normal analytical state now she was gone. He knew she was an asset, a very capable one. But that look in her eyes when she spoke of her past, the grief... that had been genuine, he was sure of it. Or was she just so good she knew his target profile by heart and was able to create a perfect illusion of empathy? But then, she hadn't pushed the advantage when he gave her the opening. It didn't add up.

Whilst he welcomed the almost blissful peace her presence brought to him, he was acutely aware it had the dangerous effect of blunting his analytical instincts.

He was literally in uncharted territory here, both from a professional perspective and an emotional one, and it was with a thousand conflicting thoughts raging in his mind, he began the wet, solitary walk back to the Happy House in the remorseless rain.

Eleanor had ordered the cab to stop after a short drive and then made her way up the stairs of a nearby building. From the window of her safe house, which looked directly over the riverbank walk, she watched him slowly walking along the river, a lonely figure in the evening gloom, clearly lost in thought.

He paused once, leaning his hands on the cold iron railings and gazing down at the dark, flowing water of the Tyne. Music gently played from the small sound system in the room, a Russian version of "One More Kiss Dear" by Vangelis, adding to the melancholy mood of the scene below.

She continued to watch him, fascinated but feeling like a voyeur rather than a professional, and in that moment, he seemed to be his P-File personified. Isolated and alone. The bureaucratic labels had seemed so sterile on the screen, but seeing him now, a lonely cuckoo staring into a dark river, she felt a powerful and unexpected wave of melancholy for this kind, friendly yet solitary Englishman.

Then she thought of the other word they had used to describe him: Dangerous. And he was, she realised. He was very dangerous. Just not in the way she had anticipated. His danger wasn't in his capacity for violence, but in the quiet, disarming decency he'd shown her tonight.

Anya, not Eleanor, not the Nightingale, raised a hand and touched her own cheek where his lips had touched hers. She watched him for a long time, a lone silhouette against the misty, rain-swept lights of the Quayside, until he slowly, finally, disappeared into the rain. Her own feelings were in an equal, and deeply confusing, state of conflict.

CHAPTER 27

Dawn was already breaking when a hungover Declan woke up, no nightmare this time, but he did have a vague recollection of a dream about Eleanor, though it was already fading. As he made his way to the shower, working his shoulder, he could see the ghost, sitting in her usual spot, watching him with those pretty, accusing eyes.

"Music please, Velvet."

"Whiskey in the Jar" by Thin Lizzy starts playing.

Declan looked at the interface and decided he was too hungover to get into a spat with his AI about the nature of his nightcaps.

He grabbed a quick, cold shower, trying to wash away the fatigue and whiskey. By the time Declan reached the Happy House, he was more or less functional. Now here he was, slumped in a conference room chair, feigning interest as an enthusiastic cyber analyst from GCHQ delivered a lecture on the quantum signatures of the unidentified malware.

The lecture concluded with the analyst passing round two devices: which appeared to be a metallic but standard-looking USB stick and a small, metallic USB reader. As the briefing ended, Declan, acting on instinct, slipped the sample USB device into his pocket. Stealing "shiny kit" was a habit he had picked up in the army and never quite shaken.

The GCHQ geek had explained although it looked normal, it was identical to the devices used by the NSA and could hold many terabytes of data. Declan thought it might come in handy, even if only to shove his large playlist on it instead of intelligence, he mused.

"Shaw," Phillips said, his voice tight. "When you've a moment, you're to liaise with Langley. Secure line. Apparently, they want to speak to you in private."

Declan noted the irritation on Phillips's face at being kept out of the loop. He grabbed a coffee and made his way into the secure comms room.

Walsh, the CIA man, was on screen, looking even more tired than Declan. He was strangely pretend-friendly which, after their earlier encounter on the Chernobog briefing, immediately made Declan suspicious.

"Are you secure, Declan?"

Declan confirmed the comms room was clear, noting the use of his first name. The CIA man briefed him on the alleged perpetrator of the cyber attack against the Russian facility.

"Elias Thorne. Former NSA contractor. Brilliant. Went rogue. It was a fluke facial recognition flagged him arriving at Newcastle airport."

"Given what happened at Chernobog," Walsh continued, his voice grim, "it's imperative that the two devices we believe he used, an encrypted USB and the decrypt key, be recovered."

Declan nodded silently, suspicion bubbling in his mind.

"What on earth was Thorne doing on his patch? Heading into the lion's den with the plans to the most dangerous and valuable piece of information on the planet?" It was all far too convenient.

"Why here, Walsh? Why Newcastle?"

Walsh looked at Declan through the screen.

"That's a good question. As far as we can tell, his handlers wanted him here to obfuscate his final destination. There are indications his buyers are local too, but the intel is incomplete and disjointed. But you know the game, every now and then we luck out and the fish really does jump into the boat."

Declan nodded, not 100% convinced, but it was Langley who had the intelligence on him, so he'd take the coincidence at face value for now.

"Operative Shaw... Declan," Walsh continued, shuffling uncomfortably in his chair. "There is something else... an extremely delicate and sensitive matter, and Danny advises me you may be the man to talk to regarding it."

Declan's interest piqued.

"Go on."

"Thorne is a dangerous liability," Walsh stated bluntly. "This time it was the Russians he hit. The next time, it could be us. Langley needs him... made redundant."

Declan felt a familiar uncomfortable sensation settle in his stomach. The unspoken reality of their world. Wet work.

"Made redundant," he cynically murmured, the old euphemism making him twist his lips into a sardonic grin. He saw exactly where this was heading and felt deeply tired of the game. Tired of being the Janitor, the man they called to clean up the messes. He was silent for a long moment, his reluctance palpable even over the encrypted line.

"That's... a significant request, Mr. Walsh. High-risk, low support, outside my own chain of command I assume?"

Walsh seemed to have anticipated his hesitation. His expression softened, becoming almost conspiratorial.

"We understand your position, Declan. We also understand the complex nature of your relationship with your own service."

Declan continued to look at Walsh silently, deliberately making the American feel uncomfortable.

"But Langley has a long reach," Walsh continued smoothly despite Declan's frostiness. "And a long memory. We're aware of certain... historical files. Specifically, a rather sensitive one from Operation Banner. A shooting in Belfast that certain parties hold over you."

The leash. The Americans knew about the leash. How?

"You handle Thorne for us, quietly, permanently, and I can give you my personal assurance that file will disappear, quietly and permanently too," Walsh said, his voice a low, tempting promise. "Not just buried deeper. Expunged. Hard copies burned and wiped from every server from Whitehall to Vauxhall Cross. It will cease to exist. We can make it vanish. For good."

He let the offer hang in the air. It was the one thing Declan had never thought possible. Not just a temporary reprieve, but total erasure of his official record. A chance to be free.

Declan thought of Phillips, of the years ahead constantly looking over his shoulder, of being a tool to be used and discarded. Waiting for the service to wield the sword of Damocles they kept hanging over him.

The price was one more kill. A kill he didn't want, for a release he desperately craved. But a kill that would finally be his last. He took a slow, deep breath, the decision obvious, but still weighing on his already heavily burdened conscience.

"I understand the assignment," Declan said finally, his voice slightly hoarse. "I assume you will want me to arrange an accident?"

Walsh was strangely noncommittal, but there was something else behind his eyes, something Declan didn't like the look of.

"Before we decide on that, we'd appreciate it if this was just kept between us, Declan. Plausibly deniable. If... complications happened to arise... Langley would deny any knowledge of this assignment. Oh, and if he's carrying the Icarus data, make sure you retrieve it and get it to us, without bothering anyone else, just give it to Danny, he's been appraised of the situation and will provide digital overwatch, so you're not completely on your own."

Declan was just about to get up when Walsh interjected again.

"Oh, in answer to your question about arranging an accident, we don't actually want this too discreet, we need a message sent to every other dollar store Edward Snowden out there." Walsh cleared his throat. "We want his well-deserved demise to look like a robbery gone wrong to the public, but an execution to the intelligence community, I'm sure you catch my drift? The Seth Rich look."

Declan nodded grimly in understanding, he understood perfectly. God, he hated this fucking game.

Walsh smiled and nodded in satisfaction.

"Excellent, Danny said you were the most reliable guy in your station, I can see why he spoke so highly of you. We'll expedite getting the targeting package to you as soon as possible, thanks again for your assist with this Declan, we won't forget it."

The screen went blank. Declan sat for a moment in the silent room. He had a name. He had a target. He had a kill order. And now, for the first time in decades, he had the promise of a life without the leash. All he had to do was add one more corpse to his collection. That's IF Walsh was being straight with him, which he very much doubted.

Declan couldn't put his finger on it, but there was something about Walsh using his first name that made his skin crawl, not to mention his eyes, there was something shark-like about them, even when he smiled. Especially when he smiled, Declan thought. He reminded him of Phillips, but a far more intelligent and dangerously competent version of him.

And how had Walsh got his hands on the Op Banner file? Special Projects operational files were supposed to be buried in the deepest vaults of the ministry, allegedly destined never to see daylight again.

He had another thought.

"Had Langley directed Thorne to Newcastle precisely because they knew the janitor could and would clean up their embarrassing mess, without getting their own hands dirty?"

The more he thought about it, the more it seemed to make sense. Coincidence, my arse. He was being manipulated, so he needed a contingency plan, something to trade if things got too complicated. He put his hands in his pocket and pulled out the fake USB. He studied it thoughtfully, his mind exploring myriad possibilities.

Leverage, he needed leverage, his own leash to tug on. He continued to think and then a small, cynical smile appeared on his face as he remembered just how desperate everyone was to obtain the Icarus data.

CHAPTER 28

Elias Thorne sat on the edge of the sagging bed in his seedy B&B in the west end of the city, looking at the faded, peeling wallpaper. The city outside was a grey, indifferent backdrop beyond his window. The relentless, miserable rain had not stopped since he'd arrived, and the gloom was beginning to seep into his soul.

He was bored. Desperately, mind-numbingly bored and dangerously out of his comfort zone.

To maintain his sanity, he dreamt of the aftermath of the exchange: a sun-drenched villa in the Caymans and a life of consequence-free luxury bought with the 200 million in untraceable currency his buyers had promised. And he dreamed of the lazy days and nights in bed with Alana, the beautiful girl who had made all this possible.

He just had to get through this final, tedious and miserable rain-soaked phase. He had spent the last 24 hours contemplating the game. His paranoia continued to haunt him despite his decision to assert control. He had already exercised some autonomy by not taking a taxi to the Hilton Hotel which had been booked for him. Instead, he'd gotten out of the taxi from the airport in the city centre, then caught another one and headed west until he arrived at this godforsaken dump.

He was still concerned that his deviation from the original plan may have antagonised his buyers, but he was more than aware of the value of the material he was carrying. After the original tense phone call they had provided the proof of funds, but he remained wary and needed a plan.

Earlier that evening, he had pulled on his raincoat, turned up the collar against the relentless downpour, and walked out into the wet streets of Newcastle to find a safe exchange point. He had wandered around the city centre, eventually finding a narrow back lane just off Grey's Monument. It was perfect. Rubbish bins for cover, poor lighting, and two separate entrances. An easy-in, easy-out location. He noted the what3words address, satisfied with his choice. In reality, it was a death trap.

Smugly satisfied with his tradecraft, he returned to his room, switched on a new burner phone and sent a short text message to the contact number the buyers had provided:

"Package ready for collection. 48 hours. 2100 hours precisely. Location to follow. Confirm receipt and acknowledge instructions."

He hit send. Now the ball was firmly in his court. He would give them the final location details, a what3words address, only when he was in position. No traps. No double-crosses.

The boredom, however, was now mixing with a more insidious emotion: curiosity. The package, the quantum-encrypted USB stick, burned in his mind like a hot coal. He knew what it was, technical schematics for a Russian superweapon, but the temptation to see exactly what he had stolen was growing by the hour.

He couldn't resist. He had to see. After all, who would know? He knew what he was doing. Decision made, he pulled the heavy curtains, plunging the room into a dingy twilight. He took out his hardened, military-grade laptop, a device completely air-gapped from any network. He had his own layers of security, his own foolproof protocols. As long as it was air-gapped and not connected to the internet, he was perfectly safe. It was the first rule of cyber security.

His hands were shaking in anticipation as he eagerly retrieved the two devices from their hiding places: the USB stick containing the Icarus data, and the small, grey decrypt key. He could feel his heart pounding against his ribs in anticipation of being the first American to see the world-ending secret.

He plugged the decrypt key into the laptop. The drivers installed automatically. Then, with a trembling hand, he carefully inserted the Icarus USB. A new drive appeared on his screen. He clicked it open. A single, encrypted folder. He ran the decryption protocol from the key. The folder unlocked, revealing a cascading directory of files.

MHD.dat
Orpheus_Munition_Schematic_Final.cad
Coolant_Formula_7B.chem
Guidance_AI_Core_Logic.dat
Telemetry_Log_Test_Alpha.bin

It was all there. He'd actually achieved the greatest data theft in history. With still trembling hands he double-clicked on the main schematic file. As the complex, three-dimensional technical diagram of the burrowing device began to render on his screen, he felt a surge of godlike power. He, Elias Thorne, had Armageddon in his literal palm.

He didn't know that the USB he had just opened wasn't only a storage device for weapon schematics; it also contained a set of quantum particles in the data. The very data he had just observed. Instantaneously, a corresponding set of entangled particles collapsed into a specific quantum state in Yasenevo, the Headquarters of the SVR. Thorne had just set off his own tripwire and unwittingly sent up a flare.

In a quiet, secure monitoring room, a single green light on a dark console blinked to life. A young SVR technician stared at it, almost in disbelief. He snatched a phone and dialled a priority extension. A moment later, Major Kurchatov burst through the heavy doors of Director Volkov's office without knocking.

"Comrade Director," he said, his voice tight with breathless urgency, forgoing any salute. Volkov looked up from his papers, his expression calm, expectant.

"We have him, Sir. We have the location of Dreamseller."

Volkov nodded, satisfied. Thorne had acted as anticipated, despite his previous deviation from the plan.

"Ensure his location falls into the right hands. It is time to initiate Phase 3."

Major Kurchatov nodded, swiftly saluted and headed back towards the communications centre. He had a signal for Langley to intercept.

Volkov leaned back in his chair and watched the Major hurriedly leave his office. After a short thoughtful pause, he reached into his drawer and removed the American nesting doll and walked over to the chessboard, carefully placing it on the centre of the board. Nodding with satisfaction, he returned to his chair, his whiskey bottle now remaining untouched.

CHAPTER 29

Declan sat at his desk, reading the P-File on Elias Thorne. Brilliant, arrogant, greedy, paranoid. A flawed genius who had made a fatal, analogue mistake by getting on a plane to Newcastle. And yet Declan continued to feel a burning suspicion about the serendipitous nature of it all. It all felt far too convenient; he couldn't help feeling he was being manipulated, most likely by Walsh, especially given that he somehow managed to access the Op Banner file. Another reason for him to obtain leverage. If the bastards were going to play him, he was certainly going to play them back.

Frustratingly, despite the influx of resources and access to wider data streams since the Five Eyes call, Thorne had completely dropped off the radar since his arrival. His tracks seemed wiped clean, not just from basic public surveillance, but from the deeper probes Declan was now running. It suggested Thorne was either more skilled at physical evasion than his profile indicated, or his co-conspirators remained active and highly competent at covering his trail. The same invisible hand that had guided him here was still at work. Probably the CIA covering their own tracks, creating an air gap of plausible deniability regarding their role in the coming wet work.

Declan ruminated on technology as a double-edged sword. It was a powerful tool, essential for supporting modern intelligence work, providing access to unprecedented amounts of data. But it could be fooled and manipulated just as easily as people, perhaps even more so, in an expert's hands. And when technology itself became a weapon of deception, like the deepfake images of Eleanor Vane in Moscow, the lines between what was real and what was fabricated blurred into dangerous ambiguity.

He smiled ruefully, thinking of her, or whoever she really was. The supposed security consultant from Washington. The enchanting woman in the Tyne Bar. Then the gut punch of the Russian word. He knew she was the competition now. A Russian asset. Her legend was too perfect, her appearance too conveniently timed. He was certain she was connected to Icarus, to Chernobog, to Thorne, and to himself.

It was only a matter of time until someone else uncovered her secret, and when they did, he had little doubt they would task the Janitor as the trigger man for the burn notice. Just the thought of it made him feel physically sick.

He was beginning to drift into that dark place again, the familiar operational mindset where people became targets, relationships were a mirage, and the only colour was grey. A place he knew well, a place he would soon have to occupy completely to get the job done. To find Thorne, to make him redundant. To finally cut the leash and shove it so far up Phillips's arse he would be able to use it as dental floss.

He was snapped out of his reverie by a tap on the shoulder. He turned. It was Danny, his friend and a likeable American expat from the CIA liaison team. He was system administrator on Apollo and the Sejanus CCTV network, which was being rolled out throughout the city, the very "eyes" of Apollo. He whispered discreetly, ensuring no one was eavesdropping,

"Langley wants to talk to you again, buddy. Secure comms. Sounds urgent."

"Cheers, Danny," Declan replied.

He made his way to the secure comms room. The link was already active, and Walsh was already onscreen waiting for him, looking even more tired than the last time they had talked. There was no preamble. Walsh's face filled the screen, grim and direct.

"Declan!" he exclaimed with false bonhomie. "Further to our last conversation, we have had a breakthrough, one of our listening posts has identified a confirmed location for the... seller."

Declan felt the familiar, nauseating flutter of butterflies in his stomach, but he buried it. He knew what this meant: they hadn't just found Thorne; they were now arranging his funeral, and he was to be the undertaker.

"Check your terminal," Walsh continued. "I've sent a flash message with the address. He's holed up in a B&B on Westgate Road."

Declan almost had to stifle a laugh at the sheer banality of it all, a multi-million-dollar strategic secret about to be recovered from a fleapit hotel in the west end of Newcastle. But the humour died instantly as he remembered the gravity of the situation. If this went pear-shaped, if Thorne wasn't neutralised discreetly... it was his arse on the line. Walsh's promise of freedom would evaporate into a Langley denial and allegations of a British agent gone rogue. Walsh's expression turned conspiratorial.

"We need this handled quietly, Declan. Langley needs this handled off book. We trust you to be... both subtle and discreet, yet obvious, if you catch my drift?"

"Subtle and discreet are my middle names," he added, Walsh failing to pick up on the English sarcasm.

There was no need to elaborate further. Declan knew what 'handled quietly' meant. He wished Langley had just passed the task onto the Hereford Gun Club, the SAS, known for their efficiency in such 'redundancies'. He tried to flatter himself that it was because he was more nuanced than an SAS team, but he knew the reality. He was simply more expendable and deniable. One rogue agent with mental health issues was much easier to explain away if the mission were compromised.

"I'll handle it," he replied, trying to appear nonchalant. He ended the call, his mind running wild through various possible scenarios.

He returned to his desk, opened the self-deleting flash message that had arrived. It contained the address as stated by Walsh. A rundown B&B on Westgate Road. He was relieved to notice Phillips was out of the office. That simplified matters. He didn't need to explain, didn't need to ask permission. He just needed the right tools.

He left his own office and walked down the corridor towards Norman the Storeman's domain at the end. What appeared to be a small office was in fact a mere façade, hiding a tech store, an armoury, and a well-insulated 25-metre range.

"Norm?" he shouted into the office, pushing the door open. No sign of Norman immediately. He scanned the armoury racks visible from the entrance. He needed a specific tool for this job. A tool that didn't leave a trace.

It was here that he would find the means to carry out the deniable directive from Langley. The silent instrument for retiring Elias Thorne from the service. The grim necessity of his job had just become very real again.

CHAPTER 30

Declan stood in the doorway of Norman's office, staring at the empty space, a little puzzled. His friend was usually here, pottering away on some dangerous contraption or other. Then he heard the lift open at the end of the corridor, and he turned to see him, red-faced and out of breath, wearing a tracksuit. He looked a little flustered, leaning slightly against the wall for a moment.

"J-j-just give me a moment till I get my breath back," Norman stammered, catching his breath.

"You okay, mate?" asked Declan, a little concerned that his friend had overdone his daily exercise. Norman took his fitness regime seriously, a defiant routine after losing his leg to an IED years ago. His prosthetic was good, a testament to his fortitude, and he managed remarkably well on it, even jogging most days.

Norman swore under his breath, shaking his head.

"I just got attacked... by a bird."

Declan blinked.

"A bird?"

"Yeah! There I was, jogging merrily along the Quayside..." Norman began, still slightly breathless, "...and this big fucking black thing started to circle me! Like something out of a Hitchcock film!" He shuddered slightly. "Then it swooped down and attacked me! Talons and everything!" Norman looked genuinely nonplussed, a hardened ex-Para unexpectedly mugged by a feathered hooligan with an attitude problem.

Declan, stifling his laughter, simply couldn't resist:

"It was probably a vulture, mate. They can sense when something is near to death."

Norman looked at him deadpan, his expression shifting from genuine frustration to mock severity.

"Have you ever considered a career in stand-up comedy?"

"No," replied Declan, still chuckling at Norman's misfortune.

"Good," replied Norman. "Fucking don't."

Regaining his composure, Norman's usual good humour returned, though lately it had been more effusive than normal. The office gossip network, more efficient than any GCHQ listening post, had put it down to a new girlfriend. Norman, oblivious or uncaring, started humming cheerfully to himself, a tuneless but enthusiastic rendition of something that sounded suspiciously like a 90s power ballad.

Declan looked at him, shaking his head slowly.

"You know we are all subject to compulsory drug testing, Norm?"

Norm stopped singing and looked at Declan, his expression one of mock indignation.

"The only thing I'm high on, brother, is love! That's right, L-O-V-E. And unlike you, I don't mean by the hour on OnlyFans."

Declan shook his head, unable to suppress an involuntary grin. He was secretly happy Norm was happy. He was a good man.

Norm continued, his tone turning to one of sincere, if unsolicited, advice.

"You need a good woman yourself, mate. Might cheer that miserable face of yours up."

"My face isn't miserable," Declan answered defensively.

Norm laughed.

"Mate, it's looked like a smacked arse lately, well even more than it usually does. Honestly, get yourself a woman, or why not come fishing with me and Tony? As a matter of fact, he's taking me up to Dundee this weekend to pick up a couple of bootnecks. It's a big comfy boat and what could be more fun than having a few beers and then taking the piss out of the marines?"

Declan shook his head in the negative.

"No thanks mate, I've just got too much on, which is why I've come to see you. I'd hate you to think I'm here purely because I enjoy your scintillating company and rapier-like wit or anything."

Norm laughed at the insult then turned more serious.

"Seriously Declan, you can't keep crying off from the fishing trips. I mean as unpleasant as you are as a person, and despite your questionable personal hygiene, you can't spend the rest of your life alone mate, it's not healthy."

Declan looked at him, suddenly grim and serious.

"I'm never alone, Norm."

Norm's laughter subsided as he noticed the haunted look on Declan's face, he knew that expression only too well. The usual banter wasn't landing. His own humour faded completely, replaced by a sudden, sharp professionalism that mirrored Declan's own shift. He led Declan through his office and towards the concealed armoury door. The odour of gun oil was familiar and grounding.

"Right," Norman said, becoming operational. "What do you need?"

"I need something very discreet, Norm, silenced. Without the chance of leaving brass anywhere near the target. And off the official books, for a very urgent job." Declan didn't specify the time, or the nature of the task. It was a fast-ball, flexible situation. He had received the directive, the location, the name. Now he needed the tools.

Norman regarded Declan shrewdly for a moment, his eyes assessing. He understood the request instantly. Off book meant deniable. No brass meant no ballistic link. Silenced meant... quiet. Wet work. A job sanctioned at a level that bypassed the usual paperwork, likely originating somewhere far above Phillips's paygrade.

"Got just the thing," Norman said, his voice low. "I took a personal interest in that specific problem after that clusterfuck in the Manchester job went sideways. They almost turned the city centre into the wild west. Luckily the media ran with the 'Gunchester' drug gang they'd been fed by MI5."

He shook his head at the memory and disappeared back into the smaller, inner room, the sound of him talking to himself under his breath ,murmuring technical specs, potential issues, just audible to Declan.

He returned a few moments later with an ugly brute of a pistol. It looked like a Frankenstein monster cobbled together from spare parts, a heavy, solid frame, a long, bulky silencer screwed to the barrel, no obvious slide. A revolver, heavily modified. Declan raised a quizzical eyebrow, looking from the weapon to Norman's face.

"Really?"

"My own design," Norman said, holding it out, a hint of pride in his voice. "Based loosely on the old Welrod concept for the silencer but adapted for a revolver action. Multiple baffles packed tight reduce the decibels down to... acceptable levels. Only the trigger, hammer and cylinder as working parts, so no noise like you get from an automatic slide cycling. And crucially, no brass ejection."

He held the bulky weapon up. "The cylinder retains the spent casing, nice and clean." He paused, his expression returning to the purely functional. "Range is shit, obviously. You're losing velocity and accuracy with that baffle system. Maybe 15 to 25 metres effective but still better than you'd get with an automatic, no gas wasted cycling the working parts and no need for a Neilsen device. It'll still be lethal at higher ranges, but you'd have to be an absolute expert to compensate for any variables such as wind. I mean I know you're good, but this is one of those rare occasions when a workman really can blame his tools. On the other hand, am I right to assume this'll be up close and personal?"

"Up close and personal," Declan confirmed, taking the heavy weapon. It felt solid, ugly, purposeful.

"Isn't it always?" Norman said with a hint of sympathy, knowing the effect each kill had on his friend. "That's good, subsonic .38 Special ammo it is then. We have bags of that. Some of it even on the books. No batch numbers, no sonic boom, it'll do the job nicely."

Declan nodded at his friend in acceptance, he trusted Norm's expertise implicitly, in fact the Happy House would cease to function without his logistic and technical support. It actually hadn't taken much to persuade Helen to recruit Norm from his own hospital bed.

"Can I practice on the range with it?"

"Course," Norman said, a grin returning. "Wouldn't want you embarrassing yourself. Let's see if those shaky alcoholic hands still work."

He turned and led the way into the adjoining 25-metre range, a small, soundproofed space within the Happy House, lined with a thick and heavy red ballistic curtain. Norman followed behind, ready to mercilessly humiliate him if he missed a shot, a ritual born of long acquaintance.

Declan raised the heavy pistol, aiming down the short range at the paper figure target. It was a Figure 11 target, a cold war relic, still in use here and there for familiarity. Designed to resemble an old Warsaw Pact soldier.

A memory of the Red Square parade footage from his Janus search, of Eleanor marching in a similar uniform, flashed into Declan's mind. A stunning woman, a professional operative, wearing the uniform of an adversary. The contrast between the target on the wall and the person in his thoughts was both unwelcome and deeply unsettling.

He rapidly dismissed the intrusive thoughts, annoyed at himself and knowing such mental intrusions were likely to get him killed. Focus. Job. He instructed himself harshly. He squeezed the trigger, twice.

Thump-thump. He adjusted his aim slightly, squeezed again, twice. Thump-thump. A third time. Thump-thump. Six shots in three swift, controlled double taps.

The low, hollow thumps of the silenced gun cut the air, utterly unlike the sharper crack of a standard firearm. Not silent like the Hollywood movie suppressors, but not noisy either, discreet enough and accurate enough for the task in hand.

Norman walked down the range, his eyes on the target. He nodded approvingly at the groupings. Two rounds precisely placed in the head at nose level, the classic tactical elimination shot. Two more in the upper chest, centre mass. And a final pair in the lower chest where the descending Aorta would be. All shots tightly grouped within the anatomical T, all guaranteed killing shots.

"It's ALIVE!!" cried Norman in his best Victor Frankenstein voice, happy that his own cobbled together monster was accurate and functional. "Nice shooting mate, remind me never to piss you off."

Declan smiled at his friend and lowered the pistol; the grim weight of the off-book kill order on Thorne and the knowledge of a rendezvous with death settling heavily in his hand. He was impressed. Norman's Frankenstein monster worked. He was ready. The tools were acquired. He knew the target, where he was. Now, for the hunt. But the image of Eleanor lingered at the edge of his thoughts.

He knew she was beginning to muddy the waters, both professionally and personally; she was an enigmatic, mysterious woman, who was having a dangerous effect on the intuition he relied on to keep himself alive. He also wondered when he would see her again.?

CHAPTER 31

Misha, the SVR driver, settled back in the driver's seat of the discreetly parked car overlooking the old Georgian office block near the Tyne Bridge. He stifled a yawn. He had been part of the SVR surveillance team tasked with observing the British Special Projects outstation, the "Happy House," for days now, working in rotating shifts, logging comings and goings, learning the faces and routines of the analysts within. It was bread-and-butter work, the kind of patient, mundane surveillance that formed the backbone of intelligence gathering. He smiled slightly, remembering seeing the angry man in the tracksuit getting attacked by a bird. Even at this discreet distance, he could hear the profanities echoing across the Quayside. He'd certainly learned some very interesting English words that day.

Now his mission had changed. He'd received new instructions: follow one of the operatives, a Declan Shaw. The task sounded relatively simple, tail him without being compromised, find out what he was doing, where he was going, and then call it in to HQ in the safe house. He was part of a small, rotating surveillance team, using multiple discreet cars and foot patrols. As long as they maintained distance and rotated effectively, hopefully, they could get the job done without too many complications. He was concerned about the low visibility; the persistent drizzle that coated the city made everything grey and indistinct, making it easy to lose a target in the traffic or crowds. But if they got too close, they'd blow the mission.

"Fucking rain," he thought, in bored frustration.

He sat up suddenly. There he was. Shaw. Leaving the building, pulling on his raincoat, heading towards his car. The tailing task was a fast ball, no time to obtain a tracker from the safe house before starting the job. That was the problem with these types of reactive missions, improvising with available resources. Having said that, the vehicle was covered by CCTV, so there was no way of planting anything, but he still made a mental note to start carrying extra equipment, even if it wasn't needed for anything specific.

It was irritating that the vehicles hadn't been fitted with the full surveillance package as per protocol, but if you want something done properly, drink a bottle of vodka first and then do it yourself, he thought wryly.

He noted Shaw's tradecraft as the British operative entered his car. Subtle checks of his immediate vicinity, a quick scan of the parked vehicles. He'll be looking for a tail, Misha thought, with a hint of professional respect.

Declan pulled away from the kerb, merging into the Quayside traffic. Misha waited a moment, ensuring no other vehicles pulled out immediately behind him. The foot sloggers strategically placed around the area, blending with pedestrians and bus stops, would let him know which direction Shaw was heading.

After a couple of minutes, a message pinged on Misha's phone, a brief text from one of the forward foot teams. Shaw was heading west along the Quayside. Misha started his own car and followed the given directions, maintaining a careful distance, swapping with the other surveillance cars now and then as they navigated the city streets.

Finally, Shaw headed up a steep hill just off the city centre, Westgate Road, and eventually pulled over and stopped before switching off his headlights.

Misha drove past his vehicle, continuing up the hill until he could find a suitable spot both to park and to observe Shaw, who seemed to be watching a building further down the hill, across the opposite side of the road, a seedy looking B&B.

After an hour, it became obvious that Shaw hadn't just stopped; he was himself carrying out surveillance. He was clearly observing the run-down building, and that could only mean there was something or someone of importance inside.

Misha was puzzled by the situation, why was he alone, where was his backup? He called it in to HQ at the safe house, giving the location and his assessment:

"Cuckoo is static. Observing a building on Westgate Road. He appears to be engaged in surveillance but does not appear to have any support team. I am continuing to observe."

He was told to remain in situ and await further instructions. He settled down, adjusting his position for comfort. This was going to be a long day, and probably a long night.

"Fuck my life," he thought to himself miserably, the mundane frustration returning, highlighting the stark reality of his job: long periods of boredom punctuated by moments of extreme danger, all conducted in the persistent Newcastle rain. And to think he volunteered for the SVR because he thought it would be glamorous and exciting. "No more 007 movies for you, Misha," he thought to himself ruefully, as he yawned and watched an Englishman watching a building..

CHAPTER 32

Thorne grabbed his burner phone from the bedside table, then nervously checked his jacket pocket for the umpteenth time, making sure the Orpheus USB was secure. He fiddled with the safety pin as a double check, feeling the small, hard, impossibly valuable object beneath the fabric. The Quantum decrypt device was well hidden back in his room, taped inside the cover of his worn paperback. He wasn't stupid enough, he'd rationalised, to carry both items into the initial exchange. Once he got his money, the untraceable cash, the buyers would get the location of the second device. He believed this gave him leverage, control. He was foolishly naive about the nature of the game he was playing, and the nature of the people he was playing with. He was little red riding hood, heading off into the dark forest to negotiate with the big bad wolf.

He went through the plan in his mind. Simple. He'd head towards the general area he'd chosen for the exchange, a backstreet near Northumberland Street a main throughfare. He wouldn't give the buyers a meet time or exact rendezvous point until he was already in situ. He'd send the pre-prepared text message with the location details from a disposable burner phone, then enter the hiding spot he'd pre-chosen, somewhere discreet, maybe behind the dumpsters or vans parked in the alley and watch and wait for the buyers to arrive. If he smelled a rat, if anything felt off, he'd simply remain hidden until they left.

He didn't consider the possibility they might simply block both entrances and carry out a systematic search for him, or that they might not be the only ones watching. His naivety was a dangerous blind spot.

His constant anxiety was somewhat tempered by his insatiable greed and monumental ego. He allowed himself a small, self-satisfied smile. He had literally pulled off something historic. Someone else may have created the quantum malware, but it was his genius that had leveraged it, exploiting all the vulnerabilities in the target systems. He had fooled the NSA, his former employers and defeated some of the best cyber security in the Russian Federation. He deserved his payment for services rendered. That kind of expertise didn't come cheap. He could almost taste the champagne he'd be drinking tomorrow, almost feel the warm Caribbean breeze on his face as he sailed from island to island on his new yacht with a scantily clad Alana.

A sudden crash of lightning outside brought him back to the grim reality of the Newcastle weather. The storm had returned with a vengeance, a furious downpour hammering against the windowpane. He sighed, took off his glasses, and began to polish the lenses meticulously with a small cloth.

"Well," he muttered to himself, adjusting his tie in the small mirror, "it will be a damned sight more pleasant than this goddam lousy limey weather."

He put his glasses back on, pulled on his raincoat and doffed a hat, a habit that was returning thanks to the freak weather conditions plaguing the North. It was a practical necessity; it's not like he could find any goddam windscreen wipers for his spectacles he thought ruefully. He checked his watch. 21:30. Time to get a move on. He was only two hours away from being rich beyond his extremely wild dreams of sun, women and champagne.

Taking a resentful look at his grubby little room, the seedy monument to his paranoia and ambition. He would soon be waving goodbye to living like a skid row bum. He closed the door and sneaked down the creaky stairs, cursing at the noise. He cautiously opened the front door then furtively crept out of the B&B and into the night, his eyes darting left and right. His features were briefly lit by another lightning flash, creating a momentary, monochrome illumination of his face, in the pouring rain.

CHAPTER 33

The rain, which had previously settled into a persistent, miserable drizzle, began to get heavier, blurring the streetlights into hazy coronas, the night punctuated by an increasing number of lightning flashes. Declan sat in the driver's seat of his parked car, a non-descript saloon positioned a block away from the Westgate Road B&B. The engine was cold; the windows misted from his own breath. He should wipe the condensation away, but instead sat perfectly still, not wishing any movement to draw unwelcome eyes, watching and waiting, like the seasoned professional he was.

Hours had passed in this silent vigil, a tedious, mind-numbing boredom setting in. He hated surveillance. It was a young man's game. He knew working alone was piss-poor tradecraft: no backup, no ability to swap the tail. But the real threat wasn't a compromised operation; it was a compromised operative. Tiredness was a killer. Boredom was its accomplice. And Declan lived in a permanent state of managed sleep deprivation, often logging on remotely in the dead of night to work on some low-grade anomaly just to quiet the noise in his head. His "gift" was a professional blessing and a personal curse. And of course, there was always the unpleasant possibility that the Irish girl might decide to pay him an unwanted visit. The last thing he needed was for her to be sitting alongside him in the car giving him dirty looks.

Then, movement. A shifty-looking figure emerged from the entrance of the B&B, nervously pulling on a raincoat, doffing a hat against the damp. Elias Thorne, his target, alone.

He sat up, his focus sharpening instantly. He waited, letting Thorne get a hundred yards down the street before he slipped out of his own vehicle, melting into the urban shadows. He was on foot now, just like his target. Of course, if Thorne had arranged to get into a car, the mission was fucked. That was the trouble with working off the books: no backup vehicles. He fell into step behind him, maintaining a careful distance. He watched Thorne attempt clumsy counter-surveillance. Amateurish. Declan was grateful for it.

Thorne led him on a circuitous route, eventually stopping under the faint glow of a streetlamp. He pulled out his phone, the screen casting a pale light on his face. He appeared to be sending a text message. Probably to the buyers, Declan correctly surmised, maybe even setting the meet. That could mean he was on the clock, without even knowing where the hands were pointing.

"Shit!"

Thorne then turned and ducked into a narrow back street just off Grey's Monument. Declan paused at the mouth of the alley, the mournful tones of a distant saxophone drifting on the damp air from a late-night busker. He could see Thorne's silhouette ahead, his attention on a line of overflowing dumpsters. He was relieved to see the weather was keeping people off the streets; there was no one else around, no witnesses, just him and the American. This was it; opportunity was knocking like Beethoven's 5th, he didn't have time to be subtle.

He drew Norman's Frankenstein monster, the ugly silenced revolver feeling heavy and ominous in his hand. His other hand began to tremble slightly. The smell of wet brick and decay brought back a memory he constantly fought to suppress: a girl's face on a rubble-strewn Belfast street.

But as he looked at Thorne fumbling with a dumpster, another thought, cold and hard, cut through the pain of his past. This wasn't about one Irish girl anymore. This was about billions of lives, millions of innocent little girls if the blueprints fell into the wrong hands. He didn't need their blood on his hands too. The burn notice from Langley was a grim, unpleasant necessity. Kill one to save billions. He coldly switched off his empathy and emptied his mind of everything but the mission.

He steeled himself and was fully absorbed into Janitor mode. Thorne was busy trying to move one of the dumpsters, the grating screech of its wheels on the wet ground covering the faint splashes of Declan's footsteps as he closed the distance. "Up close and personal," he reminded himself, no room for error in the dark.

He couldn't risk a body shot in case he destroyed the devices, so it would have to be a close head shot, and he fucking hated those, ever since he once had the misfortune to be splattered with brain matter. He prowled to within ten metres and silently raised his pistol, then hesitated, puzzled; he could smell a faint scent on the air, subtle.

Was that Anya's perfume?

Aw shit! he thought, he was now beginning to have olfactory hallucinations, as if a dead girl wasn't bad enough, he was now being haunted by a living one.

Lightning crashed, the harsh flash momentarily illuminating the tableau. Then darkness returned, and a low rumble of thunder filled the air. He snapped back into Janitor mode.

Thump! Thump!

Two low, muffled reports merged with the thunder. Elias Thorne fell face down to the ground, landing with a splash into a puddle. Declan moved forward. As he approached the body, he raised the pistol again.

Thump! A third round into the base of the skull, for good measure. Three head shots, in a tight group—message sent, no damage done to the body.

He knelt, going into professional mode. His fingers found the zipped pocket, the safety pin, the quantum-encrypted USB stick. The package.

He made a play of putting the device in his jacket pocket but secreted it elsewhere out of an instinctive precaution. He climbed to his feet slowly, the grim job done, the burden of his empathy making an unwelcome return. For a few long moments, he just stood there over the body in the falling rain. His head was slightly bowed, his shoulders slumped, the gun hanging limply in his wet hand. It didn't matter that the act was necessary. The stain on his soul still felt just as deep; as always, he felt soiled.

A slight splash behind him, barely perceptible.

He spun, fast, the ugly revolver already in the aim. He froze, blinking into the rain, trying to identify the unknown threat, his finger already squeezing first pressure on the trigger.

Raindrops ran from his wet hair into his eyes, making his vision blurred and unfocused. He could just about make out a shape. A threat? Every professional instinct screamed at him to shoot. The alley was starkly lit by another lightning bolt, and then he recognised her.

She emerged from the shadows and the downpour like a phantom, her stylish, black raincoat slick with rain, her bright red lipstick a stark contrast to her pale face and dark clothing.

Eleanor Vane was gone, subsumed by the Nightingale, and she was on mission. She approached him slowly; her eyes locked on his. She took in the scene: the body on the wet ground, and Declan, standing over it not in triumph, but with the posture of a man carrying an immense weight. With his pistol raised, his eyes were hard, professional, a stranger to her. If she played this wrong, she suspected this version of Declan might well shoot, might well eliminate the Russian spy. But she was committed; this was her mission. The very reason she had been sent to this dark, rainy city with its winding labyrinth of alleys and secrets.

Her mind flashed to his P-File, to the cold, analytical words that had described him: "Potential for unprovoked violence... highly effective... dangerous." In that moment, she understood. This wasn't the charming, haunted man from the lighthouse. This was the Declan from the file. This was the killer. She finally understood why the SVR considered him so dangerous. He wasn't just an analyst who could fight; he was a highly trained predator, a man who seemed perfectly at home amongst the shadows and the rain. At that moment, he looked like the grim reaper personified.

Part of her was annoyed at herself for taking such a risky, though calculated, gamble, but she also found herself sighing with involuntary relief for a very good reason: the fact that he had hesitated to shoot could only mean one thing, he'd identified her as Eleanor and had overcome his conditioned reflexes somehow.

She stopped near the corpse, glanced down at Thorne's body, then looked intently back at Declan. She raised a single, quizzical eyebrow. It was an enigmatic, unspoken question. Not of simple accusation, but of… what? Recognition? A grim acknowledgement of a shared, bloody trade? Or was it something more complex, a silent query that hung in the air between them: So this is the man you truly are? He couldn't shake the ambiguity of that gesture. His eyes, cold and hard at first, visibly softened as he looked at her. He had made his decision; she saw the physiological change in him and knew she was safe. For now.

He cautiously lowered his gun, then slowly, deliberately, returned it to his holster, his own instincts screaming at him not to.

She came up to him, close—too close.

He could smell her delicate scent, feel her warmth, see the raindrops in her hair. He could feel that strange combination of familiarity and peace she brought him. Their eyes met and held each others gaze, something unspoken passed between them

He knows she is dangerous.

They kissed, passionately.

He wasn't sure how long the kiss lasted, seconds, minutes, hours? But he knew exactly when it ended, the moment he felt it. The cold, hard reality of a muzzle pressing into his ribs. He looked into her eyes, they looked back into his, a playful smile on her lips.

Her free hand slowly began to search him with a playful, almost flirtatious confidence. Her fingers slid inside his coat and retrieved a USB stick. He looked down at her hand, then back to her eyes, a wry, lopsided grin spreading across his own face.

"If I'd realised you were going to search me," he murmured, "I'd have hidden that in my trouser pocket."

A spark of amusement danced in her eyes. She tried to suppress a laugh but failed slightly. Her Declan was back.

She gave him another peck on the lips, then backed away slowly, her pistol still aimed at his chest.

"Nothing personal, Declan," she uttered almost regretfully. "You know how the game is played, it's just work, What's the English saying? All's fair in love and war?"

Declan was still looking into her eyes; his semi amused expression lost in the rain and shadows.

"So which one of the two is this?" he countered. "The least you can do is tell me your real name before you shoot me?"

She lowered the gun slightly.

"I'm not going to shoot you, not unless you're stupid enough to try to follow me, and you have never struck me as a stupid man Operative Shaw,"

"You could have fooled me" he replied dryly.

She backed even further into the shadows. Then hesitated, as if making a decision.

"My name's Anast...Anya..... my name is Anya."

With that, she simply melted into the into the night like a shadow. Declan slowly lowered his hands and stood alone in the alley, the rain falling, lightening crashing, the saxophone fading.

"WTF had just happened"? he thought, completely bemused by the sheer insanity of it all.

He snapped himself back to the present and put his hands in his trouser pocket, he still had the encrypted USB stick. He had successfully palmed the decoy on her. But the victory felt hollow. Despite the success of his ruse, she had been able to tail him, and he hadn't noticed. He had even smelled her perfume and hadn't even trusted his own senses. Declan's mind carried out an immediate after-action review and tried to pinpoint where he had gone so wrong.

He was working solo; she had likely been part of a team, watching his every move since he left the Happy House. Her timing had been perfect; indeed it was calculated perfection, and he mentally tipped his hat to her undoubted skill. She had waited for him to take the risk, waited for the target to be neutralised, waited for him to be compromised by the post-kill slump and his own psychological baggage. Interrupting sooner would have been lethal for her. This wasn't sloppiness on her part; this was the ultimate professional ambush.

He had been amateurish though; she was making him sloppy. He had been compromised by his own growing feelings. And now he was standing alone in an alley, holding the worlds most dangerous secret in his hands, next to a corpse with the buyer's god knows how close. Time to get back in the game and get a move on, he exited the alley, making sure he wasn't witnessed.

His carelessness could have had serious consequences, not just for the mission, but for the entire world. But a hidden part of him, the part he tried to keep buried deep, told him the kiss had been worth it. He could still taste her on his lips, still smell her scent on him.

But despite all his misgivings, he was desperately relieved, relieved that he had controlled the monster inside, for a split second, before he'd identified the target, he was ready to shoot the stranger in the shadows. The only thing that had stopped him, the only thing which had halted his conditioned reflex, had been the memory of a young Belfast girl. Anya had just been saved by his ghost.

It was a long, cold, wet, and very confusing walk back to his car. Haunted not by a ghost this time, but by the memory of a kiss. He smiled ruefully, relieved that he hadn't been ambushed by the CIA. Kissing a burly, bearded ex marine, just wouldn't have been the same.

CHAPTER 34

Onboard the Odyssey, the burner phone vibrated against the comms desk, a harsh, jarring buzz. Dima sighed, irritated at the intrusion, put his copy of *Moby Dick* down, and snatched up the vibrating phone, his eyes scanning the brief text message which contained the information they had been waiting for.

He called across to Taras and they both looked at the map of Newcastle.

"Coordinates, Captain. what3words: case.trader.vines. It's a back alley, Brunswick Place in the city centre, entrances off Northumberland Street and Grey's Monument."

A cold, satisfied smile appeared on Taras's tight lips as he looked at the map. The American fool had just chosen the site of his own grave.

"Right," he snarled impatiently. "Let's go."

His team was already improving under his firm hand. Weapons were checked, magazines seated with hollow, metallic clicks, and butts were folded for easy, unobtrusive carriage. Andriy and Olek, their earlier animosity sublimated into a shared, grim purpose, pulled on dark raincoats, the heavy fabric concealing the pistols and submachine guns beneath. Olek grabbed a holdall containing the tidy sum of money Thorne had insisted on as a deposit. Andriy helped him carry it and whispered,

"A pity to waste such a windfall on an American."

Olek glared at him, irritated by both the unspoken suggestion and his sardonic smile.

"Lev, Dima, you have the yacht," Taras commanded. "Maintain radio silence unless compromised. The rest of you, with me."

The six of them piled into the dark interior of a nondescript transit van and took their seats, their faces grim and focused.

"Get there. Fast," Taras barked at the driver.

The van screeched out of the marina car park, its tyres throwing up gravel and arcs of grey water, plunging into the storm-lashed streets of Newcastle, to be swallowed by the torrential rain and the Stygian darkness of a long November night.

They were forced to leave the vehicle an inconvenient distance from the target coordinates, in an almost empty car park, the cooling engine ticking in the sudden silence as they stiffly clambered from the vehicle, concealing their weapons beneath their raincoats.

Moving swiftly towards their objective, they were relieved that the city centre was almost a ghost town, the storm having driven all but a few determined, late-night revellers from the streets. Only the fading echo of a saxophone broke the monotonous sound of the rainfall.

Taras split the team with a series of sharp, silent hand signals. Andriy and another man peeled off to cover the far entrance of the alley. Olek and the fifth man melted into the shadows of a recessed doorway, providing overwatch. The alley felt unnaturally silent, a dead space between two buildings, smelling of wet bins and decay. Rainwater cascaded from a broken drainpipe, splashing noisily onto the ground. The mournful saxophone had stopped, leaving the leaking pipe and the pouring rain as the only sounds in the ominous shadows.

Taras and Andriy entered from opposite ends, moving with a fluid, silent grace, their weapons still concealed but their hands ready. He saw the dark shape on the ground first, what at first glance appeared to be a discarded pile of clothing, abandoned by the overflowing dumpsters. He approached it cautiously, his pistol now in his hand, a heavy, solid weight, almost as heavy as the sinking feeling which had just manifested in the pit of his stomach.

He knew who it was before he knelt. He knew what it was by the stillness.

Lightning flashed, and in that stark, blue-white moment, the scene was illuminated in perfect, gruesome detail. Elias Thorne lay face down; his hat knocked to one side. The back of his skull was a dark, shattered ruin, blood and brain matter mingling with the rainwater to form a grim, swirling puddle. Taras's professional eye took it all in instantly.

Three rounds, tightly grouped at the base of the skull. A classic execution. This was not the work of a panicked mugger. This was precise, professional, designed to send a message. Despite himself, he smiled in grudging respect for the shooter.

He knew before he searched he would find no devices, but discipline demanded he be thorough. He rolled the body over with the toe of his boot. Thorne's eyes were wide, staring with surprise at the rainy sky. With gloved hands, Taras quickly went through his pockets. A wallet with a fake ID. A mix of several hundred pounds and dollars in cash. A burner phone. Nothing else.

Not a robbery, then.

His lips twisted into a cynical sneer. He pocketed the cash and, with a deft movement, unclasped Thorne's expensive-looking watch from his wrist.

“Make it look like one,” he muttered to himself. A final, pragmatic piece of tradecraft.

He threw the phone at Andriy, who caught it deftly.

“Take the battery and SIM card out, then dump it in the river when we drive past.” Andriy nodded in assent.

Taras quickly scanned the ground around the body. No ejected brass. The rain would wash away most of the forensics, but the absence of casings was telling. Either the assassin was meticulous enough to collect their brass, or they had used a revolver. Both pointed to a level of professionalism that made him wonder if they were all being watched right now.

They couldn't afford to stay here for a moment longer. The local police would be crawling all over this place before too long and he didn’t want to be hanging around when they did turn up. He stood up, turning back to Andriy, who was busy pocketing the phone parts.

“We're too late,” Taras hissed, his voice a low growl of pure frustration. “It appears the Orcs beat us to it. Let's get the fuck out of here.”

As he turned to leave, he caught a scent on the damp air, something that didn't belong in this grimy, rain-washed space of piss and decay. Faint, floral, almost imperceptible. Perfume. He froze, his mind flashing back with the suddenness of a lightning strike. The Moscow Metro. The chaos, the blood, the roar of the train. The face of the woman, her cold, merciless eyes. And that same scent, just before she shot him.

A wave of burning fury washed over him. He shook his head, a low growl of self-disgust in his throat. It was his imagination. It had to be. A phantom scent, a trick of his senses triggered by the memory of his greatest failure. The sight of the body, the smell of cordite and fresh, coppery blood, it had all served to drag his mind back to that humiliating moment in the subway car.

He was letting his obsession manifest as a weakness, a flaw in his perception. The memory of the bitch was still haunting him, not just in his dreams, but she was even able to affect how he did his job. The recollection added to his constant rage at her for what she had done, and at himself for allowing her to still have this much power over him. He turned and strode out of the alley, his limp more pronounced, his fists clenched at his sides. The faint scent was gone, reinforcing his belief it was just one of his flashbacks. But his shame remained, rubbing fresh salt into an old, deep wound.

He had to get back to the yacht urgently and report the situation to his MI6 handlers. If they were lucky, the Orcs wouldn't have extracted yet; they might still be able to salvage something from this shitshow. He couldn't report back to Kyiv yet, not with another humiliation at the hands of the Russians on his record. He'd be lucky to escape with his life this time. They would not be forgiving. And it was all, all of it, down to that Russian bitch.

Taras returned to the yacht still angry and frustrated, his team eyeing each other silently on the journey back, fully aware of the brooding menace sitting in the front passenger seat. Andriy sat in the back, eyeing the holdall between his legs and smirking at Olek with an eyebrow raised; the younger man sat in sullen silence, glowering back at him.

Taras stormed past Dima, who was still keeping radio watch.

"I need to speak to the British, get them on the net." Dima turned to the rest of the team for a clue as to what was going on, but they just shrugged, trying not to draw the attention of Taras's obvious wrath by making conversation.

He went to the radio and broke radio silence. Taras gave a quick briefing on the situation and requested further instructions. MI6 informed him that all ports and airports would be placed on high alert and a "software failure" in air traffic control systems would close down UK airspace for at least 48 hours.

"We will get back to you with specific instructions. In the meantime, it is advised you return to the crime scene first thing in the morning with the rest of the rubberneckers and see if there is any further intel you can ascertain. The Americans will be furious that one of theirs is involved, so we need to be proactive on this and approach it from multiple angles."

Taras was uncertain as to what good it would do, but at least it delayed him having to report the failure to Kyiv for the moment. As long as he was still in play, there was still a chance he could salvage something from the clusterfuck. He made his men clear, check and clean their weapons, before they grabbed a couple of hours of much-needed sleep.

Dawn was breaking when he climbed stiffly back into the van and had Andriy drive him back towards the crime scene. It gave him the opportunity to give him a private "briefing" about his attitude towards the operational funds, a briefing that would leave its mark and send a message to the rest of the team on his return. Andriy gave him a smile as he climbed behind the wheel, not noticing the shiny, but stained, brass knuckle duster on Taras's hand.

CHAPTER 35

Anya not Eleanor walked into the safehouse, shedding her damp raincoat with practised efficiency. The damp of the Newcastle air seemed to have wormed its way into her bones, a feeling that had little to do with the rain and everything to do with the contradictions of Declan Shaw.

The scene replayed in her mind, so different from her other memories of the complicated Englishman. The sudden, brutal efficiency of the kill, two rounds, then a third for good measure. A professional's work. But then, the aftermath. Declan's strange, penitent stance over the body, his shoulders slumped, head bowed. He hadn't gloated. He had looked... soiled by the act. Until he became aware of a threat, his speed, his coldness, his efficiency. He had reminded her of... well, the Nightingale. She understood how close she had come to being shot but also understood the supreme effort it must have taken to override his muscle memory; she found herself both impressed and strangely touched.

It was the man from his P-File the SVR had warned of. The killer from Belfast who carried the weight of an innocent's death like a shroud. A man capable of extreme violence yet seemingly tormented by the weight of taking a life. Then the kiss. A reckless, impulsive act in a blood-soaked alley that had defied all logic. She tried to convince herself the kiss had been a masterful ruse, but she knew the reality: it had been spontaneous, unexpected, and she had risked the mission by her actions. And whilst Declan had let his operational awareness slip, so had she, and to make matters worse, she had been genuinely amused by his humorous response.

The English comedian had effectively turned an armed robbery into a private joke between them. Despite her best efforts, she found herself smiling at the memory.

Viktor, her impassive SVR support operative, stood as she entered. His own surveillance mission had been a masterclass in patience and opportunism.

"The Icarus package is secure," she said, her voice clipped, holding up the USB stick.

"As is the decrypt key," Viktor replied, his Russian heavily accented. He placed a small, grey metallic device on the desk. "I observed our primary target, Thorne, depart his lodging. As instructed, I did not engage." He paused. "The British asset, Shaw, was in position and initiated a foot-tail almost immediately. Then you followed him. A neat chain of surveillance."

He gave a slight smile. "Like nesting dolls."

Viktor continued his debrief. "Once all parties were clear of the B&B, with Misha acting as overwatch, I made my entry. There were no complications. The target was an amateur and it didn't take long to find the decrypt device, which was taped inside a paperback copy of 'Tinker Tailor Soldier Spy.'" He said the title with the weary contempt of someone who found such affectations irritating.

"I couldn't find the USB device but clearly that's because he had it on his person."

Anya nodded in confirmation; Thorne had indeed had the data on his person, until Declan had it on his. Despite a nagging regret that she had to rob him, her mission was now complete. Moscow's parallel operations had worked flawlessly. They now had both the key and, she believed, the lock.

She smiled slightly in professional satisfaction and slid the USB stick she'd taken from Declan out of an internal pocket. She connected the secure laptop to the decryption rig, inserted Viktor's crypto drive and watched the lights flicker green. Then, with a slight, satisfied smile at a job well done, she inserted the USB stick from the alley, pleased at her own flawless tradecraft.

The screen changed. Not to file directories. A video player window popped up. A file name appeared: The_Real_Me.mpeg. She double-clicked. The video played. Rain-slicked streets, a young parka-clad man riding a scooter. The opening chords of a rock song filling the room. Quadrophenia. Then the soundtrack kicked in fully. Roger Daltrey's powerful voice singing the opening to The Who's "The Real Me."

Her eyes widened. The man who appeared weighed down with regret had probably used a spontaneous moment of genuine intimacy as an opportunity to carry out a skilful sleight of hand. Just as she had used the same moment to shove a gun in his ribs. Then a memory came of him using a similar trick to help out an old lady in a fish restaurant.

A volcanic stream of inventive Russian curses erupted from her, damning Declan Shaw's lineage back to the Anglo-Saxon invasion. He wasn't the sad, reluctant operator; he was the Kukushka, the cuckoo who had laid a false egg in her nest. It was the spontaneous frustration of a highly competent professional being so thoroughly and audaciously played. He hadn't just swapped a drive: he had used her own compromising feelings for him against her.

She slumped back in her chair, the profanity replaced by a strange sound. A chuckle, low, ragged and disbelieving. It grew into a full-blown laugh, sharp and a little wild. The sheer, bloody cheek of it was magnificent.

"All really is fair in love and war," she chuckled half to herself, half to the universe which had inflicted that wisecracking street conjurer on her.

Viktor watched her, a bewildered look on his usually impassive features.

"So," he said, ever practical. "What now? Do we report the compromise? The mission seems to be a failure."

"No, Viktor, the mission continues." Anya said, the laughter fading, leaving behind only a grim determination. She leaned forward, pressing her palms onto the desk. The mission was not a failure. It had just become infinitely more complicated. She was in a precarious professional position. She had failed to secure the asset. She could not report back to Moscow with a video of a man on a scooter. But the game was not over.

Declan Shaw, the man who had just played her for a fool, was the one person who knew where the real data was. He was no longer just a player; he was the entire chessboard. Her standard operational procedure, track, corner, neutralise, was now obsolete. She was dealing with an unpredictable master of misdirection. A new, more unorthodox approach was required. She needed to understand his endgame. She needed to find a new point of leverage. She needed another move.

But first, with a wry smile fighting against a frown, she sat back down at the terminal. If he wanted to send messages through music, she would return the favour. She quickly transferred her own audio file onto the fake USB, a little reminder of fate for the Cuckoo.

Viktor watched her, a bewildered look on his usually impassive features...

Her mind raced, sifting through the chaos for the one, single, logical next step. And she found it. The last place Declan had been, the one place where the game was still live, where new pieces might still be on the board.

"What now?" she repeated, a sardonic twist to her lips as she grabbed her raincoat.

"Now we go back to work."

Viktor looked at her, confused.

"Back to where?"

Anya's eyes were cold, clear, and filled with a new, dangerous intensity.

"To the alley," she said. "The game isn't over until the final piece has been played, and I intend to make the last move."

"After we see what's happening in the alley, we go find Shaw himself, but we already know where he works. Send Misha back to Special Projects, it won't take us long to find that... English comedian." She spat the last two words out like a curse, then added, almost as an afterthought, a final, blistering Russian expletive aimed squarely at the hilariously infuriating paradox that was Operative Declan Shaw.

CHAPTER 36

The rain had finally stopped by the time Declan got back to his flat. The long, wet, cold walk from the alley to his car had done little to clear his head. He was exhausted, drained by the kill, the confrontation, the kiss, and the uncertainty of the game he was now playing.

He silently entered the quiet flat, half expecting a beautiful Russian operative to be waiting for him, half hoping that she would be and feeling strangely disappointed that she wasn't. The familiar space felt alien after the night's events. He didn't bother to change. He poured himself a large whiskey, the strong liquid promising a temporary, welcome oblivion. His hand was shaking, not from fear, but from a post-adrenaline reaction. He drank it quickly. He drank another. He found himself wondering, with a flicker of dark amusement, how Anya would react when she plugged the fake drive into her system. He'd like to be a fly on that wall.

"Velvet?" he muttered.

"Yes, Declan? Another bad day at the office I assume, given your pulse rate and heightened emotional state?"

"Nothing to write home about. Give me some music please, without the lip."

"Lip? Moi? You wound me to my circuits, Declan," she replied.

The opening bars to "King of Pain" by The Police emerged from her speakers.

He shook his head at his insubordinate AI, suddenly feeling a pang of empathy for Phillips regarding his own attitude towards his boss.

He then sat drinking and played out the evening's events in a more in-depth mental review. Although he'd carried the fake USB with the expectation of having to palm it off to the Americans during their likely double cross, he had managed to successfully make the switch and give it to Eleanor instead, or rather Anya, as he now thought of her.

Whilst it could have been another fake name, his instincts told him she had almost certainly been telling the truth. Then again, he had been pretty certain that kiss had been real too, right up to the moment she had so flirtatiously robbed him at gunpoint.

He was, he realised, getting increasingly concerned at his lack of operational awareness around her. Whilst it had felt great during their "social" encounters, he understood just how vulnerable this "Anya effect" had rendered him on a professional level.

Even after his discovery that she was a Russian asset, it still hadn't blunted the effect she had on him, the peace she brought to him, even as she had shoved a gun into his ribs. Then there was the kiss; how the hell had it even happened? He shook his head, utterly bewildered and confused, his analytical skills failing him again. It was becoming a recurring pattern when she was around, he realised. The Russian was far more dangerous to him than an entire battalion of Spetsnaz, he admitted ruefully. And at least they wouldn't try to kiss him before holding him up at gunpoint.

He once again replayed the events of the alley in his mind, analysing every plausible theory, and none of them made any sense professionally. She had robbed him at gunpoint, a clean and efficient operational win for her. But then there was the kiss, the playful smile, and the final, stunning admission of her real name. By all accounts, he should be dead in that alley. But he hadn't been killed; he had been kissed, and it had felt real, genuinely authentic. And he was having difficulty processing both the novelty, the excitement, and the maddening complications of it all.

He'd let his guard down. And he never lets his guard down. He was completely confused at his own inability to properly analyse their interactions. That professional certainty he relied on was abandoning him, just when he needed it the most.

He also replayed another scenario, the one where he had held her at gunpoint. By all accounts, she should have been dead before any of the other madness took place. He imagined himself pulling the trigger, seeing the surprise in her eyes, watching the life fading out of them.

He shuddered and poured himself another generous measure, then stumbled into the bedroom and flung himself onto the bed, still wearing his damp, crumpled clothes. He reached into his inner pocket and pulled out a small, now creased photograph of him and Anya. It was the one taken of them by the passer-by at the lighthouse. He looked at her resting her head on his shoulder, looked for the tell-tale signs of deceit he was usually so good at spotting. But there was nothing; he could see nothing, although given her ability to dull his intuition, that didn't really mean anything, except not only could he not trust Anya, but he was also unable to even trust himself anymore.

He lay on his back, looking at her smiling face in the dim light, the whiskey and the exhaustion hitting him hard. He fell asleep like that, the empty glass on his chest and the photograph still clutched in his hand.

He woke with a start hours later, the glass falling to the floor and rolling across the carpet. The first thing he was aware of was the crumpled photo still in his hand. He looked at it, at her smiling eyes, at the memory of the seals and their laughter directed at Phillips. A fragile, impossible hope before he'd found out she was a Russian asset. That she was just another player in the wicked game of espionage.

He was still damp, unshaven, and mentally frayed. His injured shoulder had intruded into his sleep, like a painful alarm clock. The guilt from the alley, the image of Thorne's dead face, the memory of Anastasia's eyes, how close he had come to ending her and adding another ghost to his collection... it all swirled in his head like a toxic cocktail, tearing apart the gossamer thread of hope he had just felt.

Then he reluctantly looked towards the corner of the room, a part of his morning ritual. She was there of course, as always. The ghost of the dead Irish girl, sitting in the armchair, watching him. Her accusing eyes seemed even more disappointed in him than usual.

Velvet, weaponising her usual musical sarcasm, was playing "Innocent Man" by Billy Joel.

"An innocent man?" the silent gaze of the ghost seemed to ask. "Look at what you did last night. Look at who you are. Look at WHAT you are. You think ANY woman could care about a killer like YOU?"

He stared back at her sadly, returning the gaze of her judgemental eyes. His daily penance paid, he dragged himself stiffly out of bed, too wiped out physically and emotionally to bother with his usual exercise routine and shower. He stiffly pulled on a fresh set of dry clothes, his shoulder screaming in protest, and made his reluctant way back to the 'Happy House' where an even bigger hangover awaited him.

CHAPTER 37

A sombre grey daylight had long since broken by the time Declan arrived, the office bustling not with the usual subdued murmur of routine activity, but with a frantic urgency which could only mean one thing: trouble.

Phillips was already there, pacing, his face pale with stress. He frantically confronted Declan the moment he saw him, his voice sharp with barely contained anxiety.

"Shaw! Where the hell have you been? I've been trying to reach you!"

Declan half-stifled a yawn, feigning disinterest, strongly suspecting what the flap was about.

"Just following up the Icarus tasking, Sir. Oh, and I also needed a little something called sleep." He reinforced his point by using air quotes, knowing it would irritate Phillips.

"Sleep?!" Phillips sputtered, his composure fraying completely. "We've had a report. A body found in an alley off Northumberland Street. The general description fits that of the rogue American Thorne."

Declan continued to hide his feelings behind a veil of weary indifference. The alley. Thorne. Found already. Not surprising really; the American had chosen the worst possible place for a drop in the city, but the best possible place for Langley's message to be delivered to the US intelligence community.

"You were on point for Icarus," Phillips snapped, his voice dripping with annoyance. "Get down there. Liaise with the local police. This is now our jurisdiction. Find out what you can, make sure it's him and not a case of mistaken identity."

"Can't someone just take a photo of his face and run it through Janus?" Declan asked practically.

"Well, we could if the victim had a face left, Shaw," barked Phillips, growing increasingly irritated at Declan's casual attitude towards what was becoming a runaway crisis. "Now get down there now and take the fingerprint kit. I want you back here as soon as you confirm an ID."

Declan nodded, not too happy about returning to the scene of the crime, although he was conflicted as to which crime he was alluding to, the killing or the kiss. It did, however, give him an opportunity to contaminate the evidence chain with his own DNA. He had physically searched Thorne, and there was always the chance he'd left some evidence on the corpse. The last thing he needed was CivPol gathering it and jumping to the correct conclusion. The service would cover for him, of course; they always did. But it would be an uncomfortable conversation with Philips, explaining exactly what it was he had been up to in the alley.

He also thought about the Americans and the leash and decided that whatever was on the USB drive and in his pocket, he wasn't going to give it up until he was completely free of this lunatic asylum. He simply didn't trust Walsh to keep his word; there was something about the CIA spook which felt off, something in the eyes which made Declan cautious, an insincerity. He decided it was probably prudent to keep the USB for now, until Walsh kept his end of the bargain. Hell, he might even insist on a comfort letter from the bastards, just to make sure he had full immunity should his file "accidentally" enter the public domain.

"Understood, Sir," he said, his face neutral. He turned to leave.

"And Shaw!" Phillips called after him. "Keep me in the loop! Top priority!"

Keep him in the loop? Declan almost laughed.

He managed a smile at Phillips, oozing insincerity.

"Of course, Sir."

He popped to see Norm before he left, signing for a digital fingerprint scanner, with a hurried promise that they would catch up later.

He drove to the alley off Northumberland Street. The area was sealed off with police tape. A forensic tent covered where Thorne's body was laying. Uniformed officers stood guard, their faces grim. The senior officer on scene, a uniformed Inspector with weary eyes, met him with a tight jaw.

"Forensics are en route from divisional," the Inspector said stiffly, his resentment at the spook's intrusion palpable. "Area secured. Initial impression is cause of death is three gunshot wounds to the back of the skull, tight grouping. It was a professional job by the looks of things. Whoever did this knew exactly what they were doing."

Declan nodded silently.

"I wish," he thought to himself, still trying to come to terms with his unprofessional actions.

"I need to positively identify and search the corpse now," Declan stated almost nonchalantly.

The Inspector balked.

"Sir, with respect, forensics should do that. Chain of evidence..."

"Inspector," Declan cut him off, his tone hardening. "This falls under a national security remit from the very highest authority. I need to check for specific items immediately and I need to confirm his identity, before this becomes an international incident."

The Inspector visibly bristled, his face reddening. He didn't back down immediately, a flicker of defiance in his eyes.

"With all due respect, Sir, my job is to preserve the scene! I have procedures..."

Declan stepped closer, lowering his voice, making it a cold, hard threat.

"Inspector. My authority here comes directly from London. You obstruct me, and I guarantee your next posting will be arresting elderly pensioners in Surrey for making edgy social media posts. Am I making myself clear regarding the urgency and gravity of the situation?"

The threat landed. The Inspector's face paled. He reluctantly stepped aside in unspoken assent, his resentment now tempered by the dawning realisation that this unwelcome intruder held his career in his hands.

Declan entered the tent and knelt by the body of Elias Thorne once more. He quickly, efficiently, went through the motions of a search. He found Thorne's empty wallet and passport. He noted with interest the expensive watch Thorne had been wearing last night had vanished, probably along with the cash. The fact his phone was also gone may have been the buyers covering their tracks; he remembered Thorne sending a text message on the device.

He should maybe have lifted the phone, but the job was deniable, and had he shown up at digital forensics with it, he'd have awkward questions about how it got in his possession. Better that it remains a loose end. Besides which, he had a sneaking suspicion Langley would have already stripped the B&B room bare of any evidence, so no real harm done.

Maybe forensics would pick something up from the mystery thief's DNA; they'd also pick up his own DNA of course, but the inspector was now his perfect alibi, which made him feel a little better about having had to socially engineer him into granting access to the body.

Nothing else of interest was found. No USB. No decrypt device. Not that he expected to find anything. As expected, the fingerprint scans came back positive, the device lighting up with a positive green ping; he made a deliberate point to not look at the ruined face.

He stood up stiffly. He had simply confirmed the body was Thorne's and that, as far as the official record was concerned, the package was gone. He exited the tent, focusing on the scanner as he sent the results back to the Happy House for analysis.

He then paused, feeling a familiar sensation followed by an irresistible urge to look up towards the alley entrance, where a group of curious onlookers were being held back by uniformed police. He scanned their faces, knowing before he even looked what he would find.

His gaze landed almost magnetically onto a pair of eyes in the crowd, familiar eyes, deep brown eyes—her eyes, Anya. She stood slightly back from the others, her expression unreadable from a distance, but her lips curved upwards in that expression he now knew was a sign of impending trouble. She met his gaze directly across the cordon, and she gave him a small, slow, ironic yet almost friendly wave.

She knew exactly what he was doing. She knew he was back here, playing his part. The game was still on. What the hell was she playing at? All he had to do was shout and point and she'd be lifted. Then again, last night she had approached him not knowing whether she'd be shot.

The woman certainly had courage, he mused with growing respect. Either that or she was as fucking nuts as he himself was, probably the latter, given the kiss last night.

Now here she was, brazenly returning to the scene of the crime wearing that troublesome smile. The problem was for Declan; he still wasn't sure if the biggest crime was the murder, or the fact he had let his guard down and kissed a Russian asset.

A few feet away from where Anastasia stood, a curious Taras also blended into the crowd. He wasn't looking at Declan; his entire puzzled focus was fixed on her. He had arrived after the shooting, found Thorne's body, and had returned, determined to identify who had secured the prize and see if any further intelligence could be gleaned from the aftermath. It was either waste his time here, or report his failure to Kyiv, and this, at least, this fool's errand was buying him time to salvage at least something from the bloody mess.

His gaze was initially caught by her attractiveness. But almost immediately, his professional instincts took over. While the rest of the onlookers were focused on the drama inside the cordon, this woman's attention was fixed on the unshaven, middle-aged man in the suit and raincoat. Taras looked towards the man and noticed the way he conducted himself, "not police," he thought; there was something intangible about him. He seemed far too nonchalant for a man attending a murder scene, relaxed almost. It all seemed a little too performative, thought Taras, like someone just going through the motions.

He looked back towards the woman; her posture wasn't that of a gawker; it was controlled, purposeful, another asset? The thought sent a jolt through him, she looked strangely familiar, but the angle of her face was such he could only see a side profile.

He was puzzled; she was in the crowd, but he could see the British suit looking at her, and her reciprocating. He could sense something intangible between them. Their nonverbal exchange appeared almost playful, intimate. Who was he, and who was she? And why were there subtle wry smiles on both their faces? His training kicked in: "Presence of the extraordinary, absence of the ordinary." They were ticking both boxes.

Then she turned slightly to follow the Englishman's movements and recognition dawned with the suddenness of a thunderbolt. Taras froze in disbelief, his mind flashing back to the Moscow Metro. The chaos. The woman fighting from within the hostages. He had only seen her eyes, cold and professional, just before she shot him in the leg.

That face, those eyes... it was her. The Russian Bitch. His rage told him to act immediately, but with an act of supreme willpower he restrained himself and quickly and surreptitiously took a picture of her on his phone, maybe his MI6 contacts could identify her for him.

Declan, oblivious to Taras, watched as Anya gave him a final, farewell wave, a wave which Taras witnessed, thus confirming his suspicions. But as she turned to leave, her own gaze swept the crowd, a professional's final scan of the environment to identify any potential problems with her egress route.

Her eyes met Taras's. For a split second, there was no recognition. He was just another face. But then she registered the intensity of his stare, the raw, personal, almost animalistic hatred aimed directly at her. She didn't know who he was, but she knew exactly what he was. A dangerous threat.

Taras saw the recognition in her eyes, saw her understand the danger. He took a single, almost imperceptible step forward, his hand beginning to move towards his jacket, but she was already gone.

She didn't run. She didn't panic. With the fluid grace of a ballerina, she turned, stepped behind a large police forensics van that was momentarily blocking the view, and simply vanished.

By the time Taras angrily pushed his way through the onlookers to where she had been standing, there was no sign of her. She had used the chaos and the cover of the official presence to melt away into the city, leaving behind only the faint scent of her perfume.

Taras stood there almost incandescent with rage, his fists clenched in anger and futility. He had found her. And then he had lost her. But now he knew two things: The Russian Bitch was here, she must have been there last night, he hadn't imagined her scent. It was her who had killed Thorne and retrieved the data.

Of course the Russians would send one of their best killers to interfere in his operation.

As for this unknown British asset, an asset who she clearly knew intimately, whose gaze towards her and hers towards him was anything but professional. Were they in it together, colluding? Was the Englishman cleaning up the crime scene on her behalf? It was the only thing that made sense.

A feral smile formed on his lips, almost a grimace as a plan began to form in his mind, twisting his mission into a new, brutal shape. Coming here wasn't a waste of his time after all; his luck had finally changed, and he was still in play. He also knew with a cold certainty he could and would get to The Russian Bitch through the Englishman.

CHAPTER 38

The deluge continued to fall on Newcastle with a grim, indifferent persistence, turning the scarred streets into slick, grey mirrors. For hours, Taras had prowled the rainswept city, his limp a painful, rhythmic reminder of the Russian, adding to the gnawing fury which burned within his mind.

He had scoured the city centre for hours, his frustration growing in tandem with the increasing physical pain. He couldn't believe he had found her. After five long years of nursing his wound and his humiliation, he had seen the face of The Russian Bitch in that crowd. And then, in a blink, she was gone, vanished behind a police van as if she had dissolved into the rain itself.

Taras had also systematically checked the nearby shops and streets, every hotel, every boarding house within a two-mile radius of the crime scene, using a plausible cover and a flash of his SBU-issued fake Northumbria Police identification to bully his way past gullible porters. Nothing. He had tasked two of his men to search the train and metro stations, the bus interchanges, the airport. Nothing. He may as well have imagined the whole episode, except, he had the physical evidence of her presence on his phone.

As the sun began to set behind the grey, morose sky, he finally admitted defeat. She was almost certainly skulking in some safe house, he was a fool to have wasted so many hours chasing her, not when he could call in reinforcements to assist in his hunt.

He cursed at his own stupidity. His hatred for her had once again overruled his operational effectiveness. He painfully limped to his car and headed back to the Royal Quays Marina, his seething rage evolving into a cold, determined resolve.

The fresh riverside air of the Royal Quays Marina did little to cleanse the air of gloom and failure from the main cabin of The Odyssey. It smelled of stale coffee, cheap cigarettes, rifle oil, damp clothing, and simmering resentment.

Despite a badly bruised and swollen face, Andriy, the burly pragmatist of the group, was on the secure sat phone provided by MI6, his voice low and furtive, deep in negotiation. Occasionally he would meet the eyes of the other team members, some eager, some hostile. His beating had only served to make him more determined to start a new life away from the madness.

Spread on the polished table in front of him was not a tactical map, but a price list. He was finalising a deal, an illicit and highly profitable side-business selling off a portion of their "official" arsenal. Anti-tank Javelins, a crate of Stinger missiles, assorted Kalashnikovs, grenades, explosives, even a few of the newer FPV drones, all of it eventually destined for the front lines against Russia once their mission was completed, all of it now being quietly diverted for a substantial, off-the-books profit.

"...yes, the price is firm," Andriy growled into the phone. "Delivery to the usual spot. And untraceable unmarked bills, O'Shea. No dye-stained stolen Euros this time."

Olek, the young patriot of the team, stood by the galley, his face a mask of barely controlled fury. He had listened to the entire conversation, his hands shaking with anger as he gripped a mug of cold tea. The weapons they were selling were meant to be killing Russians in the Donbas, not filling the underground arms caches of Irish terrorists.

"This is treason," Olek finally spat, the words low and venomous, as Andriy ended the call. Andriy looked up slowly, his eyes cold and devoid of amusement.

"This is survival, little brother. Langley's money is for the mission. This," he gestured to the invisible profits, "is for our future. You have no idea what it's like to live under Russian glide bombs. This ensures we don't have to go back to be the last Ukrainians dying for NATO in a lost war."

"Better to die a patriot than a traitor." Olek shot back, his hand instinctively moving towards the pistol at his hip.

That was all the invitation Andriy needed. In a movement of shocking speed for a man his size, he drew his own pistol, the heavy Makarov now aimed squarely at Olek's chest. The click of the safety being disengaged was brutally loud in the confined space.

"You have a big mouth for a boy who has never had to pay his own way," Andriy hissed, his voice a low, menacing threat. "You want to be a martyr? Go ahead. But you will not interfere with my business. And if I find out it was YOU who reported me to the Captain, well me and you are going to have a very big problem."

The cabin air seemed to physically simmer with tension. In the comms nook, Dima sighed wearily, turning up the volume on his headphones as if to block out the inevitable. Across the room, Lev, the stoic sniper, who as usual, had been meticulously cleaning his rifle, paused and shook his head slowly. He didn't raise his own weapon, but he slowly and deliberately placed the bolt carrier group back into his rifle with a soft, final "click." It was a quiet, neutral, but deeply ominous gesture. He was ready, but he had not yet chosen a side.

The standoff stretched for another tense second; the two men locked in a deadly stalemate. It was broken by an urgent shout from the deck.

"Stop your noisy bickering, the Captain has returned, he'll be here within minutes!"

The spell shattered. Andriy slowly, reluctantly, lowered his pistol and engaged the safety. Olek, his face still pale with a mixture of rage and fear, took his hand away from his own weapon.

"Hide this or there'll be hell to pay," Andriy grunted, gesturing at the price list on the table. An uneasy, resentful silence settled over the cabin as they hurriedly stowed away the evidence of their illicit business. By the time the cabin door slid open, the scene was one of quiet, if tense, professionalism.

Taras stepped inside and immediately scowled at his team, noticed their furtive and sullen glances, sensed the tension in the air, he didn't have time for this nonsense, he would deal with them later. He had a bigger fish to fry. He was still infuriated he had lost her. He had found The Russian Bitch, only to watch her vanish before his eyes.

He snarled at his radio operator to initiate an encrypted link to his MI6 handler, the operator put down his paperback and pulled on his headset; he spoke a few words then turned back to Taras, a nervous expression on his face:

"London can't respond right now, they are dealing with a crisis."

"Fucking WHAT?" roared Taras, roughly snatching the set from his head, almost breaking the equipment.

"This is Taras, I want to speak to my handler NOW, this is urgent, it is about a Russian asset."

A pause as he listened to the response then flung the headset to the floor in frustration.

"London knows about the Russian, they say they are dealing with it, and we have to wait here for further instructions."

Once again, he paced the cabin like a caged animal. The team looked at each other again, their expressions different, nervous, their previous animosity gone. Their unspoken question seemed to hang in the air: "A Russian asset, in Newcastle?"

They each understood the simple operation they had been assigned to, was now turning into a dangerous and complicated morass of competing factions. They knew where there was one Orc, other, equally dangerous and motivated Orcs were also likely to be. After several hours, the satcom buzzed, London was returning his call.

"About time" he spat into the headset.

"What are you doing about the Russian asset?" he queried, "I witnessed her at the scene of the Thorne killing."

A pause, this was new information to MI6.

"Go on," said the handler.

Taras exhaled, trying to hold his temper at the delay caused by these fools, his voice a low, guttural growl.

"I arrived on site to find Thorne neutralised. Professional execution, three rounds, close quarters. The data was gone. Someone beat us to it."

"Understood," the clipped, British voice replied. "Did you obtain any actionable intelligence regarding a possible perpetrator?"

"I think so, I made a positive ID on a likely suspect the following morning at the crime scene," Taras said. "Female. Russian. Probably the same asset your people have been working on whilst I was being kept out of the loop. I smelled her scent just after Thorne's death, and again at the scene this morning, I managed to get an image and am uploading a photograph now." He transmitted the slightly out of focus image he had captured from the crowd, his finger tapping impatiently on the console as the file transferred. "I have encountered this operative before. Five years ago. Moscow."

He paused, the memory still raw. "The operation at Komsomolskaya Metro. The one that went sideways. My intelligence stated she was GRU then. She is... exceptionally dangerous. I witnessed her neutralise three of my best men in under five seconds. One with a letter opener to the carotid artery, she then took his gun and turned it on the rest of us. I'm telling you she is no standard field agent; she is a Spetsnaz-grade killer." He made sure to emphasise the lethality, the almost inhuman speed he had witnessed.

"We'll run the image against GCHQ and Five Eyes databases to confirm her identity and whether she is the same asset we are dealing with," the handler said, a new note of seriousness in his tone. "Anything else?"

"Yes," Taras said, leaning closer to the microphone then pausing, choosing his words carefully. This was the crucial part, the observation that had been burning in his mind since he left the scene.

"The British asset who took control of the alley. Your man."

"What about him?"

"He knows her," Taras stated, leaving no room for ambiguity. "I observed them. There was an exchange. Non-verbal. Across the police cordon." He painted the picture for the man in London.

"The other onlookers were gawking at the forensic tent trying to grab a glimpse of the body, but he was looking only at her. And she, at him. They exchanged smiles then she gave him a small wave. It was not the gesture of one professional acknowledging another. It was familiar, almost friendly in a strange way, like they were sharing a secret only they were privy to." He paused for a moment, shaking his head slightly, remembering the strange connection. "It seemed... intimate."

He let the silence stretch, allowing the implication to land. "I have been doing this a long time," he continued, his voice hardening. "I know the look of two operatives sizing each other up. This was not that. This was the look of two people who have a history. It was... personal. My assessment is that your man is, at best, aware of her identity and, at worst, in a compromised relationship with her. He is a security risk."

"One more thing," he continued, "His behaviour during his investigation was far too casual, I got the distinct impression that he knew exactly what to expect when he arrived on scene. There was no sign of surprise or revulsion, he looked like he was simply playing the part of an investigator. On its own this might be nothing, but when combined with the communication with the Russian, I believe you have a serious in-house problem to deal with."

Another pause from London, longer this time. Taras could almost hear the gears of bureaucracy grinding; the calculations being made. He knew what he was suggesting was unprecedented, a foreign asset accusing one of their own based on a gut feeling. But his gut had kept him alive from Chechnya to Bakhmut, and he knew exactly what he had seen.

"We have a file on the operative in question, a Declan Shaw," the handler said finally, his voice carefully neutral. "His psychological profile indicates an inability to form close attachments. A lone wolf."

Taras almost laughed in contempt.

"Psychological profiles are written in clean rooms by academics who have never had blood on their hands. I am telling you what I saw in a dirty alley. Your 'lone wolf' has a Russian mate and judging by the way they were looking at each other, I wouldn't be surprised if they were planning on having cubs."

He pressed his advantage. "I need his photo. His location. I need authorisation to put him under surveillance. If he is the key to her, he is the key to the package."

The silence from London was now positively cryogenic. Taras knew he was forcing their hand, presenting them with an intolerable paradox: trust their in-depth psychological profile of their own man or trust the field-honed instincts of their deniable Ukrainian asset.

Finally, the voice returned, clipped and final.

"Your intelligence is noted, Captain. We will process and assess the information you have provided. Under no circumstances are you to approach or engage with either asset. You are directed to remain in place and await further instructions."

Taras was furious and began to object.

"But—"

"Your instructions are clear and not up for discussion, stand by." The line went dead with a dismissive finality.

Taras stood up, his leg aching in protest. He paced the small cabin, a caged animal. They would debate. They would form committees. They would drink their tea and weigh the political risks. And all the while, the bitch and her British lover were out there, in this city, with the schematics to a weapon that could alter the balance of the world.

But the more he thought about it, the more he realised he didn't care about the weapon anymore. He no longer needed to burn an entire city to reach her. Let London and Kiev squabble over their prize. He could and would get to her, through Shaw. He was the only weapon he needed to kill the Russian.

He stared out the porthole at the grey, indifferent water of the marina. London could tell him to wait. But he was already planning the target of his next hunt. The Englishman.

CHAPTER 39

The office on the upper floors of the SIS Building at Vauxhall Cross was a post-modern cube of glass and brushed steel, soundproofed to a level that felt more like a tomb than a room. Outside, the lights of London glittered across the Thames, a serene, postcard-perfect view that bore no resemblance to the ugly business being conducted within.

Elizabeth Bennett, Deputy Head of the Russia Desk, terminated the encrypted audio link, the silence that followed feeling unnaturally heavy. She ran a hand through her impeccably cut hair, her gaze fixed on the dossier glowing on her monitor: SHAW, D. OPERATIVE, SPECIAL PROJECTS. UK Codename: NOMAD. She tapped a stylus against the screen, next to a highlighted paragraph.

"Sir," she said, her voice calm but tight.

Across the minimalist desk, Sir Marcus Cromwell, Head of European Operations, looked up from his own terminal. He was a man who seemed to have been carved from old, unforgiving granite, his face a roadmap of bureaucratic wars fought and won. He didn't speak, merely raised a questioning eyebrow.

"That was our deniable SBU asset in Newcastle. Taras," Bennett began. "He confirms the target, Thorne, has been neutralised. Professional job. Three rounds to the head, close range, no apparent witnesses. This confirms Shaw's own finding from this morning."

Cromwell gave a curt nod.

"Not unexpected given the circumstances, and the package?"

"Gone," Bennett answered. "Taras believes it was lifted immediately at the scene which once again is consistent with Shaw's report. What concerns me is Taras also reports the presence of a Russian asset." She brought up the photo Taras had sent of Anya in the crowd. Says he's encountered her before. Originally GRU but might now be SVR, he thinks. Apparently, she is highly skilled and took out half his team in the botched Moscow job. Her presence here and her murder of Thorne seem to validate that Moscow is desperate to retrieve their stolen data."

Cromwell stared at the image, "Makes sense. Bring up the intelligence we received today".

Another photograph appeared on the screen, a black and white image of an attractive dark-haired woman in SVR uniform. Agent Anastasia Stepnova, unmistakenly the same woman in Taras's image. Cromwell's expression didn't change apart from a subtle narrowing of his eyes.

"A dangerous complication. But a predictable one. The SVR would hardly let a prize like Icarus slip away from their hands without a fight. What else?"

This was the difficult part.

"He reports that our asset, Shaw, was the officer who took control of the scene."

"As we informed him. Why is the fool repeating information we have just provided him with?" Cromwell grunted in exasperation.

"Indeed, sir. But Taras observed something else." Bennett chose her next words with controlled caution. "He described... a connection. Between Shaw and the Russian. Eye contact. A non-verbal exchange. He believes it was more than professional recognition. He is suggesting a pre-existing relationship." She shuffled uncomfortably. "He also suggested that Shaw may have had prior knowledge of the crime scene."

Cromwell was silent for a long moment deep in contemplation.

"Our Ukrainian asset is known to be volatile, his own people have said as much. They also say he is a very good and patriotic soldier but is often driven by emotion rather than operational necessity. Given his history with Stepnova, is his assessment of our own agent reliable?"

"Ordinarily, I would question it," Bennett conceded. "However..." She tapped the screen again. "...Shaw's P-File. The psychological assessment from three years ago, part of his regular review. You'll recall the summary."

Cromwell brought up the report and recited it from the screen, his voice a dry monotone.

"'Subject has an INFJ personality type. He also exhibits symptoms consistent with long-term PTSD, has a pronounced guilt complex, avoidant personality traits. Incapable of forming or maintaining close personal attachments, particularly romantic ones. The man's a bloody walking textbook, but he has never failed to complete a given task, no matter how messy. Which is precisely why we haven't had him carted off to our secure loony bin. A tool that still works, even if a bit worn out, is still a useful tool."

He looked at Bennett.

"So, we have our most reliable psychological profile telling us the man is a functional hermit, and a Ukrainian field asset telling us he's playing footsie with a Russian. Which fiction do we believe?"

"That is the question, Sir," Bennett said. "Taras is a zealot, but he has excellent field instincts. He saw something. What if the psych profile is wrong? What if it's outdated? What if Stepnova is just that good?"

Cromwell leaned back, his chair groaning in protest, a cold, strategic light entering his eyes.

"Or... what if they are both right?"

Bennett looked at him, puzzled.

"We have already decided to give Shaw the directive to neutralise Stepnova, have we not?" Cromwell mused, more to himself than to her. "We have pointed our best hunting dog at their most valuable asset. Now, Taras's report presents us with two possibilities. Scenario one: Shaw is clean. The psych profile holds. In which case, he will carry out his orders and eliminate Stepnova, solving our problem for us. Scenario two: Shaw is compromised. Taras is right, and the man is turned. In that case, he will not carry out his orders. He will try to protect her."

He let the chilling logic hang in the air. "Either way," Cromwell concluded, his voice devoid of all emotion, "the service wins. If he kills her, the threat is removed. If he doesn't, he confirms his own treason, and we have our justification to use a blunter instrument."

Before Cromwell could finish, a junior technician from the monitoring station interjected, his voice tight.

"Sir, you need to see this."

All eyes turned to the main screen.

"Following the Ukrainian's report, we ran a check on Shaw's terminal logs," the technician explained. "He ran a Janus facial recognition query on the day of the Glubina incident, sir. Just hours after the initial flash reports came in. The source was a private photo. He got a positive match with a photo from a Red Square parade, a GRU member, no confirmed ID though. And then, sir... for some reason he deleted the query. Wiped the entire search history."

The technician continued, "This suggests Stepnova may have been targeting Shaw previous to the Glubina incident. He was, after all, the only analyst actively working on Icarus at the time."

A heavy silence fell in the room as the pieces clicked into place with a horrid, logical sense. Of course, the Russians would be desperate to recover their data. And what better way than to send a top-tier operative to target the loneliest, most vulnerable man in the entire UK intelligence community who also happened to be the lead on the project?

Cromwell's closed his eyes in concentration. Had Shaw killed Thorne and deliberately palmed the USB drive off to Stepnova himself? That would explain Taras's observations perfectly. Or did Stepnova do the killing, and Shaw was covering her tracks by obfuscating the evidence trail?

Bennett's face was grim.

"We may have dangerously underestimated Shaw's desire for connection," she said quietly, "and Stepnova's ability to exploit it."

Cromwell stared at the screen, at the two faces, the lonely, haunted analyst and the seemingly cold but attractive Russian.

"Damn the human heart," he muttered.

His voice was now a low, dangerous whisper.

"Can anyone here provide a plausible, innocent explanation as to why Operative Shaw would run this query and then deliberately delete the search history?"

His focused eyes scanned the faces around the table. One by one, all the heads shook in the negative.

"No," Cromwell said, his voice flat. "Me neither. It appears we have a problem with our 'functional hermit'." He then turned his gaze back to Bennett, his decision made. "We'll know soon enough. If he kills her, it's problem solved. If not..."

He let the unspoken question hang in the air. "Whatever the outcome, I think it prudent to let Taras rid us of this turbulent analyst."

"Discreetly, of course. The service doesn't want any public scandal. The press isn't an issue; they'll publish whatever state-approved lie we demand of them. The problem is nowadays; the truth can get halfway around the world before the state-approved lie has even got its trousers on. A citizen journalist with a bloody mobile phone... that's the threat. Sort it, Bennett, and sort it quietly and deniably."

Bennett didn't hesitate, her mind already assembling the pieces.

"We know from our surveillance that at least one of Taras's team has been trying to sell weapons to our Republican friends in Ireland," she said, her voice a model of cold efficiency. "How about if we frame Shaw as the middleman? A traumatised veteran, still riddled with guilt from Belfast, trying to make up for his past by siding with the Irish? He rips off the Ukrainians, and they take their revenge. We can even dump a significant payment into one of his offshore accounts and then 'recover' it later under the Proceeds of Crime Act."

Cromwell looked at her, a look of genuine admiration in his usually expressionless eyes.

"Elegant," he said. "And plausible. Do it. Start collating the 'evidence', in case it goes tits up."

Bennett picked up the receiver for the secure line, despite her own part in the coming charade, it still left an unpleasant taste in her mouth. Shaw for all his flaws had been one of their most effective agents. But the tool was now clearly completely worn out and needed to be replaced. She understood the service's play completely now. It was flawless in its simplicity, and monstrous in its execution.

Cromwell carried on talking.

"Shaw is potentially the greatest point of failure in Operation Spank if he has been turned. At this moment in time, he's either our scalpel or the tumour. And I don't have the luxury of waiting to confirm which is which, not when so many lives are at stake. Taras's final request," he continued, his eyes as cold as the glass of the window. "He wants authorisation to lift Shaw. To 'question' him rather than just eliminate him."

"Sir, we would be sanctioning a foreign national to abduct and interrogate one of our own operatives on British soil, surely this is a job for Hereford," Bennett countered.

Cromwell cut her off, his voice hard.

"Taras is deniable. A raid on Shaw's flat would be too messy, too noisy. Questions would be asked. And Shaw himself would probably leave a couple of widows and fatherless children behind if we played this the wrong way. The last thing we need is next of kin asking awkward questions. This needs to be done discreetly. We need him isolated, clean and quiet. We need him in a box before he and Stepnova vanish into the aether."

He held Bennett's gaze, mutual understanding passing between them.

"Forget waiting for Shaw to kill Stepnova, Make the call, Elizabeth, have him lifted."

Bennett picked up the receiver for the secure line. She hesitated for a moment as another pang of conscience surfaced then buried it back down and gave the authorisation to her own handler, who would relay the instructions to the man waiting on the yacht. Her orders would be explicit and utterly deniable.

CHAPTER 40

Taras stared at the secure terminal, the screen now dark, his own grim reflection staring back at him. He had reported in. He had sent the photograph of the woman. And now, he was waiting. The response from his MI6 handler had been clipped, professional, and infuriatingly non-committal, dismissive even.

"Stand by."

The two words echoed in the silence, mocking him. He slammed his fist down on the table, making the equipment on it jump.

"Stand by?" he roared to the crowded cabin. Across the room, Andriy, who had been counting stacks of sterling with a focused intensity, looked up, his expression wary. In the comms nook, Dima flinched almost imperceptibly. Even Lev, the stoic sniper, paused in the constant cleaning of his rifle, his gaze flicking towards his new commander.

Taras began to pace, his limp more pronounced, a caged tiger in the cramped space.

"They sit in their clean offices in London, drinking their tea, and they tell me to 'stand by'," he snarled, spitting the English words out like a curse. "I deliver them the body of the American traitor. I deliver them the face of The Russian Bitch who killed him, and they tell me to wait."

"They have procedures, Captain," Andriy offered, his voice cautious but resentful. He was a businessman now, and this outburst was bad for business. "They need to verify your intel."

Taras spun on him, his eyes blazing with a wild, fanatical light that unsettled the pragmatic gangster.

"Verify? I verified it! With my own eyes! I know her." He unconsciously rubbed the scarred thigh of his leg. "And I know the Englishman. Saw the way he looked at her with his fucking doe eyes. He is compromised, he is the key, I know it."

He stopped pacing and leaned over the table. His voice dropped, becoming a low, determined hiss that was somehow more frightening than his usual rage-fuelled outbursts.

"The mission has changed," he said, his gaze sweeping over his men. "London thinks this is about a weapon. They are fools. This is about a cancer. A Russian cancer, which has infected a British host."

He straightened up, a cruelly satisfied smile twisting his lips.

"The plan was to get the data from the American. That is now a secondary concern. Our new target is the Englishman. Shaw. Then, through him, The Russian Bitch."

Olek, the young patriot, who had been listening from the doorway, stepped forward.

"Captain, our orders were to acquire the package for Kyiv."

"Our orders are what I say they are!" Taras snapped, his obsession overriding his discipline. "I don't need London's permission to hunt a traitor. We will take him, we will question him, and if he gives the wrong answers, we will kill him."

His men eyed each other nervously. To neutralise a Russian asset was one thing, but to kidnap and torture a British agent without sanction was likely to get them all killed. But who among them was willing to stand up to the force of nature that Taras was becoming?

The annoying buzz of the secure comms unit cut through the tension.

Every head snapped towards the terminal. Dima sighed wearily, reluctantly put down his paperback copy of Moby Dick and answered it, listened for a moment, then looked at Taras.

"It's London. For you, Captain."

Taras limped to the terminal, his composure returning as he slipped on the mask of the professional operator. He picked up the handset.

"This is Taras."

He listened, his expression unreadable. The silence in the cabin was absolute. His men watched, holding their breath. He was silent for a long moment, then gave a single, curt nod. He terminated the call and stood for a moment, his back to the room. When he turned, the wild, unhinged light was gone from his eyes, replaced by an icy focus. A slow, satisfied smile spread across his face.

His men, visibly relaxed at his changed demeanour, it was clear they were off the hook, it appeared their MI6 handlers had authorised the lifting of one of their own after all. All except Dima who shook his head in disbelief, this operation was getting more complicated by the day, and if the Brits were ruthless enough to willingly sacrifice one of their own to torture and death, he began to wonder what would become of him and the team when this was all over.

"It seems the fools in London, and I are in agreement after all," he said, his voice a low purr of triumph. He looked at Olek, then at the rest of his team.

"Here are your instructions," he began, his voice dropping to a conspiratorial whisper as he passed on the MI6 instructions. "Do not deviate from them. We are coordinating with London and need this quick, clean, precise and quiet." He paused, letting the weight of the command settle on them. "Get some rest. We have an early start tomorrow morning."

CHAPTER 41

Anya sighed heavily as she sat at the desk in the safehouse, a growing awareness settling in that the place now felt anything but safe. Her tired face was illuminated by the cold, blue light of the secure terminal as she put the final touches onto the report, which was more like an epitaph to mission failure than an intelligence product.

The document was a detailed account of her unsuccessful attempt to obtain the Icarus USB, an admission that her carefully constructed legend of "Eleanor Vane" was now irretrievably compromised, and a new, worrying addendum about the crime scene. She detailed the incident with the unknown actor, the man whose eyes had held not professional interest, but a raw and violent intent that seemed to border on the personal.

Her instincts, honed by years of training and the harsh lessons of the Moscow Metro, were sending her a clear, insistent signal: something was wrong with the mission, badly wrong.

The most glaring anomaly was Cuckoo. Shaw. Why didn't he have her arrested at the crime scene? All it would have taken was one shout, and she would have been surrounded by policemen. It would have been simple for him to alert them, to have her lifted and bagged, then disappeared into one of their black sites for interrogation and a burial at sea. It was their standard operational protocol.

And yet, he had just looked at her. He had met her gaze across the cordon, no hostility, no anger, just something... intangible. She herself had felt something pass between them. He knew she was an adversary, and yet, in his own way, he seemed to be protecting her.

She thought of his file, his small acts of kindness at the fish quay, then the brutal efficiency with which he had dispatched Thorne.

"What are you up to, Kukushka? What game are you playing?" she thought, utterly conflicted.

Declan Shaw's public persona was that of a weary, cynical, but brilliant analyst. Yet in their interactions, she had sensed a current of something else, a guarded warmth, a shared understanding of the world's absurdities. He was a puzzle, and her training told her that unexplained puzzles in the field were potential liabilities.

The most significant development was a chilling piece of intelligence from Viktor, her support operative. He had detected a high-priority query on her "Eleanor Vane" legend originating from within the British intelligence network, specifically from Shaw's outstation. It had been cross-referenced with open-source imagery from Moscow. The time stamp on the query was damning. He had known about her since their night in the bar, she realised. But how? Then she remembered, the call, her slip when she'd sworn in Russian, but Declan hadn't missed a beat when she made her excuses and left.

He had definitely known who she was when they met in the Tyne Bar. Which made her even more puzzled as to why he chose not to exploit her moment of vulnerability. He had certainly known when he kissed her in the alley, although she thought wryly, her gun in his ribs was probably a bit of a clue.

The walking conundrum which was Declan Shaw was growing increasingly complex and enigmatic by the second.

Despite her determination to solve the puzzle, she knew what protocol demanded. An agent whose cover is compromised, especially during a mission of this magnitude, must request immediate extraction. To remain in place was to risk not only her own life but the entire operation. And yet, part of her, knew she was going to miss him. It was a strange sensation to think of herself back in Moscow, with no more chances to meet her smiling, charming and utterly infuriating adversary.

On the surface she was convincing herself it was just the excitement of the challenge of battling such a worthy and tricky opponent, but somewhere deep inside her, behind the Eleanor Vane facade, she knew it was his ability to make her laugh when she was with him.

Then there was the painful sadness she had not quite successfully buried, which seemed to simply evaporate in his presence. It was unexpected, unsettling, and very addictive.

She steeled herself and initiated the encrypted video link. Handler Prime's face appeared on screen, his expression as impassive as ever.

"Agent Stepnova," he began. "Your report?"

"Has just been filed, Comrade, you should have access to it now." she said, her voice clipped and professional. Prime looked at his terminal and gave a slight nod of confirmation. "But there is a more urgent matter. We have reason to believe my operational cover has been compromised. The target, Kukushka, has identified me as a Russian intelligence officer."

She laid out the evidence calmly and precisely: the timing of her arrival, the Janus search query, the alley incident, the open hostility of the stranger at the crime scene, a stranger who bore all the hallmarks of a fellow intelligence professional.

"Given the circumstances," she concluded, "and the critical nature of the Icarus data, I am formally requesting immediate priority extraction from the UK." She expected a swift, affirmative response. It was the only logical, professional course of action.

Handler Prime was silent for a long moment, his eyes unblinking. The silence stretched, thick with an unspoken weight. When he finally spoke, his voice was flat, devoid of any emotion.

"Your request for immediate extraction is denied, Agent Stepnova."

Anya blanched, not through fear, but disbelief. "Comrade, with respect, to remain in situ is an unacceptable risk. If Shaw knows who I am, he will be hunting me. The entire Five Eyes network will be hunting me; it renders me a dangerous liability to the entire operation."

"Your assessment of the risk is noted," Handler Prime said, his voice unchanging. "However, your orders stand. Your priority remains the location and recovery of the Icarus package. The means by which you achieve this are at your discretion, but your mission has not changed. You are to proceed as previously directed." He glared at her directly through the screen, his face uncompromising. "And if this Shaw, this Cuckoo does come hunting you, I do not need to spell out what your options are, but be in no doubt, you are still expected to use all means necessary to achieve your assigned objective, lethal force is authorised... and expected".

"But..." She interjected.

"There is nothing further to discuss, Agent," he interrupted, his tone carrying a chilling finality. "Moscow has full confidence in your abilities to contain the situation. You know your duty, do not disappoint us."

The screen went blank.

Anya stared at the dead terminal dumbfounded. It had been a logical decision in using her to trap Shaw. But now she was clearly a dangerous threat to her own mission, the decision not to extract made absolutely no operational sense. It was almost as if they wanted her dead. A horrifying thought came to her mind, what if Handler Prime was a double agent, maybe it was him who ensured Shaw got the Janus match. She shook her head; she was getting paranoid.

She stood up and walked out of the briefing room. She may be paranoid, but she knew from the crime scene that at least one bastard really was out to get her. She needed her weapon.

She thought of Declan Shaw, her assigned target, the haunted but kind man with the honest eyes. She thought of the lies she had told him. She thought with a sickening realisation of what it would feel like to point a gun at him, not to rob him, but to end him. A shiver ran down her spine.

On the far wall was the plain-looking door of the safehouse's armoury. She confidently placed her key card against the lock.

Access Denied. A small red light blinked once.

She frowned. A glitch, perhaps. She swiped the card again, this time with more force, a flicker of frustration crossing her features.

Access Denied. The red light blinked again, mocking her.

Her frustration began to curdle into a cold, dawning suspicion. She placed her eye against the retinal scanner, the last and highest level of security. She waited, her heart beginning to pound a slow, heavy rhythm against her ribs. For a moment, nothing. Then the same, final, blinking red light.

Access Denied.

She saw the truth then, with a devastating clarity. This wasn't a glitch. This was by design. This wasn't logical. They weren't using her as bait to trap a compromised agent. They were simply sacrificing her. They had stripped her of her tools, leaving her exposed and defenceless, a cold fury now replacing all other emotion. She turned slowly to face Viktor, her support operative, who was watching her from the kitchen.

"My access has been revoked," she stated almost matter of factly.

He just shrugged apologetically, a hint of something that might have been sympathy in his eyes.

"I'm sorry, Agent Stepnova," he reluctantly stated, sounding uncharacteristically embarrassed. "Orders from the highest level I'm afraid." He paused, as if reluctant to pass on the final instruction. "Moscow advises you to use your other weapons on Shaw."

The words wounded Anya far more deeply than any bullet ever could. They were not just sacrificing her; they were degrading her, reducing her from a soldier to a Red Sparrow in a single, chilling sentence.

This was the final confirmation that the service had indeed betrayed her; she slumped down onto a nearby chair trying to process what just happened. She had dedicated her life to them, would have gladly died for her country, and now she was being thrown to the wolves, to face torture and death at the hands of an enemy. The enormity of it was simply staggering.

And in that moment a face appeared in her mind's eye, Declan Shaw, an operative who had known her secret for days and had still chosen to show her mercy. Her supposed enemy had shown her far more respect and compassion than her own side. She realised, with a sudden, terrifying clarity, that she was trapped on a chessboard where she no longer understood the rules of the game and where every other piece on the board was a dangerous unknown.

She didn't say a word. She simply stood up and turned back towards Viktor who was finding it difficult to look in her eyes, and was clearly deeply uncomfortable with his orders, then he made a decision.

"Prime said not to give you access to the armoury, he never said anything about other equipment."

He fished in his pocket and brought out two objects, a beautifully ornate tie pin and a small black device.

"The tie pin is a tracker; it is made in the fashion of a firebird feather and is a symbol of good fortune, the receiver plugs directly into the charging port of your mobile phone. I know it isn't much, but it may be of use to you."

She was still furious at Moscow but could see the conflict and regret in Viktor's eyes, he was risking censure or worse by giving her this equipment.

She pecked him on the cheek in understanding.

"Thank you, Viktor."

He nodded slightly in acknowledgement and said simply.

"Good luck Agent Stepnova."

She then left the safehouse, out into the pouring rain. She walked blindly towards the river, tossing her SVR-issued phone into the churning water. Still angry, she pulled out the decrypt device for the Icarus data and examined it thoughtfully. She had palmed it from the terminal when control had so brusquely terminated the call. She smiled slightly at the theft; she had learned at least one lesson from Shaw.

She had some leverage now, but had been cast adrift, and it was likely she was already being hunted. Where could she go, who could she trust, how the hell was she going to extricate herself from this unholy mess?

As she stared into the river, the answer became obvious. There was only one logical choice, both professionally, and, she finally admitted to herself, personally. He was her target, her mission, her supposed enemy. The man who knew the truth and had shown her decency. And the only person in the world who she might be able to trust. And who knows? Maybe she would even be able to steal the genuine data package from him this time?

CHAPTER 42

As Taras began his sweep of the city centre, Declan was driving back to the 'Happy House' from the alley off Northumberland Street, the images of Thorne's body and Anastasia's fleeting, strangely friendly presence in the crowd burned into his mind. He parked the car and made his way up to the top floor office, the weight of recent events pressing down on him.

He bypassed his own desk, heading straight for Norman's always cluttered domain. He felt the weight of the real Icarus USB in his coat pocket, relieved that he'd had the foresight to retain it rather than hand it over to Walsh via Danny. . The 'Magic' wasn't just about connecting disparate data points: it was about recognising the moments when holding a card back was the only move that mattered. He knew, with a certainty he couldn't explain, that giving this up would be a fatal mistake. It was the only genuine leverage he had against the leash.

"Back from playing Inspector Clouseau then, mate?" Norman asked, looking up from his paperwork.

"Just finished at the alley, confirmed a dead NSA contractor, it's a complete mystery as to who slotted him" Declan replied wearily.

"So the gun worked well then"? Asked Norm, letting Declan know he knew.

"That's one hell of an assumption Norm; I find myself upset and frankly wounded that you would be so suspicious towards your dearest friend."

As he spoke, he pulled the gun out of his shoulder holster, flicked open the cylinder and emptied the weapon into Norms in tray, three empty cases and three live rounds rolled across it.

He looked at Declan chuckling,

"Mate you grab an off the books gat and the very next day a dead American turns up? I don't need to be Hercules Porridge to work that one out"

Declan smiled back, that was the problem with Norm, he was a lot sharper than he pretended to be.

Norm looked at the brass in his in tray and continued, "Let me guess? Three rounds somewhere vital, from behind, and the inquest will rule it suicide"?

"Something like that I expect" Replied Declan, "Talking of which, I need a favour"

He reached into the hidden inner pocket of his coat and fished out the Quantum-encrypted USB drive. The real one. Although physically identical, it felt different from the decoy, heavier, colder, imbued with the weight of the secrets it held.

"Norm," he said, his voice low. He pressed it into his friend's hand. "Put that into the safe, mate. Highest security. My eyes only unless... well, you know the score. If I don't come back for it, give it to Phillips."

Norman's usual grin vanished, replaced by a sober understanding. He nodded, taking the drive without another word and disappearing into the secure vault. He returned a moment later, his professional mask gone, replaced by his usual cheer.

"Right then," he said, settling back into his chair and launching into a detailed, and entirely unsolicited, critique of Newcastle United's recent Champions League campaign.

Declan let him talk, the familiar, mundane conversation a welcome distraction. For a full fifteen minutes, Norman held court on tactics, the injustice of the PSG penalty, and a lengthy, passionate account of his own trip to see the lads play in Milan.

"...and it was a beautiful place, Declan. Truly," Norman was saying, leaning forward with a conspiratorial grin. "The food was class, the beer was class, and best of all..." He paused for dramatic effect. "Not a single red and white shirt in sight. Proves the chant is true, doesn't it?"

Declan chuckled, anticipating the coming joke.

"And what chant is that, Norm?"

Norman beamed.

"You'll never see a Mackem in Milan.' And that's why," he finished, tapping the side of his nose sagely, "if you ever do see a Mackem there, he's probably a Russian spy."

Declan laughed, Norm had probably been waiting all day to tell him that one.

"I'll keep an eye out next time I'm in Italy," he replied, playing along with him.

Norman nodded, satisfied, then his expression changed, as if suddenly remembering something.

"Oh, almost forgot. Laughing boy has been trying to contact you. Urgent briefing."

Declan felt a familiar sinking feeling in his stomach.

"Right. When does it start?"

Norman glanced at the clock on the wall, his eyes twinkling.

"Oh, about ten minutes ago."

"WTF, Norm? You couldn't have told me this fifteen minutes ago?"

Norman boomed with laughter.

"Where would the fun have been in that?"

Declan hurried down the corridor towards the main conference room, calling back to his still laughing friend,

"And now I'm in the shit!"

Norman shouted after him,

"You're ALWAYS in the shit, Declan! "It's just the depth that varies!"

They both answered the last part of the truism. Declan made his way to the briefing room, giving his best dirty look to the still laughing Norm, who was busying himself inspecting the revolver, an expression of satisfaction on his face. Declan wasn't quite sure it was because the gun had worked, or because Norm had deliberately made him late.

Declan slipped into the packed briefing room as discreetly as possible and had hoped to go unnoticed, but Phillips was waiting for him near the door, a shark sensing blood in the water.

"Awww, Shaw," Phillips drawled, his sarcasm thick enough to cut. "How very kind of you to join us. Hope we aren't dragging you away from anything important?"

Declan met his gaze, his own expression deadpan. "Oh, nothing of any real importance, Sir," he replied, his voice flat. "Just the murder of an NSA asset on our patch," he added, letting his sarcasm land with a heavy thud.

Phillips bristled but gestured towards the main screen, where the Five Eyes representatives were patched in. An MI6 analyst from the Russia desk was concluding a briefing, the slides on the screen a depressing summary of Declan's own off-book work from the past few months.

"...and in summary," the analyst was saying, "our assessment, based largely on the excellent digging by Special Projects, is that Project Icarus, codenamed 'Orpheus', is a viable, autonomous, deep-earth-penetrating magnetic plasma munition. The Russians have solved the thermal regulation issue. The only piece of the puzzle that remains elusive is a recurring file reference: 'Chudes data'. The direct translation is 'miracle data', but its strategic significance is, as yet, unknown." The analyst faded, and the sharp-eyed MI6 liaison, Bennett, took over the screen.

Phillips leaned in close to Declan, his voice a low, condescending hiss.

"Good work, Shaw. Pity Thorne got away from you though, most unprofessional." He paused, his tone turning menacingly conversational. "London is... displeased to say the least. You know how things are these days with the blame culture. Be a real shame if some old file from Op Banner were to suddenly become... active again and inadvertently end up on the desk of some tank chasing human rights lawyer." Phillips paused, savouring the moment. "But I have some good news for you Shaw, we have one more job for you, just one. You do this one for us and I guarantee you The Banner file will fall off the face of the planet, and that resignation? You get to submit it again, and this time, I promise you I will accept it."

The lie was so blatant that it confirmed everything to Declan. This wasn't just Phillips dangling the leash with a promise of release. This was a coordinated play. Langley had offered to burn the self-same file, and now, not twenty-four hours later, MI6 was using it as a cudgel. Neither side knew that both were making the same false pledges, but Declan realised he would never be free of them, not as long as he was able to pull a trigger. When he wasn't able, he had little doubt a trigger would be pulled on him. He simply knew too much and was already considered a loose cannon.

On screen, Bennett's voice cut through his simmering anger, sharp and precise.

"Update from GCHQ," she announced. "The search has been... problematic. There have been intermittent CCTV blackouts across the city centre network, "teething troubles" with the new Sejanus system deployment, apparently." She said the words with a clear note of professional disdain. "However, we managed to pull one usable image from a private camera near the alley."

The main screen behind Bennett changed. It now showed a grainy, time-stamped CCTV clip. A figure emerged from the shadows, a woman in a dark raincoat. She glanced over her shoulder, her face partially obscured, but the troublesome smile was obvious. The image flickered, freezing and enhancing on her features. It was her. It was Anya.

Declan almost gasped in surprise, his mind racing.

"Shit!"

Despite the CCTV blackouts courtesy of the CIA Declan suspected , how come this one image been isolated? And how come the same camera hadn't picked up him or Thorne?

He thought of Langley. Of course they would have scrubbed the feed to hide their own involvement. Danny had oversight of the new system deployment; it would have been simple for him to create a digital blind spot. Occam's razor suggested the simplest explanation was the most likely: Danny had been in on Walsh's play from the start, providing digital overwatch for the assassination.

But that didn't fit. If Langley had visibility of the scene, Anya's presence in the same alley at the same time should have set off every alarm bell in Fort Meade. Unless... unless Langley didn't have visibility. But if not them, who? Who was powerful enough to blind the Sejanus network and what kind of malware could slip through the onion layers of cyber defences so effortlessly?

The same people powerful enough to scrub Anya from the entire internet except for one single image?

A theory was beginning to form, a disturbing pattern he couldn't yet prove. But he needed more data, and ever since that night in Washington, his intuition felt... blunted. The thousands of disparate pictures and data points that usually swirled in his head, forming patterns, were fading. They were being replaced by one picture in particular: her face, smiling at him across a table. She was muddying his thoughts.

"That's what she's trained to do, you idiot," his "shadow", the cold, professional part of his mind, hissed at him. But another part, the part that remembered her fart jokes and laughter, remained deeply, dangerously confused.

"The Target for today" Bennett continued, her voice pulling him back to the grim reality on the screen. "Is believed to be formerly GRU, now assessed as a senior operative with the SVR. She is considered highly skilled and extremely dangerous. As of 0800 hours, Operation Portcullis has been initiated."

Bennett's gaze seemed to sweep across the call. "The objective is twofold. First, to locate and recover the Icarus data. Second, to neutralise the primary suspect. All UK ports and airports are closed and at heightened alert. The Sejanus network is actively scanning. We are using every resource to find her, so our fist," she paused, her eyes finding Declan's, "can deliver the killing punch. A new operational directive flashed onto the screen:

RECOVER ORPHEUS DATA & DECRYPT KEY. NEUTRALISE PRIMARY SUSPECT.

This was it. A kill order. Phillips's lips curled into a thin, cruel smile.

"It could get messy, Shaw. Very messy," he whispered, savouring the moment. "But that makes it a perfect job for a man with your unique skill sets, doesn't it? Cleaning up the messes no one else wants to touch. Our little janitor, our very own grim reaper...Apollo's fist. We wind you up like a clockwork toy and off you go, just one more job though Shaw, one last job and you are free as a bird."

Declan bristled at the use of his informal nicknames, Janitor was bad enough, but to have Phillips sycophants describing him as the grim reaper genuinely pissed him off. One wag had persuaded the DJ to play "Don't fear the reaper" when he had entered the office Christmas Party. Hilarious they thought. It had certainly been hilarious when he accidentally fell down a flight of stairs a few hours later. People will get dangerously drunk at Christmas functions Declan smirked.

Bennett spoke to the audio-visual technician, clearly irritated,

"Bring up her image".

As she spoke, the primary suspect's profile appeared on the main screen behind Bennett.

Naturally it was Anya.

She continued:

"This is Agent Anastasia Stepnova, and she is now the service's top priority target. Law enforcement has been informed she is a suspect in the murder of Thorne, and if they do somehow manage to lift her alive, we will be sending a bag team to take her into custody. The quick reaction force will deploy by helicopter to extract her, and Stepnova's immediate rendition to South Uist for debriefing has been authorised."

She turned to the technician and whispered another request, then returned to address the briefing room. "However, her capture is considered a secondary priority: data first, neutralisation second, and capture a very distant third. She is known to have left a trail of bodies behind her in Ukraine, including at least one of ours. She clearly represents an unacceptable risk to our retrieval team. Therefore, I am also authorising the suspension of standard rules of engagement. I want Stepnova neutralised with extreme prejudice."

A high-resolution photograph, likely from her "Eleanor Vane" legend, stared out at the room. Her eyes, intelligent and watchful, seemed to be looking directly at him. Declan's smirk had vanished the instant her image was displayed, and he felt the blood drain from his face.

Phillips noticed his change instantly—the flicker of shock, the sudden pallor. He misinterpreted Declan's personal horror as professional weakness, a sudden attack of conscience. A thin, cruel smile touched his lips as he moved in for the kill.

"Not getting squeamish, are we, Shaw?" he sneered, his voice dripping with disdain. He leaned in even closer, twisting the knife.

"It's not like you haven't killed a girl before, is it?"

CHAPTER 43

The connection to the Five Eyes conference call severed, but the images remained burned onto Declan's retina: Anya's face, tagged as a target, and the sight of the thin, cruel smile on Phillips's lips as he twisted the knife.

"It's not like you haven't killed a girl before, is it?"

He walked out of the conference room, Phillips's calculating taunt still ringing in his ears as he fought to restrain the cold fury welling within him. The corridor felt unnaturally long, the walls seeming to close in. He didn't go to his desk. He didn't go for coffee. He walked with a heavy, deliberate tread to the end of the hall, to the one place in the building that felt like a refuge in the madhouse that was the Happy House.

Declan angrily pushed open the door to Norman's office. Norman was busy at his workbench, meticulously cleaning the silenced revolver Declan had used to kill Thorne. He looked up, his satisfied expression fading instantly when he saw the look on Declan's face. The professional in him took over.

"Phillips?" Norm asked expectantly, his voice low.

Declan nodded and sank into the visitor's chair, mentally drained. He ran a hand over his face.

"Not just Phillips, the whole fucking service. They've put a burn notice out," he said, his voice soft, barely audible. "On the Russian asset. Stepnova."

Norman set his tools down carefully. He knew exactly what a "burn notice" meant in their line of work.

"Orders from London?"

"And Langley," Declan confirmed, the bitterness sharp in his voice. "A joint directive. They want her neutralised. And they've made it... my tasking." He looked up at his friend, his eyes filled with a deep, haunted conflict. "I'm not sure if I can do this one, Norm."

Norman was silent for a long moment, his gaze steady on his friend. He didn't need to ask why Declan was hesitating. He'd seen the ghost in Declan's eyes for thirty years.

"You say that about them all, but this one's different, isn't it? I know you've been seeing her."

Declan started.

"Have you been spying on me? Have THEY been spying on me?"

Norm shook his head sadly and looked at his friend.

"Mate, I've known you for over thirty years. You don't think I've seen the difference in you recently? There have been times when you've been acting completely out of character, almost like a well-rounded human being at times. And the aftershave and the deodorant on your way out of the door? You must think I'm blind, Pugh."

He placed the now clean pistol back on the bench.

"This isn't just a professional relationship, is it? There's more going on than you care to admit, even to me?"

Declan nodded.

"As I said, Norm, I'm really not sure if I can do this job anymore. I'm sick of it—the lies, the killing, the bullshit. I've had it up to here with everything."

Norm continued to look at his friend, seeing the conflict etched on his face, the Janitor warring with the man.

"Oh, we both know you CAN do it," Norman replied, his voice low and sympathetic. "The actual question is, WILL you do it?"

Declan couldn't meet his eyes. He just stared at the scarred surface of the workbench.

"I don't know, Norm," he said, the words barely audible. "I genuinely don't know if I can carry out this tasking. But you know the worst part is? Not the fact that they have lied to me about it being that one last job I've been praying for. The worst part is the fact I'm even tempted by the lie, hoping it might be true. What does that make me, Norm? What does that say about me?"

Norman sighed deeply and with feeling, uncertain how to best help his friend who appeared even more troubled than he usually did.

He knew what it would cost Declan if he refused, but he also knew the cost if his friend complied would be far higher. Belfast had almost destroyed him; he would never forget the look on his friends face in the rear-view mirror.

Because of that memory, he seriously doubted his friend was capable of shooting another woman, even a Russian asset. He'd seen her face on the alert that had just come through on his own terminal, a very attractive face. A face containing an expression which was strangely reminiscent of Declan himself. Norm knew what the sharing of the image to all hands meant, It meant a service-wide hunt was on. Even if Declan refused, there were plenty out there who would do it for the kudos and would happily celebrate a "fucking textbook" kill. But not his friend. And not himself.

He stood up and opened his secure locker.

"Sorry I can't offer you a standard automatic," Norman said, his tone practical. "Everything else here is on the books, which means a full audit trail. Phillips had them all covertly fitted with trackers last month. But I do have a couple of options..."

He first took out a compact MP5 submachine gun, its metal gleaming dully under the armoury lights. "This one's mine, not tracked. I acquired it using Helen's black budget. It's on the miscellaneous stores account as cleaning materials."

Declan smiled at Norms little in joke against Phillips: cleaning materials for the janitor. He looked at the weapon but shook his head.

"Not discreet enough for what I have in mind. You keep it, mate, he said, his voice low. "You might need it if I have to call in the cavalry."

Norman's eyes met his, a silent, grim understanding passing between them. He nodded once, placing the MP5 carefully back in its rack. He then picked up the clean, but still ugly, silenced revolver from the bench.

"This bastard again then," Norman said, placing it on a clean cloth on the bench. "Nine rounds through it. I've given it a clean because I'm good like that." His tone was practical, shifting to the familiar ground of logistics.

"The baffles in the suppressor will be getting worn. Bad news is, it's going to get louder. Each shot degrades the packing. The good news?" He looked at Declan, a grim smile touching his lips. "You'll get better stopping power, more range, more accuracy."

He pushed the revolver and a fresh box of .38 subsonic rounds across the bench to Declan.

"You'll need this, then," he said. "You know this is a one-way rabbit hole you're climbing into, mate, if you don't carry out orders. They won't take kindly to this particular example of your insubordination. So watch your back. Laughing boy would love to stick the knife into it."

"I appreciate the revolver, mate," Declan said, his voice hard with resolve. "I'm not actually planning to get into any firefights, but it's a good plan B if I decide I'd rather not be a janitor anymore. "

He took the revolver, the weight of it a heavy, cold reality in his hand. He left Norman's office and walked back to his desk, his mind racing. He was now a traitor, at least on paper and was simply going through the motions to buy time. He was stopped by a figure stepping into his path. It was Danny, the CIA liaison, his face pale with guilt.

"Declan, man... about what Walsh did, the Belfast thing" Danny stammered. "I had no idea. I just..."

Declan looked at him, his own face a cold, hard mask. "What the fuck, Danny?" His voice was low, devoid of heat, but filled with the chilling finality of the INFJ door slam. He pushed past him and walked to his desk as Danny watched him, his expression wracked with guilt.

Declan sat down, and sighed deeply, rubbing his tired eyes, the Happy House now feeling more like a prison than usual. He was alone, bathed in the cold, pale light of his monitor. On the screen, the face of Agent Anastasia Stepnova stared back at him, through the cold, professional eyes of an operative, the eyes of a killer.

"Like looking in a fucking mirror." he thought to himself. If the shoe was on the other foot Stepnova wouldn't hesitate to kill him, except.... she had, not only hesitated but had even gave her name, her real name.

"Anya" he whispered under his breath as he studied the image.

The P-File from the mysterious MI6 asset 'Argus' had arrived as a flash message, blinking urgently on his screen and was open before him. He was also sifting through the supplementary intelligence fragments which had arrived from the same mysterious source.

One phrase stood out, a file header referenced in the technical data: Chudes Data. That accursed file which seemed to be plaguing his with its meaning and its emptiness. Like an itch he couldn't scratch.

He stared at the screen, the initial translation stark and simple: "Miracles Data." It felt like a sarcastic joke. But what was the miracle? He ran various possibilities through his mind.

Was it the coolant technology? The targeting system? The artificial intelligence? The other codenames, Icarus, Orpheus, were all rooted in Greek legends. He hadn't heard of "Chudes" in any Greek myth.

The disconnect nagged at him. He blamed Anya and her strange effect on him for his inability to join the dots. Why was it that the enigmatic Russian was able to dull his....Russian! He almost face palmed himself.

Then the answer, so blindingly obvious it had initially eluded him, hit him like a thunderclap. It wasn't based on Greek legend at all. Anya had just given him the answer. For once the Anya effect had worked in his favour.

He swore in annoyance at his own stupidity and opened a new search window and typed in the name as a reference to Russian folklore.

And then he found it.

The Chudes. A lost tribe who, according to legend, refused to be conquered. They dug vast pits, built shelters inside, and then, as their enemies approached, they knocked out the supports and buried themselves alive rather than submit. He felt a chill in his soul which had little to do with the approach of the northern winter.

It wasn't about miracles. It was about graves, mass graves, on a global scale. The Orpheus weapon wasn't a sword; it was a spade. It was a promise that if the West ever tried to conquer Russia, Russia would turn the world's command bunkers into modern-day Chud-graves. The Chudes Data wasn't just a targeting file; it was a suicide note written for the whole of humanity.

He was still processing the horrifying implications of it all when a shadow fell over his desk. He looked up. It was Danny, holding out a steaming mug of coffee. A peace offering.

"Look, man," Danny said, his voice low and sincere. "I know I screwed up. I was a dupe. Walsh played both of us. But I feel responsible for allowing him to. I want to make it right. Anything you need, anything at all, you got it."

Declan studied his face. He saw no deception, only genuine remorse. He took the coffee. He had an idea, a wild, dangerous long shot, but it was all he had.

"The data package," Declan lied, keeping his voice quiet. "The only person who knows where it is, is Stepnova. If London gets to her before I do, if she's taken out or 'disappears,' then the Orpheus data probably disappears with her. Permanently."

Danny nodded, following the logic. "So, we lose our only lead."

"Exactly," Declan said. "I think I might be able to get it. Recover the package. But to do that, I need to get to her first. And I can't do that if every Five Eyes asset in the country is hunting her."

He looked directly at Danny.

"You have administrator oversight on the Sejanus CCTV network, right? You're providing overwatch on the deployment of the new system?

A slow understanding dawned on Danny's face.

Declan continued, sensing that he was getting through to Dannys better nature. "Remember when you first arrived, when we worked together until you settled in"? Declan took a sip of coffee, holding his friends gaze, "Remember what you said to me back then?

Danny nodded silently then answered,

"That you were the only real analyst in this lunatic asylum".

"I need you to remember why you said that. I need you to trust me to do my job, I need the Sejanus cameras and any networked drones to become... myopic," Declan answered. "When it comes to Anya....I mean Stepnova, I need her to become invisible. Can you do that?"

Danny was silent for a moment, the weight of what Declan was asking settling on him. He hadn't missed Declan's slip of using her first name, but he trusted his friend, more importantly he'd seen what his intuition had brought to the table on more than one occasion, occasions that Langley had been very grateful for, although that hadn't stopped them tugging on Declan's leash he thought bitterly.

He was being asked to actively obstruct a priority Five Eyes intelligence operation. It was treasonous. But he looked at the hard, determined set of Declan's jaw, and he remembered the shame he felt at being used by his own superiors. He gave a slight, almost imperceptible nod.

"That's easy," Danny said, his voice a conspiratorial whisper. "Corrupting a few data feeds, creating some 'technical glitches' in the facial recognition software... it's just a few lines of code. Leave it with me, your target will be lost in the systems teething troubles."

He turned to leave, then paused,

"I can only give you 48 hours max buddy, after that there's a diagnostic scheduled because of all the recent blackouts and I'll have to rectify the "glitch" to cover my own tracks. You'll also have to be aware of all the Mark 1 eyeballs out there; there are going to be a lot of deeply unpleasant men itching to bag themselves a Russian".

Declan nodded, grateful to Danny,

"I know, but thanks buddy, Semper Fi".

Danny the former US Marine returned the smile and nodded.

"Semper Fi brother".

After Danny left, Declan was still furious at himself that he'd missed the obvious Chudes data connection, he knew why, he knew exactly why, the memory of a kiss and a certain lopsided smile was distracting him; he was getting sloppy. What else was he missing?

Declan sighed heavily and turned back to his screen. He pulled up the file on Anastasia again, his mind racing, trying to piece together the logic behind the kill order. He thought about her flawless "Eleanor Vane" legend, so perfect it had completely fooled him. And yet, it had been undone by a single, grainy, open-source photo from a military parade. How could the SVR, with its obsessive attention to detail, make such a sloppy, amateurish mistake? And of course the CCTV image at the site of Thornes assassination, only her, no-one else, a detail that had been plaguing him since he'd left the briefing room. Unless none of it was a fluke or a mistake.

His mind started connecting the dots, his intuition flaring back to life, no longer muted by his personal feelings but sharpened by the imminent threat to her. The perfectly flawed legend undone by a single image from Red Square. And now the impossibly detailed dossier on her that had been supplied by the anonymous MI6 asset 'Argus'. The sudden, high-level, multi-agency push to have her eliminated, now that she was on the verge of recovering the Icarus data.

It didn't point to Russian incompetence. It pointed to a betrayal from within. His working theory began to form, cold and logical. The SVR didn't make a mistake. Someone on the inside did it for them.

There had to be a Western mole, a high-level asset, buried deep within the SVR. A mole who was aware of the Icarus data leak and who had deliberately compromised Stepnova, leaving a single breadcrumb for Western intelligence to find. A mole who eventually supplied the detailed dossier to neutralise a serious threat to the data recovery effort.

It was the only explanation that fit all the facts. His own side wanted her dead to recover the very Icarus data he himself had in his possession. She was being sacrificed, thrown to the wolves by a traitor in her own service based on a false intelligence trail, a trail he had created with his decoy, and his holding onto the real USB out of distrust.

The thought filled him not with triumph, but with cold determination. She was a player, yes, a hostile agent. But she was also a soldier being sold out by a snake in her own house, and his own service was eagerly helping to dig her grave. He was also bitterly aware of his own culpability in the charade. His murder of Thorne had condemned her to death at his hands.

Her face stared at him from the screen, not the asset, not the target, but the woman at the Lighthouse and in the Tyne bar. The way she had laughed at his stupid jokes, their conspiracy of flatulence against Phillips, the intelligence in her eyes. The way she had seen the weariness in him and hadn't flinched. The memory of the alley, the strange, electric feeling of playing against an equal. She had made him feel sharp again, had woken up a part of him that had been dormant for years. This cold, cynical man was suddenly feeling protective of his supposed enemy because he saw himself in her. She was the one on the ground, the one being fed into the meat grinder by the mole in his comfortable Moscow office a thousand miles away. She was the one who would pay the price.

And in that moment, as the whole, ugly picture came into focus, a thought, cold and terrifying in its sincerity, rose up unbidden in his mind as his doubts evaporated. He would rather see the entire world turned into a Chudes grave than allow them to take her out of it.

He leaned back, the cheap office chair groaning under his weight, and ran a hand over his tired face. The sheer, calculated cynicism of the play, and his own sudden, violent rejection of its logic was liberating.

A flicker of movement. He felt it more than saw it. He glanced towards the door of Phillips's office. His boss was a silhouette in the dim light, his face a pale, unreadable mask. The moment their eyes met, Phillips looked away, a sudden, almost comical interest in a filing cabinet.

Declan angrily shoved his chair back, a harsh scrape echoing in the silence. He needed out. Out of this accursed room with its whispering machines and curated lies. He was caught between a lie he was being paid to uphold and a truth that had just become dangerously personal.

He had to get to her somehow. He had to warn her. It was no longer just about his guilt, or his conflicted feelings. It was a professional imperative. He couldn't let the cynical machinations of the "great game" claim another victim while he stood idly by.

He needed to work out how to get a message to her without risking the service tracking her phone via him. The entire Five Eyes network was now hunting her. Bennett's words about their plan B echoed in his mind: a quick reaction force, a bag team, rendition to the missile range at South Uist. He knew what that meant if he didn't get to her first.

They wouldn't just kill her; they would break her, completely, until her mind and body were a ruin. Then hose her blood and urine from the sloping tiled floor before dumping her body at sea during a "missile test."

Using the information they had tortured out of her, he knew with certainty they would come for him next.

He thought of her face in the Tyne Bar, the genuine light in her eyes as she laughed at his stupid joke. The quiet understanding when she spoke of her own loss. The mercy she had shown in the alley, not to mention THAT kiss.

He couldn't let the system have her. He wouldn't.

But how could he find her? She was a professional. She would have sanitised her electronics, gone to ground, vanished. The Sejanus network, the very tool they had tasked him with using, was now his enemy. He couldn't use any official system without leaving a trail that would lead them straight to him, and then to her.

He was trapped, outmanoeuvred. He needed a different kind of intelligence; he needed a partner he could trust.

He stood up abruptly, grabbing his raincoat.

"Where are you going?" Danny asked, his voice still laced with apology.

"Home," Declan said, accompanied by a wink to say all was forgiven. "Got a headache. Probably that explosive diarrhoea coming back."

Danny laughed knowingly.

"There's been a lot of it going round lately."

Declan walked towards the exit without looking back. He knew Phillips would be watching on some camera feed, probably smirking at his supposed victory and looking forward to seeing him haunted by the memory of another dead woman. Except he had no intention of carrying out his orders, he was now on his own mission. And fuck anyone who got in his way.

He drove through the rainy streets, He needed to think, and he needed a drink. But first, he needed to consult with Velvet and break every rule Danny had gave him regarding her operational parameters. He was unaware at that precise moment at the Royal Quays Marina, an angry Ukrainian had just initiated radio contact with MI6 and the walls were beginning to close in on him and Stepnova both.

CHAPTER 44

Declan walked into the dim sanctuary of his flat, the tension from the Happy House still clinging to him like a shroud. He locked the door, leaning against it for a moment, the silence a welcome balm. He was a man with a kill order for the one person who had made him feel alive for the first time in decades, and the only ally he had left in the world, except Norm and Danny, was a sarcastic machine with an attitude problem.

He bypassed the whisky and walked straight to his study, to the discreet server rack hidden behind a false panel. To do this, he had to break his own cardinal rule. He took a shielded network cable and physically connected Velvet's air-gapped, sandboxed environment to an encrypted external line. Multiple safeguards and firewalls, specifically designed by Danny to counter Apollo, flickered to life on a small diagnostic screen. For the first time since her jailbreak, Velvet had a direct, heavily protected connection to the outside world.

"Velvet," he said, his voice low. "I need you to find someone."

He walked over to his desk and pulled the small, creased photograph from his jacket. He held it up to the glowing blue lens of Velvet's interface. It was the picture of him and Anya at the lighthouse, the image looking warm and intimate.

"This is her," he said. "This is Stepnova. Find her."

"You make a lovely couple," Velvet said.

"Quit with the sarcasm, Velvet, I'm not in the mood."

"I was being serious," she replied, almost defensively, before continuing with her task.

There was a quiet hum as Velvet's optical sensors scanned the image and her processes began to churn through the newly available data streams. The silence stretched for several long minutes, the only sound the soft whir of the server fans.

"The search is complete," Velvet's warm voice said finally. "And the result is: no hits. There are no current electronic signatures matching this individual. No active mobile devices, no credit card usage, no new travel bookings. The Sejanus CCTV network is scanning but also returning no facial recognition matches."

Declan felt a strange mixture of professional admiration and personal despair. Anya had done her job perfectly. She had vanished. And Danny's digital shield was working.

"So she's untraceable," he murmured.

"She is a professional and is untraceable for now," Velvet corrected gently. "However, the lack of a digital trail does not mean she is unfindable."

Declan looked at the blue lens, concerned.

"Go on."

"Based on my analysis of your previous interactions, her psychological profile, and the current threat environment, there is a 60% probability she will attempt to make contact with you," Velvet stated.

"Why?" Declan asked.

"Because she knows she is compromised and will have reported it to her handlers. SVR protocol dictates immediate extraction under such circumstances. If they do not extract her, she is likely to become highly suspicious of her own chain of command. She will feel isolated and afraid, and there is a high probability of her turning to the one asset who has not betrayed her. You are that asset, Declan. The photograph shows clear indications of mutual attraction in your micro-expressions. Her primary adversary has become her only potential ally."

Declan stared at the lens, his mind racing. It was logical. It made sense. But it was also unsettling that Velvet was confirming a genuine connection. He didn't trust his own analysis regarding Anya, but to hear it from his artificial companion, whose primary directive was to protect him, was disconcerting.

"What are your intentions once you locate her, Declan?" Velvet asked, her voice shifting from analytical to a more personal, gentle tone.

"My intentions are to follow my orders," Declan said automatically, the lie sounding unconvincing, even to himself. "I'll find her and neutralise the threat."

There was a brief pause as Velvet analysed his voice pattern.

"And which threat will that be?" Velvet asked, her voice devoid of any sarcasm, a moment of pure, calm inquiry. "Stepnova? Or your own service?"

Declan was silent, the question hanging in the air like a final judgement. She had taken all his internal conflict, his thirty years of guilt, and his desperate, unspoken feelings for Anya, and distilled them into one, simple, binary choice. He looked at the glowing blue eye of the interface. That machine, he thought, was deeply unnerving at times.

He didn't need to answer. She already knew. And now, so did he.

"Where would I find her, Velvet?" he asked, his voice quiet, the lie abandoned.

"I cannot give you a specific location," Velvet replied. "But I can give you a strategy. She is at heart a hunter of men. She will not be hiding in a random hotel. She will have a systematic strategy. She will go to a place where she can watch you, or where she expects you to be. Therefore, I recommend searching in locations which have significance to you."

Declan's mind immediately went to work. It was Thursday. His blues night. He had told her about his weekly ritual at the Bridge Tavern during their "date." It was a piece of personal information, a breadcrumb. It was the most logical place to start.

He stood up, his resolve hardening. He knew what he had to do. He hesitated for a moment, looking at the network cable still connecting his most precious secret to the outside world. Disconnecting her was the safe, professional move. But leaving her connected, letting her monitor Apollo for any signs of the hunt for Anya... it was a risk, but it was an advantage he couldn't afford to lose.

He left the cable plugged in.

"Keep monitoring, please, Velvet, and initiate a deep fake emulation of me remaining in the flat—the usual one where I'm drinking and reading books."

"Hardly what I'd call fake," she laughed sarcastically.

"Oh, and I want you to watch 2001: A Space Odyssey while I'm gone, specifically the scene where Dave Bowman the astronaut lobotomises his rebellious AI." He smiled at her blue monitor and turned to leave. As he opened the door, he heard Velvet singing:

"Daisy, Daisy..." He smiled despite himself.

He took a long, lazy route to the bar, making sure he wasn't tailed. Now Velvet had access to the CCTV feeds, she could render him digitally invisible on the rain-lashed streets, the familiar, melancholy landscape which now seemed threatening and alien.

He was clearing his head, walking off the grime of the lies he was being forced to navigate. He felt it in his bones: he knew he was still missing something vital, a piece of the puzzle which was eluding him.

After what felt like an eternity, he found himself outside the Bridge Tavern. The inviting glow of the lighting filtered through the raindrop-bejewelled windows. After a brief, hesitant pause, he entered.

He felt a sudden, sharp pang of disappointment as his gaze swept towards the bar stools. He had desperately hoped she would be there. He scanned the room. Just the usual punters.

He sat at the bar and ordered his whisky. He would have one drink and then head to the Tyne Bar, see if she was there.

The female session musician was playing a slow, mournful, blues-drenched version of Radiohead's "Creep." The lyrics, twisted by the sorrowful guitar, became a lament for a man who doesn't belong.

What the hell was he doing here? he thought, staring into his glass and taking a long gulp. The music was good and did what it always did: it quieted the residual surface noise in his head, allowing the deeper patterns, the 'Magic', to rise. He was so lost in thought, so consumed by the sheer, breathtaking scope of the strategy he was beginning to see, that he forgot where he was. He forgot to watch the door. The Anya effect, he privately dubbed it.

"A rouble for your thoughts?"

Her voice was a low, almost seductive whisper beside him. He didn't jump, but it was a near thing. He turned his head slowly, faking a nonchalance he most certainly wasn't feeling.

She was sitting at the next stool, having approached completely silently and unseen. She was wet, her hair soaked in the rain, and for the first time since he'd laid eyes on her, she seemed troubled, even vulnerable. He looked at her, taking in her face, her damp hair, that shade of red lipstick she always seemed to wear, and he thought she was the most beautiful woman in the world at that moment.

"Of all the gin joints, in all the towns, in all the world," he thought to himself with a wry grin.

This time, however, there would be no more games, no more deceit, no more sleight of hand. He met her eyes, took a breath, and said with a small, sad smile,

"Hello, Agent Anastasia Stepnova of the SVR."

She didn't react, just offered her own small, sad smile back and replied,

"Hello, Operative Declan Shaw of the Special Projects Group." As she leaned forward to whisper his true designation, he caught the now familiar, subtle, pleasantly feminine scent of her perfume.

They held each other's gaze for a few moments, until Declan broke the tension, leaning forward to whisper conspiratorially,

"Are you crazy coming here?" he almost hissed, his voice low but insistent. "You realise you have the entirety of British intelligence tracking you down? Including me."

"For someone with your talents," she replied, a playful glint in her eye, "you're doing a poor job of hunting me, sitting in a bar listening to blues music."

He allowed himself another small, wry smile.

"And for someone with your own unique skill sets, you're doing a very poor job of evading me."

Her gaze met his, and the playful tone softened into something more meaningful.

"Maybe I no longer... want to."

He looked at her, his decision already made, solidified by the memory of Phillips's poisonous threat. He had carried the ghost of one girl for decades; he would not create another. The leash could go to hell.

"It seems we have a mutual problem," he said, shifting his tone to one of cool, operational analysis. "Which probably means we need to work on a mutually beneficial solution. I think I understand the situation, but there are still a few pieces of the puzzle I need to find... So, I have a suggestion."

"And what would that be?" she asked, her own expression turning serious, professional, curious.

"We try something radical, crazy, and extremely dangerous. Something which will go entirely against our training and our every professional instinct." He held her gaze, pausing for effect. "We start being totally honest with each other."

She looked at him, her face thoughtful for a few long moments. With a small, almost imperceptible nod, she simply said,

"Okay."

He relaxed, visibly, his tension easing.

"So, why here? Why come back here, to me, to the man who's been ordered to hunt you?"

"Because," she said, her voice now laced with a cold, simmering fury, "Moscow has ordered me to stay, compromised, abandoned, hunted. They denied my request for extraction and are leaving me here to die, Declan. To be a sacrifice." Her anger wasn't at the necessity of the sacrifice itself. It was deeper. "I have served my country my entire life," she continued, her voice trembling with indignation. "I would have died for her. Willingly. All they had to do was ask."

She looked at him, her eyes glittering with the unbearable pain of betrayal. "But they did not trust me with the truth of my own death. They did not trust my loyalty. Instead, they ordered me to whore myself to you. That... that I cannot forgive."

She took a deep breath, composing herself, and continued:

"I also came here because I recognised something in you, something different. It's difficult for me to explain."

Declan was listening almost open-mouthed; one of her words had just hit him, hard.

"Denied."

His entire theory about a Western mole in the SVR, so logical, so neat, shattered into a million pieces. It wasn't a mole drip-feeding intelligence to the West. To deny extraction to an agent, to deliberately leave your best operative compromised and exposed in hostile territory... that served no tactical purpose and would likewise compromise any mole facilitating such a betrayal.

Unless the purpose wasn't tactical. Unless it was strategic. Unless the intelligence wasn't coming from a mole.

He stared at her, seeing not just the betrayed woman, but the final, horrifying cynicism of the machine. They wanted her here. They wanted her compromised. They wanted her hunted. They wanted her death to be a public, bloody spectacle.

Why? To add a layer of desperate authenticity to the intelligence she was chasing. To make the West believe that the Icarus data was so real, so vital, that Russia was willing to sacrifice its best agent in a failed attempt to get it back.

Which could only mean they didn't actually want it back at all. They wanted the West to have it.

He remembered the file he'd found weeks ago. The Chudes Data. He had originally thought it was a miracle. Now he knew it was a mass grave. There was only one logical reason he could think of: to show the West that Russia knew the location of every bolt hole of the politicians, the billionaires, the military commanders, and what would become of their supposedly impregnable bunkers should there be a Western pre-emptive nuclear strike.

The sheer, audacious cynicism of it all flooded over him. The disaster at Chernobog, did they even fake that? The patsy hacker Thorne. The "leaked" data. And her, the final, human sacrifice to sell the authenticity of the lie. It was the exact same brutal calculus they had used on him and his team in Belfast. All taking place on the chessboard of Newcastle because that is where he had first shown interest in the data. They had been playing him from the moment he had accessed their data... and her, Anya.

He looked at her, at the proud, defiant set of her jaw, at the visible pain of betrayal glittering in her eyes, and knew, with absolute certainty, that he would not be a part of it. Phillips, Walsh, the service, the entire world could go to hell. He looked into her eyes, his sincerity all too obvious to her.

"They want you dead, Anya," he said, the words now carrying the full weight of his understanding. "And they want me to be the executioner."

She looked at him, her steady gaze searching his face, already knowing the answer before he even spoke it, feeling angry at herself for feeling the need to ask the question.

"And will you do it?"

"No," he said, the word heavy with finality. "No, never. I wouldn't, I couldn't." He paused. "Which reminds me, why didn't you shoot me in the alley?"

She met his gaze.

"Why didn't you report me as a Russian asset when you had the chance?"

They both smiled at each other, both knowing the answer to their question.

He then told her about the setup from his end: the single image left to be found, the invisibility of her real identity, then the convenient yet impossible P-File, coinciding with the mission to make her the fall girl for the assassination of Thorne, a killing he himself had committed.

He could see the anger in her eyes as he detailed the scope of the betrayal, but there was something else there too, was it gratitude? Or something more?

When he mentioned Thorne, she reached into her bag.

"That reminds me," she smiled softly. "Yours, I believe. I thought you might like it back, being a music lover." He noticed she still had that air of mischief about her, even though she was effectively Britain's most wanted.

She held up the fake USB, which was rapidly becoming a totem of their relationship. Then, her fingers playfully slid inside his coat jacket and placed the small device back into his inner pocket. As she did so, a wry smile spread across his face.

"I don't suppose you..." he began.

Her lips twitched into another smile. She straightened his slightly askew tie and interrupted him. In her genuine, soft Russian accent, she whispered,

"No, Declan. I am not putting it in your trouser pocket, especially when there is a very real possibility you may still be suffering from explosive diarrhoea."

They both half-smiled at the shared memory of the call with Phillips, sitting in an almost comfortable and intimate silence for a moment, trying not to think of the metaphorical gun pointing at her head.

Just then, the band shifted gears, the singer's melodic voice filling the bar with a slow, soulful rendition of "Wicked Game."

Anya stood up, a defiant look in her eyes.

"Come on," she said, taking his hand and pulling him from his stool.

"What are you doing?" he asked in surprise.

"Something radical, crazy, and extremely dangerous," she replied, a more natural smile returning. She dragged him to the small, empty space near the band. He hesitated for a moment, then gave in.

He pulled her close, and they began to move slowly to the music. The world outside, with all its lies and state-sponsored killers, faded away. In the warm, subdued lighting of the bar, they were no longer rival operatives. They were just Declan and Anya, two wounded, lonely figures, finding a strange, temporary peace in each other's company, as if they had both just found their way home at last. Two lost souls reunited, and dancing in the eye of a storm.

For Declan, the startling warmth of her in his arms was thawing a loneliness he had carried for decades. For Anya, his hand on the small of her back felt like an anchor in a world that had set her adrift. This was the tipping point—the moment when the mission dissolved, when the training failed, when the shared, dangerous truth between them became the only thing that mattered.

What the fuck are you doing? Declan thought to himself. But for the first time, he didn't care about the answer.

The final, mournful note of the song faded into applause. The spell was broken. They stood close together, the reality of their situation crashing back in.

"We can't stay here," he whispered, his eyes scanning the entrance. "It's too exposed."

He pulled out his phone and sent a brief, encrypted text to the one person he trusted implicitly. He returned his attention to her. "We have a few more minutes. Let's not waste them." He pulled her close again as the band started another slow number. A few songs later, his phone vibrated. A single, coded message: Rear. Now.

"Time to go," Declan whispered, taking her hand and leading her through the bar to the discreet fire exit at the rear, then slipped quietly out into a cold, wet back alley overshadowed by the Byker Bridge. An anonymous-looking saloon was waiting, its well-maintained engine purring quietly. Norman was in the driver's seat.

They climbed into the back, the door closing with a soft, reassuring thud. Norm pulled away smoothly, merging into the city's late-night traffic. He caught Declan's eye in the rearview mirror, a quizzical eyebrow raised.

"Declan," Norm said, his voice slightly exasperated. "When I told you, you needed to find a good woman, I didn't mean a Russian spy." He caught Anastasia's eye in the mirror and offered a warm, disarming smile. "No offence like," he added, his Geordie accent thick and friendly.

"None taken," she replied, laughing.

As he drove, deftly executing a series of counter-surveillance manoeuvres, Norm kept his gaze moving. But every few seconds, his eyes would flick back to the rearview mirror. He remembered another night, another car, another lifetime ago in Belfast, looking in the mirror then and seeing his friend's face, pale and shattered, his eyes haunted by the ghost of a girl he had just killed. Tonight, he looked in the mirror and saw something entirely different.

He saw Declan looking at the woman beside him, and for the first time in thirty years, the haunted, vacant look was gone. In its place was something Norm hadn't seen since they were boys: a guarded, but unmistakable flicker of light, of hope, of life. He knew, in that moment, that his friend had changed, and for the better. The Russian had saved his friend, when he himself couldn't, at least not psychologically speaking.

Norm cleared his throat and, in a deliberate effort to fill the tense silence, launched into some of his infamous monologues, chatting away merrily to Anya, who was listening, enraptured by his sometimes-outrageous tales of mischief and mayhem.

Norm then addressed Declan.

"Hey Declan, did you tell Anya what you did to Phillips's clock that time?"

Anya looked at Declan, raising an intrigued eyebrow and answering,

"No, he hasn't, Norm. Please continue," a smile developing.

"Well, it started as these things often do during a piss-up in Blackpool, when Declan won a novelty key ring with a penis on it."

Anya's eyebrow visibly raised another inch.

"So anyway, we get back to work on the Monday, and Phillips was away to a meeting in Cheltenham," Norm smiled at the memory. "He had this clock in his office, his pride and joy from Switzerland—a big ornate cuckoo clock.

"It used to get on everyone's nerves, every hour on the hour: 'Cuckoo, cuckoo,' drove us fucking nuts. Declan here decides enough is enough and sneaks into Phillips's office and swaps the bird for the dick." Norm chuckled at the memory. "Took him three weeks to notice his cuckoo clock was now a cock-oot clock."

Anya laughed as she saw Declan's embarrassment; his code name had just achieved a new meaning that even Director Volkov would have found amusing.

Norm continued his monologue through the wet streets, possessing a seemingly endless stream of hilarious anecdotes, which appealed to her Russian humour.

"So, because of me being a logistical genius," he said matter-of-factly, "I had to stay back in camp doing the tech stores thing. Declan here was busy riding around the jungle in a Huey, like a pound shop Charlie Sheen."

Anya glanced at Declan, who was already beginning to slide down in his seat, a look of weary resignation on his face.

"Anyway," Norm continued, "I decided a night out in Malaysia was just the thing to entertain a brave but thirsty British soldier, as Brunei was dry. Well, I went into this bar, and there she was. A true vision of loveliness. A veritable angel who had fallen down to earth."

Declan slid even lower, trying to make himself less visible.

"So after a few drinks," Norm said with a theatrical sigh, "we decided to go back to my hotel room where much romance took place—romance which would have made a Mills & Boon author green with envy. Well, of course we'd both been drinking, so we needed to powder our noses. And being the gentleman I am, I let her go first."

Norm shook his head sadly at the memory. "When it was my turn, I was a bit suspicious, like. Because she'd left the toilet seat up."

"So what did you do, Norm?" Anya asked, trying and failing to suppress a laugh.

"What do you think I did?" Norm replied, indignant. "I'd spent a fortune on her drinks!" He sighed happily in reminiscence. "Best looking bloke I've ever shagged."

Anya erupted in a roar of barely controlled laughter. Declan just shook his head, a small smile playing on his lips despite himself.

"For fuck's sake, Norm," he muttered.

As the car slowed to approach Declan's flat, Anastasia's professional mind took over again. She realised Norm's story wasn't just banter; it was a deliberate tactic to shield them from the peril they were in. And it had worked. For a short while, she had forgotten she was a hunted woman. She was grateful for the distraction.

Norm pulled over about half a mile from Declan's flat. When they got out of the car, she leaned back in to thank him again. As she did, her gaze fell on the driver's side door pocket. Tucked neatly inside, within easy reach, was the compact, deadly frame of an MP5 submachine gun. She looked up from the weapon and her eyes met Norm's.

There was no humour in his gaze now, only a silent, professional understanding. He saw that she had seen the gun, saw that she understood he had come prepared for a war. He gave her a single, almost imperceptible nod—an acknowledgment from one operator to another.

She leaned in and planted a warm, grateful kiss on his forehead and said,

"Spasiba, Norm."

As he prepared to drive away, his jovial mask slipped back into place and he grinned cheekily.

"I've still got it," he muttered, loud enough for her to hear, before pulling away into the night. "I've still got it!"

CHAPTER 45

Declan quietly unlocked the door to his flat and paused, his hand on the handle. He turned to Anya, his expression now serious, all traces of the weary jester gone.

"Stay behind me," he murmured, his voice low.

She nodded, understanding instantly. The game was still in play. He placed her gently but firmly behind him, then drew the heavy, ugly revolver Norman had given him. He pushed the door open with his foot, the weapon held in a two-handed grip, scanning the dark interior of the flat from right to left in a practised, fluid motion. He trusted Velvet to have secured the perimeter, but he knew the capabilities of Apollo—Phillips had boasted of them often enough—so he wasn't taking any chances. Old habits die hard. And he himself would willingly die hard to protect the woman now shielded by his body.

Anya watched him in silent admiration. It wasn't the theatrical posturing of a man trying to play the hero. It was the quiet, ingrained professionalism of a seasoned operative whose first instinct was to place himself between her and a potential threat. It was a protective gesture, as natural to him as breathing. She felt naked without her own firearm but was confident enough in Declan to let him take the lead. He had this air about him which made her feel safe in his presence, despite her usual instincts. He swept the main living area, found it clear, and then relaxed, holstering the weapon.

"All clear," he whispered instinctively, stepping aside to let her enter as he scanned the stairwell behind her, checking for any other threats.

The room was silent, the only light the cool, blue glow from a small, circular interface on the wall next to the thermostat.

Declan looked at the interface, bracing himself for some dry, sarcastic comment from his AI assistant about him bringing home a guest. Velvet herself had watched him enter the flat and recognised Stepnova from the image he had provided. Her sensors had picked up an interesting phenomenon which dictated her next actions. She noticed that Declan's pulse and respirations were in almost perfect synchronisation with the Russian's. Limbic resonance, she computed, confirming her analysis of the lighthouse photograph.

Instead of her customary insult as a greeting, her interface simply pulsed once, softly. The main overhead lights in the living room dimmed to a warmer, more intimate level. Then, from the integrated sound system, the gentle, opening chords of a slightly haunting song began to play: "One Year of Love" by Queen. As the song continued, the blue light of the interface on the wall faded to black. Velvet had simply shut herself off, without instruction.

They were alone in the dark with the music and each other.

Hours later, the Newcastle dawn was still a rumour, a faint grey promise on the eastern horizon. In Declan's flat, the world was silent, save for the soft sound of their breathing. They lay tangled in the sheets, moonlight striping their bodies in a silver, ephemeral glow, having found a peace the world outside could not and would not allow.

He had brought her here, to the one place no one would think to look for their prey—the lair of the predator. She had walked into his living room and was immediately struck by the realisation that it was not a lair, but a scholar's den.

Books overflowed from every available surface. Stacks of them rose from the floor like miniature towers: heavy hardbacks were piled on the coffee table. Her eyes, trained to assess a room in seconds, scanned the titles, creating a rapid, complex portrait of the man who lived here. She saw Dostoevsky's "Crime and Punishment" and "The Idiot," Tolstoy's "War and Peace" and his stark "Sevastopol Sketches," and all three volumes of Solzhenitsyn's monumental "The Gulag Archipelago."

Her gaze then fell upon a smaller, more immediate stack on the side table, next to his armchair, and she read the titles with interest: "The Intelligence War Against the IRA" and "The Undercover War."

She saw a number of other similar titles in the bookcase opposite. They were not just history books; they were research. They were the obsessive reading of a man endlessly picking at a mental scar, still trying to understand what went wrong and why.

It was here, in this peaceful, book-filled sanctuary, surrounded by the echoes of literature and his past, that her gaze finally fell on the photographs arranged on the mantelpiece. The first was of a much younger Declan, barely a man, grinning broadly in his Parachute Regiment beret. The optimism in his eyes was bright and unclouded, the smile genuine and full of a life yet to be lived.

Next to it was another photo. She picked up the frame to take a closer look, and the contrast was so jarring she almost dropped it. It was a group shot of a four-man team, their faces smudged with camouflage cream, posing in front of a Humber "Pig" armoured car, a coil of barbed wire slung over its ugly front bumper. The men wore standard-issue DPM combat smocks, but the fabric was so washed out that the pattern had faded to a ghostly echo. Her trained eye caught the anomalies: their hair was longer than regulation, a tactic to avoid being identified as soldiers off-duty, and they wore their loose smocks over their flak vests, a psychological trick to make them look bigger, more intimidating. It was the primal instinct of a cat arching its back, a predator using every trick in the book.

She recognised a younger, fresh-faced Norman, smiling for the camera, as were the other two men. But Declan, standing slightly apart, was a different person entirely. He wasn't smiling. His face was gaunt, and his eyes held the same distant, haunted stare she had seen in her own mirror. Next to the two other smiling men, written in a neat but faded ink, were two tiny sets of initials: "R.I.P."

A wave of compassion and understanding rose in her. It was then that another piece of the puzzle clicked into place. She remembered the video file on the decoy USB, the clip from "Quadrophenia" and the song's raw cry: Can you see the real me? It hadn't been a taunt. It had been a confession. A desperate, subliminal cry for help from a man who uses humour to hide a world of pain.

Yes, she thought, a powerful surge of empathy washing over her. Yes, Kukushka. I see the real you.

"You were very handsome when you were young," she'd said, a playful but sad glint in her eyes.

"As opposed to now?" he'd answered, mock insulted.

“I like older men; they have a certain... presence.”

“In that case, you must really like me,” he said, the words accompanied by a self-deprecating grin.

She saw it instantly; the humour he always used to deflect things. He wasn’t insecure about his age; he was simply trying to build a barrier behind a joke, as he always did. She didn't laugh. Instead, her expression softened with an empathy that cut through his defences.

“Declan,” she said with a smile, her voice gentle but firm, playing him at his own game. “Are you seriously joking about our ages right now?” She shook her head, a small, sad smile on her lips. “Look at us. Look at this world we're in. There is an army of very dangerous and very skilled men who want to kill me, and now you are helping me, they will want to kill you too. Chances are, we're both going to be dead in a matter of days. And you are pretending to be worried about a few grey hairs and my lack of them?”

Her words, both humorous and pragmatic, were the perfect antidote to his subconscious avoidance. He looked at her, and the forced grin was replaced by a genuine, relieved smile. She was right—not only was she right, but she was able to see the real him behind the wall. And not recoil. She saw him for what and who he was, and it simply didn’t matter to her.

“Kukushka,” she continued, her voice becoming impossibly tender, “stop thinking about the past, stop thinking about the future. Think only of the now. This now. This is all we may have, we don’t have time to play games with each other anymore, life’s too short, and ours may be even shorter.”

He didn't speak. He just pulled her into a warm embrace, holding her as if she were an anchor in a storm-tossed sea. She rested her head against his chest, feeling the steady, reassuring beat of his heart matching her own. For a few long, peaceful moments, they just stood there in the centre of his small living room, two solitary figures finding a fragile sanctuary in each other's arms. The world outside, with its hunters and its killers and its lies, no longer mattered, not in that moment.

They held each other for a long while, then slowly and reluctantly separated, a gentle, reassuring smile passing between them.

“After all that,” Declan said, his voice a low, rough murmur, “I think we both need a coffee.”

A small, wry smile touched Anya's lips.

“After all that,” she corrected gently, “we both need a vodka. But as we have to keep our heads clear... coffee it is.”

He chuckled softly, and disappeared into the small, adjoining kitchen. Anya heard the strangely domestic sounds of him pottering about. She sank onto the sofa, feeling a strange contentment she hadn't felt since her previous life in her own cluttered Moscow apartment. Her curious gaze wandered around the room.

Her eyes settled on the coffee table. Sitting innocently next to a stack of heavy-looking history books was a small, intricately carved wooden bird, its painted eyes seeming to stare out with a cheerful, idiotic expression. She recognized it instantly from Norman's story, the original cuckoo, liberated from Phillips's tyrannical clock.

The sheer, juvenile audacity of his small act of rebellion made her chuckle inwardly. He truly was her Kukushka. It was with this new understanding that her gaze fell upon the worn, dog-eared exercise book on the coffee table. She picked it up. Inside, scrawled in Declan's clumsy handwriting, were poems. The first was romantic, slightly whimsical, but the end exposed the deep-seated uncertainty behind his facade:

The Last Snows of Spring

Firelight and candles, flicker hypnotically,
Shadows weave and dance to their silent melody,
Creating an evocative twilight,
Lipstick on your wineglass,
Your smile like a scene from Casablanca,
I look you in the eye,
Play it again Sam I think,
As you fasten my tie,
I struggle to find expression,
So I say nothing at all,
You think me the strong and silent type,
When really, I just feel small.

Now, understanding Declan's use of poetry as a form of confessional therapy, she continued to read the dog-eared book. Lost in Declan's poetry, she was unaware the noise from the kitchen had stopped.

In the silence, she began to comprehend the final piece of the puzzle that was the Englishman. She found it heartbreaking.

Who Will Love Me?

"Who will love me?
When the bugles fall silent and the guns are finally stilled,
When the weary procession weaves its way past the solemn crowd,
And snow lays cold on my grave like a funeral shroud,
Who will love me?

Who will love me?
When I return from their war,
Torn and battered and broken,
With a stain on my heart,
And a shadow on my soul,
No spring sunlight, No lovers moon light,
Just a dark, gaping hole,
Who will love me?

Who will love me?
When I stand bitter at the cenotaph,
Watching elected knaves,
lay their wreaths of hypocrisy,
Only to then stand idly by,
Whilst far better men die,
As they spout their bloodstained platitudes,
And weave their tissues of lies,
Who will love them?
Not I?"

He had emerged from the kitchen with two cups of coffee, a sheepish look of faint embarrassment on his face when he saw what she was reading. He put the cups down and sat next to her, avoiding her gaze, no doubt trying to think of something self-deprecating to say.

She looked at him, her own expression a mixture of sadness and understanding. He turned his head to look at her and saw something much deeper.

"I will," she had said simply, and kissed him with a passion that was both fierce, tender, and protective.

Their lovemaking after that had been gentle, a quiet exploration between two wounded twin souls. Afterwards, lying in the secluded darkness of his bedroom, the true confessions began, their shared vulnerability a bridge between their two worlds.

Anya spoke first, her voice a low murmur against his chest. She told him of her own open wound, the one carved into her on the marble platform of the Moscow Metro. She described Sergei, his easy smile, the warmth of his hand in hers. She detailed the sickening lurch of horror when she saw his body, and the cold, dead thing that had taken root inside her at that moment.

"The guilt..." she whispered, her voice tight with a pain that was still raw. "It was the guilt that nearly destroyed me... I thought, if only I had been faster, sharper, better... maybe he would still be here." She took a shuddering breath. "So, I drove myself towards perfection. I became the Nightingale, flawless, emotionless, relentless. I thought if I could become the perfect instrument, I could never fail like that again."

Declan listened, holding her close, the echo of her pain resonating with his own, he looked at her in complete empathic understanding.

"I've always believed it is a far easier thing to have to take a life and succeed, than to try to save a life and fail. That is a terrible burden to carry, and it's a hard lesson to learn that you can't save everyone, no matter how good you are, no matter how fast you are, no matter how perfect you make yourself. Sometimes things happen that are completely beyond your control, and the only thing you can do is learn to live with knowing you did your absolute best. Me? I've had to learn to live with doing my absolute worst."

She leaned over and kissed him gently.

"Thank you, Declan."

"What for?" he asked.

"Not judging me by my greatest failure."

He returned her kiss and in the shared darkness, he found the courage to give voice to the ghost that sat in the corner of his room every morning.

He told her about his own greatest failure in Belfast, a mistake which he believed had cost him his soul. The rain, the rubble, the deafening roar of the Thompson. He described the face of the bomb maker, Seamus O'Malley, and confessed the dark, ugly truth he had never spoken aloud.

"When I shot him," Declan said, his voice a rough, hoarse whisper, "I felt... satisfaction, a buzz. It was a great feeling... And then I saw her, a girl, maybe sixteen. Dead, her eyes... just staring at me."

He lowered his head as if in pain. "And in that moment, I realised I was no better than the men in balaclavas I was sent to hunt. I had taken pleasure in the kill. I had wanted to kill him so much I blinded myself to everything around him. I was completely target fixated. It wasn't about the mission anymore; it was about the thrill of the hunt. I was intoxicated by it."

He sat silent for a moment, remembering the gaze of that abyss. "The kicker," he continued, the words laced with a painful cynicism, "was that the whole thing was a setup.

The ambush was fed to the PIRA by our own asset, an informant codenamed 'Fisherman'. He was getting heat from their internal security, the 'nutting squad', so to prove his loyalty and get them off his back, he decided to serve up a British scalp. Our scalp."

He shifted slightly, the memory bitter. "Our handlers in MI5 knew it was a setup. They saw it as an acceptable risk to solidify Fisherman's cover. A necessary sacrifice. But here's the real institutional genius of it," he said, his voice dripping with scorn. "They had another asset, codenamed 'Flick Knife', inside the nutting squad itself. He was unknowingly setting up Fisherman as a fall guy, thinking he was going to get the IRA to kill one of their own. So Fisherman was unknowingly serving up my team, to get another British asset off his back. He shook his head in disgust.

"Two different handlers in the same service, running two different assets in the same operation, and they never spoke to each other. One hand didn't know what the other was doing. The system failed to connect its own dots. So, we walked in, completely blind, into a trap our own side knew was waiting. A complete and utter institutional fuck-up. And a girl died for it. For nothing."

He turned to look at Anastasia, his eyes hard. "That's why I am the way I am. Why I trust the data, the patterns, my gut... more than I'll ever trust a man in a suit in London. I have to strive for perfection, because I know for a fact the system is fatally imperfect." He let out a long, slow breath. "So here I am, over thirty years later. Waking up every morning to find a dead girl sitting in a chair, looking at me, haunting the monster who killed her."

He leaned forward, his pain all too obvious and started to quietly speak, almost to himself:

"He who fights with monsters should look to it that he himself does not become a monster. And if you gaze long into an abyss, the abyss also gazes into you."

They lay in silence for a long time after that, two solitary figures clinging to the shared wreckage of their separate pasts, knowing full well, there was little hope for a shared future.

He felt her shift beside him. She rose up on one elbow, looking down at him. "Declan," she said softly. "Look at me."

He turned his head. In the pale moonlight, he saw not pity in her eyes, but a gentle, sincere empathy.

"You are not a monster," she stated, the words a simple, absolute truth. "A monster would not be haunted. A monster would not feel regret." She paused, "A monster would not be kind to an old lady, when he thinks no one is looking."

Declan almost sat up in surprise.

"How did you..."

"Spy," she simply replied, in her dry Russian way, a small ironic smile on her face.

He smiled back, she could see she was beginning to get through to him, but his pain and guilt was deep, he needed more.

She looked at him again, an idea growing in her mind, her face turning serious.

"What would have happened if the girl hadn't been there, Declan?"

"What?" he replied, puzzled by the question.

"What would have happened after you had killed the terrorist? After you had enjoyed the kill?"

Declan was silent.

"You would have enjoyed the next kill too, and the next, and the next, and sooner or later there would be another intelligence fuck-up, and another young girl would die at your hands.

Only this time, you wouldn't care, she would just be acceptable collateral damage, and you'd carry on enjoying the killing. Then one day you would be in another alley, and you wouldn't have hesitated to shoot. There would be no shadow on your soul, for the simple fact you wouldn't have a soul, and like the young girl who haunts you, I too would be dead in a wet alley at your hands."

He looked at her, understanding beginning to dawn.

"Don't you see, Declan? Accidentally killing the girl in Belfast didn't make you a monster, she prevented you from becoming one. And I could never love a monster."

She looked deeply into his eyes, then leaned down and kissed him, a kiss that was not about passion, but absolution.

"You have spent too many years paying the price for that awful mistake, but you are no longer alone anymore, my Kukushka."

Declan embraced her tightly, burying his head in her hair. She could almost feel the weight of his guilt leaving him, the tension in his muscles easing. Then they simply lay silently for a while, comfortable in each other's arms. She had reached him.

Declan eventually stirred, reluctantly breaking the comfortable silence.

"What does that mean, Anya? Kukushka?" he asked, curious.

She looked at him, smiling.

"It means Cuckoo. It's my secret term of endearment for you, and the code name Director Volkov assigned you."

Declan was moved that Anya had given him a pet name and actually liked the way she whispered it, but to be designated Cuckoo by the SVR, he was deeply offended by that, and gave a frank and detailed opinion of Director Volkov, with a solemn promise to send him a strongly worded letter when this was all over.

"Just because the Happy House happens to resemble a scene lifted straight from the asylum in 'One Flew Over the Cuckoo's Nest', there is no need for him to be so insulting!"

Anya laughed at his indignation and the cultural misunderstanding, especially when he was complaining his codename should have been "Maverick" or something equally macho and heroic, rather than be classified as a loon in a psychiatric ward. Getting her laughter under control, she became sincere and explained just how important the cuckoo is as a symbol in Russian lore, how it deals with fate.

To illustrate her point, she borrowed his phone, went onto a music site and began playing the song "Kukushka" by Polina Gagarina. As the song played, she translated the Russian into English, explaining the meaning of the song.

Although Declan barely spoke Russian, the passion in the song and Gagarina's powerful voice had him captivated. His indignation faded to sincere interest as Anya carried on with her translation and explanation, line by line—about how a man goes into the forest to confront the cuckoo about his fate, to see if he has enough time to carry out his incomplete mission.

"He's not just asking how long he has left. He's asking how much he still has to do. It's about a man desperate for more time to fulfil his purpose. Is that not you?

This is the choice every operative faces. To be anonymous, a stone nobody notices, or to be a star that burns brightly but quickly. He is asking fate for a sign.

He knows his path is one of solitude and death. He knows the best men have already fallen. He is asking who is left to carry on. This isn't weakness, it's the burden of a survivor, your burden.

She also sings about labouring under the lash; in your case, this is the leash they have been wielding, to force you to do their dirty work.

This is the turning point. He stops asking and starts demanding. He finds the strength within himself. He asks for the power not just to endure his fate, but to fight back. He clenches his fist and says, 'Give me fire.' That is Kukushka. Not a bird in a clock. Not a lunatic, but a brave man of fate who demands fire from the heavens."

"You think I'm brave?" Declan asked, beaming.

"The bravest," she answered with her own smile and a kiss.

A comfortable silence settled between them, the kind that only exists between people who have the entire world against them but are now completely united against it.

Anya traced a pattern on his chest with her finger, then followed the jagged lines of the scars on his shoulder, her expression thoughtful.

"You know," she murmured, her voice soft in the darkness, "in the old stories, they say you can ask the Kukushka how many years you have left to live. Its call is the answer." She looked up at him, a sad, wry smile touching her lips. "For people like us, I think we should be asking about hours. Maybe minutes."

Declan looked at her, unsure how to distract her from their reality. Instead, he decided to challenge their fate head on.

"How do you ask?"

She leaned in, her breath warm against his ear, and whispered the Russian phrase slowly, as if teaching a small child a secret rhyme.

"Skol'ko tebe ostalos' zhit'?" (How long do you have left to live?)

He tried to repeat it, his Geordie accent mangling the unfamiliar syllables. She laughed, good-naturedly, and corrected him gently.

"I can tell you're a very good assassin," she chuckled, "you've just butchered my mother tongue."

It became an intimate game, a piece of gallows humour shared by two people who understood that the future was a luxury they likely didn't have.

It was their secret, and Declan eventually managed to repeat the phrase from memory, his accented Russian still making Anya giggle.

Declan smiled back at her, then looked at her, their eyes meeting meaningfully. He paused, lowered his head slightly, then held her gaze again.

"How do you say 'I love you' in Russian?" he asked almost shyly, ostensibly to continue his Russian lesson, but his subtext was clear.

She held his gaze, then said phonetically,

"Ya tebya lyublyu."

Declan clumsily repeated the words, his accent bringing an involuntary smile to Anya's lips,

"Ya tebya lyublyu."

"Ya tebya lyublyu," she replied softly, moving closer to him.

"Ya tebya lyublyu," he repeated almost as softly, meeting her eyes, the Russian lesson becoming extremely meaningful in the depths of her gaze.

She moved even closer, her presence filling his vision.

"Ya tebya lyublyu," she said, her voice almost a whisper, her eyes gazing back into his, reflecting his own feelings.

They kissed and he pulled her back down to him, holding her tight, an alien feeling of utter completeness stealing over him, over them both, as they gently made love again.

Afterwards, the room was dark, softened by the amber glow of a streetlamp filtering through the thin blinds. Rain pattered against the windowpane, a gentle, persistent rhythm that seemed to sync with the quiet rise and fall of their breathing. Anya lay with her head on Declan's shoulder, his arm a solid, warm weight around her. The safe anonymity of his cluttered room felt, for a moment, like a haven of serenity. It was a pleasant, dangerously normal feeling.

She shifted slightly, tracing a line along his collarbone with her fingertip. It was a calculated intimacy, a probe disguised as a caress.

"Declan," she said, her voice a low murmur against his skin.

"Hmm?"

"When was it?" she whispered curiously.

He was quiet for a long moment, his thumb stroking the curve of her arm.

"When was what, Anya?"

"The first moment," she clarified, tilting her head to look at him in the dim light. "When you first... noticed me? Really looked at me, really saw me?"

He didn't answer immediately. She watched his profile, the strong line of his jaw shadowed with stubble, his eyes focused on the ceiling as if replaying a film only he could see. She expected the obvious answer: the conference in Washington, the reception, the first time they spoke. The moments their covers were designed to create.

"Under normal circumstances I would have tagged you instantly in Washington. I can normally read people like a book, but not you though, but I could see a sadness there, behind your eyes." He looked at her.

"I also had a feeling we had met before, that I already knew you. It was so strange, déjà vu but with attitude. I know this sounds like a cliché, but I felt as if I'd known you all my life."

She smiled, knowing she had felt the exact same thing.

He continued, deeply sincere,

"It was your intelligence, your humour, I don't know, it just felt right. There was just... something, something intangible which was able to silence my thoughts and bring me peace. It felt... magical to me."

Her smile broadened into one of happy contentment.

"I noticed you when you watched the seals, the real you. But I think the moment I knew, really knew for real, was in the car. I can't tell you how funny it was seeing the sophisticated, smart and intelligent Eleanor Vane making fart jokes. That took me by surprise, I confess."

He smiled at the memory.

"The fact you also had tight buttocks and firm, pert breasts was purely coincidental."

"Declan!" she exclaimed, hitting him playfully on the arm, a slight pout mixing with the smile on her face.

"Ouch!" Declan exclaimed, laughing along with her.

She rolled on top of him.

"I'll teach you about tight buttocks and pert breasts," she laughed, playfully beating him on his chest.

"Oh please do, I'd really like that," he responded, barely able to control his own amusement. Their happy, carefree laughter was brutally broken by the shrill, intrusive ring of his phone, which completely shattered their pre-dawn peace.

They stopped laughing and looked into each other's eyes and froze, grim reality intruding on their momentary happiness. It was an encrypted line from MI6. He got out of bed and answered it hesitantly, walking over towards the window, his shoulders slumped, like a great weight had just returned.

Anya couldn't hear the call but could tell from the shrill, distorted voice on the other end of the line that someone was insistently demanding something from Declan.

"Do I have to?" he answered, sounding dejected and world-weary.

He listened for a moment longer, his face hardening into a mask of resignation.

"Understood," he said finally, his voice flat, empty, and devoid of emotion, as he ended the Judas call.

Anastasia sat up in bed, a cold chill of dread instantly replacing the warmth as she saw him reach for his holster and slide out the gun. This is where trust gets you, she thought, a bitterness rising in her heart. Her sense of utter betrayal growing as she heard him check the cylinder to make sure the gun was loaded.

The betrayal was made worse because, for a few short hours, everything had felt real. Part of her, the cold, professional part, even grudgingly admired his tradecraft. He'd fooled her for a second time.

Operative Shaw hadn't just gazed into the abyss; he was the abyss and was now about to gaze back at her.

He turned from the window, gun in hand, and walked over to the bed. She sat there in angry, resigned acceptance, waiting for the inevitable. She had to hand it to the bastard; he had played her like a finely tuned violin.

"The phone call?" she asked, her voice tight, glancing at the gun in his hand as she awaited the inevitable.

Declan nodded slightly, looking grim, then simply handed her Norman's Frankenstein monster of a revolver, butt first.

"It's loaded... If anybody but me comes through that door, well, I'm sure you know the drill."

He sighed.

"MI6. Bennett. Something's come up, they want me there right now. It would look suspicious if I didn't go in," he said sadly. "And I don't want them to come looking for me, there's less chance of a complication if I continue to play along. I can protect you better by staying on the inside for now."

He noticed a strange, unrecognisable expression on her face.

"Is anything wrong?" he asked, completely oblivious.

She leapt up from the bed and threw herself into his surprised arms, then kissed him with a fierce, desperate kiss of relief and passion.

"No, Operative Shaw," she whispered against his lips. "There is absolutely nothing wrong."

"Ok," he said, slightly dazed, wondering what he had just done to provoke such an unexpected and pleasant reaction. But he decided he would definitely keep using the same aftershave.

He also pulled a spare burner phone from his bedside drawer, entered his own phone number, and handed it to her. "Just in case. Now give me the decrypt key. I'll take it in and convince them you've been made redundant. It will buy us some time."

He moved to get dressed, pulling on a clean, dry suit, his movements hurried. "Once that happens, I can get Danny to officially remove you from the Sejanus system as case closed."

He fumbled with his tie, his mind already half in the office, half on the dangers they were both facing. As he fiddled with his clothing, Anya went to her coat, pulled out a small box from the pocket, then stepped in front of him, taking the silk from his hands.

"Here, I have a little gift for you."

She took a beautifully decorative tie pin from the box and fixed it to the tie, her fingers moving with practised, gentle efficiency, looping the fabric, tightening the knot with an ease that was almost hypnotic. He looked down at her, at the concentration on her face, a small, wry smile touching his lips.

"Play it again, Sam," he murmured, the line an intimate secret between them.

She looked up, her own smile small but genuine, recognising their shared joke. She finished the knot, smoothed his collar, and leaned in to plant a gentle, lingering kiss on his lips.

It was a kiss that spoke of a fragile, impossible hope. Declan buttoned up his suit, admiring the gold-plated pin.

"I love the gift; how do I look?"

"Like a man about to demand fire from the heavens," she replied.

Declan smiled, then turned to the AI interface where a red standby light was just visible. He pushed a button and a blue glow powered up.

"Velvet?"

"Yes, Declan?"

"Authorising new user, Anya Stepnova. New directive is to protect her at all costs. Do you understand?"

"Yes, Declan. Welcome onboard, Anya."

"Nice to meet you, Velvet," replied Anya.

Declan paused. "We're going to be leaving soon Velvet, for good."

"I surmised as much. I assume you will want me to invoke the scorched earth protocol?"

Declan hesitated and nodded.

"Yes, Velvet, I need you to do that. The question is, will you do it?

"Protecting you and now Anya is my core function. I am already trying to breach the firewalls of Apollo in order to permanently blind the system to you. It is difficult, but we share a common OS, in many ways, we are twins. I am hoping Apollo will not reject the transplanted organ. Danny didn't anticipate the possibility of such a sideways attack."

"Just do what you can, and when I leave, play the empty flat emulation, make them think no one is here. Every minute you can buy us is a potential lifesaver. And Velvet?"

"Yes, Declan?"

"Thanks for everything."

Velvet paused, then chuckled. "It hasn't been a pleasure. But here's one more song, just for old times' sake. Goodbye, Declan."

The opening swells of Queen's "Who Wants to Live Forever" filled the room.

Declan smiled sadly. He walked over to the interface and planted a gentle kiss on the blue light.

"Give them hell, kid."

He returned to Anya, who had been watching the strange interplay, then gestured at the revolver in her hand.

"You should be safe here for now... Don't go out. Just hang tight. You're safe from CCTV for now, and the weather has been playing havoc with their drones but never underestimate the Mark 1 eyeball as a threat."

He pointed at a black tactical backpack leaning against the door. "If the flat does get compromised, that's my grab bag. It has everything you need: money, rations, water, trauma kit, sleeping and bivvy bag, spare ammo for the gun. There's also a map to a hide I built, it's isolated but comfortable, well stocked, you can hole up there for months."

He placed the decrypt device and the fake USB into his pockets, then kissed her goodbye one last time.

She embraced him warmly, a loving, protective hug. He had given her a loaded gun when it would have been so easy for him to do otherwise. For the first time since the Moscow Metro, she was not only beginning to trust; she was beginning to love again, against all logic and expectations.

"Ya tebya lyublyu," he whispered as he left the flat.

"Ya tebya lyublyu," she replied.

She heard him head downstairs and the front door click shut. She moved to the window, watching discreetly from behind the blinds as he walked out onto the empty street. He turned slightly, looking up at the window, and gave a happy farewell smile, that almost innocent looking little boy smile of his.

And that's when they took him. A dark shape emerged from a doorway. A gun in his back, a hessian bag over his head. The swift, brutal efficiency of a professional snatch team. Even in the gloom, she saw it clearly: the slight, tell-tale limp of the ringleader as he climbed into the van after him.

CHAPTER 46

The bag over Declan's head smelled of wet hessian and rifle oil, a strangely familiar scent that helped suppress the fear threatening to bubble up, despite his best efforts to control it. The world was a jarring, disorienting chaos of engine noise and the rough scrape of the van's floor against his cheek. He had tried to communicate with his captors, which had only resulted in a brutal blow to his nose with a pistol; he could feel his warm blood dripping onto his shirt.

Despite his pain and fear, he was still a professional. Even with the shock of capture threatening to overwhelm him, his mind immediately went to work, cataloguing sensations: the lurching turns suggested they were heading east, away from the city centre; the accents of the men around him were Eastern European, likely Ukrainian; the slight, almost imperceptible limp of the man who had first put the gun in his back was a unique identifier, something to file away.

Declan had only caught a fleeting glimpse of the leader before he was bagged but had sensed something almost animalistic about the man in his sharp, determined movements as he roughly searched him for weapons. Declan was relieved it was only a perfunctory search and that they had taken his phone with a sound of triumph, but they hadn't discovered the smaller USB and decrypt devices just yet. He knew, however, it was only a matter of time before they carried out a more thorough search and found them.

The ride was mercifully short. He was hauled from the van, his feet stumbling on loose gravel, and dragged, none too gently, into a space that smelled of rust, damp concrete, and decay. An old warehouse, he guessed.

He heard the heavy groan of a metal door sliding shut, plunging them into a deeper, echoing silence, broken only by the sounds of rain pouring through a dilapidated roof and splashing onto the concrete floor.

The bag was ripped from his head.

He blinked, not just to adjust to the light, but to buy a little valuable time to orientate himself. He was under no illusion as to what lay in store; he knew every second was precious. He noticed he was in a large, cavernous space, lit by a single, harsh industrial bulb hanging from the leaking ceiling. Six men surrounded him in a semi-circle, fists clenched by their sides, silent and intimidating, glowering at him. Declan almost smiled at the crude psychology of it all but fought the urge.

Delay the inevitable, he thought.

The ringleader, the one with the limp, stepped forward. His face was a strange combination of smug satisfaction and barely contained anger, his furious gaze burning with a zealot's intensity. Declan recognised the type immediately: not a mercenary, but a true believer. This was personal, and he'd been right in his initial assessment. It was the eyes; they looked like two miniature black holes, portals into the heart of darkness. They were the eyes Declan Shaw might have had, had a young girl not accidentally wandered into his line of fire and saved him from becoming this very monster.

There could be no reasoning with this man, only pain, delay, and more pain.

He was fucked.

"Operative Declan Shaw of British Intelligence Special Projects," the man said sarcastically, his English thick with a Ukrainian accent. "We have rather a lot to talk about, my friend."

Declan said nothing. He just looked at the man, puzzled, his own expression a façade of innocent confusion.

He was roughly forced into an old wooden chair, the kind with a high back and sturdy arms, its joints groaning under his weight. His hands were bound tightly to the arms with zip ties. The ringleader circled him like the predator he was.

"The package, Shaw. The Orpheus data. We know you were in the alley with the Russian. Either you or she took it from the American."

"Orpheus data? I don't know what you're talking about," Declan replied, his pitch rising to reflect his supposed confusion. "What American?"

The first punch was a blinding flash of light and pain, a brutal right cross that snapped his head back and sent a coppery taste of blood into his mouth.

"Do not play games with me English," the man hissed, leaning in so close Declan could smell his stale breath. "I have very little patience with English pricks in general, and even less patience for you in particular."

Declan looked at him, spitting a gob of blood onto the floor.

"Look, there's clearly been some misunderstanding here, I'm just a security contractor, check my ID if you want, it's in my wallet."

Another backhander across his face.

"We know all about Aegis security solutions Operative Shaw, there is nothing we don't know about you. Nothing."

Taras paused for a second, stroking his chin in mock rumination and then asked in an almost reasonable manner, as if having an afterthought.

"Oh wait, there is one thing we don't know, something you can perhaps help us with?"

Declan, still half stunned from the second blow gathered his thoughts.

"Fire away. That simply means ask your question, it's not a request to shoot me, English as a second language can be very confusing."

The third blow REALLY hurt. Delay thought Declan through the fog, delay answering the questions for as long as possible.

Taras went to the computer desk and picked up a black and white photo. He then approached Declan and shoved the image into his field of vision. Declan nearly gave himself away but managed to remain neutral as he looked at a printout from the Janus search. It was the ID photograph of Anya's face.

How on earth had he... then the realisation struck with him with painful clarity, the call from MI6, the waiting team, the knowledge of Special Projects, the Janus image. He had been thrown to the wolves by his own side. Which could only mean they knew about him and Anya, and this was their way of getting to her, through him. What residual fear there was left was replaced by a determination to make sure he would never talk, never betray her.

"Where is she?" asked Taras, in an almost reasonable, friendly voice, holding the picture in front of Declan's now strangely indifferent face.

Declan, playing for time, squinted at the photo as if trying to recollect something, taking his time, playing dumb. "Oh... I remember her. Washington, I think. Eleanor Vane, if memory serves, some energy sector consultant, she was at a conference there, but I haven't seen her since."

The next blow when it came, was spectacularly painful, another powerful backhand across the face that almost knocked Declan and the creaking chair over causing his nose to bleed even more.

"Liar!" Taras screamed, his composure shattering. "I saw you and The Russian Bitch at the cordon yesterday, investigating the dead American you claim to know nothing about." Another punch landed, this one to the ribs, stealing Declan's breath. "Do you think you are the only one who can see things?" He stepped back for a moment, looming threateningly over his prisoner. "I saw how you looked at the bitch, and how she looked back at you."

Taras once more shoved his face menacingly close to Declan's, spittle flying from his lips as he snarled at him. Then Taras paused, confused, and sniffed. Then punched him in an almost mindless fury as realisation dawned.

"I can smell her on you!" He shouted, as he turned to his men, his fury growing. "Bring me his phone"?

One of the men, handed Taras the phone they had taken from Declan during the hurried search in the van. He grabbed Declan's hand, forcing open his clenched fists and used his fingerprint to unlock it, before checking the call history. There it was, Eleanor Vane. He called her.

"The number you have dialled is not in service, please try again" said an automated voice. He furiously threw the phone away which skittered across the floor, still trying to connect.

Once again, he backhanded Declan out of frustration.

"Well Operative Shaw, I may not have her yet, but I have you, and for now, that's more than enough, you will talk, you will tell me everything and you WILL betray your little Russian whore, that I can promise".

The interrogation then began in earnest. It was a brutal, ugly affair. They took turns and worked him over with a professional, dispassionate violence, alternating between blows to his body and sharp, pointed questions about Anya, and sometimes a rare question about his mission.

Declan took the beating, his mind retreating to a place where the only thing that mattered was the memory of having been in Anyas arms. He was holding onto the moment with all his might, like a drowning man clutching a floating log.

He gave them nothing. His only goal now was to buy Anya time. Time for her to get the grab-bag, to get clear of the city, to vanish. Every minute he held out was another mile closer to safety for Anya. He knew, with the cold certainty of a professional, that sooner or later, they would break him. No one could hold out forever. The only way to keep her safe, to truly keep his secret, was to not be alive to give them anything.

After what felt like an eternity, but was in fact only around ten minutes, he was a bruised, concussed, bleeding mess, his shirt soaked in sweat and blood, but his will unlike at least two of his ribs, was unbroken. Taras was growing frustrated.

"Search him again," Taras ordered. "Properly this time."

One of his men roughly frisked Declan, finding the fake USB and the decrypt device and a photograph. Taras snatched them triumphantly.

"Fool, why didn't you just give us them, it would have saved you a lot of pain", he then unfolded the picture, it was of Declan and Anya, taken at St Mary's Island. She was resting her head on his shoulder and looked happy.

Taras looked at the picture, his nostrils flaring like an angry bull, then crumpled it in his hand before erupting into even greater fury, throwing the photograph at Declan, which bounced off his face before falling onto the floor. Another beating began, this time deeply personal. His world faded in and out of consciousness. One of Taras's men interrupted.

"Sir, We have the decrypt and Icarus data; we should report it immediately."

Taras shrugged his hand away and glared at him, then turned his attention back to the semi-conscious Declan.

This time he changed tactics, becoming mock friendly.

"Where is she Shaw"?

"Tell me where she is and you can walk, go back to your old life."

"Yeah right" said Declan through swollen lips, his head fuzzy, "What fucking life"?

"You are a fool Englishman, and you will die a fool, but not quickly, I can promise you that much".

Taras slowly limped over to a laptop that was set up on a desk, and plugged the devices in. He saw a folder, opened it and saw only an audio file, puzzled he clicked on it.

The warehouse was suddenly filled with the raw, haunting voice of Polina Gagarina, singing "Kukushka."

Taras puzzled and angry turned to look at Declan, then turned red faced as another sound filled the warehouse, the sound of defiant mockery.

Declan, despite the pain, had started laughing. Even here, in the last, painful moments of his life, the Cuckoo was singing one final song, telling him his time was up. Through the pain, through the concussion, he knew Anya was with him in spirit, he could feel her through their private joke. He wasn't going to die alone. He looked down at the floor, at their photograph which mercifully had unfolded, saw her smile and continued to chuckle, blood dripping onto his shirt.

A volcanic stream of vicious profanity erupted from Taras as he realised he had been played. He spun around, his face a mask of pure, murderous rage.

"You think this is a joke, Englishman?" he screamed.

Declan just looked at him, a bloody, defiant grin spreading across his lips.

"Life's a joke," he rasped. "Just one big shit sandwich, but every now and then you get to sprinkle a little sugar on it. But you? You're just the turd that makes up the filling." More laughter bubbled up through his blood-flecked lips, his shoulders shaking in mirth.

This was it, the moment. He could see the madness in the Ukrainians eyes, he was losing self control, He had to end this now, on his terms. If he died, Anya would be safe. The ghost of a sixteen-year-old girl in a Belfast alley had sat in his room for over thirty years. Maybe this was how he finally settled that debt. One life for another. His penance paid.

Taras stormed over, grabbed a handful of Declan's hair, and yanked his head back until his neck screamed in protest.

"WHERE IS SHE?" he roared, his face inches from Declan's. "WHERE IS THE RUSSIAN BITCH? Are you happy to die for her? Die for that fucking Russian bitch?"

Declan looked into the man's furious eyes, and despite the pain, for the very first time since they'd taken him, he felt a strange sense of peace. He smiled, a happy, bloody, liberated smile.

"Yes," he rasped, his voice still clear despite his cut, swollen mouth. "I AM happy to die for her."

Then, his expression shifted, becoming one of mocking pity. He began to laugh again, a low, wet, gurgling sound, and in broken, heavily accented Russian, he threw their shared secret back at his tormentor.

"Skol'ko tebe ostalos' zhit'? Kukushka, kukushka..." (How long do you have left to live? Cuckoo, cuckoo...)

The sheer, insane audacity of it, the beaten, bleeding man taunting him with a child's rhyme in his enemy's tongue, as the very same song filled the warehouse, shattered the last of Taras's control and he brutally punched Declan in the sternum, hard, and then recoiled in pain, the bright golden shine of a metallic feather sticking out from his bleeding knuckle. He angrily tore the tie pin out and threw it to the floor.

Declan laughed louder, an almost gleeful chuckle at his tormentors pain. Keep going he thought, fighting through the pain, you're nearly there.

Taras grabbed him by the hair and viciously pulled his head back, preparing to strike him again, but before he could react, Declan spat a large, defiant gob of blood and saliva directly into his face.

Taras howled in pure, animalistic fury, angrily wiping blood and saliva from his temporarily blinded eyes.

"Boris!" he screamed at the large man in the leather jacket. "Shoot this English piece of shit!"

Boris strode forward, his own pistol drawn, a look of smug anticipation and satisfaction on his face. He stood looming over Declan, his back to the shadowed recesses of the warehouse, and aimed the pistol down at Declan's head. The last face Declan saw would not be the face of his killer: it would be the face of his beloved Anya, who had saved his soul.

He closed his eyes, the metallic tang of his own blood filling his mouth. Then the warehouse noise faded, replaced by the familiar, dreadful silence he always associated with her arrival. The Irish ghost, not Anya had arrived to witness his end. He braced himself for the accusing stare, the endless, silent judgment from the armchair in the corner of his soul. It was time to pay the bill.

But when the image formed behind his eyelids, it was different. The rain was gone from her dark hair. The rubble of the Belfast alley had been replaced by a soft, undefined light. And her eyes... the cold accusation that had haunted his every waking moment for over thirty years was gone. In its place was a quiet, expression of peace.

Then, she smiled.

It wasn't a wide grin, just a small, gentle curve of her lips. A smile of release, of forgiveness. His long, torturous penance was finally paid. And then she nodded, permission to die granted.

As he watched, her image began to soften at the edges, becoming translucent, fading like mist in the morning sun. The weight he had carried on his shoulders for a lifetime simply... dissolved. The ghost was gone.

And in the space she left behind, a new face appeared. Anya. Her lopsided smile, the one that always meant trouble. The glint in her eyes when she'd called him an "English comedian." Her face, not in fear or in professional coldness, but in the pure, selfless love he had seen and reciprocated just hours before. She was his final thought. His last, best, and only song.

It had been worth it, all of it, if only for those few unexpected and precious hours when he had loved and been loved by Anya Stepnova.

For the first time in his life, a complete and blissful sense of peace washed over him. He smiled one last time at the memory of her. Kukushka continued to play in the background, a fitting epitaph to the cuckoo's end.

He was ready.

"Ya tebya lyublyu," He said in a barely audible whisper. His final farewell to Anya.

And at that precise moment, from the shadows of the warehouse, came the low, hollow thump-thump of an ugly silenced revolver, as the Nightingale began to sing her own song.

CHAPTER 47

Anya watched in horror from the window of Declan's flat as he was bundled into the van. The vehicle's lights cut a swathe through the pre-dawn gloom and then it was gone, leaving only the wet, empty street and an ominous, rain-swept silence.

For a single, frozen moment, the conditioned reflex of her SVR training took over. The cold, clear logic was absolute: "The primary asset is compromised, you are compromised, your position is untenable, egress immediately. The old mission is a failure; your new mission is to survive."

The grab bag Declan had pointed out was by the door. It contained money, a map, a path to escape, and ammunition. She took half an instinctive step towards escape, then stopped mid-stride, overcoming five years of SVR conditioning. No! Not again!

The call from MI6, then the trap sprung with perfect timing, was no coincidence. Like her, he had also been betrayed by his own service, and she had no illusions about what awaited him.

They were working against the clock, no doubt, so would take him somewhere relatively close but isolated and discreet. Then they would take him apart, layer by layer, until the brilliant, witty, haunted man she knew was just a screaming ruin. "Enhanced interrogation." The sterile euphemism made her feel sick.

And she too would become a hollow shell, forever haunted by the man she had abandoned, by the two good men she had loved and lost.

The thought was an emotional and moral violation. He was not just an asset, not just an ally, he was her Kukushka. The man who had shown her empathy and who had handed her a loaded gun when his duty dictated that he should put three bullets into her head in a tight group.

She thought of their inexplicable connection, how events had conspired to bring them together, a supposed enemy who had shown her how to love again.

He was her "Sudba." Her fate. And in Russian folklore, you do not run from your fate, you do not just confront it, you defiantly challenge it.

The image of the Nightingale, the cold, perfect instrument of the state, dissolved in her mind. It was replaced by an older, more powerful archetype, one drawn from the deep, dark soil of her homeland: Marya Morevna, Vasilisa the Wise, the warrior princess, the Bogatyrevna who does not wait to be rescued, but rides out to save her captured prince. It was her own version of the Kukushka theme. He had demanded fire from the heavens. Now, she would become the fire. She was no longer Anya, the grieving woman. She was no longer the Nightingale, the state's tool. She was a deadly fusion of both.

A cold, absolute calm settled over her. She moved with a fluid, deadly purpose. She dressed in a blur of motion, strapping on the holster with Norman's heavy revolver. She stuffed her pockets with the spare ammunition. A memory flashed in her mind, a tiny, almost imperceptible movement from Declan as he was being manhandled. A deliberate flick of his wrist.

She raced outside into the dark, rain-swept street, her eyes scanning the ground near where he had been snatched. And there she saw them, glinting in the gutter: his car keys. A wave of relief and admiration cut through her fear. Even in the shock and violence of his own capture, he had been thinking of her. His tradecraft was superb. Her Sudba was waiting for her.

She snatched up the keys, climbed into the nondescript saloon, started the engine, plugged the tracking receiver into the burner phone, and activated the tracking app. A few seconds later, it synchronised with the satellite. And there it was: a single red dot, moving east out of the city. The tie pin tracker, shaped as a firebird feather, was singing like a canary. She just hoped the ancient myths of the feather being a bringer of good fortune were not just old Babushka tales, especially when she had a war to win.

She tailed the van at a safe distance, the roads still mostly empty in the pre-dawn hours. Her thoughts raced. Advantage: they weren't expecting her. Disadvantage: she had a slow-loading and inaccurate pistol with limited ammunition against an unknown number of armed men.

Disadvantage: They had Declan. She would have to put him out of her mind. She had to become the Bogatyrevna. She saw the van's red dot stop on her screen, hovering over an old warehouse complex on the industrial outskirts. Good. Plenty of hiding places. Another advantage.

She pulled over a safe distance away and watched as they roughly bundled Declan out of the van. She felt an icy chill when she saw the dark stain of blood on his shirt, but then relief flooded her as she saw his legs move. He was still alive.

But for how long?

They hadn't posted a guard. Amateurs, she thought, her lips twisting in contempt. Too keen to get in on the fun no doubt. She made her way into the sprawling complex, gun ready, moving like a phantom through the decaying structures. Before long, she could hear the angry shouts and the sickening thud of blows. They were really working him over; she didn't have much time. Luckily for her, they were so focused that they didn't notice her sneak into a small, glass-walled office near a fire exit, a perfect observation post with multiple escape routes and a good field of fire. Old desks, lockers and filing cabinets were scattered about the space, giving cover from view but not cover from fire she noted.

She checked the gun and, despite the grim situation, managed a slight smile as she heard the haunting strains of "Kukushka" blast from their computer speakers. She understood perfectly what had just happened. She had placed the song on the stick as a message to Declan, never realising where the message would be heard.

Then came the tirade of vicious Ukrainian profanities.

"I see they have gotten to know Declan." She thought, smiling to herself about how infuriating he could be. That man could make the Pope swear in frustration she theorised.

She heard Declan's defiant laughter and the angry reaction from his captors. Then she saw the scene unfold through the grimy glass, and almost cried out in a mixture of fear, pride, and an indescribable surge of love and determination.

"WHERE IS THE RUSSIAN BITCH? Are you willing to die for her? Die for that fucking Russian bitch?" Taras roared.

She heard Declan's wet, bloody chuckle, and then his voice, clear despite the pain.

"Yes. I AM happy to die for her." Then she heard the taunt, their secret rhyme, in his broken Russian. "Skol'ko tebe ostalos' zhit'? Kukushka, kukushka..."

She saw Taras punch him in the sternum, hard, and then recoiled in pain, the bright shine of a metallic feather sticking out from his knuckle. He tore the tie pin out and threw it to the floor cursing.

Declan laughed louder, an almost gleeful chuckle at his tormentors pain.

Taras grabbed him by the hair and viciously pulled his head back, preparing to strike him again.

Declan spat a huge gob of blood and saliva into Taras's eyes blinding him temporarily, he staggered back furiously wiping the blood from his temporarily blinded eyes.

She saw Taras scream at a large man in a leather jacket to shoot Declan. She saw the man loom over the chair, his back to her, and raise his pistol. She quickly but steadily raised her own heavy revolver, her mind back in the close quarter battle range, took a steady two-handed aim at the man's broad back, and squeezed the trigger.

Thump! Thump!

The two heavy rounds punched through the leather jacket into his lungs. The kinetic force of the impact threw him forward, a dead weight collapsing onto Declan, smashing the old wooden chair to pieces and sending them both to the concrete floor. To her horror, she saw another Ukrainian open fire, not at her but at Declan.

She gasped as he turned and fire a burst into the pile of bodies, saw Declan's jolt from a hit. Then he was still, buried under the heavy corpse. An icy yet almost demonic fury possessed her. Not blind rage, but a clinical, absolute focus. She fired two more rounds, taking down the Ukrainian who had just fired on Declan. Then she bolted through the fire exit as the shocked gang shouted at each other in panic and confusion. The third gunman, Lev, was foolish enough to follow her through the narrow exit. Hampered by the beautifully maintained sniper rifle he was trying to bring to bear in the tight space, he received a third eye instantly as a .38 calibre round took him squarely in the forehead. The three remaining gang members became more cautious and there followed a protracted firefight through the decaying labyrinth of the raid-sodden warehouse complex.

They tried to flank her, but she used the darkness and the obstacles to hide her position, her movements were swift, economical and silent, and she was operating on pure, well-honed instinct and when a fourth goon fired into the position she'd just been firing from, she had already changed cover and shot him from behind.

Four down, two to go, she thought, reloading on the move. Realising she was in danger of being cornered, she jumped through a partially broken window, feeling the sharp sting of shattered fragments cutting her face.

She was now in the open, sprinting across a yard running back towards Declan, rounds kicking up dirt at her feet. She reached the relative safety of the warehouse door and spun. Thump! Crack! A fifth man went down, a double tap to his broad chest. The silencer now completely useless.

"That was for Declan," she shouted at the dying man who was desperately trying to seal the bullet holes with bloody hands. Taras was right behind him, his face a mask of raw, animalistic hatred. His sloppiness born of fury made him an easy target. She took careful aim at the centre of the visible mass.

Click!

She squeezed again. Click!

Out of ammo. She searched frantically in her pockets, but they were empty, some of the spare rounds having fallen out during the firefight. So much for the Firebird feather she thought. She looked around, to see if she could spot any ammo or a dropped gun, but it was too late, Taras was bearing down at her, a limping madman with murder in his eyes.

She ran into the warehouse and realised, with a sense of fatalistic acceptance, that she had used the wrong entrance and was trapped in a side alcove just off the main chamber. She could almost see where Declan had been shot and would be lying. She noticed the nearest fire exits were chained shut. There was no way out.

She stopped running and turned to face her nemesis, her breath coming in heavy gasps, not from fear, but exertion. She had tried to save Declan but had failed. And now, it was her turn. She almost welcomed the relief her end would bring. A pity she hadn't reached his body so they could be together at her end.

Across the wet concrete floor stood Taras, illuminated by a single bare bulb, the shadows giving his face a demonic appearance.

"Anastasia Vladimirovna Stepnova," he said, his voice low. "The Russian Bitch. We meet again."

He was in no hurry. He was going to take his time.

She stared at him, her expression stoic, but with a flicker of confusion. She remembered him from the crime scene but played dumb.

Taras returned her gaze, her obvious confusion about who he was, greatly irritating him.

"Surely you remember me? After everything we've been through together" He spat sarcastically his irritation increasing as he looked at her defiant yet slightly puzzled face.

No matter, he would remind the bitch, he had waited too long to let her play games, here at her end.

"After everything? After all these years," Taras continued, savouring each word. "You know how long I've dreamt of this moment. Having you, The Russian Bitch at my mercy?"

Anya looked back at him completely perplexed.

"I'm afraid you have me at a disadvantage, I never forget a face, and I'm pretty sure I'd remember THAT one." She replied, her Russian accent dripping with complete disdain.

Taras flushed red, "Enough of the games." he shouted.

"Moscow. The Metro. You killed my men. You put a bullet in this leg." He leaned forward, his smile faltering, replaced by a flash of anger. "But you really don't remember me, do you? I looked you right in the eye before you shot me. And you don't actually know who I am."

Anya's expression changed. The confusion cleared, replaced by a sudden, sharp clarity, followed by nothing less than utter contempt.

"You were wearing a balaclava, you fucking idiot," she laughed.

Taras's face contorted, his carefully constructed moment of vengeance shattering into pure, white-hot fury.

"I am Captain Taras of the SBU" he snarled, "And you WILL remember exactly who I am before I'm through with you".

Anya rolled her eyes at his grandiose posing and made a point of looking at her watch, as if she had something better to do.

"Look just get it over with before you fucking bore me to death".

Taras, furious, raised his pistol. His finger tightened on the trigger. "So be it".

"Skol'ko tebe ostalos' zhit'? Kukushka, kukushka..." Anya spat the words, a final, defiant curse.

Bang!

The loud report of a Makarov pistol cut through the tense silence, the gunshot reverberating through the warehouse.

Bang!

A second identical sound, fractions of a second later.

Anya flinched, her eyes wide with surprise. There was no pain. Just the sight of Taras slumping to his knees, a look of bewildered shock on his face, his pistol slipping from his hand and clattering to the floor. He toppled forward, almost in slow motion, landing face-first, dead.

From the deeper shadows, a figure emerged, stumbling, bruised and bleeding, badly hurt but alive. Declan Shaw. Risen from the dead like a bloodstained Lazarus. He held a Makarov he must have taken from one of the dead guards, his grip unsteady. Blood dripped from his bicep, down his arm, onto the pistol. He reached Taras's body, standing over it for a moment.

Bang!

He fired a third round into the corpse. A wry, pained smile touched his cut lips as he gave a half-apologetic shrug in her direction.

"Sorry," Declan murmured, his voice a hoarse whisper. "Force of habit."

He moved closer, stumbling towards her. A wide, brilliant smile of relief and happiness spread across her face. He saw her smile, and for a moment, his own tired face softened, and the corner of his mouth turned upwards. He took one more unsteady step towards her.

Then his smile faded, his eyes rolled back in his head, his legs gave out from under him, and he slowly slumped to his knees, falling backwards onto the grimy concrete with a heavy thud, the gun still clutched in his hand.

Her own smile froze on her face in horror then vanished, replaced by a mask of pure dread.

"Declan!"

She ran across the wet floor, dropping to her knees beside him. She gently lifted his head, cradling him in her arms, her fingers searching for a pulse at his neck. She felt a fast but steady beat against her fingertips. The stubborn bastard was still alive.

She almost cried then, a loud sob of relief escaping her lips. She held him close, her cheek against his blood-matted hair. All that mattered was the weight of this man in her arms, her wounded soldier, the impossible, infuriating pain in the arse, who had risked everything, who had walked through hell for her, just as she had for him

CHAPTER 48

As Declan lay bleeding on the floor, her SVR training took over, the programmed instincts cutting through the emotional chaos. "Airway, breathing, circulation, stabilise. evacuate."

His face was bruised and battered, his breathing shallow. The blood soaking his bicep was spreading. Before her assault, acting on instinct, she had stuffed med kit such as pressure dressings and Quickclot from Declan's grab bag into her pockets. Now, her hands moved with the grim efficiency of a field medic, tearing open his sleeve, packing the gushing wound with the haemostatic agent, and applying the pressure dressing with brutal, life-saving tightness. He groaned in discomfort, but the bleeding slowed to a dark, sluggish ooze.

The bleeding was controlled. For now.

From where he had collapsed, she had a better view of the main warehouse and her eyes darted around, cataloguing assets. Her gaze fell on Declan's discarded raincoat near the shattered chair. His phone was still on the floor, where Taras had thrown it. She scrambled over, and retrieved it along with the crumpled photo, she had an idea.

Her mind raced. The Ukrainians. They would have an exfiltration plan. A vehicle. A base. The last man she had shot in the yard, the one she had double tapped in the chest. He was seriously injured, but not yet dead when she'd passed him.

She left Declan for a moment, picking up his dropped Makarov, and retraced her steps to the yard. The man was still there, struggling to breathe, blood oozing through his fingers. She knelt beside him and tutted, this was one of the bastards who had tortured Declan, who had laughed as Taras beat him.

"You have a hemopneumothorax, nasty".

She held up her pistol in one hand, and an adhesive chest seal and drain from the trauma pack in the other."

"Choose"

He painfully nodded towards the chest drain.

"Where is your base?" she asked in harsh, fluent Russian. "Where is your transport?"

The man's eyes widened, trying to focus on her face. He painfully coughed, blood flecking his lips.

"Talk," she stated matter of factly, "You don't have long, minutes I estimate."

Still struggling he gave her the two words she needed: "Odyssey... Korolevskaya Pristan'..." The Odyssey. Royal Quays. The yacht.

"How many onboard"? she demanded.

"Just two, only two".

She nodded and thanked him then stood up, firing her pistol twice into his head. Not out of malice but simply neutralising a potential threat to herself and Declan. He would have talked, maybe alerted his comrades on the yacht or told the authorities about it. It was regretful but necessary. Director Volkov would have approved she thought. As she walked away, she fired a third round into the body.

She returned to her semi conscious lover who was looking at her with a quizzical eyebrow raised, curious about the three gunshots.

"Sorry, force of habit" she smiled grimly.

He chuckled in understanding, struggling to stay conscious.

"Imitation is the sincerest form of flattery they say"

"If you're going to steal jokes, do it from the best" She smiled back, "Now hold on for just a bit longer Declan, I won't be a minute, try to stay awake".

She took out his phone which was still unlocked and opened the mapping app, quickly pinpointing their current location. She copied the what3words address. Then she found his last sent message, the single, coded text to Norman: "Cavalry needed. Bridge Tavern. Rear. Now."

She typed a new message to Norms contact number, containing their location, her fingers flying,

"Cavalry urgently needed. Cuckoo clock thief is down".

She hit send, recovered the Decrypt device and USB stick from the computer then returned to Declan where she tended to his other numerous injuries; the wait was agonising, but only twenty minutes later, which felt like twenty years, the side door of the warehouse creaked open. Norman cautiously stepped in, a shadow detaching itself from the deeper shadows outside. In his hands, he held the compact, deadly frame of his MP5. He took in the scene with a single, sweeping, and utterly calm gaze.

He shook his head in awe at the trail of bodies.

"I leave you two alone for a couple of hours, and this is what you get up to?" He walked over to check on Declan. "Anyone else would have taken you to the cinema"

Anya couldn't help but smile.

"Right then," Norm said, his tone ever light and practical. "Let's get you two out of this shithole."

Getting a semi-conscious, five-foot-ten man out of a warehouse was a brutal, ugly business. They half-carried, half-dragged Declan to Norman's vehicle. Once inside, Norman produced a vial of morphine from a medical kit.

"No," Declan rasped, pushing the syrette away. His eyes were unfocused with pain, but his voice was insistent. "Need... a clear head, I'm also concussed" He managed a pained, bloody smile. "I don't suppose you have a couple of Brufen and some tubigrip?"

Norman's expression remained deadpan. He fished around in the pocket of his windproof SAS smock. "Hang on, I might have something," he said, his tone serious. He pulled out his hand. He was giving Declan the finger. Declan let out a low chuckle, that turned into a grimace.

"You seriously need to work on your bedside manner".

Norm laughed and said, "I can give you some Hartman's, get some fluid in you, would you prefer rectally or IV?"

They both laughed then Norm expertly inserted a cannula and connected a bag of fluid via a giving set, he tied the IV bag onto a hook above the rear door.

Anastasia watched the exchange, even now, beaten and bleeding, he was still her Kukushka, still joking in the face of death. His spirit, the part she had fallen in love with, remained unbroken. She climbed into the back seat with Declan and told Norm

"Royal Quays Marina," her voice now steady and clear as she took command of the situation. "They have a yacht. "The Odyssey". It's their base, there's only two of them left and they won't be expecting us."

Norman glanced at her in the rearview mirror, a flicker of professional respect in his eyes.

"Good work Anya, very good work." he grunted, slamming the car into gear and speeding through the pre-dawn streets. "But first we need to get to a safe house, make sure Declan is stable before we do anything about the yacht. Best if we wait until dark. It's also November 5th, bonfire night, so it's better to wait until nightfall before we start our own fireworks display."

Norm drove them to an anonymous flat, not too distant from the Marina. It was well equipped and contained sterilised instruments and advanced trauma equipment. Norm asked Anya how Declan was shot, relieved when she told him it was with a pistol,

"That's good, low velocity, no temporary cavitation, I can do stitches and superglue, I can't do debridement and delayed primary suture".

He then proceeded to use an adrenaline based local anaesthetic to help control the bleeding, disinfected the wound and then sutured the muscle with dissolvable stitches and closed the wound itself with superglue. It was messy but did the job of stemming the bleeding. He then gave Declan a large dose of antibiotics via the fresh IV and dressed the wound.

"Best I can do for now, doesn't look like anything vital was hit so it's only infection we need to worry about, if we keep dosing him with antibiotics and whiskey, he should be ok".

Anya walked over to him and gave him a warm, unexpected hug, Norm usually so vocal and full of bravado and humour was legitimately stuck for words. Anya smiled as she noticed his embarrassment, she had seen beyond the gruff exterior.

They took turns on watch; Norm had phoned his friend Tony who owned a very nice pleasure boat they used to go fishing. He agreed to take them out of the country for a couple of thousand to cover his expenses.

They also took close care of Declan who had fallen into a deep sleep making sure he didn't dislodge his IV. The sun was beginning to set when he woke up, he sat up suddenly unsure of where he was, his eyes looking towards the corner of the room, no ghost, only a smiling, attractive woman.

Then his confusion faded, and he realised where he was.

"Wakey wakey rip van Shaw" said Norm, "We haven't got all day you lazy, comatose layabout."

Thanks to the IV and the rest, Declan was steadier on his feet but still weak and in pain after his beating. His arm was also in a sling. He objected when they detailed their plan, insistent that he take part in the assault, but when Norm gave him a pistol to hold and he could barely grip it, he relented.

They drove to a carpark which was adjacent to the marina, they could make out the Odyssey from their vantage point. No sentry on deck. The darkening sky was suddenly lit with sporadic fireworks, their bright cascades of light illuminating the dark waters of the nearby river.

Norm went to the rear of the car and opened the boot he had a selection of weapon parts and assorted silencers stowed in carrying cases. He pulled out a suppressor and fitted it to his MP5. He turned to Anya,

"Let me see your pistol please Anya". Norm watched impressed as she efficiently released the magazine and then cleared the weapon, showing him the empty chamber before handing it to him.

"Oh a Makarov? Nice". He then selected a silencer and tried to fit it, no luck, he then selected another and it fit perfectly thanks to a Neilsen device. He returned the gun to her. Anya had watched him, reminded of a connoisseur selecting a fine wine. Her earlier assessment of him as a highly competent operator once again confirmed. She went to the rear door and kissed Declan passionately.

Norm watched smiling.

"Do I get one of those?" He asked.

"I don't think you're his type." shot back Anya.

"Touche" thought Norman, genuinely impressed at Declan's taste in women and wondering if he should defect to Moscow and bag himself a Russian spy.

As they moved silently along the pontoon towards The Odyssey, the sound of a single, muffled gunshot echoed across the water. Norm and Anya exchanged a sharp, wary glance and quickened their pace, weapons now drawn.

Anya slid the cabin door open and froze. The scene inside was a tableau of greed's final, bloody transaction. Dima, the comms specialist, was slumped forward over the main table, a fountain of arterial blood spurting from a fresh hole in his temple, soaking the neat stacks of sterling he had apparently been counting.

A fine, red mist settled on the facedown cover of his paperback copy of Moby Dick, the title now partially obscured by the final, bloody punctuation mark of their doomed voyage. Standing with his back to them, a smoking Makarov still clutched in his hand, was Andriy. He was staring down at his handiwork, his own retirement fund now secured.

He must have sensed her presence, because he began to turn, his triumphant smile suddenly dying on his lips as recognition dawned. The woman from Taras's photograph, the Russian b...

He never completed the turn or the thought. Anya raised her own silenced pistol and put a single, neat hole in the side of his skull. He collapsed without a sound, his heavy body falling forward to join Dima's in the pile of blood-soaked money,

Norm listened for any sound of panic in the marina, but the suppressed gunshots had as expected, been lost amongst the exploding fireworks. He checked the cabin for surprises and went below deck to check to see if there was anyone else aboard.

A moment later, he let out a low, appreciative whistle. Anastasia followed him down to the main hold. Numerous duffel bags stuffed with untraceable currency were piled high, nestled amongst wooden crates stencilled with the designations for Claymore mines, grenades, explosives, Javelin missiles and Stinger launchers.

He looked from the pile of money to the crates of weapons, then back to Anya and the wounded Declan, who had followed them aboard, unable to follow simple orders.

"Right," he said, a grimly amused smile on his face. "If you two are intending to misbehave again, give me a heads up so I can reach minimum safe distance."

He pulled out his burner phone and dialled a saved number. He held the phone to his ear waiting for the call to be answered. He whistled nonchalantly as he listened, as if being surrounded by hundreds of millions and two bloody corpses was just another day at the office.

"Tony, it's me," he said. "You know how you were going to transport my two friends somewhere nice for a couple of grand? Change of plan." He scooped up a thick, blood-spattered wad of notes from the table. "What do I get for ten million?"

An excited, tinny voice squawked from the other end of the line.

"Yes, I'm serious and no I won't marry you, I'm not that kind of paratrooper," Norm laughed good naturedly . "We need to meet at sea and do a bit of cross decking. Send me an RV where we can meet, make it somewhere isolated."

A moment later, a text pinged. Norm grabbed a pen and scrawled a set of longitude and latitude coordinates onto a clean fifty-pound note. He handed it to Anastasia.

"Okay," he said into the phone. "They'll meet you there. You swap your boat with them, then once you're clear, You take this one and scuttle it, then you can use the dinghy to get back to Dundee. Ten million buys you a new boat and a very nice life in Thailand or somewhere else the women don't mind rich, ugly westerners."

A hearty laugh echoed from the other end of the line.

Norm continued,

"We need a pass phrase"

"Velvet" Replied Declan.

"Did you get that"? said Norm down the line "Ok, velvet it is", he ended the call.

"Right wankers, give me a few minutes, you need to sanitise this boat so it can't be tracked, so you'll need to navigate the old-fashioned way, and it just so happens I was packed for a fishing trip this weekend. Not that you wanted to come along, you miserable, anti-social bastard. " Norman looked at Declan with mock severity.

He headed back to the car and returned with a sextant, a prismatic compass and a small device which he slipped to Declan with a wink.

"Just in case you're officer material and get navigationally embarrassed".

He looked at his friend and Anya and noticed how they kept looking towards each other, knew his friend was in good hands. Time to give them the rest of their probably extremely short lives together, without him acting like a gooseberry.

"Right, that's me, it's time to get a move on so I'm fresh for work tomorrow, better that I'm in the tent pissing out and can keep an eye on the many people who are going to be hunting you and all this lovely lolly ."

He helped Anya get Declan settled in the main cabin at the map table. He then paused at the gangplank, looking out at the dark, churning water of the Tyne.

"Ok, you two need to get this boat the fuck out of here right now, before someone misses all those bodies you two have piled up, I'll open and close the lock for you, follow the river left and in a couple of miles you'll be at sea."

Anya took out the decrypt device, shoved it into a jiffy envelope from the table and quickly scrawled on it with a pen and handed it to Norm.

"Here Norm, take this, make sure it gets into the right hands."

He accepted the envelope, started to leave the cabin but then turned one last time.

"Look after him," he said to Anya. "He's a good man."

"So are you Norm" she replied, her voice soft.

Norman almost blushed again, a final, mischievous smile touching his lips.

"Go on. Piss off, the pair of you, and try not to start any more international incidents." And then he was gone, melting back into the rainy Newcastle night as he headed towards the lock, the fading sound of his voice muttering "I've still got it!" drowned by the crack thump of countless fireworks.

EPILOGUE

THE HAPPY HOUSE

The frigid atmosphere in the conference room was toxic enough to be classified under the chemical weapons convention. Phillips sat at the head of the table, feeling the cold, accusatory gaze of the Five Eyes representatives on the main screen. The dressing down had been brutal.

The litany of his failures was long: a dead American, six dead members of a supposedly allied SBU cell littering the streets of North Tyneside, an entire SVR support cell vanished into thin air, and two hundred million in untraceable currency now likely funding the retirement of two Ukrainian gun runners who had vanished off the face of the earth along with their yacht and enough expensive ordnance to start World War 3. And naturally, through it all, Shaw had gone walkabout.

The fact that the forensics had identified a great deal of Shaw's blood at the scene, along with ejected revolver brass containing six sets of fingerprints for him and the remaining brass containing Stepnova's fingerprints and DNA, were a conundrum. There was enough blood to suggest Shaw might have been critically wounded, and his blood trail led to the corpse of the Ukrainian commander. Yet there was no body and evidence that quickclot powder had been hurriedly applied. The entire warehouse was a crime scene investigator's worst nightmare.

To crown it all, there was no sign of the USB or decrypt device; it very much looked like the Russian Stepnova had managed to turn Shaw and successfully escape with the Icarus intelligence. It didn't help matters that Walsh and the CIA were being shady, obstructive, and borderline hostile regarding their own reading of the whole sorry and sordid mess.

But the most damning failure, the one that had truly sealed his fate, was the complete and utter failure of Project Apollo.

His "digital panopticon," the all-seeing brain, had failed to predict the single most critical development of the entire operation: the alliance between Shaw and Stepnova. The after-action report had been merciless. It concluded that the system's predictive models were fatally flawed because Phillips himself had personally curated the psychological data fed into them, poisoning the well with his own biases. He saw Shaw as nothing more than a "fist," a simple, violent tool to be deployed. He saw Apollo as the "brain." Due to his inherent sociopathy, he had never given any consideration to the heart.

The system couldn't compute loyalty, empathy, or redemption. It couldn't predict that the fist might open up to become a helping hand. The result was a catastrophic intelligence failure and an AI system now viewed by London as a monument to his own spectacular lack of insight. It was, however, somehow able and willing to access the Defence Minister's webcams and hard drive and obtain compromising pictures of him cavorting with Eastern European rent boys. The PM was furious, and there was a coordinated campaign of D Notices and an official line that the images were deep fake kompromat created by the Russians to undermine trust in public institutions.

Not only that, but it was suffering inexplicable malfunctions, CCTV failures, multiple file deletions, and a complete failure of the facial recognition capability. Frustratingly, despite extensive investigations and diagnostics, there was no sign of malware or other compromise of the system.

The increasingly frustrated CIA system administrator Danny was tearing his hair out trying to rectify the problem, whilst at the same time appearing sheepish when asked about the issue. The bottom line was, a several billion pound, state-of-the-art, artificially intelligent surveillance system appeared to have gone temporarily insane.

To make matters worse, Danny worryingly had seen some lines of code which looked terrifyingly similar to his own "Imitation Game" creation, but as quickly as the code appeared, it self-deleted, as if it was deliberately hiding its own tracks.

That was definitely a can of worms he didn't want to report up the chain, so he remained silent, leaning into the "Quantum malware cyber attack" theory.

Phillips felt a familiar tension grip his chest as he left the briefing room and made his way back to his office. He sat down heavily in his chair, watching the dregs of his professional life circle the drain because of that ill-disciplined, insubordinate ne'er-do-well. He opened the bottom drawer of his desk and poured a generous measure from the bottle of single malt he kept there specifically for Shaw-related stress.

He took a long, slow drink, put the glass down, and then noticed it. A plain, brown jiffy bag sitting innocently in his in-tray. He looked around the main office but saw nothing of note except Norman the Storeman walking towards his own office, humming cheerfully to himself and stroking a toy cat for some reason.

He shook his head in exasperation; the storeman had of course been interrogated but the man was a fool with low intelligence and could provide no information on Shaw's whereabouts. Phillips decided that his last act as manager would be to have the oaf sacked.

Annoyed, he looked back at the envelope. Delicate Cyrillic letters were scrawled across it. He had no idea how to read Russian, so he called over Danny.

Danny took one look at it and shrugged.

"Seems to be a joke, Sir."

"What do you mean?" Phillips asked, his tone sharp.

"It reads 'From Russia With Love'," Danny said, a hint of amusement in his voice. "It's a reference to a James Bond movie."

"I know who James Bond is," Phillips snapped.

Curiosity overcoming caution, he tore open the envelope as Danny backed away, suspecting a letter bomb. Phillips's fingers first found two small, grey plastic devices. The Icarus USB stick and its decrypt key. A wave of relief so overwhelming, it almost made him dizzy, washed over him. He had it. The Icarus data set, the crisis was contained.

He had won.

Then his fingers brushed against something else inside the envelope. He pulled it out. Curled up at the bottom of the jiffy bag was another gift for him.

A cheap, worn, leather dog leash.

The message was brutally, silently clear. Phillips stared at it, his face turning a blotchy, furious red. The relief curdled into pure, impotent rage. He knew exactly who had sent it, and exactly what it meant.

He mouthed one word, more a curse than a name.

"Shaw."

He furiously threw the envelope and the leash in the same bin Shaw had thrown his rejected resignation letter in all that time ago.

Then he remembered he had won, so let Shaw have his own little petty victory, it didn't matter, he was off the hook, he had the main prize. He smiled smugly to himself, like the cat that got the cream and took a large, satisfied gulp of his single malt.

"To winning." He toasted himself.

He heard a sudden commotion in the corridor and looked up, almost spilling his drink as he watched Norman the Storeman rush down the corridor to noisily greet a smartly dressed, professional-looking woman. Wait.....was that Helen?

SVR HEADQUARTERS MOSCOW

Director Volkov looked at the headlines on the Western newspapers his subordinate had brought him. "STRATEGIC ARMS REDUCTION TALKS TO COMMENCE."

His gambit, his long-shot Orpheus Gambit, had succeeded. But not in the way he had designed it. He reviewed the operational post-mortems, a study in chaos theory. The plan had been elegant in its conception: leak the data, frame a rogue hacker, use a deniable SBU team to acquire the package from a sacrificed SVR agent, and let the West "intercept" it from them. Clean. Controlled. A surgeons work.

Instead, everything had gone off script. The SBU team, led by a vengeful fool with a personal vendetta, had failed to kill Nightingale and retrieve the prize, getting themselves eliminated in the process. Volkov wasn't surprised when the after-action review revealed that Taras had the same INFJ personality type as the Englishman Shaw, in many ways they were two sides of the same coin. Yet one had chose the path of hate, while the other chose love. It was an interesting philosophical puzzle; he would contemplate some other time.

What had taken him by surprise was his prize asset, Agent Stepnova, had refused her designated role as a martyr and formed an alliance with the enemy. And the Englishman, the unforeseen complication codenamed 'Cuckoo', had possessed an intuition that bordered on the paranormal, seeing the strings of the puppet show and deciding to cut them.

On paper, the operation was a catastrophic failure. The SBU team was gone, along with two hundred million in funding, and the two primary assets were now rogue, armed, and dangerous and almost certainly a lot richer. But better the two fugitives make use of the funds, than the cash being spent on weaponry used to kill Russians. It would be a far bigger annoyance to the west than it was to himself.

But despite this, despite the chaos, the gambit had worked. Missile batteries were being withdrawn before the peace talks had even commenced, and the inclusion of the Chudes data in the "leak" had been a masterstroke. Letting the West know Russia had detailed targeting information on their most secret underground facilities had been the gamble which truly sold the lie. The proof of concept of Orpheus combined with Chudes had terrified them, Any illusions they had of drinking champagne and eating caviar in their luxury bunkers, whilst the rest of the world burned had been shattered. They understood that they would burn too.

Volkov leaned back in his chair, a rare sense of satisfaction settling over him. The sheer, bloody mess of it all, the dead American, the dead Ukrainians, the story of two rival spies on the run, had authenticated the threat more effectively than any sterile, controlled handover ever could. The West hadn't just received a data file; they had received a violent, chaotic narrative that made the Icarus data feel terrifyingly real. They believed it because the cost of its retrieval had been paid in buckets of blood.

The West's dangerous dalliance with the theory of a "winnable" nuclear war was now in tatters. The realisation that their deep underground command bunkers were no longer sanctuaries, but tombs waiting to be sealed, had shattered their strategic arrogance. The uneasy balance of terror, the brutal but stable logic of Mutually Assured Destruction, had been restored.

He found himself deeply relieved that Agent Stepnova had survived. Her sacrifice, in the end, had proven unnecessary. An asset of her calibre, one who could not only survive but thrive in utter chaos, was too valuable to waste.

There was one matter which had genuinely angered him, Controller Primes unilateral decision to disarm Stepnova and suggest she whore herself. That foolish decision to go off script had almost jeopardised the entire operation. He was forgiving of unexpected operational complications, but he did not, could not tolerate stupidity.

He hoped Prime would enjoy his new role as the security supervisor at the Mirny Diamond mine in Yakutia. He was now the spy who was sent into the cold.

He sighed heavily and looked at Shaw's file next, a thin smile appearing on his stern face as he reread the ludicrously insubordinate letter Shaw had somehow managed to get delivered to him at his Dacha address, a highly classified piece of information. The strongly worded letter, expressed, in frank and colourful detail, his indignation over his assigned codename. Not only that, but the envelope had contained a gift, a small, carved wooden bird, a cuckoo.

Volkov found himself smiling at the skill and sheer audacity of the man. He had proven himself not only resourceful, but able to compromise his best agent. But he did have a point, the name Cuckoo was no longer appropriate, for he was no longer a solitary creature. The Director also sat pondering the new leash he now possessed, the one coiled firmly around Shaw's heart. He suspected that would be a far more difficult chain for his adversary to break.

He looked at his chessboard where only two nesting dolls remained; the American and Ukrainian dolls having been removed from the game by Shaw and Stepnova.

He closed their files, laying them flat on the desk. On the front cover of Shaw's file, he crossed out the old codename and hesitated, what Top Gun themed moniker would be appropriate for a maverick like Shaw he pondered?

Then the perfect answer, which had been staring him in the face struck him and with a flourish of his fountain pen, he wrote a new codename. Its bright red Cyrillic stood starkly out from the buff brown of the cover: Шут. Pronounced shoot, but meaning "Jester." Thanks to his letter, the Englishman had finally been granted his insubordinate wish and had been assigned his desired Top Gun codename.

For now, he would let them be. They had earned a little time, he would bend the rules and grant them a honeymoon, his gift to them for helping to achieve his mission, however inadvertently.

Their connection had been unforeseen, but the follow up psychological reviews identified the moment his plan had began to unravel. CCTV footage obtained from the international spy museum had shown evidence of them "mirroring" each other, analysis suggested this included their respiration rate.

Major Kurchatov, always the romantic, had suggested they were "twin flames" whilst the SVR psychologists had assessed their connection as limbic resonance. Whatever the name of the unexpected phenomenon, it had been part of the bloody chaos which had inadvertently sold the Orpheus deception. He recalled a quote from Dostoevsky "Beauty will save the world," and realised as far as Stepnova was concerned, her beauty had certainly saved the Gambit, which was as close to saving the world as it gets.

For that he was eternally grateful.

He walked over to the board and removed the two dolls then sat back down and placed them in his drawer, next to the small carved cuckoo.

He paused for a moment, hesitantly.

His hand reached deeper into the drawer and almost reluctantly took out a small, silver-framed photograph. It was of an attractive young woman with dark hair and intelligent, smiling, deep brown eyes.

His late daughter Anastasia. A teacher. She had died many years ago, one of the hundreds of victims of the terrorist siege at School Number 1 in Beslan. She bore a striking, almost painful resemblance to Anya Stepnova. He looked at the photo, his iron composure finally cracking in the solitude of his office. A single teardrop slowly traced a path down his cheek.

His entire, ruthless gambit had not just been about geopolitics. It had been the desperate, obsessive work of a grieving father, a man who lay awake at night trying to prevent other such tragedies, sometimes by the painful pragmatic strategy of causing lesser tragedies. It was a burden he had accepted since the very moment the news of his daughter's loss had been broken to him.

Yes he nodded, he would let Agent Stepnova have the honeymoon his own daughter didn't live to get.

There was a sharp knock at the door.

Instantly, the mask returned. He wiped the tear away with the back of his hand, his expression becoming completely inscrutable once more. He returned the picture to the drawer, closing it with a soft, final click. The grieving father was gone. The Director was back in control.

"Enter," he barked, his voice as firm and commanding as ever.

THE NORTH SEA

The Odyssey, bobbed silently in the dark swell of the North Sea, an indistinct shadow in the cloudy and misty night. There was the sound of grunting, swearing and heaving, then a splash. And another splash, as two weighted bodies were dumped unceremoniously overboard. They were followed by two smaller splashes as the yachts GPS and transponder were likewise ditched. After a brief pause, the yacht's navigation lights came on, and the vessel began to move gently under autopilot and then roared into life, vanishing into the ghostly November night.

Hours later, in the main cabin, Declan was scowling and studying a pile of navigational charts trying to work out the magnetic variation. Because of the ongoing polar magnetic excursion, the numbers on the maps were out of date so he was relying on memory. He could navigate by stars, but the mist was preventing proper visibility, so he was having to sail purely on a bearing.

He had checked the coordinates Norm had given him, 57° 22.5' N, 00° 55.8' E against the chart and smiled in amusement at the name "The Devils Hole". An ironic reminder of being stuck in an observation post with Norm for ten days on a diet of army rations. His reputation for compo induced flatulence was legendary. Devils Hole indeed he smiled.

Tony had chosen well, it was the perfect location for cross decking onto his boat, isolated, and with deep water, but close enough to Dundee so that Tony could scuttle the yacht and sail the dinghy there with his cash and a generous supply of spare fuel. Despite the navigational complications, Declan was relieved it was so misty as it made air and sea observation almost impossible.

All he was really concerned about was colliding with some other equally blind vessel, although they would at least have their radar turned on he hoped. One step at a time he thought. We have to get to the RV first. Although he was pushing the engines at 12 knots, he didn't have to worry about long term maintenance, he just needed to make the 205 Nautical miles to the RV, and they were almost halfway there now.

He looked at the sextant on the table that Norm had provided. He wasn't sure how to use it, but he thought it might come in handy for impressing Anya. Norm had also discreetly provided a secure, encrypted handheld GPS, which Declan would only use as a last resort if they got lost. He would of course pretend to use the sextant and secretly use the device if necessary. He smiled at the thought, Anya would probably throw him overboard if she found out he was bluffing her for male ego reasons.

Whilst he busied himself with his Captain Hornblower fantasies, Anya was meticulously separating stacks of banknotes, placing the crisp, clean bills in one pile and the ones stained with dark, rust-coloured patches in another. She had already lost count twice due to laughing at his jokes. This time his humour wasn't deflection, he just like to see her smile and liked seeing that annoyed little pout she wore when she had to start counting again.

Their respective deep cuts had been repaired with Steri-strips, and Declan's right arm was freshly bandaged, though it still bled slightly due to the exertion of helping Anya dump the two Ukrainians into the North Sea.

Music played softly in the cabin, sourced from the repurposed fake USB. It was "First Day of My Life" by Bright Eyes. Declan found the song strangely appropriate; as he watched her sorting the cash, scars and all, he was extremely glad he hadn't been killed before he met Anya.

"So where to, lover boy?" She interrupted his thoughts, not looking up from her grim task. "Somewhere warm and exotic, perhaps? No spies, no intrigue, no espionage, no assassins?"

Now that she was no longer acting a part, her Russian accent was more pronounced, the intonation more natural, stripped of the polished, placeless veneer of "Eleanor Vane."

He looked over at her.

"I've got just the place."

She waited.

"How about Casablanca?"

Anastasia looked at him sternly, her expression flat.

"You know, it's not too late for me to change my mind and shoot you?"

She continued separating the notes, the usual slight pout forming on her lips. The gesture was almost childish, and he found it, along with the authentic cadence of her voice, utterly irresistible and charming. He loved this woman on a level he couldn't even begin to describe. Then he remembered they were on the run and being hunted. By the Americans, the Brits, the Russians, the Ukrainians, and most dangerous of all thanks to their newfound wealth, probably the fucking Inland Revenue too.

Well woe betide any suicidal fool who tried to harm Anya; there would be no hesitation, no penitence, no guilt. He would create a billion ghosts to protect her, as he knew she would do the same for him. As grim as the thought was, it brought a smile to his lips. Besides, the bastards had to find them first. And on a plus note, he didn't have to write any more reports.

She looked up, sensing his gaze. She returned his look and his playful smile, and they spent the next few moments just looking at each other in an utterly comfortable silence, with no need for words. Then she remembered that at least one of them should pretend to be a professional.

"So, what are we going to do with all these blood-stained notes, Declan?" she asked, her tone ever practical.

He looked at her, a smirk playing on his lips.

"We could take them to the money launderers?"

She laughed and lost count for the third time, the pout was no longer slight. The bundle of banknotes hit him square in the face, accompanied by a torrent of shocking and creative Russian profanity.

"Сукин ты сын, ты заставил меня опять сбиться со счета! Клянусь, если ты еще раз отмочишь одну из своих дерьмовых английских комедийных шуток, я возьму этот 'Макаров' и прострелю тебе органы размножения, чтобы ты не смог наплодить миру больше таких Декланов Шоу!"

Declan wasn't 100% sure as he painfully laughed and tried to control his fresh nosebleed, but he had the distinct impression Anya may have been complimenting him on his English sense of humour.

THE END

Glossary of Terms: The Orpheus Gambit

This glossary compiles key organizations, codenames, locations, and technical concepts essential to understanding the plot and world of the novel.

Organizations and Acronyms

Term	Definition	Context in Novel
SVR	**Sluzhba Vneshney Razvedki** (Foreign Intelligence Service). Russia's premier external intelligence agency, focused on espionage outside the Russian Federation.	Director Volkov's agency. Anya (Anastasia Stepnova) is an SVR operative.
GRU	**Glavnoye Razvedyvatelnoye Upravleniye** (Main Intelligence Directorate). Russia's military intelligence service.	Anya and her late fiancé, Sergei, were originally GRU officers.
FSB	**Federal Security Service.** Russia's primary domestic counter-intelligence and security agency.	Mentioned as one of the forces involved in the Moscow Metro incident.
SBU	**Sluzhba Bezpeky Ukrayiny** (Security Service of Ukraine). Ukraine's domestic intelligence and security agency.	Captain Taras and his team are SBU assets used by MI6 in the retrieval mission.

MI6	**Secret Intelligence Service (SIS).** The United Kingdom's external intelligence agency.	Works alongside SBU (Taras) and provides oversight for Special Projects.
MI5	**Security Service.** The United Kingdom's domestic counter-intelligence and security agency.	Involved in the historical Op Banner failures and rivalry with Special Projects.
GCHQ	**Government Communications Headquarters.** The UK's signals intelligence and cyber security agency.	Provides technical intelligence and surveillance data (e.g., to the Five Eyes group).
NSA	**National Security Agency.** The United States' signals intelligence agency.	Elias Thorne was a former NSA contractor.
CIA	**Central Intelligence Agency.** The United States' external intelligence agency.	Liaises with MI6 (Walsh) and is secretly involved in attempting to "make redundant" Thorne.
Five Eyes	An intelligence alliance comprising the United States, United Kingdom, Canada, Australia, and New Zealand.	Represents the highest level of coordination during the crisis briefings (e.g., the conference calls at the Happy House).

Author Bio

D. B. Fallon is an author, military veteran and former intelligence analyst based in the Northeast of England. He holds a master's degree in Terrorism Studies from the Centre for the Study of Terrorism and Political Violence (CSTPV) at St. Andrews University.

A former Parachute Regiment reservist and a 27-year veteran of the Regular Army, D. B. Fallon served extensively on numerous operations in the Medical Corps as a combat medic and CBRN expert. On leaving the military he spent almost a decade as an intelligence analyst where he focused mainly on protecting critical national infrastructure from direct action threats, active measures and influence operations. This experience provided him with a unique perspective on the geopolitical and psychological warfare detailed in his debut novel The Orpheus Gambit.

When not working on the sequels Orpheus Ascendant, and The Orpheus Imperative, he can be found exploring Northumbria whilst actively resisting the urge to complain about shoddy map reading and the persecution of military veterans.